Lena put her hand on her arm. "I'm sorry, Evelyn. I'm sure you miss him."

"I do."

"Seventies is still too young to die."

"It is, isn't it? We could have had twenty more years if we were lucky." They drank in silence for a little, then Evelyn said, "So, how about we set you up on one of those apps."

"Oh, for heaven's sake, Evelyn! We were having a nice moment."

"We're still having a nice moment."

"What about you, then?" Lena said. "You said you would be up for a new romance. Let's get you signed up. I'm sure there's a hook-up app for old folks."

Evelyn narrowed her eyes. "Why do we need a special old folks app? Some people are into wrinkles."

Lena snorted.

"I'm serious. My friend, Mavis, her third husband is ten years younger than her. I want my next husband to be younger. And, if you can manage it, I'd like him to be ripped."

Lena bent over laughing. The timer dinged for the muffins and Evelyn slid off her stool and grabbed her oven mitts. "I'm serious," she said, banging the oven shut again and placing the tray on the stove. "A young, ripped husband. He doesn't have to be too bright or wealthy—in fact, better if he isn't—but he must be handsome."

"I didn't take you for a cougar, Evelyn."

"I think you'll find I'm full of surprises."

The Widows' Pact

by

J.L. Cole

The Widows' Pact

Cover Art by *Kristian Norris*

The Wild Rose Press, Inc.
PO Box 708
Adams Basin, NY 14410-0708
Visit us at www.thewildrosepress.com

Publishing History
First Edition, 2023
Trade Paperback ISBN 978-1-5092-4733-2
Digital ISBN 978-1-5092-4734-9

Published in the United States of America

Dedication

To Paige, my partner in crime since the beginning.
Thank you for always lifting me up when I am feeling
low, and for all the laughs.

Acknowledgements

The first person I want to thank is you, Reader. I can't express how grateful I am that you picked up this book and took the time to invest into Lena and Evelyn's story. It is such an honor every time someone tells me they read my work. I truly, deeply appreciate it! A big thank you also goes to the Women's Fiction Writers Association. I love being a member and all the connections I have made through WFWA. Thank you again for the support! To The Wild Rose Press, thank you so much for getting 'The Widows' Pact' out into the world. To my editor Morena Stamm, thank you for believing in the story and for your work improving it! Also thank you to Kristian Norris for the wonderful cover art!

I also need to thank Shauna-Lee and Darvy for being the first beta readers and for your generous encouragement. Thank you to Anita Kushwaha and Maggie Smith for the advanced blurbs, I so appreciate your feedback and that you took the time to help me out! Also, a big thanks has to go to Paige and my parents for their endless support—especially for reading early drafts and letting me talk through ideas and riding the roller coaster that is writing with me! Thank you also to Brooke for answering police related questions, and to Raelyn for the graphic and web design work and Mya for your support. And of course, a big thank you to my girls for sort of letting me work, and to my wonderful husband, Matt, for working so hard for our family. I wouldn't be able to stare at a computer screen all day trying to make words appear without your support.

Until the next one!

CHAPTER ONE

She was here again.

The old woman.

It was the fifth or sixth time Lena noticed her at the movie theater. She was alone, like Lena was. She always seemed to come alone.

Most nights they ended up picking the same movie, which was a strange coincidence because Lena picked her movies randomly, usually deciding on the spur of the moment as she bought her ticket. She'd watch almost anything—action, romance, comedy...She even tried a horror one once, but after having to sleep with a kitchen knife on her nightstand for a week she decided that was the limit.

It crossed her mind that maybe the old lady was stalking her. She dismissed that thought quickly, though. It was ridiculous. First off, why on earth would anybody want to stalk her at a movie theater of all places? Her life was pretty uneventful any other time but stalking someone while they sat still for two hours had to be the most boring time to stalk. Secondly, the probability of an elderly person being some sort of movie stalker must be slim. For some reason, stalking seemed more like a young person's hobby.

Anyway, it was probably just a coincidence she and this woman kept crossing paths. Red Deer wasn't that big even though it was currently the third largest city in

Alberta. It only had around a hundred thousand people or so. She was bound to run into the same faces a few times.

Today the woman's long silver hair was braided back and rested between her narrow shoulder blades. It was rare to see a woman her age with hair that long. It made her look trendy, or maybe a little like one of those old hippie women who would serve home-made herbal teas and wear long skirts and have feathers in their hair. She didn't dress like that though, she wore her usual white sneakers, black pants, and a sweater made for someone much larger making her look smaller than she probably was. Tonight, it was a dark navy blue one with the sleeves rolled up to her elbows.

Lena named her Helen, an elegant, sort of hippy name. She was terrible at guessing ages, but Lena figured Helen must be somewhere in her sixties. She imagined Helen was one of those quirky people who was always in their own little world. She probably kept birds as pets and candy in her purse and was always overly nice. Lena didn't know why she assumed this. Maybe because Helen was always alone and usually people who are always alone were either depressed or quirky.

What did that make her then?

Depressed.

Definitely depressed.

Lena tended to always sit in the back of the theater. Helen usually sat around the middle, a small bag of popcorn on her lap and a small pop resting in the cup holder to her right. Always smalls, always popcorn and pop. Never candy, or chocolates. Never a different size. Lena liked to mix her treats up; it made her feel spontaneous.

She was pretty sure Helen recognized her too. Lena had noticed the woman's eyes lingered a tad longer on her than on other people. Once, she thought Helen might come over and say something. For a second, Lena actually wanted her to. Only for a second, then she got nervous and stepped out of line to retreat to the washroom. By the time Lena came out again, the show she was planning on seeing was full, so she had to go to one she'd seen before.

Lena only ever went to the movies on Cheap Tuesdays. She could get her ticket and a snack for almost half the price. She and her late-husband James used to always go together.

Late-husband. That made her sound like she was a billion years old. She should be sitting in a rocking chair telling her great-grandkids about her darling late-husband James and how they used to go on weekly date nights to the movies. But here she was, not even thirty yet and already a widow. After three short years of marital bliss, she was dried up and heartbroken, going to the movies alone and thinking she was being stalked by the elderly.

How terribly depressing.

Today, Helen was two people ahead of her in line. She turned to look for something in her purse, glanced up and caught Lena's eye. Lena quickly looked away and pretended to study the movie posters on the wall.

"Excuse me. Please, go ahead."

Lena glanced back and to her horror, saw Helen waving others ahead of herself, inching her way closer.

Oh, don't. No, don't. They had a good thing going, she and Helen. There was no need to ruin it by actually acknowledging each other. But too late, Helen was suddenly standing right in front of her and Lena had no choice but to smile politely.

"I see you here a lot," Helen said. Her voice had a faint English accent. Lena hadn't expect that.

"Yeah, I've seen you too." Lena felt a blush warming her cheeks, probably turning them as bright as cherries. Damn her stupid cheeks, always giving away her social awkwardness at every opportunity. A childhood curse she never seemed to outgrow.

Helen did the polite thing and ignored it. "Are you alone tonight? You're often alone."

"So are you." That sounded defensive. Lena shifted, trying to will herself to relax. She was never very good with small talk. In fact, she loathed it. Probably because she always got the sense that she wasn't doing it right. She never followed the right protocols or stuck to the correct script. She always was left scrambling to assemble answers to the simplest of questions, her uneasiness oozing off her, infecting the other person who was just trying to be nice. Like at her brother's wedding when their aunt asked her while they were in line for food what she thought of the flowers. Lena had blubbered on about how she wasn't sure, that she didn't know much about flowers. Nice color though, but she knew her mom didn't like the color, she liked more of a pink shade—but they seemed nice, so yeah, they were nice. Her aunt just stared at Lena like she was a mental patient. Lena still cringed thinking about it.

"I don't see the point going to the movies with other people," Helen said. "Why get together only to sit there not talking? If you make the effort to get together with someone, you should at least be able to talk."

"I guess so." Lena shuffled forward and pretended

to read the snack menu.

"Do you agree?" Helen edged closer to her.

"I don't know. I guess it gives you something to do together."

"Yes, I suppose."

"And the company can be nice," she offered. "Someone to laugh with or whatever."

"You don't look like a girl who laughs a lot."

Lena's eyebrows lifted. What was that supposed to mean? That she looked as miserable as she felt? Nice. Maybe it was time for a haircut and dye. She could do something drastic; blonde and short instead of her regular brown and long. Spice things up a bit. Although, she wasn't sure she could pull off blonde—that might be too bold for her. Maybe she could start with highlights.

It could be because of her skin too, the reason she looked so miserable. She'd noticed this morning the bags under her eyes seemed particularly awful. She made a mental note to get some new concealer when she went to get her hair done.

"You look sad is what I mean."

"Okay," Lena said, because what else does one say to such a comment?

How interesting that Helen was not a quirky, nice-all-the-time person. She was actually an overly forward British lady. Guess one can never really know a person from staring. Wasn't it a British thing to be rude? Or was that supposed to be a French thing…

"Sorry, am I making you uncomfortable?"

"Yes."

She laughed. "I'm good at that. My kids and grandkids always say I talk too much. They said I don't have a filter. I'm Evelyn, by the way."

Evelyn, not Helen. Close though. Evelyn might be better anyway. It suited her British accent.

"I'm Lena."

"Lena. That's pretty. Is it short for something?"

"Selena."

They took another step forward.

"Selena, like the singer."

"Yup."

"I rarely talk to strangers at the movie theater," Evelyn said. "It's kind of my 'me time', you know? But I said to myself today, *if I see that girl again I'm going to say hi*. So, here we are."

Lena smiled politely. She never talked to strangers either.

Anywhere.

"So, what are you planning on watching tonight?" Evelyn said, clearly trying to keep the conversation limping along.

"Um…the new romance one."

"Me too!"

Great. No escaping her now.

"I love romance movies," Evelyn said. "I mean, you need to be in the right mood. They all have a similar feel don't you think?"

"Yeah. They're a little cheesy, but I like that."

"Yes, I agree. Nothing like a classic star-crossed lovers' story."

It was Evelyn's turn to order snacks. She went up to the young boy with acne and unfortunate frizzy hair stuffed under an ill-fitting cap who was working behind the counter. He asked her deadpan what she would like, and she ordered her usual in an overly chipper voice. Evelyn got her popcorn and pop and, as Lena feared, waited while she ordered.

Lena asked for fuzzy peaches and orange pop. The boy, his name tag said Chris, said to enjoy the show with as much gusto as a deflated balloon. Lena said thanks and tried to give him a little smile, but it might have come across as a grimace. She wanted to tell him it gets better, give him a little hope to hold on to, but she'd feel like a hypocrite because she didn't actually know if she believed it would. Maybe working the register, standing on a sticky cement floor with bits of crushed popcorn sticking to his feet wearing a frumpy uniform was the best life had to offer him. It would be a better life than some, maybe better than what most had in this world. Maybe even better than hers.

She and Helen—Evelyn—walked together into theater number three and paused uncertainly at the foot of the stairs.

Evelyn smiled. "Do you want to sit together? I promise I won't talk. Much." She laughed.

"Okay," Lena said. Because really, what else could she do? The French might get away with being rude, but she was Canadian. Polite to her very core and the thought of telling Evelyn to leave her alone was more mortifying than sitting through a movie with a stranger.

Evelyn led them into the third row from the back. A sort of middle ground from where they usually sat. Lena leaned back in her chair and was relieved to see the pre-show was ending and the previews were starting. Maybe now there wouldn't be any more awkward conversations. More to avoid looking at her companion than anything, she glanced around the theater. There weren't many people there tonight. Everyone was probably watching the new superhero movie. Lena planned to see that one next week when the hype died down. She liked to pretend she differed from the masses, but in truth she was just the same.

The movie was, as predicted, a typical romance plot. A girl and boy fall in love only to be driven apart for a while, but it all worked out in the end. Even though she could guess most of the plot twists, by the end she was still sniffling and was so wrapped up in the movie she almost forgot Evelyn was sitting beside her.

"Ugh...that got me." Evelyn stood and stretched as the credits rolled across the screen. "I swear I almost shed a tear, and I never cry in movies."

Lena grinned, forgetting to feel self-conscious for a moment. "It was good, wasn't it? I love that actor."

"He is dreamy." Evelyn agreed. "He reminds me of a boy I went to school with. Every girl fancied him. I was obsessed with him from primary school till we graduated."

"What was his name?"

"Edwin. Isn't that a dreamy name? Like a character from a romance novel. He could have been too. He looked just like that actor; dark hair, blue eyes..."

"Did you go out with him?"

"Heavens no. I was a shy little thing, barely said two words to him." Evelyn caught the skeptical look on Lena's face and laughed. "I know, hard to believe, isn't it? I was though. I don't think I talked to boys till Uni. You couldn't shut me up after that."

They walked out of the theater together. Evelyn paused by the washrooms. "I have to use the loo, so I guess this is where we part. Maybe I'll see you next week?"

"Yeah, maybe. I'm not sure what I'm doing next

week." That was a lie. Lena knew exactly what she would be doing, which was what she'd done this week and the one before and the one before that. She would go to work at a job she hated, then after work she would waste away the hours until it was a reasonable time to go to bed. Then she would start the day all over again until Tuesday came, and she would go see a movie.

"Well, it was nice to finally meet you, Lena. I'm sure we will run into each other sometime."

"It was nice to meet you too," Lena said automatically. She turned and headed towards the exit. In the parking lot she got into her car and sat for a minute, trying to recall the last time she'd made plans with someone.

CHAPTER TWO

Evelyn knew what initially drew her to the girl.

She looked like her daughter, Alice, had when she was that age. They had the same light brown hair falling to their chest, and they shared the same small, freckled nose and wide blue eyes.

Alice got her eyes from Doug, as did their other daughter, Sarah. Evelyn's own eyes were brown—the color of mud. They were insignificant, much like the rest of her looks. This wasn't a self-conscious criticism—it was a simple fact. She hadn't been especially pretty or terribly unattractive in her younger years. Not overly thin or fat, or, smart or dumb. Just an average girl living an average sort of life, and, besides never receiving much attention from boys when all her friends were juggling dates, she had been pretty fine with it.

In fact, Doug had been her first real love interest. They met at Uni when they were both nineteen, and for reasons unknown to Evelyn, Doug singled her out amongst a group of her friends. They had gone to a house party at a mutual friend's place.

Back then, Evelyn had been quite awkward and introverted, raucous parties were not her style. She usually stayed in her dorm room on weekends reading or studying. Somehow her friend, Betty, convinced her to tag along.

So, she found herself awkwardly sitting in a corner

pretending to drink a beer, which after her first sip she'd wanted to discard. Beside her, Betty was throwing her head back, laughing at something some boy had said. The music had been so loud Evelyn didn't know how anyone could hear a single thing, but then again most of them weren't there to talk.

Then, just like in a movie, across the haze, Evelyn spotted Doug.

He stood out in his brown suit and tie while everyone else was more casually dressed. His blonde hair was carefully parted and slicked back, as it would be every day of their marriage. In his hand he held a cigarette, but he looked about as comfortable with it as Evelyn did with her beer.

She instantly liked the look of him, how put together he seemed. He had an organized air about him—like this was a man who wouldn't go out in a stained shirt, who wouldn't leave dishes in the sink, and his socks on the ground. That was high qualities to find in a man (she had been very pleased to discover in time that her assessment of his character had been correct).

She gave him a tentative smile, which must have encouraged him because next thing she knew he was standing next to her, yelling something in her ear. Evelyn had laughed and shook her head, indicating she couldn't hear a thing. He gestured for her to go outside and, relieved for a reason to get out of there, Evelyn followed him out to the yard.

"That's better," Doug had said. He extended his hand formally. "I'm Doug. You looked like you needed to be rescued back there."

"Evelyn," she replied taking his hand.

That was it, all it took. A formal handshake outside

a party neither of them had wanted to be at. She hadn't known it then, of course, but that was the start of Doug rescuing her over and over again. From her disorderly life in the seaside town of St. Ives, Cornwall, to flat tires on the side of the road, nights she couldn't cope with the girls, disappointments and heartache, Doug always rescued her.

Until he couldn't anymore, and Evelyn finally had to rescue herself.

She did a damn good job of it too.

Evelyn was in an excellent mood when she got home that evening after the movie. She hummed a made-up tune as she took the elevator from the parkade up to her floor. She didn't pass anyone in the hallway on the way to her apartment door, but that wasn't unusual for this late at night in a sixty plus building.

In fact, the peace and quiet was one thing that drew her in when she was touring apartments. That and the smell. It had that brand-new, out of the box smell. Not like some other apartments where, despite the upkeep, the smell of years of human inhabitants stained the air. In places like those the carpets had lost their fluffiness, the walls were tired with layers of paint trying to disguise the dents and markings, and the chipped counter tops were not able to mask their age. When she walked into this building, into her apartment, for the first time, she had breathed in deep and known this was going to be the place for the next chapter in her life.

The feeling was solidified when she walked into the kitchen. It was small, but beautiful. A floating island with room for sitting and for preparing dishes. A place to hang her pots, a beautiful gas stove. She had known exactly where she would put all her things. The apartment was a brand-new place for a brand-new era. They were made for each other, she and her little one-bedroom apartment.

It actually reminded Evelyn of the place she and Doug rented when they first got married. She loved their time together in that tiny condo. They couldn't walk around something without their hip hitting a wall. After Alice arrived and all their stuff seemed to multiply, it was so crammed, they couldn't fit another person in there even if they tried. For their little family, though, it was perfect. They didn't stay there long, barely a year before they ended up moving, but Evelyn always longed for that time again. It was a simple, undistracted time of life.

The years have tumbled by since those days, gaining momentum and passing by faster and faster. Now the face in the mirror was barely recognizable, although Evelyn did think her looks got better with age. She had never tried to fight aging like most of her friends did with their bottles of hair dye, special face cream, and secret plastic surgeries. She didn't mind the gray hair and wrinkles, the slower pace of life. It was better than the alternative, wasn't it? Nothing to be ashamed of.

Still, it was a little startling whenever she slowed down enough to really look at herself in the mirror. Despite what she looked like outwardly, she didn't feel like an old person. She never even considered herself a senior until the day she looked at Alice and saw the roots of her eldest daughter's hair turning gray. How strange to see her child getting gray hair and the beginning of wrinkles, like an old lady.

And what on earth did that make her? Was she really turning seventy-one this year?

Well, anyway, Evelyn firmly believed she was

going to live to be a hundred. So, she still had a good thirty years or so to go. All the signs were there. Her mind was still sharp, and her body was still functioning as it should.

Evelyn kept humming as she hung her keys on the hook under the mirror in the entryway. She put her shoes neatly on the rack and smoothed the creases of her jacket on the hanger. She stopped humming and squinted at the picture of a vase of lilies hanging in the living room. Was it crooked again? She could never get it quite right. In a few strides she was across the room and adjusting it.

There. That was better.

She continued her humming as she walked down the hallway to her room where she changed into a blue pajama set, pausing to run her finger across the top of the silver picture frame on her nightstand. Satisfied when her finger came away clean, Evelyn kissed her fingertips and gently touched the image of Doug.

"You would have liked the movie tonight, my darling," she said. "You always loved the romantic ones, even if you pretended you didn't." She let her gaze linger, then forced herself to look away and leave the room. She tried to only let herself feel sad once or twice a month. It took careful thought and great vigilance to achieve this, but she knew it was important. She didn't have very long left on this planet (even if she managed to make it to a hundred) and she couldn't afford to spend it being sad. Doug wouldn't have wanted her to. He was a cheerful man who made it his mission to help anyone who crossed his path. He would have been devastated if he knew how things ended up…

But there was no use going there. Evelyn was doing the best she could to set things right.

Life was too short for anyone to go through it broken-hearted. She firmly believed that. So, when she saw poor Lena's sad looking face in line at the movie theater again, Evelyn had gathered her courage and approached her. It had gone well, she thought. A good beginning.

She was too buoyant about her recent social success to wind down for bed just yet, so she went back down the hall, turned the TV on in the living room and crossed over to the kitchen. With the noise from the news filling the silence, she took her flour dusted apron from the hook, tied it around her waist, and began taking out a few ingredients to whip together some biscuits. Baking had always been the most reliable thing in her life, ever since she was a child, too young to be using a hot stove but having no one care enough to stop her. She never understood people who struggled with it. It was easy. All one needed to do was follow the recipe and there was a predictable, guaranteed outcome. It soothed and reassured her, whenever she needed it.

As she whisked the flour in with the eggs, she felt very optimistic indeed about the night's events. She probably could have talked less. Next time she would try to be more careful. Lena was like a scared little bunny rabbit, ready to bolt if Evelyn moved too quickly. She would need to be strategic in order not to mess this up. Because whether or not Lena knew it, Evelyn was exactly the person Lena needed.

CHAPTER THREE

Lena was fairly certain Chad, the new ad sales rep, and Amy, the graphic designer, were having an affair.

She had no solid proof, of course, but they did take smoke breaks at the same time three times a day and would come back with smug little grins on their faces. That and the fact that Amy hadn't even smoked before Chad joined the newspaper was enough evidence for a conviction in Lena's opinion. Because who just randomly started smoking in their thirties in this day and age? With all the information about cancer and those terrible pictures on the boxes. It didn't make sense unless she was trying to impress somebody.

Lena was privy to all that went on in the newspaper, being the front receptionist. Not that she shared any of her observations with anyone, but it kept her mildly amused in her otherwise boring day.

She watched them head outside together, casually avoiding eye contact as they rounded the building away from the big front windows where Lena could have still seen them. That's where everyone usually smoked—in full view of Lena, unflatteringly squishing their butts against the glass. More evidence. They were totally doing it. Why else would they go out of sight? They were probably hooking up in Chad's disgusting little car right now.

Amy could do better in Lena's opinion. She had the

cute, artsy thing going on with her black frame glasses and chin length hair, dyed bright pink on the ends. Amy was the kind of girl that probably went to concerts on the weekends and lived in a loft style apartment with a beanbag chair in the living room. Chad, on the other hand, was the kind of guy who thought he was the show, but all he had going for him was a whole lot of confidence. He was decent looking enough, Lena supposed, but when she met him with his overconfident swagger and his too much hair gel slicking back his thinning locks, she couldn't help but think, *sleazy*. She hadn't been able to shake that impression yet.

The phone started ringing, Lena snapped it up immediately. "Mirror Chronicle. This is Lena."

"This is Devin. I live at 119 Eastview Ave."

"Hi, Devin, how can I help you?"

"You can help by telling your damn couriers to stop leaving your fucking newspapers at my door."

Ah great. Another one.

"I'll pass it on to circulation. What was your address again?"

"I have called three times now. If I get one more damn paper, I'm gonna come over there and throw them at *your* building on a windy day. How would you like that?"

"I certainly hope it doesn't come to that. Can I get your address again?"

Lena jotted down the address, then held the phone away from her ear until Devin Dickhead was done with his yelling. Then she wished him a pleasant day and hung up quickly.

Those calls used to bother her and make her face flame up, but she'd grown used to them over the four years she had worked for the paper. She got at least three calls a day complaining about something. It was part of the job. The complaints varied; a story they didn't like, the paper delivery person leaving the paper in the snow, wanting the paper, not wanting the paper…Didn't really matter what it was. They were all pissed about something. She'd had no idea newspapers had such an emotional effect on people before she worked at one.

At least it was mildly interesting dealing with angry individuals. Other than that, she answered emails, entered ads into the filing system on the computer, took messages and payments for ads, and stared at the wall— in between checking social media pages and playing computer games, of course. It was the first job she'd landed when she and James moved to the city after the wedding. Lena had figured the job would be temporary, something to pass the time until they got pregnant, but it turned out James hadn't wanted kids right away. Now he was gone, and here she still was.

"Martin!" Jerry, her boss, said rounding the corner. "How are you this morning, lovely? Brought your A-game today?"

Lena flicked her gaze to the slightly pudgy, bald man in front of her and tried to swallow the automatic irritation that rose whenever she heard his voice.

Jerry had played hockey growing up. He would brag to anyone who would listen that he could have made it to the NHL, but 'politics' got in the way. Whatever that meant. Now he was a typical fifty-year-old washed-up jock who couldn't let go of the 'good ole days'. He referred to everyone by their last name and was always using sports analogies, like how they all needed to be 'team players' and 'go for gold'. Lena had never been a fan of sports and found this type of talk exceptionally maddening. The fact that he flirted with every female in the vicinity wasn't half as annoying as his sports talk.

"I'm good, Jerry. How are you?"

"Terrific. You're looking stunning, as usual."

His eyes slid down to her neckline, as usual. She knew her skin was turning red under his stare and hated herself for it. He loved to make her blush. It must have fed his little ego somehow. She was used to it; the boys growing up made a sport out of her blushing. They used to pull her hair, sing songs about her kissing someone in a tree, snap her bra straps. Once, Johnny, a bigwig in grade seven, sat beside her on the bus and said he had a secret to tell her. When she leaned closer he kissed her on the cheek. Her face had instantly turned crimson and the whole bus laughed.

Jerry smiled the smug smile of a man who had no clue how he came across. "Listen. We are gonna have a team meeting on Thursday. Make sure everyone gets the memo and order some pizza. Not from that place you got it last time."

"Sure thing."

"That's my girl." He winked at her before disappearing down the hall again.

Lena might have hated her job a little less if Jerry hadn't been her boss.

Chad and Amy came back in just then. Amy gave Lena a brief smile before rounding the corner. Chad lingered, watching Amy go as he leaned against the front counter. Lena wrinkled her nose against the smell of tobacco easing off him. So, they did do a bit of smoking out there…along with whatever else they did.

"Need something?" Lena asked.

What she wanted to say was, "How's your wife, Chad?" In a pointed, *I know what you're up to,* voice. In her daydreams, she could pull it off.

"Yeah." Chad snapped his gaze away and gave her a big smile. "Hey, listen, I got a client coming in at three to pay a bill. I put it on your desk this morning."

"I got it."

"Good. And if you got some spare time, I'm gonna email you a list of photos to find for some ads."

"Okay."

"Awesome. Thanks." Chad turned to go, then hesitated. "Hey, Lena…couple of us might get drinks after. Do you want to…?"

"Oh." Lena's face heated. "Thanks, but I'm meeting up with someone later."

Her co-workers used to ask her out now and then. She used to always say no until one night she decided to say yes. Just for the hell of it. It went terribly. Seeing her co-workers in a setting outside of work had been unsettling. She couldn't help but think as she watched her colleagues order another round of drinks that she spent enough time as it was with these people. Why then was she wasting her evening in a loud bar where she could barely hear anything, watching them drink and having nothing to say? She went back to saying no after that.

When James died she didn't have to worry about it anymore. She took two months off. When she returned they gave her a condolence card, then avoided eye-contact. Something about death scared people off. Like they thought they could catch it if they spent too much time with her. Or maybe it was the vibe she gave off, the tragic   leave-me-alone-to-wallow-in-my-widowhood feeling she emanated. Chad mustn't have gotten the message yet.

"Yeah, okay, no problem. Maybe next time." He shifted awkwardly. "I just heard about how you lost your husband last year. That sucks."

Or maybe he had.

"Yeah. Thanks." Lena automatically started fiddling with her wedding ring, as she tended to do whenever someone unexpectedly brought up her marriage, or lack thereof.

"It was a car accident?"

"Yup."

This was the very worst small talk topic ever. *Go away now*, Lena pleaded.

"I had a cousin, well a friend of a cousin who—"

The phone ringing cut him off. Lena leapt for it. "Mirror Chronicle. This is Lena…Sorry about that, I'll pass it on to circulation for you. What's your address?" Lena scribbled the address down with great concentration. She could see Chad make a hasty retreat in her peripheral vision.

She found two things generally happened when people found out her husband died. Either they avoided talking about it, or they started sharing about everyone they knew who had died and how, as if it was a club. Lena should have been used to it. That's what bonded her and James after all, sharing about the loss in their lives at a college group grief counselling session. Not the most romantic beginning. He'd just lost his mother to cancer, and she'd lost her friend Cheryl to—well—an *accident*. That's what everyone said: that it was an accident.

Anyway, now she knew to avoid eye contact with

Chad.

The day slowly dripped by afterwards. She ran completely out of work by three and spent the last two hours in acute boredom, waiting for the phone to ring or for someone to come in. When five o'clock finally rolled around, Lena was the last to leave as usual. The sales reps were almost all reliably gone by four, claiming meetings with clients, while the reporters kept such odd hours covering stories no one kept track of where they were. Lena said goodbye to the last of the graphic designers, turned off the lights, locked the door behind her, and hurried to her car.

The heat of summer was beginning to turn to the chill of fall, the days slowly getting shorter and shorter. Soon she would leave home and arrive home in the dark, but right now the sun was still reasonably high, warming her skin as she crossed the parking lot. It was a relief summer was almost over. She used to love the warmer months, but now it just made her feel restless and guilty. Like she should be outside doing something instead of hanging out in her condo watching TV. Lena found she now preferred the long, snowy days of winter, when it was usually so cold she didn't have to have much of an excuse to stay indoors and roll up in a fuzzy blanket.

By the time she made her way across town through the slow-moving traffic, it was almost six. Her downstairs neighbor, whose name she had yet to find out, was sitting on his step, smoking. His long lanky frame was stretched out and shaggy dark hair fell over his forehead.

"How's it going?" he asked her.

"Good, you?"

"Good."

Lena gave him a little smile, then let herself into her condo. Same conversation every day. Maybe she should switch it up next time and say 'great' instead of 'good'. That might add some spark to the interaction.

It was an improvement, though. When James was here, the neighbor and her had said nothing at all to each other. His hostility towards her husband had naturally rolled onto her. His affinity for loud music and louder friends made James on more than one occasion bang his fist on the neighbor's door and unleash some choice words. Which—fairly—made every interaction she had with him quite awkward.

James and her never could figure out what he did for a living, he always seemed to be home. Judging from a suspicious-looking plant in the window and the occasional smells seeping through the floor, they had a few guesses. Now, Lena never went down and complained about his music or his friends, so their interactions had grown friendlier. Even when the bass was so loud her floor vibrated, she let him carry on and do his thing. It actually comforted her some, knowing there was another living person so close. Sometimes when he was having one of his parties, she laid on the floor and listened to the murmured voices, the high-pitched laughter. She let it surround her, breaking apart the usual sounds of nothing. This usually led her to sinking into a very low mental state and consuming a bottle or two of wine.

It worked out to get drunk in sync with her neighbor. That way they would both be quiet in solidarity in the morning.

Lena kicked off her shoes inside the door, then locked the three door locks. She listened to the satisfying safety of the clicks. She had them installed a couple months after James had died.

She'd never actually lived by herself before; she'd gone from her parents' place, to college dorms, to living with James. The first few weeks of silence had been unsettling enough, but then her water pressure started acting up and she had to call a plumber. It was the first time she'd been alone with another man in the condo and she'd been highly aware of just how much bigger and stronger the forty-something man kneeling under her sink was. Lena had the terrifying realization that, with just the two of them there, he could turn and grab her, and do whatever he wanted. And she couldn't stop him. It was all she could think about as he politely made small talk.

She wondered if those thoughts ever occurred to men. If even the most upstanding, well brought up man ever thought, *huh, I could hurt this girl if I wanted to. I could pin her down and take what I want, and no one could stop me.* She imagined it did. The terrible stories she'd heard about cab drivers taking advantage of vulnerable women, or the unsettling stories of women being grabbed on their runs… The man must have thought, *well, what the hell,* and just did it because he could.

After that moment with the plumber, Lena had gone out and bought the three locks and decided to ask her brother or father to come over if something needed maintenance again.

After making sure the door was securely bolted shut, Lena trekked up the flight of stairs. A ground floor unit would have been more convenient, but both she and James had loved the upstairs condo when they first saw it. It had a bit of a mountain cabin feel to it with its own door and entryway that led directly into their space. The vaulted ceiling in the living room helped the place feel bigger than it was. It was only nine-hundred square-feet; one bedroom, a den and bath, but it was perfect for the couple years until they could move into something larger. The only flaw was it was right next to a busy intersection, so there was a constant hum of traffic in the background. This was especially noticeable at night (a fact they hadn't realized until after they bought it). It also got almost unbearably hot in the summer. And, of course, there was the very thin floor between them and their downstairs neighbor…so maybe there were a couple flaws. But, it was home…because she didn't have anywhere else to go and it probably would take forever to sell the condo if she tried.

Just as she pulled her blouse over her head and flung it onto her bedroom floor, her cell phone rang.

Lena answered it without looking at the caller I.D. "Hey, mom."

"Hey, hon. How was work?"

"It was fine. What are you up to?"

"I'm at your brother's, watching Noah, while Carrie and the baby sleep."

In the background Lena could hear her five-year-old nephew yelling about something. She grimaced. "You're a good soul."

"I know," her mom sighed. "But Carrie's mom is still in Mexico and Carrie needs help. Imagine being in Mexico when your only daughter has her baby! I would never do that to you."

"How is little Leslie?" Lena asked, padding into the kitchen. She opened the fridge and stared, uninspired at the few contents. Half a jug of milk, some leftovers from take out. A block of cheese. Half a bottle of red wine. Wilted grapes.

Lovely.

She sighed. Every day the same dilemma. She hated the fact humans had to eat so damn much in a day. She wished there was some sort of injection that would give a person the feeling of being full and all the sustenance needed. She would take that in a heartbeat.

"Not sleeping very well, I'm afraid," her mom was saying.

"Oh?" She grabbed the bottle of wine and shut the door.

"I wonder if maybe she isn't eating enough." Her mom's voice dropped to a whisper, "I want to ask…if maybe the *procedure* might hinder things. But you know…"

"She's still not admitting to the boob job?" It was a strange, unspoken thing between Carrie and the rest of the family. Clearly, she hadn't been born with her double D sized breasts that barely moved when she walked. She had a tiny frame that didn't quite suit the enhancement. Yet she talked about plastic surgery with an air of disdain, as if she hadn't been one of the many women to get work done.

Whenever she did this, Lena and her mom would be careful not to make eye contact. Lena didn't know why Carrie didn't just own it.

Lena had actually looked at getting breast surgery herself. Before the accident, James had been hinting she should look into it.

Afterwards, she never thought about it again. She wasn't really on board with the whole idea, if she were being honest with herself. She just couldn't imagine showing up to work one day with new, massive breasts and having a normal conversation. Jerry already gave that area of her body enough attention. He would never leave her desk if she showed up like that. And what about her dad? How could she look him in the eye? She didn't know how girls did it. The thought of being stared at like that, at having her breasts be the first thing people noticed about her…it just didn't seem appealing at all.

"Yes, exactly. It's awkward." Her mom said. "I did google it, and google says you can breastfeed even if you have the…um."

"Implants?"

"Yes. Apparently you can breastfeed, but it can affect the amount of milk—oh it's okay, love." In the background Leslie began to cry.

Lena went to the pantry and began rummaging around for a box of chocolate chip cookies. "Are you going to swing by here before you head home?"

"I would, but I'm in a bit of a rush. We have the Wrights coming over tonight. I'll see you Sunday though, right? You're still coming to help pack the house."

"Um…"

"Selena, you promised. You and Roy both said you would be there."

Lena sighed. "Yes, okay. I'll be there."

"Great," her mom said. "Listen, I have to go. Roy is getting home. I'll call you tomorrow. Bye, love."

"Bye, mom."

"And don't just have cookies and wine tonight. Make a proper meal, okay?"

"You got it," Lena said, bringing the two offending

items to the couch. She tossed her phone aside and turned the TV on. Flicking through the channels, she settled on a home renovation show.

As she systematically ate through the box of cookies between sipping the red wine from the bottle, she watched the two interior decorators' debate about wall colors and pictures.

Lena surveyed her own home. Maybe she needed an upgrade: something fresh. The place was basically the same as it was when she and James had moved in. The den still had a large Oilers poster tacked on the wall that James had insisted on hanging. The living room had about five pictures that James had thought went with the couches that Lena's mom hated. The walls were still painted a light brown that was badly chipped. Lena had wanted to paint it a nice light gray, but James thought it had been fine the way it was. In their bedroom, hanging above their bed, was a massive, framed photo from their wedding day.

About seven months after his funeral, Lena and her mom had carefully sorted through James' clothes: keeping a couple items and donating most of the rest. They never talked about taking down the wedding photo, or any of the other things that were obviously his. Lena didn't want to then, but now that she had hit the year mark, maybe she should consider it. His fingerprints were still so clearly around the condo. It was definitely more his style than hers.

Though to be fair, she wasn't completely sure what her style was. Besides painting the walls gray, she wasn't sure what else she would do with the place.

How did people get on these renovation shows? Did a person have to apply? She'd bet she had a good chance of getting picked. She had a pretty good tragedy story. It would definitely be a tearjerker episode. Maybe she should look into it.

Not that she wanted to remove every trace of him. She would be fine existing like this for a while longer. Maybe forever. But whenever her mom came over she was starting to give Lena looks. There was going to be a conversation soon. Lena could just see it, how her mom would gently try to tell her it was time to make the place her own. And she was probably right.

Lena grabbed the remote and changed the channel. She didn't want to think about all that right now. She wanted to think about nothing. Taking longer swigs from the bottle, Lena laid down and lost herself in the blue light of the TV, slowly twirling the diamond ring still on her finger.

CHAPTER FOUR

Evelyn's life was very scheduled.

Sometimes this bothered her—she hated to feel like she was in a rut—but it was just so convenient to know what was coming next and when it would happen. If she didn't keep things in a routine, she couldn't possibly spend time with everyone she cared about. And at her age time was precious, indeed.

On Thursdays she met with her friends at the mall food court. Weekends were for her family—usually someone had some event happening on Saturday that she would attend: lacrosse, hockey, etc. Though these things would get less frequent now that all her grandkids had almost graduated. Sundays were reserved for church and having dinner with whoever could make it. And, Tuesdays, of course, were movie night at the cheap theater.

She kept some days free so that she could fit in her various volunteer duties. Evelyn was on the library board and the Senior Center board. She served at the soup kitchen twice a month, volunteered at the old folks' home when they did their teas, and helped the community drama club when they needed people to be ushers.

In her spare time, Evelyn liked to go for walks around the city parks. They had the most wonderful walking paths in the clumps of forest spread throughout

Red Deer. She found she enjoyed walking outdoors as opposed to the track at the gym. It felt healthier for her soul to breathe in fresh air instead of stale sweat and air-conditioning.

It was important to stay active, especially at her age. Folks could go downhill quickly in their latter years. Her mother had been walking with a cane at the tender age of seventy-two, and was wheelchair bound by her eighties. Amazing, the extremes. Alice had just shown her an Instagram account of a woman who was seventy-seven doing some strange upside-down pose, her muscles bulging against her wrinkles. She had a six-pack and everything. It was a little disconcerting; it looked like someone had taken an elderly person's head and photoshopped it onto a younger, muscular body. Evelyn wasn't trying to be that extreme, she just wanted to be able to move from point A to point B with some degree of ease.

Today was Thursday, so she was at the mall with her friends June, Mavis, and Nora. In solidarity with her quest to not be an invalid (and because Nora had a health scare last year that made them all feel quite paranoid) they started their little meetings with a brisk walk around the mall just as it was opening.

"Come along, Mavis, Nora. You two are falling behind," Evelyn said, arms pumping.

"I'll…kill her. I swear. I'll kill her." Mavis huffed.

"Your threats don't scare me. You've had plenty of opportunities to off me in the last forty years, and here I am."

"Maybe," Mavis breathed. "I've just been…biding my time."

"Hush both of you." Nora gasped, head down, her

pudgy legs working twice as hard to keep up. "I'm concentrating."

June, ahead of everyone, looked over her shoulder. "Almost there, ladies."

As they reached the bed and bath place another group of elderly comrades' power-walked by. Evelyn nodded to them in solidarity, then focused on her breathing as they reached the last stretch. They rounded the corner, the food court straight ahead. The coffee shop they usually sat by was just opening.

"Thank god. Thank god." Mavis got a sudden burst of speed.

They made it to their table and Nora collapsed down. "Water, please, Evie dear. And a coffee."

"Yes, ma'am. For you, Mavis?"

"Vodka. Stat."

"That's the last thing *you* need." June said with a sniff.

"And probably just the thing *you* need, Junie."

Evelyn chuckled and moved with June to go get the coffees. They brought them back and settled in their seats—Evelyn beside Mavis, June across from her and beside Nora. The four of them made quite the group. Mavis and Evelyn had been friends since Evelyn had arrived in Canada. They managed all the big milestones together. Their kids had attended the same school, so they had bonded over field trips and high school basketball games, then they helped each other through menopause and adjusting to being empty nesters. Nora, who was sweet and plump with a hint of her red hair still streaking her gray, joined them twenty years ago after Evelyn met her in an aqua-size class. She had instantly admired Nora's sunny nature, and her genuine appreciation for baked goods (hence the need for the aqua-size). June was the last to join, having connected through the senior center just five years ago.

June was the eldest of them and looked it with her short fluffy white hair and wrinkled face (clearly, no one had told her about the benefits of face cream in her younger days, that, or Evelyn suspected she'd overdone it with the tanning beds). June had a slightly harsh disposition. Evelyn often thought they would not have been friends in their younger years, but age gave her grace for all types of people, and she found she could even appreciate June's frankness in a world that was turning more and more to flattery and falsehood.

Nora rubbed her lower back, moaning. "Why do you make us do that every time, Evie? I swear you are hasting me to my grave."

"We do it, so that we have the ability to wipe our own asses for as long as possible," Mavis said.

June frowned. "Must you always be so crass?"

"Must you always have a stick up your—"

"Alright, ladies, if I wanted to listen to bickering I could have gone for breakfast with my daughters," said Evelyn.

"How are your girls?" Nora asked. "I worry about them, poor things."

"Good, I think. Sarah and Cam are doing marital counselling." *Again*, she added privately. They'd been in and out of counselling for years. Separate from the personal therapist Sarah had been seeing since her early thirties. Evelyn often wondered what sort of things Sarah told her therapist. No doubt they discussed her childhood memories to death—as if Sarah had anything to complain about. Her girls had wonderful childhoods, thank you very much—but if complaining to a stranger about the minuscule hardships of growing up in a stable, loving, well-adjusted family helped with her—*issues*—then Evelyn supposed that was what mattered.

"I think it's helping." Evelyn continued. "They seemed better last I saw them. I know she is on some new medication, which seems to be helping with the depression."

Nora nodded. "She took the loss of Doug hard, didn't she? They were close, weren't they?"

"Yes, but—"

"She's always struggled with depression, hasn't she?" said Mavis, "I remember when she was in college, didn't she have a month there when she barely got out of bed?"

"Doug was always good, helping her get back on her feet." Evelyn sighed. "It's hard, watching her struggle. There's not much I can do, though. That's what Alice keeps telling me, at least." She couldn't keep the bitter note from creeping into her voice. She didn't like being told there was nothing to be done. There was *always* something to be done. One just needed to be creative enough to find it, which Evelyn always was. The problem here was that her sure-fire plan of helping her second born had always been her husband.

"There isn't," said June. "My Albert struggled horribly with his mental health when we were first married. Course, back then it wasn't talked about like it is now. Just being there is all you can do, really. Especially, you know, considering Sarah is…what now? Forty-five?"

"Forty-six," said Evelyn.

"Right, forty-six. It's not like you can coddle her

like some lost twenty-year-old."

Evelyn nodded, pretending she agreed, when she, in fact, did not. It didn't matter what age her daughters were, if they were struggling, she would intervene. Give her some time, she would come up with something to help Sarah. There was no doubt in her mind.

If only Doug was here.

The longing hit her hard, as it did now and then. She took a long sip of her tea then turned and pretended to look through her bag for something so she could collect herself, letting her friends' discussion wash over her.

When she felt her voice was stable again, she piped up with a change of topic, "Anyway, I'm sure she will be fine. Alice at least is doing great. She is loving being a grandmother."

"Doesn't that make you feel ancient?" Mavis clucked. "Your daughter a grandmother? Lord, we are getting up there."

Nora sighed. "Please, let's not talk about dying. I feel like we are always talking about dying."

"Dying, failing health, the grandkids, that's what life is now," June said. "Might as well accept it."

Mavis frowned. "Must you be so pessimistic? You know, you are why us elderly have reputations for being cranky old biddies."

"Why *do* people get so cranky at the end of life?" Evelyn mused. "Is it because of unfulfilled dreams, you think? Regrets?"

Mavis cocked her head. "Do you have unfulfilled dreams? I don't think I do."

"I don't think it's that. It's because we are finally tired of putting up with everybody's crap," said June.

"Maybe," Nora cut in, "It's because we are so sore

all the time. I swear every day I have a new ache and pain. The other day I actually needed Phil's help, just to get off the couch! I'm going to end up with a walker, I just know it."

"You won't," Evelyn declared. "That's why we power walk, Nora."

June circled back, ignoring them. "Or maybe it's because most things worth living for have already been accomplished and there just isn't much to look forward to anymore."

Mavis snorted. "Maybe that's the case for you, June, but the rest of us still have some zip in our zazz. For instance, Dave did the most amazing thing to me last night in bed, he—"

Nora and Evelyn groaned as June scowled. "No! No, no, no. We are not going to listen to another one of your disturbing sex things."

"It's hardly disturbing. You know, I think I'm having the best sex of my life with Dave. That's saying something because back in my twenties I was with this man who was so incredibly talented with his hands. Just thinking about it makes me—"

Evelyn snorted.

Nora turned pink. "Stop, Mavis!"

"Nora, out of everyone here you should be most interested. At least you're still having sex. You could learn a thing or two for you and Phil."

"I'm married still as well, in case you forgot," said June.

Mavis smirked. "Your point?"

June glared.

"Alright, ladies." Evelyn intervened. "Let's change the topic. What's the book this month, Junie?"

"*Still Alice*. You have three weeks to read it, so I don't want to hear any excuses."

"Oh good, a heart-warmer," Mavis said. "Couldn't you have picked something a little cheerier?"

"We read one of your horrible romance one's last month," June said. "Or at least I did. Is anyone going to read this time? If you all don't start taking it seriously, I'm going to start a book club somewhere else."

"That would be devastating," Mavis said.

"We'll do our best, Junie." Nora stood and started gathering her things. "Sorry, ladies, I should get going. I'm meeting Phil for brunch."

They all got to their feet and said their goodbyes— Nora and June headed out the nearest exit as Mavis and Evelyn left the food court to leisurely peruse the stores. They always parked at the farthest exit, so they had an excuse to do some shopping on the way out. Not that Evelyn ever needed an excuse, Doug had never harassed her about shopping like some husbands were prone to do—obsessed with money as they all seemed to be. For them it was quite the opposite, Doug used to always encourage her to spoil herself more. He would sometimes give her cash to go on shopping sprees (as if she couldn't access all their money herself, but she appreciated the thought behind it). She didn't like excessive amounts of clothing and things though.

Every spring she went through all her possessions from her clothes to her closets and donated anything that had not been used within the year. It was a very strict policy she stuck to, one that used to drive her family batty (no doubt her obsessive purging made it into Sarah's therapy talks), but Doug had understood it. He had seen Evelyn's mum's house after all—seen the piles of magazines, boxes of unused dishes from some garage sale or other, the stacks of clothes, takeout containers piled around the house with trails of ants around them…Her mum had been what Evelyn called a low-grade hoarder. Not enough to warrant a place on those awful TV shows, but just enough to make it so Evelyn had never invited her friends over.

Sometimes the smell of something rocketed her back to those days—old pizza, the musty scent of dust, sour milk…the scents of her childhood. Funny how thinking of those days still made her feel sick. She read somewhere that life was top heavy. That what happened during childhood was so significant that it affected and echoed through the rest of a person's life. It seemed unfair—talk about putting pressure on parents—but Evelyn knew it to be true. Here she was at seventy, and still she was haunted by arguably the shortest season of her life.

So, while Mavis would be laden with shopping bags by the end of their time, buying who knows what with the divorce money she'd accumulated over the years, Evelyn kept her shopping in check, selecting only a few things for her kids and grandkids if she came across something interesting. She took great pleasure in purchasing them things; she was always supplying them with clever knickknacks from the TV commercial store, as well as candles, fancy chocolates and colorful scarves. Her latest obsession was bath bombs. She'd seen them around, but not until recently had she tried one. She was not a big bather, preferring the efficiency and cleanliness of showers, but just last week she'd spotted this multi-colored bath bomb that smelled like roses. That night she took her first bath in her condo. She watched the ball frizz and shrink, turning the water a murky pink with floating blue hearts. Her skin felt shimmery and soft after, and she smelled like she'd dipped herself in a bottle of perfume. It was heaven. Now she planned on bathing once a week, each time with a different bath bomb. She got some for her daughters and granddaughters too.

It was a funny thing between them all: her buying them these little gifts, and them saying a heartfelt thank you and then exchanging looks behind her back. They would never tell her to stop, but she'd seen a few items she had given them for sale on Facebook (as if she wouldn't notice—now and then she would comment on them, just to make them squirm). It wasn't like she got them *junk;* it was almost always something useful, something they needed even if they didn't know it yet. Perhaps that was part of the problem though…like last month Evelyn bought Alice a trimmer for her upper lip. Lord knew the girl could use it. Her hair there tended to get a little on the fuzzy side. Alice had seemed very offended by the nudge and didn't hide it very well. Oh well. That was a mother's job, after all, to look out for the best interests of her family even if it was unpopular.

Maybe she should get a little something for Lena while she was here. She considered this as she followed Mavis around a clothing store, half-heartedly listening to her ongoing commentary about what clothing items she *desperately* needed to find. Evelyn could get Lena something simple. A candle, perhaps? It was always nice to have candles, especially during the fall. A nice pumpkin spice candle, or perhaps an evergreen scented one. Once she came across a roasted marshmallow scent that was just lovely. That might be nice…but she didn't know much about Lena. Maybe she had an abundance of candles, or maybe she was one of those people who got headaches from aromatic smells.

Something edible, then? Chocolates or candies? Maybe Evelyn could bake her something, biscuits or what not. That might be weird though, to give Lena a gift on their second meeting. Evelyn didn't want to be overbearing. It was probably best to wait until their third or fourth get together before she gave anything, give herself a chance to get to know Lena a little better.

Happy with this plan, Evelyn picked up a shirt that said, 'I'm Not For Everyone' and chuckled as she tried to decide how offended Sarah would be if she got it for her.

CHAPTER FIVE

Lena hated weekends.

She wasn't always this way. She used to be a normal person, excited on Fridays, reveling in the novelty of wearing jeans to work and doing nothing productive after the noon hour until home time. It was silly really, it was only two days of the week, yet it fueled such enthusiasm with its possibility of freedom and life. In reality, weekends weren't even that exciting. What did people do? Stay up late, sleep in, binge watch TV, clean the house? That's what she and James did at least, though a lot of times he was busy showing houses to potential buyers, so she would be by herself—quite bored— waiting for him to come home.

Then on Monday everyone went back to the same old same old, all melancholy because the weekend was so far away again. A depressing cycle at the best of times. Maybe it was different for people who actually had a passion for their jobs—but that has to be, what? Twenty percent of the population? Thirty? She had no idea, but it seemed like most of humanity were just working whatever jobs to make money so they could waste away the weekends in some level of leisure.

Except now she dreaded the weekend because she didn't have anyone to waste it with. She was just alone, sometimes not talking to anyone from Friday night at five till Monday morning at eight. She had her parents, sometimes Roy and Carrie, but she couldn't rely on them every weekend. They had their own things going on, like every other person except Lena it seemed.

The question that plagued her during the week and especially on the weekends was, what *was* she working for? It wasn't to support her active lifestyle, not to support a family, not because she loved it…She actually didn't even need the money. She had enough life insurance from James that if she wanted to she didn't have to work for a couple years—more if she was frugal. But the thought of having an eternal weekend stretched a head of her, with nothing to do, no reason to get out of bed…it was not in the least bit appealing.

So, she reported for duty every Monday to a job that was only slightly more amusing than watching paint dry. She wondered what young Lena would have thought of her current self. She often wondered this about people— if she saw an obese woman waddling down the sidewalk, or a sketchy looking man with a beard down to his chest and a cigarette hanging from his lips. What would their childhood selves think of these adults if they saw them? Would they think they were intimidating? Sad? Embarrassing? Would they have pointed and whispered to their friends about them as they passed?

She was pretty sure her childhood self wouldn't be overly surprised at her outcome. She had never dreamt big, even back then.

Her mom thought she should travel, discover herself or something. Like the *Eat, Pray, Love* woman. But what was the difference going somewhere to be alone, or just staying home and being alone? Either way, it was the same result, her staring out some window, alone.

That's what she was doing now. Staring out the

window at all the traffic roaring through the intersection, slowly sipping coffee. The honking and revving engines filtered through her cracked window, along with a slightly chilly breeze. Where were all those people going on a Saturday? So purposeful, so needing to be somewhere. Good for them.

Come on, something happen. Please.

Someone text and not pay attention. Fiddle with the radio. Nothing too devastating, just a good T-Bone, or fender bender. Something to add a little spark to her day. Once or twice a week there was usually an incident on this intersection.

One time she even saw two men get out and have a fist fight at the red light. She could see them from her place at her window grappling with each other, getting a few good swings in before getting stuck in a sort of awkward embrace. Not nearly as impressive and thrilling as the movies made fighting seem. It actually looked more embarrassing than anything. No one moved to intervene, everyone just sat in their cars until the light changed, then they drove around the men who eventually broke up and went to their own vehicles. Stupid men. A person would never see two women get out and start punching each other over road-rage. Right?

Maybe it could happen…if it did it would probably end up on YouTube or something with a bunch of creeps making comments. Women do not get any respect when they get physical. Men always label it a catfight and try to turn it into something sexy. She never understood what there was to be turned on about when women fight.

It was quite sexist, actually.

A woman should be able to punch another woman and be taken seriously. She should tell the feminist people to get that on the list, maybe in between fair wages and the free the nipple movement.

She took another sip of coffee and wandered away, back to the couch. More out of habit than anything, she pulled out her phone and began scrolling through Facebook. Why she had an account, she didn't quite know. She never posted. What would she even say if she did? *Another night alone on the couch! #Eternallyandmiserabllychilling!*

No, she was a more of a silent social media lurker. Never liking anything, never commenting—just looking. Watching people she went to high school and college with age, their families grow, their hair change. She supposed it sort of felt like a way to connect to people, even if she never actually engaged. At least she knew what was going on: who was getting married, who cooked fish for supper, who got a new car...

At the very least, it was a type of amusement— another mind-numbing activity that helped the minutes pass by. She especially enjoyed following the social and political debates people started. It was cheap entertainment reading, all the heated comments. Sometimes she would type out her own response if something was offensive enough, but she always deleted it.

She scrolled meaninglessly for several minutes, then paused on a hair salon ad with an impossibly gorgeous model, silky hair blowing in the wind.

Hmm.

Lena fiddled with her hair, quite long now. She'd dyed it once in high school, out of a box. The color had faded away within a year. Last time she cut it was nearly two years ago. James had been working an open house on a Saturday, so Lena had decided to get her hair done. The hairdresser had been less than enthused when she unraveled Lena's hair from its braid, it swung down almost the length of her back.

"You know, you have a face shape that would look so good with short hair," she had said, drawing out the word 'so', her penciled in eyebrows not moving an inch. Her own hair was cut to her chin in a stylish bob. It looked alright, and since Lena didn't really care (and she wasn't very good at saying no) she let the hairdresser do whatever she liked.

Lena left feeling so light she could have floated away. The hair swishing around her cheeks looked quite trendy, she had thought. She looked like a different person, like the type who could pull off knee-high boots and a black leather jacket. It was a bit exhilarating. By the time she got home, James was sitting on the couch watching TV. He took one look at her hair and had said, "What did you do."

"I got it cut," Lena answered, her hand going to her head. Already her heart had sunk and her face heated.

He stared at her a minute longer, then looked back at the TV. "Maybe you can get extensions."

Lena hadn't cut her hair since.

Maybe it was time, though. Not for a chop—she wouldn't be doing that again—but maybe for those highlights she'd been thinking of…

Yes, why not? A trip to the salon would waste away a couple hours at least. Maybe she would pick up a pizza on the way home and then settle in for a movie. Not a bad Saturday at all.

It was meant to be. Lena called the hair school downtown and was able to get in that afternoon.

According to some eavesdropped conversations between Amy the graphic designer and some others at work, it was the best and cheapest place to get hair done if a person didn't mind being a bit of a guinea pig.

Lena arrived downtown fifteen minutes early. It took ten minutes to find a parking space, which unfortunately ended up being on the other side of downtown than the salon. She was five minutes late and completely out of breath by the time she burst through the door. The receptionist, a bored-looking student, barely looked up from her phone at Lena's arrival.

"I'm Lena. Martin. For two o'clock?" Lena huffed.

The girl, who looked exceptionally young with too much eyeliner and horribly dyed blonde hair, glanced at the computer and said, "Take a seat." Then, with a put-upon sigh, went around the desk to presumably go find Lena's hairdresser.

Lena sat on the edge of the plastic chair, her knee drumming up and down. She was feeling uneasy after seeing the receptionist's fried bleached hair…maybe she should've gone to a place with fully trained people. She wasn't as adventurous as Amy, who Lena was sure could pull off a hair disaster episode with a laugh. Women with sparkling, confident personalities could pull off anything. It didn't matter what they looked like; they attracted people to them like magnets, good hair notwithstanding.

Cheryl had been like that.

Ever since they were kids, she had that irresistible air. It was something people were born with, if they were lucky. Lena hadn't been lucky. She had to work hard to make some sort of impression on the people around her. She wasn't sure she could survive, with grace, another bad hair decision. After the big cut she'd lost her mind a little, googling how to make hair grow faster, which resulted in her laying upside down on the couch to get more blood flow to her roots, washing her hair with rosemary herbs, and rubbing coconut oil in her scalp. Not to mention the expensive pills that promised exponential growth, which in truth were just an exponential waste of money.

She was considering fleeing when a woman dressed in black, who looked to be Lena's age or older, rounded the corner with bad-blonde-job trailing behind.

The woman tucked a piece of dark hair behind her ear. "Lena? I'm Stacey, I'll be your hairdresser this afternoon." She gave Lena a friendly smile showing off perfectly white, straight teeth. "Follow me."

Lena sat in the chair Stacey stopped beside. After she fixed the choker cape around her neck, Stacey clapped. "Right, what are we doing today?" She smoothed Lena's hair with her hands, playing with the ends.

"I think, just some highlights?"

Stacey nodded. "Alright, bit of a trim too?"

"Not too much," Lena said quickly.

"Half an inch?" Stacey held up a chunk of her hair to show. "Just to make it healthy. One sec, I just need to grab my teacher." Stacey disappeared for a moment then came back with another woman in tow. After explaining what she was going to do and how she was going to do it, the teacher left, and Stacey mixed some color.

Lena watched in the mirror as Stacey dabbed color on and covered the pieces with foil. Lena tried to avoid studying her own reflection too much, hairdresser light always made her feel especially pale and dull. Maybe because most of the women who worked in salons had such vibrant hair colors and heavily applied make-up, Lena felt like a child next to them. Stacey didn't seem like that though, her make-up was simple, and her hair was done up in a loose ponytail. She hummed as she worked, not asking the usual bunch of questions hairdressers asked.

Normally, Lena would have appreciated this, but as she watched Stacey's hands gently applying the color with expert speed, she felt a bit curious. Most of the students working the salon looked younger. This woman had to be in her thirties.

"How long have you been a, um, student here?"

Stacey smiled proudly. "I graduate in two weeks!"

Well, that was good. She must have a fairly good idea what she was doing then. Lena relaxed a little. "What made you want to become a hairdresser?"

"I'm getting divorced." Stacey said it as if she just announced she won a free vacation. "I have a little boy who is two. His daddy will help with childcare, but I wanted something I could do out of my home until he is in school."

"Oh…I'm sorry."

"Don't be. He was an ass." Stacey laughed.

"Oh."

"I'm the happiest I've been in years actually," Stacey continued. "It's been kind of exciting. I never thought I would start over at thirty-two. But here I am, new career, new life, dating again…"

"I can't imagine dating again." Lena said without thinking.

"You're married?"

"I'm…yes. I am." Lena clenched her hands together

under the hairdresser's robe. It was easier than going through the usual, *no, I'm not anymore. Divorced? No widow. Oh my gosh, I'm so sorry.* And then all talk turns to death, how did he die, who she knows who died. How hard it is. Until that piddles out into awkward silence.

"Are you happy?" Stacey asked.

"Um."

"It's just, no one ever asked if I was happy. Now I try to ask every married person if they are happy."

Lena had a sudden flash of a few months after her wedding. Her mom taking her out for coffee and staring at her with a serious expression. *Are you happy, Lena?* She remembered the question had felt odd, weighted almost. *Of course, I am, mom.* Her mom had looked down at the table, then moved on. The air strained between them.

What an odd memory.

Lena pushed herself back to the present. "Um, yeah. I'm…happy." She couldn't quite pull the right tone to sell it. Stacey could tell, she glanced up and gave her a little smile, then continued working in silence.

After all the foils were in, Stacey left her with a stack of old magazines. Lena thumbed through them for what felt like an overly long period of time. Stacey came to check on her a few times until finally she and her teacher deemed her ready to be rinsed. Soon she was rinsed, blow dried, trimmed and watching as Stacey finished straightening the last few pieces.

Lena turned her head from side to side as the teacher came by and nodded approvingly before signing off on Stacey's piece of paper. Her hair looked…nice. The highlights were subtle, giving the color a slight golden sheen. When she looked in the mirror she still saw herself though. She felt oddly disappointed at that.

Stacey walked her to the counter and punched in the total. Lena ended up tipping enough that it made it cost the same as a regular salon.

"Thanks a million." Stacey beamed. "Have a good one!"

Lena watched Stacey walk away. She had a sudden urge to call out to her, ask her maybe if they could go for drinks sometime. Ask if they could be friends. She seemed like someone who would make a good friend. Sunny and positive. A take-life-by-the-horns type of person. Lena didn't know how to ask without coming across as weird or needy, so instead she zipped her coat up and pushed the door open to the outside.

She walked with her head down, watching her feet slap the pavement with each step. She was debating which pizza place to order from when suddenly someone called her name. Startled, Lena looked up and stared with confusion at the elderly lady in a black jacket walking quickly towards her.

It hit her as the woman stopped in front of her, silver braid swinging. "Evelyn?"

Maybe the old woman was stalking her after all.

CHAPTER SIX

What luck! What absolute, glorious luck.

Here Evelyn was, leaving the library after finishing helping with the reading program, as she did whenever she had a free Saturday, and there Lena was—right in Evelyn's pathway. The Good Lord definitely orchestrated this one.

"Fancy running into you!" Evelyn said. "Your hair! It's different, isn't it?"

Lena's hand flew up to her hair, her face coloring. "I just got it done. Just some highlights."

"It looks wonderful. A nice change for fall coming. I wasn't into the dyeing thing myself—too much upkeep—but I like what you've done."

"Thanks." Lena shifted on her feet.

"Nice day, isn't it? You can feel the chill coming though. Can hardly believe summer is almost over."

"Yes, it is nice."

"I love fall though. Such a beautiful time of year. All the colors, the pumpkin spice…"

Stop babbling, Evelyn! Surely, she could do better than the *weather,* of all things. She cast her mind around for a more engaging topic but couldn't land on anything fast enough.

"Well, I should be off." Lena made to move past.

No! Not yet! Evelyn shifted, blocking her. "Oh, where are you headed? Got some exciting Saturday night plans?"

"Um."

"I've got nothing on myself. A lovely rarity actually, for Saturday." A thought struck her just then, "Say, why don't we get a bite?" That would be the perfect scenario. A nice, relaxed atmosphere where they could properly connect.

"Now?" She sounded panicked.

Evelyn pressed on hurriedly, "Why not? Unless you have plans?"

"I...um..."

"We don't have to do supper, maybe just a quick tea?" She consulted her watch. "Although, it's already past five. Are you hungry?"

"Oh...well, I have an early start tomorrow, so..."

"Oh, come on, we won't party all night, I promise. Just a quick bite." Evelyn could see Lena was still hesitant, so she switched tactics. "Please? I would so love the company, and I'm harmless, I swear! If you're nervous you can text your friends where we are going. Actually, you should do that anyway, it's a good practice isn't it? You never know these days...course you'll be perfectly safe with me. That would be quite the twist wouldn't it? *Old lady is actually a kidnapper.*"

Lena's eyed widened slightly.

"Not that I am, or you know, that's very plausible." This wasn't going very well. Evelyn tried to give her a reassuring smile. "What do you say? Make an old lady's night? Where are you parked?"

"I'm down a ways." Lena gestured in the general direction of forward.

"Oh, well, I'm right here. Why don't we take my car, I know a place near here."

Lena hesitated, then finally gave in, "Okay, I guess…Maybe just something quick."

"Excellent." Evelyn stepped off the sidewalk and unlocked her car.

As Lena slid into the passenger seat, Evelyn was suddenly very aware how close they were in her tiny little car. She thought, not for the first time, how there was something rather intimate about driving with someone else. Sitting closer to someone than a person normally would and trusting that they weren't kidnappers looking to sell humans on the black market.

Evelyn always hated riding in taxis and Uber and things. It felt like she was giving up control to some stranger, her safety in their hands. Doug had thought she was ridiculous. But he was a man. He didn't have to worry about things like being kidnapped and sitting next to a stranger the way a woman did. It was why she'd taken self-defense lessons with her girls when they were teenagers. A woman had to know how to defend herself in this day and age. It's just the way it was.

They didn't talk much on the short drive. Evelyn let the radio fill the silence. She pulled up and parked outside of a little Irish pub right on the corner of a busy intersection. "Here we are. This is my favorite pub in the city. Reminds me of home." She chuckled, "I mean, I'm Cornish of course, but this is close enough."

They slid into a booth by the window. Evelyn wasn't actually that hungry yet. They always had a delightful display of snacks at the reading program: plates full of cookies, veggie trays, and, occasionally, mini cinnamon rolls. She'd helped herself to plenty of it during the program, so she just ordered green tea and some nachos. Lena asked for a glass of red wine.

As they stared at each other with little smiles, Evelyn was a bit mortified to discover her mind was completely blank. She couldn't seem to come up with a single topic to discuss. What did two complete strangers with several decades between them talk about? She should have prepared some ice-breaker questions. Of course. this was a spontaneous event so she wasn't as prepared as she could have been...she had to say *something*.

"So." Evelyn spoke just as Lena started to say something. She waved her to proceed more than a little relieved, "Oh you go, after you."

"I was just wondering, what were you doing downtown?"

"I volunteer at the library now and then. I'm on the board." Evelyn answered enthusiastically. "We have a reading program for young tots on Saturday. It's quite a lot of fun, reading to the kids. They are so interested, their little mouths hanging open, studying each page." She chuckled. "I get a kick out of it."

"Nice."

"It is, it's fun. I've been volunteering at the library since I moved to Canada."

Another pause, then Lena asked, "How long has that been? Since you moved?"

"Oh, what's it been...forty-seven, forty-eight years now? I think I was twenty-three when we moved here. I can't quite remember. My husband was an entrepreneur. His cousin lived here and was starting up a business. Things hadn't taken off in England, so we packed up our belongings and our little family and came here."

"What sort of business?"

"They opened a restaurant, of all things. Doug could

barely boil a pot of water, but he was good with the business end. His cousin took care of the menu. They eventually franchised it and have locations all over Canada. Donna's? The breakfast place?"

"You own Donna's?" Lena's eyes widened. "We used to eat there all the time."

Evelyn nodded. "Donna was Doug's Nana. They named it for her."

"Wow." Lena said, clearly impressed.

Evelyn smiled, a little uncomfortable. She generally tried not to mention to people that she was part-owner of Donna's. They tended to look at her differently and make assumptions about her financial situation—completely accurate assumptions, but still.

They leaned back as the server set the nachos and drinks down. Lena wrapped her fingers around the stem of the wineglass and asked, "Do you ever miss England?"

"Sometimes." Evelyn confessed, swirling the tea bag. "I try to visit once or twice a year. Course, most of my family are gone now. I still have some friends there, though. But, enough about me. Let's talk about you." She leaned forward. "What's life like for you?"

"What's life like?" Lena flushed. "I don't know. It's fine, I guess."

"Married?" She prompted. Might as well get to the good stuff.

"I used to be. He died in a car accident last year. His Uber driver got distracted and drove into a guardrail."

Evelyn clenched her hands together. "That's awful."

Lena took a sip and shrugged. "Yeah. I assumed you were going to ask. People like to know how it happened."

"I'm sorry," Evelyn said. "My husband passed away

too. It's been difficult, but we had a lifetime together so I really can't complain. How long were you married for?"

"Three years. We met in college."

"Ah, college sweethearts. That was Doug and I too." Evelyn smiled. "How have you been coping?"

"Fine." Lena shifted in her seat and took another swig from her wineglass.

"Do you go to grief counselling? I tried it at first. It was alright, but not for me."

"No, I haven't. I did that before. It was good but—"

"Before?" Evelyn cocked her head. "Have you lost someone before?"

Lena fiddled with her glass. "Um…yes. My friend in high school."

"Oh dear. What happened?"

"An accident. She drowned. Sorry, I don't usually talk about this. Do you mind if we don't talk about it?"

"Of course." Evelyn nodded as her heart contracted. This poor, poor girl. So much loss at such a young age. Life could kick the ballocks out of some people. She couldn't understand how things could be so unbalanced. How much could one person cope with? No wonder Lena was the way she was—reserved and awkward. Evelyn lowered her tone. "I'm sorry for the interrogation. I'll stop now."

"It's okay."

A silence descended on the table. Evelyn nibbled at her nachos, trying to think of something to say.

Lena cleared her throat. "I'm sorry about your husband."

"Oh, thank you. I do miss him."

"What was his name?"

"Doug."

"Mine was James."

"Well, look at us. Two widows. Only you're much too young for widowhood. Have you thought about dating? You probably miss sex. I do."

Lena choked on her wine. She wiped a dribble that slid down her chin. "What?"

"Of course, I shouldn't assume, you might be having plenty of sex. Maybe that's how you cope with grief or something—that helps some people I hear. That casual thing isn't for me though, I know that much."

"I—no. I'm not…"

"Oh, that's what I thought. You don't seem the type to, you know, *sleep around* as they say. Not that I would judge you, of course. To each his own and all—or *her* own, I should say. It is a downer though, isn't it? Not being able to have sex anymore? Or at least, have someone you can just roll over and proposition without all the fanfare."

Lena blinked. "You're quite forward, aren't you?"

"Forward? Yes, I have been accused of that. I used to drive my kids nuts when they were teenagers. I think I still do, actually."

"I bet." Lena signaled for another drink from the server.

Evelyn watched her take the full wineglass and sip it generously. She pushed the nachos towards her. "You better eat something if you're going to keep that pace up."

"I'm fine." Lena said, then took a nacho.

"So? Have you thought of dating?"

"No, of course not. It's only been a year…"

"That's a suitable length of time, you could dip your

toe in. Maybe internet dating. Don't they have apps for that nowadays?"

"I don't want to date." Lena said, firmly.

"Why ever not?"

"Because…what James and I had…It was special."

"All relationships are special, in some way or another."

"No." Lena shook her head. "No, it wasn't like that. It was different. Like, it can't be replicated. It was like winning the lottery."

"The lottery?"

"Yes, once in a lifetime. "

"Wasn't there a guy who won it twice?"

"I don't know. But that's not the point. The point is most people don't win it twice—or even once."

"I see…" Evelyn narrowed her eyes. "So, being with your James was like winning the lottery."

"Yes, exactly. I won't get lucky twice. So, why try."

Evelyn cocked her eyebrow. "My goodness. The sex must have been amazing."

"What?"

"To say he was like winning the lottery, the sex must have been amazing."

"No, well, I mean it was fine…you don't get it."

"I do get it. But Lena, no man is the lottery. No relationship is perfect. Do you think you might be putting him on a pedestal? That's what people do, you know, when someone dies. They forget all their flaws and just remember the good things. I do it too, with Doug. Now and then I have to remind myself that he wasn't God's gift to humankind."

"I'm not saying he was perfect."

"Well, I'm just saying if you fell in love once you

can fall in love again."

"So, you would feel fine, getting married again after being with Doug for so long?"

"Why not? A new romance might be exactly what I need. Get the old heart thumping again."

Lena looked at her, one eyebrow raised.

"What? You don't think a woman my age could fall in love again?"

"No, it's not that. Wouldn't you feel you are betraying him though?"

"Of course not. He was my whole heart—but he is gone now, and I am not."

Lena swished her drink around, watching the red liquid slosh up the sides. "You make it sound simple."

"It is, for the most part. If you can take the emotions out of it."

"I can't do that."

"Maybe one day." Evelyn grabbed another nacho and dipped it in the salsa. "What made your man so special, anyway? If the sex was 'just fine'."

"I didn't say it was just fine." Lena's face was a delicate shade of red. "It could be good, really good sometimes."

"Uh-huh."

"He was, like, he made me feel…safe." She paused, then added, "I didn't need anyone else, because I had him. You know?"

"What do you mean? You didn't need anyone else?" Evelyn frowned. "You have friends, don't you? Girlfriends?"

"I don't know. Not really. We didn't need that, we had each other."

"One person can't be everything for someone else."

"Well, he was. That's why he was the lottery," Lena said. A little testily, Evelyn thought.

She bit back her reply. That didn't sound like the lottery to her. That sounded unhealthy. But she needed to be more careful, or she was going to mess things up. "Right, well, if you say so."

Lena snorted.

"What?"

"You're not good at hiding your opinions."

"I don't generally try to be." Evelyn smiled. "Doug used to say I should have been a lawyer or a food critic. Something that I could spout my thoughts doing and get paid for it."

"Did you have a career?"

"Not really. I was a mother first and foremost—in my day that was more common than not. Then I volunteered quite a lot which felt a bit like a career. I don't have regrets about any of that."

"You don't—like—wish you had a more career type thing?"

"No." Evelyn answered honestly. "I know I am supposed to, but I don't. It was a privilege being able to stay home with my girls, to have the freedom to pursue my various passions and hobbies and not have to worry about making money. Course, I supported the franchise—supported Doug—as best I could."

"That sounds—"

"I know it probably sounds frivolous," Evelyn continued. "Some days it feels like it was, other days I feel like I spent my life in servitude." She laughed. "Both my girls have careers. Alice, my oldest, is a Recreation Therapist at an old folks' home and Sarah is in marketing. I think they look down on me, sometimes.

What about you? What do you do?"

"I'm a receptionist at a newspaper."

"Do you like it?"

"I hate it."

"Then why do you do it?"

"Because it pays the bills. And I don't know what else I would do."

"I see." Evelyn tapped her glass. "Well, we have covered a lot of ground, I'd say."

"Yes." Lena pushed her glass away. "I should get going. Thanks for…this."

"Have I scared you off?" Evelyn asked. "Will we still meet Tuesday at the theater?"

Lena stared at her for a moment. "Why? Why do you want to?"

Evelyn shrugged. "I think we should be friends."

"Why?"

"Don't you want a friend? Don't you get lonely?"

Evelyn watched the emotions dance across Lena's face.

"I guess I do," she said finally.

"There you have it. I'll drop you off at your car. Will you be alright to drive?"

"Yes, I think so."

"You think so, or you know so?"

"I know so."

"Maybe you should call an Uber."

"I don't do that."

Evelyn flushed. Of course, Lena wouldn't take an Uber. Stupid of her to say. "Neither do I. How about I drive you home?"

"Evelyn, I'm fine. Honestly. I can handle two glasses of wine."

"Alright then." Evelyn paid the bill, and they walked out to her car. They drove back downtown. Lena instructed her where she parked. Evelyn pulled in beside her car.

"Take care then, Lena."

"You too," Lena said. She got out, then leaned down, "I'll see you, maybe Tuesday."

Evelyn smiled. "See you then."

CHAPTER SEVEN

On Sunday, Lena made the forty-minute trip from the city to Redwood, the small town where she grew up. The drive was a familiar one down a long straight highway with few curves in the road and fields stretched out on either side. Unless one ventured over to the mountains, most the drives in Alberta were like this— long, dull, and straight.

She'd been to the mountains a handful of times, a few times as a kid with her family, once with James. The vastness of them always scared and fascinated her. Something about their wild beauty stirred something in her, but it was almost an overwhelming, suffocating feeling.

She preferred the breathable freedom the prairies offered her. It was more comforting. Probably because it was what she knew.

It would be strange when her parents no longer lived out here. She supposed she wouldn't have much excuse to visit Redwood after they moved to Red Deer. Part of her felt relieved. She had many happy childhood memories wrapped up in the small town, but most of them were also wrapped up in Cheryl.

Cheryl, who was the sister she never had. Who could tell stories that left Lena gasping for air from laughing too hard. Who convinced her to sneak out at night and take their bicycles around the dark deserted Main Street, both of them pedaling down the middle of the road, hands in the air and their heads thrown back, like they owned the night. Cheryl, who was found face first in the river, her bright pink grad dress floating around her, tangled with strands of her blonde hair…

No matter all the happy memories Lena thought of, they all led there, to that last moment which haunted her dreams still. James had understood. He was the only one she would talk to about that night. He helped her make sense of it, to lock it away and focus on other things. Now that he too had left her, she felt exposed and vulnerable. Like her protective layer had been stripped from her, and now she had even more pain to deal with than before.

She felt it now, the tightening of her chest, her breath starting to catch in her throat. It came on fast. She gasped, her vision blurring. Lena pulled over on the shoulder of the road and grabbed the steering wheel hard. Wheezing as she tried to breathe.

It's okay, it's okay. Breathe, just breathe. It was just a panic attack. She'd gotten them a lot after Cheryl. Then they started again after James. She just needed to calm down.

Lena took in a shuddering breath, in through her nose, out through her mouth. Again, and again, until her body responded and started to relax. She took in longer and deeper breathes then wiped the tears from her eyes, her fingers coming away black. She flipped down the mirror and scrubbed at the mascara smeared on her cheeks.

"Great," she mumbled, clicking open the glove compartment and grabbing some napkins she kept stashed there. She poured some water from her water bottle to dampen one and scrubbed until the make-up came off. Her face was now red and blotchy, but at least the melting look was gone. She carefully checked to make sure the road was clear, then pulled out on to the road again.

It had been a couple months since her last attack. She thought maybe she was over them, but apparently, she wasn't. She would have to be more careful not to let her thoughts wander like that.

When she finally reached town, she signaled to turn and rumbled over the railway tracks. The telltale sign of entering Redwood. The tracks stretched the entire length of the town and was home to many romantic high school dates and first kisses. When the train came through, everyone knew it. The blast of the horn could be heard no matter where someone was in town, and the houses nearby the tracks would shake with the vibrations—it felt like the train was going to come straight through the living room wall. It used to be a source of annoyance; she used to cringe every time the train rumbled through town, but after moving away she found she missed the obnoxious sound. Funny the things that become normal.

She drove past the gas station, past her old high school, and down a residential street. The houses were old but cheery, the lawns well cared for, and fences freshly painted. Kids played outside on the street, pent up energy spilling out of them as they scrambled to enjoy the last free days before school started. There were a few couples walking along the sidewalks holding hands and a handful of joggers dutifully running along.

It felt relaxed and friendly, something Lena missed now and then. Red Deer always felt busy and full of strangers. Exchanging tentative smiles with someone she wouldn't see again wasn't the same as waving hello to the neighbor she'd known for twenty years. Who she'd see at church that Sunday and then bump into at the grocery store on Tuesday. But that was exactly why Lena left. People here knew too much.

Across the way there was a soccer field that was overgrown with wild grass. If she crossed it, it led to a forest with walking paths, and beyond that, the river. The river was usually so low it barely brushed her knees, with a few deep spots that might reach her waist. It was full of sharp rocks, beavers, and muskrats. Muddy banks lined the sides, well-worn from kids slipping and sliding down to go floating on the water with inner tubes during the summer.

As far as Lena knew, there had been no major incidents with the river before or since Cheryl. She would have approved of that, the drama of her exit. The ripple of shock that tore through the town, the fear that still lingered around it.

Lena hadn't been to the river since.

She kept her eyes firmly ahead, signaled down her old street, and finally pulled up to her parent's house. Roy's truck was already parked outside.

She sat for a minute staring at her home. She still considered it that, even though she hadn't lived here since before she left for college. It was an old house, the blue siding's color was faded from years in the sun. The porch was freshly painted white when it was put on sale, to give it new life. It looked good. Safe.

Her heart squeezed in her chest thinking of all the times she had walked up to that door. As a girl after school, Sundays after church, after basketball practice in high school, home visiting from college…would she ever see the inside again after her parents moved? It felt like a loss, knowing it wouldn't belong to her anymore. Another loss added on top of a pile of losses that pulled her down harder than gravity ever could.

Lena shook her head firmly and blinked away the wetness in her eyes. She couldn't think like that. Life moved on and so must she. She got out of her car and almost immediately was accosted by none other than Mr. Wright.

"Hey there, Ms. Wilson." Mr. Wright said from the other side of the hedge that separated the two properties.

Mr. Wright always called her by her maiden name, ever since she was in school. He was a large bull of a man who had recently retired from teaching math at the high school. How a man who looked like Arnold Schwarzenegger was his body double ended up a math teacher was beyond anyone. He should have been a personal trainer, or bodybuilder, or maybe a bouncer. Not teaching kids how to understand a math problem most would never need to use again.

He leaned over the hedge, holding a pair of hedge trimmers that looked a little foreboding in his massive hands. He was always working on that hedge, it seemed. It was like a weird retirement obsession or something.

"Hi, Mr. Wright," said Lena.

"Helping the folks pack up?"

"Yup." Lena inched towards the door.

"It's a shame. We sure are gonna miss having them around."

"They'll visit, I'm sure." Almost there…

"So how have you been? Still working at the paper?"

Lena sighed inwardly, clutching her purse. Maybe it was just the idea of small-town friendliness she missed.

The reality of it she could do without. There was nothing worse than small talk. "Sure am."

"Painting still? I remember you being quite the painter back in the day."

"Not too much, no. Sorry, Mr. Wright, I should get in there. I'm a little late."

"Course, sure. Don't be a stranger, Ms. Wilson, alright?"

"You got it." She gave him a terrible fake smile, then let herself in the house with a relieved sigh. "Hello? Mom? Dad?"

"Lena!" Lena's dad came around the corner holding a large box. "Welcome to hell. I hope you're prepared for a day of torture."

"Oh, stop it." Lena's mom called out. "It's not that bad."

Dad rolled his eyes. "We are packing up thirty years' worth of crap. Of course, it is."

Lena smiled. Her dad looked the same as ever, clean shaven, recently grayed-hair still thick and combed back, plaid shirt tucked into dark jeans, and his eternally friendly attitude radiating off him.

Both her parents were optimists on steroids. They didn't deal well with cup half empty feelings, preferring everything to be jolly and fine all the time. Which meant they didn't deal well with Lena, as she was not jolly and fine any of the time. Even before all the horrible things, she'd been more of a serious, quiet kid. An introspective introvert amongst a family of loud extroverts. Family holidays had been excruciatingly painful, usually always ending with Lena hiding in her room listening to the laughter of others through the walls.

Lena followed him into the kitchen where her mom

and Roy were having a cup of coffee around the table. Boxes surrounded the floor beside them. Walls which used to have pictures hanging on them were bare.

"Just taking a break," Roy said. "Been going for two hours already."

Lena gave her mom a hug and ignored Roy. "Sorry I'm late, Mom."

"No problem," Mom said, brushing her dyed chin length hair behind her ears. "There's still plenty to do. Did you do something to your hair? It looks different."

"Highlights," Lena said.

"You know, you can hire people to do this," said Roy.

"What, pack for you? Why would you do that?" Mom asked.

"So, you don't have to."

Dad grunted. "Yeah and spend your entire life savings because you were too lazy to pack your own underwear. No, thank you."

"Besides," Mom said. "It might be fun for you kids to go through your old rooms. You both still have a lot of stuff here."

"Fun isn't the word I would use," Roy grumbled.

Lena looked at her older brother. His hair was rumpled, dark bags lined his eyes, and a scowl was etched between them. "You're unusually grumpy. Leslie still not sleeping?"

"Nope. And Noah has decided to get up at six every morning."

"Why don't you sleep in the basement if Leslie is waking you up?" Mom asked.

"Because Carrie needs help in the night," said Roy.

"She needs help with what? Breastfeeding?"

"I change her, and she feeds her."

Mom looked aghast. "Well," she huffed. "When you were little, I was lucky if your dad held you, never mind changed you. Not that I minded, your dad had to work in the morning, so of course I handled you at night."

"Times are different, mom."

"Apparently."

Lena grinned. "You're not sounding very feminist, mom."

"I am a feminist. Which is why I know women can handle a baby at night by themselves."

"You just don't like Carrie," Roy said.

"What? Of course, I do." Mom shot Lena a sideways glance. "Why would you say that? Has she said something? Of course, I like her."

"Let's stop talking about this." Dad interjected. "We are going to be packing all day if we don't get going."

"When do you have to be out of here?" Lena picked up an empty box.

"Possession date is in two weeks, but we are going to move some things to the new place next week. So, we aren't packing up the kitchen just yet, or our room." Dad grinned. "It's going to be fun, eh? Living close to you two again? Maybe we can do family brunch on the weekends."

"Yeah. Maybe…"

"Who is buying this place, anyway?" Roy asked. "Do we know them?"

Mom and dad exchanged a glance.

"What? Who is it?"

Mom fiddled with her cup. "It's um…well, believe it or not, it's Sean."

Roy and Lena paused.

"Sean who?" But she knew from the looks on their faces.

"Sean Whitmore."

Her stomach dropped at the sound of his name.

"No." Roy looked between his parents. "You sold our house to Sean Whitmore? Lena's sketchy ex?"

"He wasn't sketchy. You didn't even know him." Lena's mind raced. Sean was back? Last she'd heard, he was living on Vancouver Island. A thrill shot through her, and she wasn't sure if it was excitement, or dread, or maybe…fear? Her hands trembled. She folded her arms, trying to hide them.

"I know enough," Roy said.

"You were at college when he moved here. You don't know anything."

"Everyone knew Lena, about his druggy mom and abusive dad they were running away from—"

"Shut up." Lena snapped, the old habit of defending him coming back to her as naturally as breathing. "You don't know anything. All you know is the stupid gossip people judged him by."

"Well, there had to be some reason he was high half the time—"

"That's enough," Mom said.

Roy shook his head. "I can't believe you sold it to him."

"It doesn't matter who bought it," Dad said. "We are going to have a new home now."

Mom nodded. "Besides, I'm sure he has grown up a lot."

"He wasn't that bad," said Lena.

"Lena, you would probably say that about Bill Cosby. You have the worst taste in guys I have ever seen." Roy snorted.

Lena's blood turned cold. Sean darted from her mind. "What does that mean?"

"It means what I said. You suck at picking guys."

"Roy…" Mom warned.

"Are you saying you didn't like James?" Lena stared at her brother.

Mom, Dad, and Roy all froze. Then reacted at once.

"No, no, sweetheart, that's not what he meant."

"Course, he liked him, Lena. Don't be ridiculous."

"I didn't know him very well."

Lena glared. "What do you mean you didn't know him well? I was with him for seven years."

Roy shrugged. "Yeah, but it's not like we saw you two much. You guys kept to yourselves a lot."

"What are you talking about?"

"He just means," Mom interrupted. "That…well…you both liked your space and…"

"That James was a fuckin' control freak," Roy said.

"Roy!" Mom gasped.

Lena stared at him. "Excuse me?"

"Roy, stop it," Dad said.

"Look, I'm sorry to 'speak ill of the dead' or whatever, but can't we say it now? We all knew it."

"You all knew what?" Lena said.

Roy sighed. "Look, Lena, James had a way of…he just wouldn't let you do much without him. Or with him."

"You don't know what you're talking about." Lena's voice shook. "Just because we were homebodies doesn't mean he was controlling."

"It was more than that. He—" Roy began.

"Enough, Roy," Dad said. "You two came here to

help us pack, so let's pack."

Lena grabbed an empty box and went down the hall to the staircase. Taking them two at a time, she went up and entered her old room and slammed the door behind her, like she was a teenager again. She flopped down on her twin size bed and stared up at the slanted ceiling. Her body feeling hot then cold, tears filling her eyes for no good reason. She angrily wiped them away.

Roy hadn't liked James. Her *parents* hadn't liked him…How could she not have known that? She searched in her mind for the times they'd been all together.

She was certain her mom and dad had approved when she brought him home from college the first time. James had confidently shaken her dad's hand and charmingly complimented her mom's looks. Lena remembered her mom beaming at her and whispering that he looked like a Hemsworth brother, which wasn't at all accurate. Her mom referred to every attractive man as a Hemsworth, which made Lena doubt that she even knew who they were. James had more of a slender build. He had that boyish, approachable look: high cheekbones, smooth skin, probably no hope of growing a decent beard, but she didn't care for beards, anyway.

When did her family start feeling differently?

Lena rolled the uncomfortable question around in her mind. Honestly, she couldn't remember ever noticing anything off between them and James. Everyone liked him. Didn't they?

There was a gentle knock on the door before her mom entered. "You okay, hon?"

"I'm fine."

Mom smiled. "You always say you're fine."

Lena sat up. "I mostly always am."

"I don't know if that's true." Mom sat on the edge of the bed. "I'm sorry if Roy upset you."

"You guys really didn't like him?"

Mom sighed. "It's not that we didn't like him. It's just…he was a bit dominating. I worried he might be taking up too much of you."

"What are you talking about?"

"There were just little things…what does it matter now?"

"It matters," Lena said. "What little things?"

"Just…like, the way you dressed changed. You didn't do things you used to love doing. Like painting. Remember how painting used to be such a big part of your life?"

"Maybe I just grew up. People change, you know, mom. Maybe it had nothing to do with James."

"Maybe…" Mom sounded hesitant.

"What? Just say it."

"Well, he did like to dictate what you did a bit…a lot of times when I called your phone, he would answer. Or I would text, and you wouldn't reply, and I'd think…maybe he was deleting them."

Memories surfaced of times Lena came out of the bathroom and James was holding her phone, another of him grabbing it while she drove, scanning her texts. They hadn't kept their phones private from each other. Lena could have done the same if she'd wanted. It was part of their trust. She hadn't known he answered her phone sometimes, though. And deleting her texts? Surely, he wouldn't have. She would have known.

"Why would he do that?" Lena said out loud.

Mom shrugged. "I don't know, hon. I just know we all noticed that he…liked to have you to himself a lot.

And sometimes the way he talked to you…we just weren't sure about it."

Lena shook her head. "You guys had it wrong. We were great, I was really, really happy with him." Emotion choked off her words. She looked away from her mom and wiped at her face.

"Oh honey, I know. I know you loved him." Mom moved and put her arm around Lena, which only made it harder to hold in her tears. "I'm so sorry you lost him. After all you have been through, you didn't deserve this."

"No one deserves it." Lena hiccupped. After a moment, she composed herself and offered her mom a watery smile. "Sorry about that. I actually am fine. I'm doing a lot better these days."

"You never need to apologize, sweetie."

"Thanks, mom." Lena looked around her room. "I guess I better get going with all this."

"Alright, call your dad if you need help bringing anything down." Mom gave her another smile and quietly left the room.

Lena sighed, then forced herself up and started the mundane task of clearing away her old things. She had taken everything she wanted to keep when she moved out the first time. A lot of this was going to go to the junk pile. She didn't have any sentimental attachment to her old trophies and medals from team sports she got for being a benchwarmer, or for the posters of bands she didn't care about that decorated the walls of her room. Her mom bought her those, trying to get her interested in normal teen stuff, she supposed.

She worked fast, boxing up her small collection of books and textbooks, throwing in old report cards and school projects that were still laying in her closet. She cleared away the various odds and ends on her little wooden desk, pausing as her eyes traced over the pictures that were tacked to her bulletin board. Cheryl and herself, grinning in various stages of youth. Going through bad haircuts and embarrassing fashion styles, the two of them always together. Then there was that one picture. Cheryl on one side, her on the other, and with his arms casually thrown around both their shoulders, Sean.

Lena pulled it off and brought it to her bed, staring down at the three of them. That must have been, when? A month or two after Sean moved here? He came in their grade twelve year. It was an exciting thing to have a new kid in school. All the girls of course were giddy over the handsome new guy. In truth, he wasn't even that good looking—he was fine; he had some of that swagger, blonde hair, blue-eyed thing going—it was more of the newness that made him attractive.

It quickly became apparent to everyone that he was going to join in with Cheryl and Lena's little group. He wasn't into sports like most of the school was, which made him stand out even more. Just a week or so before this picture was taken was when Lena and Sean had started going out. He was her first proper boyfriend. Her first for a lot of things. He had been a bit wild, sneaking booze, smoking pot. He excited Lena, he felt dangerous and sexy. But for Cheryl, he did something else to her. Made her crazier. Challenged her. They had this weird connection between them, a competitive spark that morphed from liking to hating in seconds.

Toxic.

Lena had been in the middle. A calming agent for both. She just hadn't been able to do a good enough job.

Lena stood up and moved to add it to the junk box. But then changed her mind and tucked it in her back-pocket.

CHAPTER EIGHT

Evelyn stood shock-still, keeping her eyes fixed on the theater's entryway doors. Her heart pounded faster every time someone entered, then deflated a bit when it wasn't Lena. Maybe she'd came on too strong on Saturday. She'd been a little nervous, probably a tad too chatty. Maybe Lena decided Evelyn was a crazy old bat and wanted nothing to do with her.

Evelyn fiddled with the long sleeve of Doug's sweater that she was wearing as yet another person entered who wasn't Lena. If Lena didn't show up, how was Evelyn going to find her again? She couldn't very well drive around the city calling out her name. All her carefully laid out plans were for not.

"Are you alright?"

Evelyn jumped, then quickly smiled at the woman staring at her with concern. "Oh! Yes, I'm fine, thanks. Just waiting for a friend."

"Oh nice. Have a good evening." The woman gave her a brief smile, then hurried after the man waiting for her.

Nice of her, Evelyn thought. *Probably checking if I had dementia or something.* She noticed things like that were happening to her more often: someone offering to help carry her groceries, asking if she was alright when she was out doing things. Her age must finally be showing.

But for heaven's sake, she was only in her seventies! Seventies were the new sixties, were they not? Perhaps a shorter haircut would help her look more modern. She fiddled with her braid, imagining it gone and feeling the wisps of her hair against her cheeks. It would look quite chic, like Helen Mirren…but Doug had always loved her long hair. She wasn't sure she could do it. Besides, she saw some very with-it celebrities in their seventies who had nice long hair still. Just look at Cher, she looked fabulous. Course, she probably had a team of people complete with some discreet plastic surgeons whose job it was to make her fabulous. But still.

Evelyn decided she should move to keep from being mistaken as senile. She nonchalantly walked along the wall, pretending to scrutinize the movie posters while keeping the doors in her peripheral vision. The sweet smell of popcorn teased her nostrils, making her mouth water. She had a very light supper in anticipation for her popcorn. If Lena didn't hurry it up, Evelyn was going to have to go without her.

Just as she was about to give up and go buy her ticket, there Lena was. She pushed open the door and entered the foyer, shoulders slightly hunched, the hood from her gray sweatshirt bunched around her neck and her hair fell over her face.

Evelyn's plan was to act casual, but as soon as she was close Evelyn broke into a smile and waved like a maniac. "Lena! Over here! I'm so glad you came."

Lena's face flushed a deep red that squeezed Evelyn's heart.

"Hi, Evelyn." She came slowly over.

"I wasn't sure if you were going to come. I was going to text you, but then I realized I don't have your contact info. We really should exchange numbers."

"I don't know if we're there quite yet," Lena said, but then gave her a grin.

Evelyn laughed. "This feels a bit like dating, doesn't it? Kind of the same awkward, vulnerable, I-hope-they-like-me thing."

Lena shot her a look. "You're not going to start on that again, are you?"

"What? Dating?" Evelyn put her hands up innocently. "No, no. I'll behave, I promise. Shall we pick something to watch together? It wasn't too traumatic last time, was it?"

Lena grinned. Evelyn felt some awkwardness dissipate. "No, it wasn't," she said.

They moved in line. "So, how have you been?" Evelyn asked.

Lena shrugged. "Fine. I helped my parents pack up their house this weekend. They're moving into the city."

"Oh, that's nice. It's so good to have family live close. I had a pretty uneventful weekend myself, besides bumping into you of course. My—"

"You know what." Lena said suddenly, then flushed. "Oh, sorry. I cut you off."

"No, go ahead."

"I just…I found out something and I can't stop thinking about it." They took a step forward. "It turns out, no one in my family liked my husband."

"Huh. And you didn't know that?"

"No, I didn't have a clue. It's strange…" Lena choked on her words, her eyes looking teary.

"Are you alright?"

Lena nodded. "I'm fine. I'm just feeling on edge lately. I'm not sure why."

"Time of the month?" Evelyn ventured.

"Evelyn."

"What? I don't know why women are so afraid to talk about it. It's natural."

"You're sounding like my mother. And no, that's not the issue."

"I don't miss those days, I can tell you. Although, menopause was no laughing matter. Doug and I barely made it through." Evelyn chuckled, recalling how poor Doug would cautiously eye her in the kitchen as she sweated through a hot flash, angrily punching down dough for cinnamon buns. The mood swings hit her hard. There were a few years there where Evelyn didn't even recognize herself. It is tough being a woman, during much of the female life hormones wage war with the body and mind. There is always a need to constantly justify emotions, while secretly wondering if the emotions were indeed, justifiable.

"Although, you know what always bothered me?" Evelyn said, thinking out loud. "Why do women have the reputation for being moody? Men are terribly moody too, and they don't even have the excuse of the hormones! It's *humans* who are moody, not women. How about that? Women are just better at expressing ourselves. That's why we get the rep."

"You should write a book, you know that? Filled with all your wisdom."

"I should, shouldn't I?" Evelyn cocked her head, considering. "Though that seems like an awful lot of work. And I'm a baker, not a writer. Maybe I could get a ghostwriter."

"You could call it, 'Unwanted Advice 101'."

"More like, 'Wisdom That Should Be Heeded by the

Ignorant and Ungrateful Younger Generation'."

"Too long."

"Anyway, why does it bother you that your family didn't like your husband?"

"Because it's like…" Lena's voice trailed away. Then in a flash, her chest started heaving, and she burst into tears.

Evelyn stared at her in alarm. "Oh, my."

"I'm…so-sorry."

"No, no. It's quite alright." Evelyn patted her on the shoulder. Seeing the concerned looks from people around them, she steered Lena out of the line. "Why don't we get some air?"

Evelyn led her across the foyer, trying not to notice the people staring. Public displays of emotion always made her feel uncomfortable. This North American thing of processing every feeling one has publicly was something Evelyn was never going to get used to. Everyone needed a good cry now and then, but she always thought one should do it dignifiedly in their own home. She supposed that's why the English had a reputation for being cold and unfeeling. She liked to think of it as being civilized and stoic. Self-control was never a bad thing, in her opinion. It was stereotypical of her to think this way, but she had embraced this side of her British nature long ago.

She led Lena, sniffing, outside into the crisp cool air.

"Take a deep breath. There we go, darling."

Lena breathed in and out, slowly calming down. She shook her head. "Wh-what about the movie?"

"We'll catch it next week. Are you alright?"

"I'm fine." Lena leaned against the building, her hair falling over her face.

Evelyn resisted the urge to push it behind her ear as she would have her daughters when they were younger and upset.

"I get these, panic attacks, sometimes," she mumbled.

Poor thing, Evelyn felt a wave of sadness for the girl. "That's quite normal for what you've been through, I'm sure."

"I was fine for a while. They went away, but they seem to be coming back now."

"Why does your family not liking your husband upset you so much?"

Lena blew out her breath and shrugged her shoulders. "I guess, it's just things weren't how I thought they were. I don't know. It's stupid."

"It's not stupid if it upsets you."

Lena gave her a watery smile. "I'm sorry about all this. You must think you picked an insane person to be movie friends with."

"Oh, don't worry about that. I haven't shown you my skeletons yet." Evelyn straightened up. "In fact, why don't you come over to my place? I know just the thing to make you feel better. I don't live far. Come on." She turned on her heel and hurried across the parking lot. "Coming?" She called over her shoulder, unlocking her car.

After a moment, Lena hurried after her and slid into the passenger side. Evelyn hummed along to the radio as she twisted the wheel to back out.

"I should maybe follow you in my car, so you don't have to drive me back," Lena said.

Evelyn waved away her worry. "It's fine. I live close by."

Five minutes away, to be exact. Her little condo was close to almost everything. Situated near downtown Red Deer, she was within walking distances to most things, and a short drive away from the rest. Selling their house and downsizing was the best decision she'd made for herself after Doug passed.

They had lived in this ridiculous upscale house for years, with more bedrooms than children. It was in a part of town that just screamed money from all sides. Evelyn had found it over-the-top and not at all her style. But Doug, drunk with the success from Donna's, had insisted it was right. She suspected he regretted the decision over the years, especially after their kids moved out, but the silly man had been too proud to admit it. They were simple people who believed in hard work, and the house hadn't reflected their values at all.

Evelyn pulled into her underground parking lot and parked in her spot. They walked over to the elevator, and she punched the top floor button. Lena seemed nervous. She kept her arms crossed tightly over her chest and looked everywhere but at Evelyn. Like she couldn't decide if she was going to stay or bolt.

"Here we are." Evelyn exited the elevator and walked three doors down and let herself in. "Welcome to my home."

Lena walked slowly in and took in the modest surroundings. "It's nice," she offered.

"Thank you."

"It's different then I thought it would be."

"What did you think?"

Lena shrugged. "When you told me you owned Donna's, I thought…"

"That I would be in a penthouse?" Evelyn chuckled.

"I have money, but not that much. I don't really like fancy things, anyway." She felt a little guilty after she said that, like she was being misleading. After all, she had led a pretty fancy life, even if it hadn't been her decision too. She quickly added, "Doug was more liberal than I. He drove new vehicles and liked designer clothes and things. He wasn't a snob or anything. He was a hard worker. He didn't believe in retirement. He wasn't like one of those people who wanted to get rich so they could sit around and golf. After he stepped back from management at Donna's he would do these odds and ends jobs, just because he liked it."

"Like what?" Lena walked slowly along, looking at the family photos on the walls.

"Oh, this and that," Evelyn said airily.

"This is Doug?" Lena asked, gently touching a framed photo of the two of them.

"Yes, that's him."

Lena studied it. "He looks nice. Sort of reminds me of someone, I think…"

"Oh, he had one of those faces. You know, everyone thought they knew him. Come to the kitchen." Lena followed her in. Evelyn grabbed two aprons from the hooks in the corner and passed one to her.

"Are we cooking?" Lena took it cautiously.

"We are baking. It will make you feel better, I promise." She tied hers quickly around her waist and proceeded to gather the ingredients needed. "How about some lemon bread? Or lemon muffins? I'm feeling like lemon. What do you think?"

"Um, sure."

Evelyn hummed a little tune as she grabbed her mixing bowl and measuring cups. "Baking is good for the soul. Cooking too. Do you cook?"

"Not really," Lena leaned against the counter. "I used to a little for James, but he was a picky eater so we only had a few different meals we would cycle through. We ate out a lot."

Evelyn tutted. She always thought what someone was willing or not willing to eat said a lot about their character. It was a more accurate depiction of them than horoscopes. Aggressively picky eaters were stubborn and unapologetic. They expected the world to revolve around them and their wants. Passively picky eaters—those who would try something with enough encouragement—were the self-conscious sort who tended to be unsure of who they were and what they wanted. Whereas people who tried everything, like herself, were the more adventurous, ready for anything types.

There were exceptions, of course, for every scenario, but mostly, her food theory had proved correct over the years. Her father was a picky eater. Her mother, too. It had been an unpleasant combination. They got divorced almost as soon as Evelyn moved out for college. Not that she blamed her father. She had gotten out of there too, as fast as she could, and hardly looked back.

Interesting that James was a picky eater, an aggressive one if he limited their menu to a few items. And Lena, obviously being shy and reserved...it must have been an interesting dynamic.

But here Evelyn was, judging a dead man's marriage like it was any of her business. No sense in paying the past too much attention when the present needed so much effort. Evelyn pushed away her suspicions of the deceased and for the next half-hour she carefully guided Lena through the recipe for her favorite lemon poppy seed muffins.

It was a simple enough recipe. Evelyn found most were if you paid enough attention. Just as she hoped, the act of measuring, pouring, and mixing helped calm Lena, whose shoulders relaxed as easy conversation drifted between them. After they divided the batter into a large twenty-four muffin tin tray and placed them in the oven, they chose wine over tea and sat at the island sipping from their glasses.

It was quite pleasant to sit and drink with the sweet smell of muffins filling the condo. Evelyn only ever drank wine when she had someone over to share a bottle with, so within a few minutes she could feel the alcohol warming her blood and buzzing in her veins.

"How old are you, anyway?" Lena asked, already refilling her glass. "Is that rude to ask?"

"I don't think so. I'm turning seventy-one this year."

"Huh, I would have guessed you were in your sixties."

"How kind of you."

"How many grandkids do you have?" Lena nodded over to the family photos hanging in the hallway.

"Five grandkids, one great-grandkid, and two kids," she answered.

"Wow, a great-grandkid already."

Evelyn nodded. "We have three generations of marrying young and having kids young. My mother just passed away two years ago actually, she came very close to being able to meet her great-great grandchild."

"That's pretty amazing."

"Do you want kids?"

Lena shrugged. "Yeah, I think so. I thought James and I were going to have some right away, but he wanted to focus on his career first. He was a realtor."

"You know, in order to have kids you need to shag. And to shag, you need to date again."

"What is with you and that?" Lena frowned. "I thought you said you weren't going to bring it up again."

Evelyn held out her hands innocently. "I'm sorry, it's the wine. It's loosened my tongue."

"I have lots of time, you know. I'm only twenty-seven. A lot of people don't even get married till they are thirty."

"I had a nine-year-old when I was thirty."

"That's just ridiculous."

Evelyn laughed and topped off their glasses. She was overindulging a bit, but the tipsiness in her head was making her feel reckless. Goodness, would she be hung over tomorrow? She hadn't been hung over in years. The thought made laughter come again, and she nearly slid off her chair.

Lena cocked her eyebrow at Evelyn, "You alright?"

"Fine, fine." Evelyn waved her concern away.

"Don't fall and break a hip or something."

"Wouldn't that just be awful?" Evelyn giggled.

"It would definitely make a memory."

She leaned towards Lena, confidentially. "I have never broken a single bone before. I think I might be invincible."

"Really."

"Yup. I've suspected it for years. I'm going to live to be a hundred."

"Everyone thinks that."

"Not true. Doug didn't think so. He would always

say he would save a place for me in heaven, because he wasn't going to stick around that long. He was scared of growing old. He didn't want to get senile." Evelyn sighed. Her giddiness deserting her a bit. "I wish I could have seen him get senile. I mean, I wish I could have seen him get old. Older, that is. That probably sounds selfish, to you. He was old."

Lena put her hand on her arm. "I'm sorry, Evelyn. I'm sure you miss him."

"I do."

"Seventies is still too young to die."

"It is, isn't it? We could have had twenty more years if we were lucky." They drank in silence for a little, then Evelyn said, "So, how about we set you up on one of those apps."

"Oh, for heaven's sake, Evelyn! We were having a nice moment."

"We're still having a nice moment."

"What about you, then?" Lena said. "You said you would be up for a new romance. Let's get *you* signed up. I'm sure there's a hook-up app for old folks."

Evelyn narrowed her eyes. "Why do we need a special old folks app? Some people are into wrinkles."

Lena snorted.

"I'm serious. My friend, Mavis, her third husband is ten years younger than her. I want my next husband to be younger. And, if you can manage it, I'd like him to be ripped."

Lena bent over laughing. The timer dinged for the muffins and Evelyn slid off her stool and grabbed her oven mitts. "I'm serious," she said, banging the oven shut again and placing the tray on the stove. "A young, ripped husband. He doesn't have to be too bright or wealthy—in fact, better if he isn't—but he must be handsome."

"I didn't take you for a cougar, Evelyn."

"I think you'll find I'm full of surprises."

"What about that guy you told me about? Your old crush? The one who looked like the actor in the movie we watched."

"Who, Edwin?"

"Yeah, what's he up to?"

"I have no idea. He's probably still in England."

"You haven't looked him up?"

"Why would I?"

Lena pulled out her phone and began tapping away. "What's his last name? Where did he live?"

"Edwin Peterson. We grew up in St. Ives. What are you doing?" Evelyn peered over Lena's shoulder as her fingers danced across her screen.

"That him?" Lena pointed to a profile picture.

"No…he was much handsomer. Wait, scroll down." Evelyn peered at the screen, and suddenly she was fourteen again, her heart in her throat. "Oh. My. God. That's him! That's Edwin. How did you do that?"

"I just searched on Facebook."

Evelyn took the phone from Lena and sank down in her seat. A thousand memories assaulted her. Edwin walking down the hallway at school with his easy saunter and slow smile. Her staring at the back of his head when he sat ahead of her in class, and at the way his hair curled over the back of his collar. Nights lying in her bed journaling about her unrequited love. Giggling with her girlfriends getting ready for school dances, each dreaming they would be the one he asked to dance. They had all been obsessed.

And look at him now! The years had been kind. His hair was still full, salt and peppered gray with a hint of the dark it used to be. He was leaning over the side of a boat, grinning at the camera, that same grin that lit up his face. His eyes had crinkles around the corners and his face was a little more slack than before. But she could clearly see the handsome boy he had been. She clicked on his picture and scanned his About Me section.

"What's it say?" Lena asked.

"He...still lives in St. Ives. It doesn't say anything about a relationship."

"That's a good thing. If he had a wife, it would probably be on there."

"He has a wife. Don't be silly. A man like him doesn't walk around single."

"He could be divorced. Or widowed. Or maybe he turned out to be an addict or something and stayed single."

"He did not."

"You should message him."

Evelyn stared. "Message him? And what on earth would I say? Hello, Edwin, you probably don't remember me, but I used to be your classmate. I live halfway across the world now. Want to shag over video chat?"

"Definitely not the last part. Unless you know, that's what you're wanting..."

Evelyn put the phone on the counter and stood up. She grabbed two plates out of her cupboard and served them both each a muffin. "Just...exit out. Don't do anything."

"Message him! What do you have to lose?"

"My dignity, for one thing."

Lena pushed Evelyn's wine cup towards her. "Have a drink, relax. Let's just think about this."

Evelyn gulped it down, then took a bite out of the muffin. "Oh, these are good. I've done it again. Have a taste."

Lena popped a piece in her mouth. "Oh wow, you weren't kidding."

"I never kid about baking."

"I think you should message him."

"I think I should not."

"Why not?" Lena said. "You're the one who said you would like to get out there again."

"I never said I wanted to. I said I would. There's a difference. Besides, it's you we should concentrate on. You're the one with the ticking clock. Mine's already timed out. I'm done."

"You're living till you're a hundred. You have quite a ways to go."

"That's true…"

"Come on, Evelyn! I'll buy your movie ticket next week if you do."

"I can afford the eleven dollars."

"You don't have to hit on him. Just see how his life has been. Aren't you curious?"

She was curious. Edwin had flitted in and out of her mind throughout the years. He was tied to her childhood memories as much as her friends were. Had he always stayed in St. Ives? Did he ever go anywhere else? Did he and Marie, his high school sweetheart, stay together after college? Evelyn had lost touch with a lot of her classmates after they graduated. When she met Doug she became obsessed with him, and any lingering longing for Edwin was boxed away with all her other juvenile wants.

But what would be the point of messaging him? What interest would he have connecting with someone he used to be in school with, but never talked to? He probably had a young, perky second wife by now.

"I'm not sure…" Evelyn said slowly.

Lena sensed her weakness and pounced. "Let's just write something out and see where it goes. No harm in that. Here, login to your account. You do have Facebook, don't you?"

"Of course, I do." She took the phone. "I don't know why I'm listening to you," she said as she typed in her email and password. She grabbed a second bottle of wine and filled their glasses as they peered at the screen.

"You have a very nice profile picture." Lena paused, considering. "Actually, it doesn't look a thing like you."

"What do you mean?" The picture was of her sitting on her daughter's porch swing last summer. She was laughing at something with a cup of tea in her hand, her hair up on the sides and flowing over her shoulders. Evelyn thought she looked rather pretty, but of course wouldn't say that out loud.

"You're dressed different."

"I'm wearing a dress. It was a Sunday."

"I've only ever seen you in a big sweater, like what you're wearing now. Or in a coat, I guess."

"Oh this. This is Doug's. I like to wear his sweaters to the theater. It still smells like him. We would always go to the theater together."

"Oh. I thought you didn't like to go with others to the theater. You said you didn't like how you couldn't talk."

"Doug didn't count as others. We already knew what each other would say."

"Uh-huh. Okay. Anyway, let's start." Lena did her search again and found Edwin easily.

Evelyn couldn't believe how after all this time Edwin was just a few clicks away. It never occurred to her to look.

"Alright. How should we begin?" Lena gulped more wine. "Dearest handsome Edwin, who looks like a movie star. How good are you at cyber-sex?"

"That's a strong beginning. Then just say, 'don't reply if you turned out to be an addict. Or if you want perky boobs.'"

"You could get perky boobs. I heard of a woman who was seventy-five who got breast implants."

"You did not."

"Did so."

"Whatever for?"

"To attract a younger man, I suppose. Maybe that was Mavis's secret," Lena said.

"Please, Mavis could tuck them into her belt if she wanted."

Lena snorted and choked on her wine.

"Okay, let's focus. You got me started and now I'm committed." Evelyn straightened up as best she could. Her vision shifted from the movement. "Dear…To…Dear, Edwin."

"Here you do it." Lena passed her the phone.

Evelyn squinted down at the letters. She began tapping away and after a few minutes she passed it back. "Done. Sent."

"What did you say?"

"I said, 'hello, we used to be classmates, and I thought you were terribly attractive. How has your life been…'something like that."

"Good, good. I like that."

"Me too." Evelyn got up and went to the living room. With great concentration, she pulled the cushions off the couch and unfolded it into a bed.

"What are you doing?"

"I'm not driving," Evelyn said. "Sleep here."

Lena stumbled in and fell down on the couch. "Fine. Night…thanks for the muffins…" and almost instantly was out.

Evelyn covered the muffins so they wouldn't get stale, then made her way to her own bed, using the walls to propel herself forward. Then she too flopped down and let the world fade away. Her dreams that night were a confusing blur of Doug turning into Edwin, turning back into Doug, who held a lemon muffin out to her…

CHAPTER NINE

Lena woke up with a sick feeling in her gut and a velvety texture on her tongue. She lay still for a moment, unwilling to open her eyes and face the assault waiting for them. Waking up queasy from too much alcohol was not a new feeling, but Evelyn's wine had been more potent than Lena's usual cheap brand and it hit her differently. Reluctantly, she opened her eyes, squinting against the morning light, and fumbled for her phone.

Dead.

Perfect.

With a movement that was not overly graceful, Lena managed to get her feet on the ground and heave herself vertical. She swayed in place, then felt herself steady. Her head hurt, but not bad. She mostly felt sick. Some water would help with that. She shuffled forward into the kitchen and on her second try found a glass and filled it with water from the tap. She drank it slowly then held it to her forehead, the cool of the glass soothing her pounding head.

"Morning," Evelyn croaked, coming into the kitchen.

"Morning."

"Feeling alright?"

"Okay. You?"

"Better than I thought, actually." She looked a little pale, and her braid had come loose around her face.

Other than that, Evelyn didn't look like she was suffering too much.

Maybe she was invincible.

"Want pancakes?" Evelyn grabbed her own glass and filled it with water.

"Maybe just an aspirin."

"You should eat something."

"I need to get going…what time is it?"

Evelyn nodded at the stove clock. "Eight-thirty."

Her heart slammed into her ribs. "No, it's not."

"It is."

"Oh shit, shit, shit. I was supposed to be at work half an hour ago! I can't believe I slept in." Lena dashed down the hall to the bathroom, splashed water on her face and twisted her hair into a bun. "I need to go." She came tearing out again, grabbed the sweatshirt she discarded last night and stuffed her dead phone in her jeans. Jeans! She couldn't show up to work in jeans. "I don't have time to change," she said out loud. "Shit, shit, shit."

"Come here." Evelyn led Lena to her bedroom and yanked open the closet door.

"I can't wear your clothes," Lena said.

"Do you have a better option? You'll wear my clothes and take my car."

"Oh shit, my car. It's still at the theater." Lena took the offered dress and quickly stripped off her shirt and slipped it over her head. It was maroon colored and went a hand past her knees with lacy half sleeves. It actually didn't fit too bad, but she hardly had time to care about that.

Evelyn passed her a pair of black heels. "Take my car then after work leave it at the theater with the keys on the front wheel. I'll walk over this evening and get it."

Lena put the heels on. They were a half size too small and immediately caused pain. She ignored the pinching feeling and hobbled out of the room towards the door.

"Here are the keys, and a muffin." Evelyn stuffed both in her hands.

"Thank-you. See you later." Lena walked as quick as she could down the hall and stabbed at the elevator button till the doors opened. In the parking lot, she pressed panic on the keys in order to locate the car and drove as fast as she dared out onto the street. After cursing at every red light and stuffing the lemon muffin down her throat, Lena finally pulled into the parking lot and hurried towards the building. A chunk of hair had escaped from her bun and she impatiently pushed it behind her ear. She burst in, exactly one hour and ten minutes late, to find Jerry sitting behind her desk with the phone pressed against his ear.

"Martin, thank God." He abruptly hung up. "I thought you might have been in an accident."

"No...sorry," Lena said, breathless. "My phone died and..."

"You look like hell."

"I know, I'm sorry I—"

"You know, this really isn't acceptable. In order for the team to work, we've all got to do our part. The people on the bench are just as important as the starters. More even, some could argue."

"I know, it won't happen—"

"Are you hung over?" Jerry eyed her disheveled appearance. Then a smile crept over his face. "You weren't out partying last night, were you? What is this, the walk of shame?"

"No, I—"

"You know, Martin, if I knew you were the type, I would have invited you out more."

"That's not—"

Jerry laughed. "You're full of surprises. I like that in a girl. Keeps things interesting. It's always the ones you least expect that are the best at...things." He winked at her.

Lena stared, her mouth falling open and blood rushing to her cheeks.

"No need to be embarrassed. It's a compliment."

And then, Lena bent over and vomited lemon poppy seed muffin all over the floor.

****

Two hours later, Lena was sitting in her car, having just parked Evelyn's car and left it with the dress and heels on the passenger seat. She plugged her phone into the new car charger she had bought and waited for it to come to life.

After the mortifying moment when all thoughts of her being a viable sexual partner must have flown from Jerry's mind—the only possible upside of the incident—Lena apologized profusely, said she was ill and shouldn't have come to work and quickly left the building. It had definitely made the top five of the worst moments of her life. Ranking right up there with wetting herself in kindergarten and the first time she got her period (in public, white pants, every girl's nightmare). With humiliation burning her face to cinders, Lena debated going home, but then changed her mind and went to the mall. She bought herself a new dress, sandals, car charger, and some aspirin. Then she got her hair washed and styled, hoping that getting her head massaged by expert hands would help dissolve her lingering headache and mounting shame. Feeling more human, Lena went to the theater to get her car and now here she sat trying to decide what to do.

She had never played hooky from work before; it felt like a shame to waste it. She was feeling much better after emptying her stomach all over her workplace floor, and the thought of going home just to sit and re-live it again and again—as she knew she would—was not appealing.

When her phone finally turned on, she tried calling her mom, but it went right to voicemail. Lena hung up and sent her a quick text saying she was coming over for a visit. Sad that the only thing she could think to do was go visit her mother. It was better than going home though. She followed the traffic out of the city, the cars in front of her melting away the farther she got until she had the road all to herself.

Thick clouds that looked like they should be as dense as brand-new marshmallows sat in heavy groups across the sky, swirling and forming loose pictures of animals and mythical creatures. Lena had always been fascinated with the sky. She loved how it changed, how the colors could break her heart at the beginning and end of the day. How the clouds were a window into the emotions of the earth: sometimes moving so slowly and peacefully, other times expanding with pent up energy like a giant about to exhale. She used to paint it all the time. Along with trees, rivers, fields…She had done portraits too sometimes, but landscape art was her favorite. Every emotion ever felt by the human race could be felt looking at a painting of nature. She felt sure about this.

She'd studied art in college. Impractical and totally useless for the real world, but art had a way of taking her out of herself. It helped her express things that words just couldn't and it was the only thing she had any interest in learning about. She'd thought vaguely maybe she would teach art one day (indeed, what else did one do with an art degree?) but she didn't have any real plans besides getting through university.

She couldn't remember when she stopped painting. Funny how something could seem like such an integral part of herself, only to melt away with time. It wasn't James' fault, though.

He hadn't been into art, but that had been fine. Lena had taken him to an art show once. He looked so bored and miserable she never tried to get him to go again. He had been far more of a realist than her—smarter, too. He never read much, but when he did, it was biographies or self-help books. He hadn't liked movies that were too unrealistic, and he didn't like spending money. These were things Lena thought were good for her to have in a partner. Someone practical, who wouldn't drown them in debt. Someone who would take care of her. Someone completely different from Sean, who had given Lena the exhausting task of being the responsible one.

When Lena had first seen James sitting in the grief circle, fiddling with a foam cup, she felt a flare of attraction. It wasn't like a thunderclap or gravitational pull or anything. It was just a mild acknowledgement that she was in the same room as a man she found good looking. It hadn't crossed her mind in the slightest that he might look at her the same way until at the end of the third session when he cornered her at the snack table.

"Lena, right?"

"Yeah. You're James?" She'd said it like a question, but of course she knew who he was. James Martin, first-year student. His mom died of cancer the summer before college. She had been a single parent, and the loss was a hard one for him to accept. He shared it all with the group while staring at his hands, his voice serious and almost impersonal. At first Lena thought it was odd. Everyone else cried when they talked, but he sounded more angry than sad.

After a bit of small talk, he asked her out for a coffee. She agreed, though completely taken off guard. Every time he called her after, she was genuinely surprised. Between their dates she barely thought of him, sure that he would fade away soon.

Their fourth date, exactly two weeks later, he took her back to his place, and they had sex. She hadn't intended on sleeping with him so soon. It just sort of happened. He asked if she wanted to come up for a drink; they had just gone out to a movie. His roommates were out—that should have been the first clue. The apartment had the typical grungy bachelor pad look and smell. Dirty dishes in the sink, beer and pizza in the fridge. Not a single picture hung on the bare white walls. He'd grabbed two beers and led her to his bedroom, which was surprisingly clean. The bed was made, and no clothes were on the floor. She still had no thoughts of sex as the springs creaked under them when they sat on the edge. It was like the first time he kissed her; she was completely taken aback, as if it had never occurred to her that kissing was something he might want to do with her.

He had finished his beer quickly. A couple quick slugs and it was gone.

"Almost done?" he asked her. She looked at her barely touched drink and back at his face. His cheeks were flushed, eyes bright.

Oh.

Then she knew. She briefly considered leaving, but then thought, why not? Why leave? Wasn't this what people did in college? Wasn't it supposed to be part of the experience or something? And she had just shaved her legs, so she was prepared that way.

She'd let him take the bottle from her and push her back on the bed. They undressed themselves. Then he moved on top of her and after some impatient, awkward handling, and pausing to put a condom on, he was in, moving fast. A few minutes later he collapsed on top. That was it, their first time. Not even a kiss.

It had occurred to her later that maybe that was weird, to not even be kissed during their first time together. She remembered lying there wondering how long until she could get up and get dressed again.

After that, they had sort of became an official couple without much discussion about it. He was just always there, always calling, always showing up. He told her he loved her two months later. Lena said it back. It was so simple. She had appreciated that about their relationship. No games or guessing.

They'd both graduated with their degrees at twenty-one, moved in together, got married two years later, and then three years after that Lena was staring down at his grave.

Horrible.

Tragic,

Completely unfair.

But that was life.

Lena pulled into Redwood and finally parked outside her house. She got out and went to let herself in, but the door was locked.

"Mom?" She knocked sharply on the door.

After a pause, there was the sound of a lock being turned then the door swung open and suddenly Lena was face to face with a tall, tanned man with closely cut dirty blond hair. It took her a second to register what she was seeing, then her heart slammed in her throat. "Sean!"

"Well, hello." Sean grinned at her. "Long time no see."

"What the hell are you doing here?"

"Didn't your mom tell you I bought the house?"

"Yes, she did…I just…" Lena scrambled, trying to collect her thoughts. "I thought they had possession for a couple more weeks."

"They do. Your mom was gone today, so they let me move some stuff in."

"Oh." Lena shifted. "Okay. Well, bye."

She turned to go, but Sean reached out and grabbed her arm. "Hold up." Lena stiffened, he let her go and held up his hands. "You don't have to rush off. It's been what? Ten years almost since I've seen you?"

"Almost."

"You look the same."

"You look different." The boy she remembered had long hair swept back, his frame and face edging towards too skinny. The man in front of her was filled out more, his arms and torso thicker, and his muscles more defined.

Sean leaned against the door. "Good different?"

Lena shrugged. "Just different. Why are you back here? I thought you were on the Island."

"I was, but I needed a change."

"You bought my house."

"I know. Kinda weird, isn't it? But I had so many good memories here…" He grinned again, and Lena knew exactly what kind of memories he was thinking about. She was sure the skin on her cheeks was going to melt off any second.

"Bad ones too," she said.

And just like that, Cheryl floated between them.

Sean's grin slipped. "Yeah, some bad ones too."

Lena looked down at her feet. "Sorry. I shouldn't have brought it up."

"It's fine." He shifted.

A million questions flooded her mouth, but cowardliness overtook them. For ten years she had imagined what she would say if she ever saw Sean again. She had questions. She wanted to know exactly what he remembered about that night. After she found Cheryl in the river, they were both questioned by the cops. When it was ruled an accident, Sean disappeared. He didn't even stay for the funeral, no note to Lena or anything. Though it's not like she needed to hear from him that they were over. She knew it the second it all happened.

It all hung over them now. Cheryl, him leaving, the years of silence. She couldn't do it though, she couldn't will the words she wanted to ask to come.

She could feel Sean studying her, and suddenly she felt angry. "What the hell were you thinking? Moving back here? Buying my house? What is wrong with you?"

Sean straightened. "You have a right to be angry."

"You didn't answer me."

"Why don't I tell you over dinner."

"Dinner?" Lena stared.

"Yeah. Dinner. It's what people do when they get

hungry."

"I'm not going to dinner with you."

"Why not? Come on, Len. For old times' sake."

Hearing the nickname he called her sounding so familiar and easy threw her off guard. It brought a whirlwind of memories—walking down the railway tracks, holding hands for the first time, sharing slushies from the gas station, skipping school to go lay by the river, his mouth touching hers, his hands sliding over her…God, how easily she had given pieces of herself to that reckless boy, now a man, standing in front of her asking her to dinner.

"I-I don't know."

"Just coffee then. It's too early for dinner, anyway."

"Okay. Fine. Just a coffee, but we are having it here." She couldn't imagine going to Main Street for coffee with Sean. It would for sure get the entire town whispering. She walked past him and led him into the house to the kitchen. He sat on a stool by the island while Lena rummaged through the cupboards and grabbed two mugs and set the coffee brewing.

He chatted as they waited for the pot to fill. He was staying in the hotel on the edge of town until the possession date. Moving back had been spontaneous. He wanted to get off the Island: he had a bad split with his girlfriend, and he didn't care for his job as a mechanic, so he decided to start over. When he saw Lena's house for sale, it felt like a sign, a weird one, but he took it as a confirmation that it was time to return to Redwood.

"I heard about your husband passing." Sean took the offered cup. "That's shitty. I'm sorry."

"That's an understatement, but thanks." Lena leaned back against the counter.

"I shouldn't have left like that, Len. After what happened. I was a messed up little fucker. It's been my biggest regret. Leaving you to deal with all that alone."

"It's fine."

"It's not."

"How's your mom?"

Sean blinked. "My mom?"

"I saw her after you left. She was devastated."

"She's fine. She's had a new boyfriend for a few years now, I think. We don't talk."

"That's too bad."

Sean shrugged. Still a touchy subject then.

"Anyway, it's probably best you left," she continued. "I don't think you would have been very helpful."

"No. I wouldn't have. I spent the better part of two years high and drunk after that. I don't even remember most of it."

Lena shook her head. "That's exactly what I pictured you doing."

"I missed you though. I never stopped missing you."

"Really."

"You don't believe me?"

"Not even a little bit."

"You never forget your first. Isn't that what they say?" He slid off the stool and went around to stand in front of her. Lena's heart drummed in her stomach as he reached around her and set his cup in the sink. So close she could feel his breath on her face. "You've thought about me too. Admit it."

She tilted her head to see him. It would take little effort to reach up and kiss him, to feel his soft lips against her own. They would move slowly at first, then with urgency. They would grip each other and tumble to the couch like teenagers. Like ten years hadn't passed with a million heartbreaks in between.

No, she thought, *you never forget your first.*

She could feel the tension throbbing off him and knew he was imagining a similar scene. Her lips tingled with the near contact. She felt almost dizzy. It had been so long since she'd been kissed. She hadn't thought about it much before today, but now the months without intimacy suddenly felt very long indeed.

She needed to get out of here.

"I'm going now." She set her cup down and went to move past him.

He stopped her with a hand on her arm. "Can I have your phone number? You know, in case I have a question about something in the house or I find one of your old diaries or something?"

She shouldn't. She should walk out of here and never see him again.

"Fine." Lena took his phone and put in her number.

"It was nice to catchup, Len."

"Yeah. Have a good one." Lena walked out of the house and to her car. She got in and put the car in drive, all the while conscious of Sean's eyes following her and the thrill running up and down her spine.

CHAPTER TEN

"Mom, go sit down. I've got this."

"I'm perfectly able to help."

Alice gave Evelyn a perfected exasperated look and swiped her hair out of her face. "I know you are Mom, but you don't have to. Please, just sit."

"Just because I'm getting older doesn't mean I have to be waited on hand and foot like I'm the Queen."

Her other daughter, Sarah, came into the kitchen just then and kissed her on the cheek. "But wouldn't that be nice?"

"I suppose." Evelyn eyed Sarah as she sat down beside her at the island. She seemed good, eyes bright and alert. Her pixie short dyed blonde hairdo freshly washed and styled nicely. She was even dressed in the nice blue sweater Evelyn had bought her and clean black pants. When she was feeling well, Sarah had wonderful style, age appropriate and trendy.

Alice didn't seem to put much effort into her clothing unless she was going out. Not that Evelyn would ever comment on her style, or lack thereof. She had learned the hard way many years ago that Alice didn't appreciate receiving feedback on her clothing, or on any other topic Evelyn tried to bring up.

"Still on the pills, Sarah?" Evelyn asked.

"What?"

"The depression pills. You said you started taking

some new ones?"

"No, they made me really groggy. I'm fine though."

"Did your doctor clear you to go off?"

"I'm fine, mom."

Evelyn and Alice exchanged a look. How many times have they heard that?

Evelyn tried another approach. "How are things with you and Cam?"

Sarah sighed. "Mom, could you please stop prying?"

"I'm not prying, honey. It's just a question. I know things have been difficult lately and—"

"It's fine. I'm fine. Cam is fine."

Evelyn felt the tension rising but couldn't help herself. "It's just, last time you were struggling with depression you and Cam did that separation thing for a while and I don't think—"

"Mom, I don't think Sarah wants to talk about all that right now." Alice intervened.

Evelyn gripped her hands to keep her cool. So like Alice to side with Sarah, she always preferred things to be all flowers and sunshine even when they weren't.

"What's this?" Sarah picked up a bag on the seat beside Evelyn, determined to change the subject.

Fine. She would call Sarah tomorrow and get a proper update. "Oh, yes. I picked up a little something for you. And you, Alice. Have a look." Evelyn bit back a grin at the quick glance between them.

Sarah reached in and pulled out two small items wrapped in paper. She carefully unwrapped one and held it up. "A…shot glass?"

"It has measurements on it," Evelyn said. "So you know how much you're mixing. Remember last Sunday you made me that—what was it? Rum and coke. I nearly died. There's one for you too, Alice."

"I don't usually make mixed drinks," Alice said.

"Well, keep it for when we do, so Sarah doesn't give us all alcohol poisoning."

"Please." Sarah rolled her eyes, then said, "This is nice, isn't it? Quiet for once."

It definitely was quiet. Usually their Sunday get-togethers were slightly chaotic with her daughters' families packed into one house. Alice and Brent had three kids: two who lived close by, one who just had their first baby. Sarah and Cam had two, the youngest who was graduating this year. While not all could make it every week, there were usually enough people to make the place fairly loud. This week, however, it was just Alice and Sarah and their husbands who were able to meet for dinner. Evelyn loved seeing her family all in one place, still amazed that all of it had exploded from her and Doug saying 'I will' all those years ago. But she had to agree with Sarah that the quieter atmosphere made for a nice change.

It would have been a good night for her to host, come to think of it. That was her one regret to downsizing—she couldn't host her whole family anymore. She had comforted herself when she moved that it just meant she could have quality time with members of her family instead of having them all over at once. The family get-togethers had shifted mainly to Alice's house now. Which was fine, of course. Evelyn wasn't the type to be so controlling that she couldn't pass the reigns. She was very happy to let someone else take the lead.

It's just. It could be a bit much was all. Poor Alice looked so flustered, buzzing around the kitchen. It would be easier if she would just accept some help now and then. Look at her, her ponytail falling out, dirty apron due for a wash tied around her hips…oh dear, was that a make-up line on her chin? Should Evelyn tell her? Probably not.

Alice could be so touchy, so ready to assume Evelyn was critiquing her. She'd always been like that. Since Alice was a little girl she'd easily feel hurt, and always read in between the lines in the simplest conversations. Evelyn didn't know where she got it from. She and Doug had always been fairly easygoing, though Doug had a habit of getting too involved in other people's business. He constantly had an opinion to share—from what the kids should go to college for, to how the neighbor decorated the lawn for Christmas. Course, he would have said the same thing about her.

Learning how to manage her eldest daughter's feelings had been a challenge, one she wasn't sure they handled correctly. Even now, she still had to be careful what she said and did. It was hard to say nothing—to do nothing—all the time. If they were at Sarah's house, Evelyn would've been able to help with supper—she could even help tidy up the house and perhaps suggest some new decor tips. Sarah wouldn't care. That might be Sarah's issue though, she didn't care enough about things. Like feelings, people's opinions etc…Evelyn was a little worried Sarah was going to end up like June in her old age, harsh and direct when her filter finally gave out.

Oh well. There were worse things one could be, she supposed. Besides, she wouldn't be around to see it.

Evelyn sat on her hands, trying to keep from tidying up the island. It was a massive one, six feet long and could easily fit six people on one side. Evelyn had tried to warn Alice when she bought this place that an island that big could turn into a dumping ground for clutter. She hadn't listened, though.

Like look, there was a box of—what was in there? Jars? A stack of mail, dishes, computer cords…magazines? Evelyn leaned around the box to see the stack of celebrity gossip magazines. She clicked her tongue. "Alice, what are you buying that trash for?"

"What?" Alice looked up from the potato salad she was mixing.

"These, trashy magazines. It's a waste of money, you know. Half the stuff is lies."

"I like them." Alice turned back.

Sarah said, "It's just for fun, mom."

"It contributes to the unhealthy worship of celebrities," Evelyn said. "Look at this, 'Their Just Like Us!' Of course they are just like us—they pass gas, take dumps, and look like crap in the mornings, don't they?"

"You've always had a love/hate thing with celebrities," Sarah laughed. "What with your obsession with movies. I think you're just jealous of them."

"I am not. I think it's ridiculous how people idolize them. That's all." She looked down at one title about some celebrity coming out about their secret 'tortured world.' No doubt about the perils brought on by being so rich and glamourous. Please. She had little patience for celebrities and their superficial problems. She rolled her eyes whenever one moaned and complained about the lack of privacy being a rich celebrity came with. Or recently, the new trend of being body-shamed for being too thin and perfect. 'My body type counts too!' whined the flat stomach, big boob model posting naked pictures two weeks after giving birth. Being too beautiful, too rich, too popular. Those were not *actual* problems. Actual problems were wondering how to afford rent or put food on the table. Not that Evelyn had those particular problems either. But still.

"You shouldn't buy this garbage, Alice. If you want to waste your money, you should—"

"Hello my favorite mother-in-law." Cam, Sarah's bear of a husband, came up and gave Evelyn a side hug.

Evelyn smiled up at him. She always got a kick out of her sons-in-law. They were extreme opposites. Cam stood over six feet, wide chest, big arms whereas Brent wore glasses, was as slender as a beanpole and not much taller than Alice. They were good men though, good husbands to her girls and fathers to her grandkids.

She felt very fortunate her daughters hadn't married one of those first boyfriends they dated, the ones who drank too much and had tattoos up and down their arms. There had been some concerning years there for a while, but in the end, Evelyn was quite happy with the sons who joined their family—Cam had a wonderful sense of humor and Brent was quite handy with fixing things. It certainly wasn't by chance, though. She was the one who set Alice up with Brent, and she knew for a fact Doug scared off more than one of Sarah's boyfriends. All in a days' work when one had daughters.

"Hello, Cam," she said. "Your beard is getting long."

Cam ran his hand over his dark beard matching his wavy dark head. "Thanks, Sarah hates it."

"I do." Sarah agreed.

Evelyn sensed a bit of tension there. She moved on quickly. "Where is Brent?"

"Downstairs watching the game. I'm just grabbing some beers." He moved to the fridge, "Mind if we eat there?"

"Um, *yes*," Sarah said. "We are here for a *family* meal, Cam. I told you that."

Evelyn waved her hand. "Oh, it's fine. Go on, Cam." She pretended she didn't see Sarah roll her eyes.

"Great, call us when it's ready," Cam said, before disappearing downstairs.

"*Call us when it's ready.* What are we, their servants?" Sarah said.

Alice and Evelyn exchanged another look. Looked like the marriage counselling was still very much needed.

Alice's phone rang just then. She seized it quickly and moved into the living room to answer. Evelyn made sure her back was turned, then slid off the chair and went around to assess the state of supper. Alice, bless her heart, inherited Evelyn's enthusiasm for cooking, but sadly not her talent.

"Mom, she'll kill you if you touch anything," Sarah said.

"Shush, I'm just taking a peek." Just a dab more mustard in the potato salad might fix it…and a tad more BBQ sauce to the pulled pork, it was looking a little dry…and what did she put in that salad? It was looking very soggy…

"Mom!"

Evelyn jumped and spun around as Alice reemerged, hands on her hips.

"For the love of God! Stop criticizing and go sit down."

"What? I'm not, honey. I'm just helping a bit."

"Sarah, please get her out of here so I can finish."

Sarah grinned. "Come on, mom, leave her be or we will never be able to eat."

Evelyn frowned. "Fine." She started following Sarah to the porch but paused to say over her shoulder. "You have a make-up line, by the way, under your chin."

She dashed out before Alice could react. It felt easier to breathe out here, away from the clutter in the house. It was on the verge of too cool for eating outside. Soon they wouldn't be able to do it any longer. Evelyn sat down on the slightly uncomfortable patio chair and placed her hands on the glass table.

"Do you want some wine?" Sarah asked.

"Oh no, I'm fine. I'm off wine for a bit." After overindulging with Lena a few days ago, the thought of having another glass made her stomach twist.

They chatted for a few minutes until Alice came and announced, a bit stiffly, that dinner was ready. After dishing up, they settled back around the porch table. The pulled pork *was* dry, but the buns were excellent, and Evelyn heartily complimented Alice on them, who took it with a suspicious thanks.

Oh dear.

Resolved not to ruffle any more feathers, Evelyn finished and sat back, listening to the sisterly banter flowing between her girls. Alice was fifty years old and a new grandmother. Sarah was forty-seven and almost an empty-nester. They were both firmly middle-aged women, yet when they got together they always reverted to their teenage ways, bickering over the silliest things, bossing and teasing. She liked to imagine them old and gray in a nursing home one day, driving the nurses nuts with their constant chatter. Watching them made her wish—not for the first time—that she could have had a sister. It was a bond unlike anything she had with her friends. Her girls had the complete freedom to say what they liked, how they liked, and know the other one would always answer the next time they rang.

Well, Evelyn had that too with her daughters—sort of. That was the next best thing to having a sister. Daughters could make the best of friends, actually. It had come as a bit of a surprise, her own relationship with her mum when she was alive could be described as 'distant' at best. Evelyn used to call her mum now and then, visit her in London once a year, and when the time came Evelyn helped settle her into a nursing home. It was all very polite, very formal. Done out of duty, not really out of love. When her mum finally did pass, it felt like a bee sting. It hurt for a few minutes, but then it dulled, and life carried on. It was kind of sad.

She was the only one—as far as she knew—who had any feelings about her mum passing. Dying should make more of an impact on people, shouldn't it? Doug's certainly had. His funeral had been huge. She hadn't even recognized half the people who showed up, each with a story of how they knew him, how he made them laugh, how he had helped them…

Well, her mum had made her choices. There were consequences to actions, after all. Though it occurred to Evelyn after she flew back for the funeral and was working on her speech, that she didn't know her mom well at all. Surely, there was some reason for her being the way she was? Clearly, she had mental health issues. There must have been some trauma in her past, something to make her so…thoughtless. Anyway, it was too late to find out now.

What was Lena's mum like? Were they close? Was she loving? Was she there for Lena, to help her cope with her grief? Evelyn hoped so. A girl needed her mum—that was another strange thing. Even with the physical and emotional distance between them, a part of her longed for her mum. Maybe not as she was, but as she could have—should have—been. Evelyn thought she would've been over it by now, at her age. Apparently, it was one of those things that never went away.

She would have to ask Lena about her mum next time she saw her. It would be a good topic to discuss, help her find out where Lena's family life was at…

"Mom? Are you listening?" Alice said.

"What? Oh sorry, I was thinking."

"What about?" Sarah popped the rest of her bun into her mouth.

"You remember I told you about Lena? I was just wondering what her mum is like."

Alice and Sarah both stilled. Sarah swallowed. "You…saw her at the movies again?"

Evelyn nodded. "We've actually hung out a couple times."

Alice's mouth dropped open. "You did? Why?"

"What do you mean why?"

Alice and Sarah exchanged looks.

Evelyn frowned. "What?"

"Mom," Alice began. "Sarah and I—we don't think you should see her again."

"Why ever not?"

"It's not a good idea mom," said Sarah. "It's weird. Does she even know about, you know, everything?"

"It hasn't come up."

Alice sighed. "Mom. I know you want to help her,

118

but I don't think you two hanging out is a good idea. Dad would've—"

"Your dad would have wanted me to look out for her," said Evelyn. "Tell me, who else do you think is qualified to help her? I know the pain she feels. In fact, it's been nice talking to someone who understands."

"We understand, Mom—"

"You don't," Evelyn said. "I know you loved your dad, and you miss him. But you don't know the same heartache I do. The heartache of losing the love of your life—your partner. The one person you want to talk to at the beginning and end of every day. You don't understand."

Alice's eyes filled with tears. Sarah stared down at the table.

Evelyn sighed. She should never have told them about Lena. She knew the second she saw their faces the first time she told them about Lena that they didn't approve.

"Okay mom," Sarah said, finally. "Just be careful, okay? Don't stir things up…"

"You both are making this more dramatic than it needs to be."

Alice wiped her eyes, sniffing. "We're just worried about you," she said, her voice high.

"Well, don't. I'm the last person you should worry about. I'm one of the dullest people on the planet." Just then, Evelyn's phone dinged, and she fished it out of her pocket. "Really girls, you have your own families to look after. Alice, honey, please don't cry. It's not—" she paused, looking at the notification on her screen. Then she gasped. "Oh. My. God."

"What?" Sarah asked. "What is it?"

"Nothing. Nothing at all." Evelyn's face heated. She quickly put the phone back in her pocket.

"What, mom? What happened?" Alice said.

"Nothing. Mavis got a lot of scrabble points on our online game we are playing is all. Speaking of Mavis, I forgot I'm meeting the girls bright and early tomorrow. I better call it a night."

Sarah's eyebrow rose. "I thought you did that Thursdays."

"Oh yes, well, tomorrow is Nora's birthday, so we are doing it then. Thanks for the lovely, lovely meal, Alice, dear." Careful to avoid their surprised faces, Evelyn quickly stood from the table and hurried through the house and out to her car.

She started the engine, then pulled out her phone again. The notification was still there, *Edwin Peterson sent you a message*. God, what did she send him again? What had she been thinking? She'd felt foolish the next morning after Lena convinced her to message him, but quickly shook it off and put it entirely from her mind. She'd assumed if he did check his messages he wouldn't bother getting back to some random woman whom he hadn't seen in over fifty years.

Evelyn threw the phone on the passenger seat like it was made of fire. She wouldn't look at it now. She would wait until she was in the comfort of her own home where baking supplies were a fingertip away should she need it.

She could think of little else during the drive home and was scarcely aware of parking and getting up to her apartment. She sat on the couch and cradled the phone in her hands. Taking a deep breath, she swiped it open, first looking at the message she'd sent to remind herself how mortified she should be. It was worse than she had remembered.

Dear Edwin,

This is completely out of the blue, but you crossed my mind the other day. We used to be classmates way back when, I used to sit behind you in English. I always thought you were terribly attractive and judging from your profile picture you haven't aged too badly. I was wondering what you have been up to these past fifty some odd years?

Sincerely,

Evelyn Williamson (Webb)

Evelyn groaned. She supposed it could have been worse. She seemed to recall there being some discussion about including something to do with cyber-sex. Thank goodness that hadn't made it in. She collected herself and continued reading.

Hello Evelyn,

It's nice to hear from you. Believe it or not, I do remember you. You were one of the smartest kids in class. I remember you always wore your hair in braids. Thank you for the generous compliment, though I must admit I am much less attractive in real life. Since we are being frank, I looked at your profile picture too and you look lovelier than ever. I saw you are in Canada now, when did you move there?

He went on about what he did after high school (he did marry Marie; they divorced twenty years ago and they had two sons together). He'd worked in finance in London until he retired and bought a pub with one of his sons back in St. Ives. He helped manage it now and enjoyed being home, living close to the sea again. He wrote a lot more than Evelyn would ever have expected.

She read his message twice and sat back, feeling a bit dazed.

After a moment, she got up, made herself a cup of tea and then sat down to craft her reply. She hesitated for a split second, then her fingers started tapping away. She told him about Doug, about their college romance, moving to Canada, the restaurant franchise they owned. She told him of her kids and grandkids, and how Doug had passed away. Feeling giddy, she pressed send then sat back against the cushion of the couch, one hand on her chest, feeling the quickened thumping of her heart.

Edwin Peterson.

Messaging her.

Thinking she looked *lovely as ever.*

Huh.

Life still had some curveballs for her yet.

CHAPTER ELEVEN

It had been four days since running into Sean. Four days of pretending she wasn't obsessively checking her phone to see if he texted. She couldn't stop thinking about how he looked. The way his lips curved into that familiar smile. The way her body tingled when they stood close...

She hated how much he was on her mind. It was pathetic. Just a few minutes with him and she was back to that gawky teenager, so struck by the notion a guy wanted her that she lost all common sense. It was ridiculous, especially because she'd barely thought of him in years.

Well, maybe she had a little now and then.

Not really, though.

She'd tried not to. Anytime he had come to mind, she firmly pushed him away. He was tied to so much hurt and confusion. There was no possible good that could come from letting him back in her life.

A sentiment her mom seemed to share. She called, frantic, after Lena left the house Wednesday. She had been in a massage apparently and was mortified when she realized Lena had gone to the house with Sean there. Lena had told her she barely said hi and then left, which was true enough. She didn't tell her mom that she gave Sean her number, or that the reason she declined to get together this weekend was that a part of her thought maybe he would text and maybe they would hang out…Not that she wanted to. Or would say yes. Or would even admit to herself that's why she sat alone at home all weekend. It was Sunday now, and she was sitting on the couch staring at the phone, wondering why he hadn't reached out yet, and feeling more and more pathetic that she so clearly wanted him to.

Was she so lonely that even the slightest bit of attention made her desperate for more? There had been something in the air between them that she hadn't felt in a long time. It was almost intoxicating.

It was better that he hadn't texted, though. He probably wasn't going to. That would be for the best. She clearly wasn't someone to be trusted to have good judgement right now.

Still, it was fine to be curious about an ex, wasn't it? Nothing wrong with just wanting to find out what he has been up to, who he is now. She didn't have to talk to him again to find out that. Lena took out her phone and began sleuthing. She'd resisted the urge to look him up before—Facebook was just becoming a thing when they were in high school. He didn't have it back then, but surely he would now…A quick search on social media proved her wrong. Not only was he not on Facebook, he also had no Instagram or Twitter, or at least none that she could find.

She clicked her phone off, feeling very dissatisfied. If she could just get a little more information, it might quench the obsession she was starting to feel.

He seemed different at the house…grown up, maybe. Maybe time helped him mature. Maybe he turned out to be a decent guy… Even as she thought it, she couldn't quite convince herself. It was more likely that he was still the same old Sean. Still a partier, still wild, still dangerous. People didn't change, wasn't that common knowledge? She certainly still felt like the same person she'd always been. She even still looked the same. There was very little difference between her pictures at eighteen and what she looked like now.

Maybe he has changed though, surely some people do. The optimistic thought floated through her mind.

No. No, no, no. Stop trying to make him an option. But an image flashed through her mind, overtaking her objections. Sean kissing her, unbuttoning her shirt, his hands on her breasts. Hers drifting down to unbuckle his pants...

Stop it!

She forced the images away, her cheeks burning.

What the hell was wrong with her? She hadn't thought about...that—doing that—with someone since James...And it was *Sean* who was bringing out these...things? Her pothead, ex-boyfriend who abandoned her after Cheryl died? God, she had issues.

Not issues. She was just lonely. That's all this was. Lonely and bored and sad. Mix in a complicated ex and it was a recipe for an absolute disaster.

Lena leaned back against the couch and firmly clicked the TV on. What she needed was to relax and stop thinking about things. That was the danger, she found, with living alone. She was constantly thinking. Thinking, thinking, thinking which almost always made things feel worse, and sadder and a whole lot lonelier. No good came from too much thinking.

She forced herself to focus on the movie, a rerun of an old rom-com. The two impossibly good-looking characters were fighting one minute, then they were intertwined in a passionate kiss the next. Lena watched them, her body tightening. The slightly sick, sloppy wet sound of lips smacking together in movies usually made her cringe, but now…now it made heat spread from her mid-section down in a distracting throb. It had been so long, so freaking long…

This was not helping.

She snatched up the remote and furiously clicked the channel button, pausing when it showed two police officers breaking into a house, guns drawn. Lena settled back, ready to sink into the crime TV show when she heard it. A thump from the condo below her. Then another. Then the unmistakable sound of a female moan, high and building with each rhythmic bang.

For fuck sakes.

The bloody world was conspiring against her.

She turned the volume up, face completely aflame. It wasn't the first time she'd heard her neighbor in the throws of lovemaking. It happened now and then (probably not as often as her neighbor would have liked). This time felt louder and more obnoxious than usual. It was only two in the afternoon! What were they doing down there? Screwing against the living room wall? They had to be for her to hear them.

That seemed in character with her neighbor. He looked like the kind of person that would have sex in the middle of the apartment, blinds wide open. He had that sort of mischievous, rough look to him. She and James had been strictly bedroom lovers, and both completely fine with that. Lena had no desire to make love in adventurous places. Give her a mattress in a properly darkened room any day. Unlike her neighbor, who seemed to be picking up speed. He probably had the girl pinned against the wall, his hands curved around her backside, her breasts jiggling as he enthusiastically pumped into her.

Holy hell. Stop picturing it! Lena clasped her hands over her ears, as if that would stop her thoughts from going there again. She was absolutely losing her mind.

The noises finally subsided. She kept her hands to her ears an extra few seconds then cautiously removed them. Thank the good lord. She turned the volume down and got up for a glass of water, her hands trembling. Maybe Evelyn had a point. Maybe she should go on a date…No, she wasn't ready for that.

She should take up exercising. Start going for some nice long runs, maybe lift a few weights. That should help burn off…things. Plus, it would shape up her body, which would be good if she ever…did whatever again.

She gulped her water down, set the cup on the counter, then sat again and determinedly stared at the TV. The scene switched. The two police officers were now looking at a dead body lying on a cold, metal table, the coroner explaining the results of the autopsy.

Any heated thoughts melted away, and were replaced by ice. She stared at the perfectly still, waxy, pale body displayed on the screen, neat stitches making a Y on his exposed chest.

That's not what it looked like.

At least, that's not what Cheryl had looked like.

TV hadn't prepared her for what dead bodies were actually like. They still looked human in the shows, just pale and sleeping, like marble statues. In real life there's no mistaking it, they weren't sleeping. They were dead. That person she was staring at, trying to recognize, was gone. It's almost too hard to describe. She was looking down at Cheryl's body but it wasn't her, she knew it wasn't her. It was just this empty shell that sort of resembled the person she loved, rapidly becoming less and less her as the seconds ticked by. It was a very real, jarring reminder that bodies really were just vessels for souls, or whatever it was that truly made up a person.

It haunted her still. She'd come to accept it always would. She was the one who had found Cheryl, after all.

She could remember it as clearly as if it happened only moments ago instead of nearly ten years. Lena had woken up on the banks of the river, groggy and confused. Her purple grad dress was bunched around her, damp and muddy. Her feet were numb, her bare heels just touching the ice-cold water. That was the first thing she remembered thinking, that her feet were cold, followed quickly by how much her head hurt. She'd pushed herself up on her elbows, slowly, feeling sick, and looked around for Sean and Cheryl. No one was there. It wouldn't be the first time she'd woken up from one of their parties alone. She'd been mildly annoyed, but mostly she'd just wanted to get home and curl up in bed.

She was sure, thinking back, as she often did when it was late and she drank too much, that she had felt something was off when she was sitting there on that riverbank. Like a foreboding feeling that something was wrong. Maybe she just liked to think she did though, maybe she liked to think that she didn't wake up feeling all was fine on the day her best friend was no longer existing on the planet. It made it feel worse, somehow, that Lena hadn't known the moment Cheryl was gone. Lena should have been able to feel it, the absence of her life. They had been close like sisters, closer even.

When Lena had sat up fully on the banks of that

river, she blinked against the morning light. Then her eyes settled on something in the water. Something pink. She had sat staring at it for a minute, not understanding what she was seeing. When she finally did realize…

It was one of the worst moments of her life.

One that revisited her in her dreams. She always woke with a start, drenched in sweat and tears. She could never unseen it, Cheryl's face: her eyes wide, the color of her skin…James used to rub Lena's back, hold her until she calmed down.

Now he starred in his own dream. She never actually saw his body after the accident, but she had a very vivid imagination that did a fine job picturing him. The police identified him at the scene, a funeral home had been called, and he had been cremated. All she saw was the box in which his ashes were placed. She sometimes wondered if it would have been better to see him, if it would have helped it feel more real. She'd felt like she was in a state of numbness for so long after, a part of her fully expecting him to walk in the door at any moment. Maybe they had made a mistake—it had all just been a horrible mistake, and she wasn't actually a widow. She wasn't actually alone…

Lena clicked the TV off. Her stomach felt twisted into a knot. She went over to the fridge and grabbed her bottle of wine. Not quite two-thirty yet. Well, she had started earlier than this before.

She took a few swigs from the bottle, then sat on the couch again. There was a buzzing in her ears, the kind that becomes loud in silence. Outside a horn honked, an engine roared. Below there was a sudden loud female laugh followed by a rumbling male voice and then music began to play. The bass beat against her feet. Lena took another drink and leaned back, listening to the sounds of others living.

She had almost finished the bottle off when her phone buzzed with a text.

She glanced at it, then froze.

An unknown number.

—Hey, whats up—

Was it? It had to be. Who else would be texting her? A second later it was confirmed.

—This is Sean lol—

Lena's heart drummed against her chest as a thrill shot through her.

He texted.

So what! The still resistant side of her screamed for attention. *Don't text back, don't open that door. Sad, lonely, and the ex equals bad news, remember?*

Lena stared down at the phone, the wine making her feel sluggish and slow. One heartbeat, then two. Then her fingers started moving, as if on their own accord.

—Hey. How's it going—

She hit send.

CHAPTER TWELVE

It was chilly in her condo when Evelyn got out of bed. She wrapped her fluffy white robe around herself and slid her feet into a pair of soft pink slippers. She shuffled into the kitchen and glanced out the window. It was dark and gray outside, a nasty wind howled and moaned, doing a fine job of pulling the dying leaves off the trees, leaving them naked and colorless. It was appropriate weather for October being just around the bend. She wouldn't be surprised if it was another snowy Halloween this year.

With a sigh at the wintry days ahead, Evelyn turned to her stove and set the water kettle on. She waited patiently for it to boil, then poured herself a cup of tea. She took it to the table and then did what she'd been doing for the past week straight—she opened her laptop and loaded her messages from Facebook.

A new one was waiting for her. She couldn't help herself, her lips pulled into a smile at the sight of Edwin's name in her inbox. They'd been faithfully writing to each other every day, sometimes several times a day, since last Sunday. Their messages got longer and longer as memories flowed freely between them. They reminisced about their school days and caught each other up on what they knew of their old classmates. It was odd to hear stories of their school from his perspective—it was the same in a way to hers, but also different coming from someone who'd been a good deal more popular.

Reading his messages, Evelyn was transported back into another time, another life. She could almost feel the cobblestone streets of St. Ives beneath her feet. Could almost taste the thick, rich, sweetness of clotted cream and jam smeared over a warm scone that she used to have after school. She could clearly picture the shops lined together with signs proclaiming they had the best Cornish pasties in all of Cornwall and the street artists working on their paintings throughout. The more they talked, the more her heart ached for it, the place of her childhood. For the sound of the sea that gently played underneath the noise of the market town. For the rocky beaches and fresh fish and chips.

There was something innocent about those memories. It wasn't even that she had a particularly good childhood, but there was an attachment there. Good memories mixed in with the bad, love mixed in with the hardships. It was home.

She rarely went back to St. Ives when she visited England. Her dad had moved back to Ireland and her mum to London shortly after the divorce. Evelyn had expected that of her dad, who spent as much time away in Ireland as he could—but her mum had completely stunned Evelyn. She never seemed like the type to up and leave, but there she was, living in the largest city in England, having hardly packed a suitcase to bring with her. Part of Evelyn wondered if her mum's neurotic ways were actually her attempt to get her father to leave. She continued with the same habits though, after the move, until she ended up in a home by seventy. Evelyn had tried to visit once a year at least, her father too, until he died of cancer at sixty-seven.

Evelyn loved London when she went. She loved going to live theater performances, eating lunch outside Buckingham palace by the Queen Victoria Memorial, and walking through Covent Garden—but now, re-living it all with Edwin, she found she missed St. Ives.

Their messages had progressed from memories into thoughts about life that felt a little personal. It was strange to write to someone instead of talking in person. She felt she was being more open and honest than she probably would have been, were he across the table instead of across the ocean. They discussed their families and spouses, his career and her volunteer work. She found herself checking her inbox frequently throughout the day, even when she knew the time change meant he was probably long asleep.

She read his message now, feeling a pleasant hum in her body as she did so. She blew on her tea and took a sip, then went about responding. After re-reading the message she typed three times she pressed send and snapped the laptop shut.

The day stretched out luxuriously before her. It was rare that she had no plans on a Saturday, but here she was, free as a bird. Then tomorrow she would go to Sarah's after church and then to Alice's for the big family meal. Almost everyone was going to be there this week, so it should be loud and busy—nicely balancing out the quiet day she had ahead.

She felt some uneasiness then, thinking about seeing her family tomorrow. So far, whenever she had interactions with any of them this week, she had not yet mentioned her new pen pal. It was unlike her to keep something to herself. Usually she couldn't stub her toe without telling someone about it, but she just couldn't imagine what she would say. It felt personal, though it shouldn't. They were just emailing for goodness' sake. She was just catching up with an old friend…and yet, it felt different than that. Course, that could all be in her head. It was impossible to tell tone from emails. Maybe Edwin was just lonely and wanting someone to talk to. Which was fine. That was basically why she was enjoying talking to him…

She'd almost told Lena about it when they met on Tuesday at the theater this last week. The words had been on her tongue, but she'd bit them back. Maybe this week she would. She was being silly after all. There was no need for acting all special and secretive.

Shaking herself from her nonsense, Evelyn turned the TV on to the morning news station, then went about making herself some eggs and toast for breakfast.

After having a shower and combing her hair, she let it swing wet and loose down her back as she set about doing a thorough deep clean of the apartment. She usually saved her deep cleaning for the third Wednesday of every month, but she had time and cleaning was a relaxing way to spend a few hours. Once that was done she had a light lunch, a long nap that was bound to keep her up late that night, then she attempted to read the book club book she was supposed to have done by this Thursday.

It was well written, but Evelyn just couldn't get into the rhythm of it. She found the story quite depressing, and she didn't generally like spending her time making herself depressed. After trying to keep at it for half an hour or so, she snapped it shut. There was a movie on this one, wasn't there? She would watch that and google the summary. That should give her enough information to answer any questions June threw at them.

Evelyn went over to her computer, intending on google searching about the book, but she found herself automatically typing in Facebook. Another message! Sent shortly after she'd replied this morning. She scanned his note, then paused at the end, rereading the last line.

Would you like to video chat this week? I'd like to see you.

Evelyn felt tingles up her arms. Video chat? That was a whole new level. She tapped her fingers on the keyboard, considering it. Thoughts and questions ricocheted around her skull. What on earth was she doing? Where would all this lead? What did Edwin think this was?

Then another thought that had been lurking in the back of her mind since the beginning of all this exploded to the front—what would Doug think?

She'd been trying not to think of it. For all her brave talk to Lena it still felt odd to Evelyn to be getting this connected to another man. She had male friendships before, of course, but always within the carefully constructed loop of her marriage. She and Doug had been overcautious about friendships with the opposite sex. If one had a friend, they brought the other in, always meeting them together for dinners or informing the other if they were going to text them about something. As far as Evelyn was concerned, it was common sense to be careful with that sort of thing if marriage was to last.

Never had Evelyn had a correspondence with a man on this level that wasn't Doug, and never with the possibility of it turning into something more…Something more? What was she even saying?

She lived in Canada, he in England…he probably wasn't even thinking of anything. Why would they upend their lives at this stage? This was ridiculous. She was getting far too invested. She should just end this and be done with it…

Evelyn shut her computer and strolled around her apartment, trying not to spiral.

What she needed was an outside perspective. Yes, someone not so emotionally invested would help her figure this out. She grabbed her phone and quickly scrolled through her contacts then clicked call. It rang four times before she finally answered.

"Hello?"

"Lena. He wants to video chat."

There was a pause. "Who is this?"

"Who do you think? It's Evelyn. Didn't you save my number?"

"Oh, hi Evelyn. Who wants to video chat?"

"Edwin!"

"Edwin? Oh right! He got back to you. That's great!"

"He got back to me a while ago. We've been emailing."

"You have? Why didn't you tell me?"

"I don't know, but we have. We have been emailing, but now he wants to video chat."

"Is he a druggie? Married?"

"Divorced. Drugs haven't come up yet."

"When will you video chat?"

Evelyn pressed the phone to her ear. "I don't know if I should."

"Why not?"

"I don't know."

"You definitely should."

"You think so?"

"Absolutely."

"Won't it be awkward?"

"I don't think so."

Evelyn chewed her lip, thinking it over.

"It's just a video chat," said Lena. "Hardly different from emailing. You should do it."

Evelyn paced back and forth, then stopped. "Okay. I'm going to say yes."

"Good for you. Tell me how it goes."

"Right. Chat soon." Evelyn hung up and before she could change her mind, grabbed her laptop, opened it, and typed back: *I'd love to see you too, name the day.*

Oh God, what was she doing? She felt like a nervous teenager again. Lena was right though; it wasn't a big deal. Besides, nothing would come of it.

If that was true, why wasn't Evelyn telling her kids about it? And what about Doug?

Alright, enough. She wasn't a woman to go into distress over a man like this. She was seventy for Pete's sake. Surely the time to be stressed over romance (or whatever this was) had passed. Her mind made up, Evelyn grabbed her coat and thrusted her arms into it. She buttoned up the big black buttons and tied the sash tight around her waist. She pulled her leather driving gloves on and fixed a stylish fake fur hat on her head, the kind that only a woman of a certain age with English roots could pull off (so Sarah informed her). Then she headed out of the apartment.

She made the twenty-minute drive through the city to where the cemetery was located. There was about two hours until the sunset, but the thick clouds overhead were already darkening the sky. The days were getting progressively shorter. Soon it would be pitch black by five o'clock. She wasn't looking forward to that. It felt harder living alone when darkness came so early.

She parked the car and got out. The wind had died down some throughout the day, but it still stung her cheeks. Evelyn wrapped her arms around herself and made her way down the familiar trail. Dry dead grass and shriveled leaves crunched beneath her feet. Her gaze slid over the names and dates etched into the stones as she walked. So many people from all walks of life—women, children, men young and old—resting together in this patch of dirt. How strange to think they had all once walked around, feeling, thinking, crying, and laughing. Now they lay in rows of silence. Stranger still to think she would join them one day. Thank God she believed there was more to come after this life, or she would get terribly depressed.

She finally stopped beside Doug's grave. She knelt down beside it, ignoring the pang of cold on her knees. Evelyn gently ran her hand down the side of the cool cement tombstone bearing his name above his date of birth and death. *Loving husband, father, and friend*, was inscribed below with his favorite Bible verse underneath; *To live is Christ, to die is gain (Phil. 1:21)*.

Seventy-two years of life on this earth, boiled down to a few etchings in stone. It didn't feel like enough.

One of the kids or grandkids must have come recently because there were fresh flowers carefully placed at the base of the grave, a beautiful arrangement of yellow daffodils. It warmed her heart to know he was visited by them. She visited the grave once a month since she'd buried him. It was hard coming here. She didn't like to think of his body resting under the ground, tucked in a dark, silent coffin. She didn't want to think of him as gone; she wanted to remember him as alive. She felt his presence much stronger wrapped in one of his sweaters in the darkness of the movie theater than she did here. He had loved the movies. He always said his dream job would have been to be a director. He could talk for hours analyzing this movie or that one. God, she missed him.

"Hey, hon," she whispered. "I've been meeting up with Lena, like I told you I was going to. She's doing pretty good, all things considered. You would have liked her." Evelyn moved from her knees to sit more comfortably. The wind picked up and blew hard against her back. She reached up to hold her hat and then spoke again when it relaxed. "Everyone's doing good. We all miss you. Sarah and Cam are still in couples' therapy, but it's going well. I think they will be fine. She's been battling some depression again, since you passed. She's taken it hard, of course. You know she was closer to you than me…The grandkids are good. They are all so busy I can barely keep track of them, living their little adult lives…"

A piece of her hair blew across her face, Evelyn tucked the silver strand behind her ear and hunched her shoulders. "I've been thinking about home a lot lately. I know you never missed it; not like I did. I'm missing it a lot these days."

She paused then, not sure what she wanted to say next. She cleared her throat, finally continuing, "I guess I came to tell you, not that it's really a thing. Just that I've been talking to someone. Just silly emails, but you know…thought you should know. I know you always said if something should happen to you I should feel free to…well, anyway, not to get ahead of myself, but I just wanted to tell you."

She stared for a minute at the tombstone, her hand gently touching the petals of the bouquet. With a sigh, she got up and brushed the dirt from her pants. She turned to go, then hesitated and turned back. "I love you, Doug. You were the love of my life."

Her voice caught and her eyes grew wet. She cleared her throat once more, then straightened her shoulders and walked back across the cemetery to her car. The silence of the graves and the whistle of the wind was loud in her ears.

CHAPTER THIRTEEN

There was a click as Evelyn hung up. Lena put the phone down on the counter, smiling a little at Evelyn's obvious excitement for her video chat date. She leaned in again close to the mirror and blinked against the mascara brush. She kept her eyes wide, letting it dry before moving back and assessing her overall appearance. She had curled her hair, making it fall in waves around her shoulders and had gone a little out of character with a subtly pink lipstick. The dark navy dress she wore with half-sleeves fit slim. A carefully selected strapless bra gave the suggestion of cleavage and made her look a little more endowed than what she was. She turned this way and that, trying to decide if it was too much, if she was giving off the wrong impression.

And what impression was she aiming to give off exactly?

Confident would be good. Maybe looking confident would make her actually confident and squash the butterflies shooting up and down her stomach. And maybe she also wanted to appear…sexy? Did she want to be sexy for Sean?

"What the hell am I doing," Lena said.

Her phone dinged, and she grabbed it, a text from the man himself.

—*Can't wait to see you tonight.*—

The butterflies pounded harder, and she took a

breath to steady herself. It was just dinner. Two old friends meeting for dinner. That's it. Nothing to get worked up about.

Except it was more than that. And she knew it.

They had been texting on and off since he reached out last week, catching up on all the missing pieces. They talked about college, her job, his work as a mechanic, her family...they never talked about James. Lena was careful not to mention him, and Sean never brought him up. It felt too weird—her old life clashing with her new one. She wanted to keep them separate, though she wasn't sure why.

And, of course, they never talked about Cheryl. They mentioned her now and then as they played back some memories, always in a casual way. It was impossible not to—she had been there in almost every moment—but they never talked about that night.

She was planning to tonight, though. Part of her rationalized that's why she was even talking to Sean, to find out what he knew. After that she wouldn't keep texting him. It was starting to feel like a burning itch in her mind, her desire to know what he knew, to see if there was any new information. After so many years of trying to repress her memories and thoughts about it, it had become impossible to bury any longer. It suddenly all felt fresh. He must feel that way too, she reasoned. He must want someone to talk to about it as well. It must haunt him the way it haunted her.

She hadn't told anyone that she was talking to Sean yet. Evelyn would be far too enthusiastic that she was talking to a man and would read too much into it. Lena didn't have the energy to explain the complicated history. She wasn't sure what Evelyn would think if she knew about everything. Her mom, she knew, would be worried. When she asked if they were talking, Lena had made a noncommittal sound and changed the subject. She told herself it was nothing anyone needed to know about, but in reality she just didn't want to deal with her mom's not-so-subtle disapproval. She already knew how that conversation would go. She argued with her mom in her head about it all the time.

You can't judge him based on who he was at seventeen, mom!

I'm not sweetie, I'm just worried. You're in a vulnerable place and you need to be careful.

"I am being careful," Lena muttered, fiddling with the ends of her hair. With one last look, she left the bathroom and wandered into the kitchen. She didn't have to leave for the restaurant for another thirty minutes.

What to do, what to do…

She paced back and forth, feeling on edge. Sean offered to pick her up, but she'd been firm about meeting at the restaurant. If he drove her, then he would have to drive her back. If he did that then he might ask to come up and see her place. The thought of him standing in her little condo was too confusing to think about.

She turned on the TV to the national news station, trying to distract herself. After the weather predicted a frosty week ahead, a solemn-looking newswoman began talking about a missing woman from British Columbia. Lena didn't pay much attention until they showed a picture. Her heart contracted, then thumped hard. For a confusing moment, she thought she was staring at Cheryl. They had the same face shape, same short light blonde hair. Lena's body tingled with recognition. *Cheryl.* The hair on her arms stood on end, but a breath later she remembered it couldn't be, Cheryl was lying in a graveyard in Redwood. A closer look revealed differences, the nose wasn't quite right, the eye color brown instead of blue, the forehead higher…

This happened now and then. Sometimes Lena would be at the mall shopping, or going for a walk, and someone so eerily similar would knock the breath out of her lungs and make the past come rushing back. It wasn't just Cheryl. Sometimes she thought she saw James too. It was like her mind longed to see them again, so it jumped at the slightest similarities it spotted in complete strangers. She wondered if this disconcerting experience would happen the rest of her life, or if one day her brain would catch up with reality and stop trying to bring them back.

Lena watched the news story for a minute longer. It flicked to an interview with a tearful woman who was the girl's mother. She'd been missing for two months, today would have been her twenty-sixth birthday. Her mother was pleading with the police to do more, they were desperate that she not be forgotten. How horrible. Losing someone was bad enough, but to never know what happened…Lena couldn't imagine the terrible anxiety that came with that. The never-ending grief, the what-ifs…

Lena felt tears building in her eyes and clicked off the TV. She shook her head, trying to clear away the image of the Cheryl-looking girl. The last thing she needed right now was to be triggered and lose control. Not to mention she was not wearing waterproof mascara and had spent too long carefully grooming her eyelashes to wreck them now.

Gathering her purse, she zipped up her coat and

slipped on a pair of black heels that looked cute but were guaranteed to make her feet ache and freeze. She clunked down the stairs and stepped outside, gently closing the door behind her, and shivered as the wind threatened her carefully styled hair. She started towards her car but faltered slightly at the sight of her neighbor, sitting on the doorstep to his condo, faithfully smoking his cigarette. His cheeks were shadowed with stubble, the wind played his hair across his forehead as the end of his cigarette glowed, dangling from his lips. She tried to avoid eye contact. The image of him and the mystery woman from last Saturday burned in her mind's eye. Every bloody time she saw him now, she couldn't stop the image from coming. It was making their awkward social interactions feel even more damn awkward.

"How's it going?" He asked as she walked past.

"Good, you?" Lena stared at her feet and kept walking as her blush threatened to show through her makeup.

"Good." Was it just her, or did he sound amused? He probably told stories at his parties about the socially awkward widow from upstairs. He probably found her entertaining, which was why he always made a point to talk to her when he saw her. The shame of that, of being the butt of someone's joke, made her feel sick.

Unlocking her car, she dove into the driver's seat and jammed the keys into the ignition. Careful not to look up at him, she backed out and steered towards the street. She took a very long, scenic route to the restaurant, all the while concentrating on her breathing, willing herself to relax. Fifteen minutes before the agreed upon time, she was yanking back the heavy wood door to the restaurant. It was a seat yourself kind of place, so she chose a booth in the back corner where she could watch the door and slid her coat off.

A minute later a chesty, blonde waitress with dark smoky eyes in a very short, tight black dress appeared, menus in hand. "Just you?" She asked.

"Someone's joining me." Lena leaned back as the waitress placed the menus down. Her forearm, Lena noticed, had a colorful watercolor tree tattoo covering most of it. It looked artsy and bold. The kind of tattoo someone would get because they liked it, and they truly did not care what other people thought. Lena always felt a bit of admiration for people who had tattoos. They were brave, to decide to mark their bodies so permanently. Brave or stupid, she supposed.

"Can I get you anything while you wait?"

"Gin and tonic, please." Lena watched, a little worried, as the waitress walked away on her teetering high heels. How was bending supposed to work in a dress that short? Clearly the owner of this restaurant chain was a male, judging by how all the waitresses were similarly dressed. The things women had to do to make a buck…

Her gin and tonic arrived just as Sean did. She watched him scan the room, then grin as he spotted her. A thrill shot up her stomach and into her throat as he weaved between the tables towards her. He was wearing an open leather jacket over a deep green collared shirt and dark jeans.

As he slid into the booth and greeted her, she was suddenly very aware of how masculine he was—how much taller his frame, bigger his arms, and deeper his voice was. The flare she'd felt the last time they were together came back in a rush. It had been so long since

146

she was aware of the opposite sex. She had almost forgot what it felt like to be attracted to someone. It was thrilling. Addicting, almost. Like she'd been sleepwalking for a year, wrapped up in grief and heartbreak, only to be woken up by seeing the only other man she had been close with. She was going to have to be very careful tonight.

"You look beautiful." His eyes flickered down her body.

Lena's cheeks colored. She crossed her arm over to rub her other one, casually trying to hide the view. Stupid of her to wear this dress. She should have gone for something less exposing.

"I missed that." Sean grinned. "Your blush. I always loved how you turn red."

"You teased me about it all the time." It had been a source of entertainment for him, trying to make her face flame up when they were with people. Like eating supper with her family, he would rub her leg with his foot or snake his hand across her thigh...

Lena stopped that thought in its tracks. That would lead to other thoughts, and she didn't want to think about that right now, sitting across from him in a public place. Her head would surely burst into flames. She took a generous sip from her drink.

"I'm glad we're doing this," he said, leaning forward.

His gaze was too intense. Lena looked away and tried to steer them to a safe topic. "How's the house? Are you settled in?"

"Almost unpacked. I got an interview with the garage in town next week too."

"That's great. Things are coming together."

"Yeah, they are. It's weird being back. Lots of memories in Redwood."

"I bet."

The waitress came right then and asked for their order. Sean asked for a beer and a steak sandwich. Lena opted for the broccoli cheese soup. She watched as Sean's eyes followed the waitress as she walked away, then his gaze snapped back to her. "So," he said, "tell me about your husband."

Lena jolted. "Sorry?"

"Your husband, the one who got you to say, 'I do' and commit forever to him. What was he like?"

"The opposite of you."

"Terribly unattractive and a bore?"

"No, responsible and smart."

"Ouch."

"Well, you weren't the wisest guy around back then."

"That's a kind way of saying I was an idiot."

She shrugged.

Sean laughed. "I guess I did get us into some trouble."

"I'm surprised you even made it to graduation. You know, I never skipped class until you came along. Not even Cheryl could get me to skip. My parents were not your biggest fans."

"Yeah, I taught you a thing or two, didn't I?" He wiggled his eyebrows suggestively.

Lena's blush deepened. "I guess."

"So." He leaned back. "You went from exciting to boring."

"He wasn't boring."

"The first word you use to describe him is

'responsible'. You can't get much more boring than that."

"You would think that."

Sean grinned. "Where did you meet this upstanding young man?"

"College."

"Classmates? Was he an artist too?"

It had been a long time since Lena thought of herself as an artist. Another piece of her past foreign to her life now. She felt a twinge of sadness at that but pushed it down. "No. We met at a grief group."

"Oh. Because of Cheryl?"

"Yeah." Lena swirled her drink around. "Do you…think about it? That night?"

They paused as the waitress came and set Sean's drink down. He held the bottle in both hands, not looking at her. "I try not to."

"Do you remember much? Because I—"

"Let's not talk about this."

His change of tone jolted her. She looked at him, surprised.

"I don't like talking about it," Sean said.

"Neither do I, but you're the only other person who—"

"We will talk, okay? Not tonight, though. Let's just have fun tonight."

Lena looked at him, then shook her head. "You're exactly the same."

"What do you mean?"

"Avoiding anything serious. Always wanting to just have fun."

"What's wrong with that?" Sean leaned towards her again. "When's the last time you just relaxed and had fun? Not for a while I bet."

"I've been busy with the whole grieving my dead husband thing."

"You can't spend your life sad, Len."

"A lot of sad things have happened."

"Cheryl wouldn't want you to—"

Lena gripped her hands tight around her drink. "You can't do that."

"What?"

"Refuse to talk about what happened, then bring her up like that. And how would you know what she would have wanted? She was *my* friend—"

"She was my friend too. I miss her too."

I loved her too. Lena could practically see the words on his mouth. Old unease surfaced—the wild connection Sean and Cheryl had shared, the uncertainty of why Sean picked Lena to date and not Cheryl. The way she would laugh and touch his arm while Lena watched, feeling oddly on the outs with the two people she cared about the most. It was stupid, stupid high school drama she'd put behind her ages ago. She felt sick sometimes, thinking of the weird triangle relationship they had going on. It was embarrassing to think about, so obvious now that time had given her clarity. She didn't want to remember any of that—she wanted to remember her friend as the girl who had her back in everything, who made her laugh and live life to the fullest. Not as the wild girl who made her feel small and uncertain, who made people raise their eyebrows and guess which girl Sean was with, or if he was with both...

Then the way it all ended...Snapshots of that night surfaced. Wild laughter, slamming back drink after drink. Her grad dress bunched around her as she laid on the bank of the river. The smell of weed, booze, and muddy grass mingling together...There had been some sort of fight, she was sure of that. Why couldn't she remember...

"Stop," Sean said, grabbing her arm.

Lena jerked, spilling her drink. Her hands shook.

"Don't go there. Don't think about it, that's why I said I didn't want to talk about it."

"I—"

"You always did that. One minute you would be here, then the next you would disappear so far into your thoughts that I wasn't sure you would come back."

"I—I'm sorry. I think this was a mistake." Lena moved to get up, but Sean tightened his grip.

"Don't go, Len. Please. Can we start over?"

"This is all...it's too much. It's too weird."

"It's not."

"There are these giant elephants in the room, Sean. How can you ignore them?"

"Look, how about tonight we do. We ignore the bastards and just enjoy tonight. We will deal with it all sometime, okay? I promise."

"I don't—"

"Come on Len, please?"

Lena hesitated, wanting to go but equally wanting to stay.

Sean could sense her weakness. "Look, the food is here. Let's at least eat."

"Okay. Fine." Lena relaxed back as the food was set in front of them. Sean let go of her arm, letting his fingers trail down her skin before pulling away. She felt the weight of his fingers against her flesh even after he let go.

After they finished Sean insisted on paying, then he walked her to her car. "I wish you'd let me pick you up," he said, "We could go somewhere."

"And do what?"

He shrugged. "Anything. You look too good to be going home this early. Unless I went with you, that is."

Definitely had been a good call to drive herself. She opened her door. "Have a goodnight, Sean."

He held his hands up in defeat. "Alright, alright. I'll see you soon though, okay? How about Saturday? I'll text you."

"Okay. Fine. See you then." Lena got in her car and carefully backed out, wondering if it was wise to see him again so soon.

CHAPTER FOURTEEN

"Now *that* is a man."

"Where?" Evelyn craned her neck as she sat down at their table.

Mavis, still breathing heavily, took her tea from Evelyn and nodded discreetly towards the smoothie place where, apparently, a real man was located.

"The one in the black t-shirt?" June asked, peering over the top of her bifocals.

"No, the one working."

"What?" Nora frowned. "The man bun?"

"Mm-hmm." Mavis nodded and patted down her freshly styled hair, cut short and dyed dark on the sides with gray left in the fringe. Very modern. Evelyn didn't like it at all.

Nora snorted. "Oh, for heaven's sake, Mavis. He's young enough to be your grandson!"

"So? Just because my body is old, doesn't mean my eyes are."

"Ladies please, can we focus?" June tapped the cover of the book in front of her, eager as ever to lead the book club discussion.

"Don't talk about being old," Nora said. "If your body is old, then mine is ancient. You haven't even hit seventy yet."

"Denial isn't healthy, Nora, dear," said Mavis.

Evelyn chuckled. "Says the one checking out a

twenty-year-old." Same old Mavis. She'd always been very appreciative of the male gender. Which may or may not have led to the demise of her first two marriages. Evelyn was sure that on her deathbed, Mavis would use the last of her strength to flirt with the doctor.

"I can look at the menu, it doesn't mean I will order," said Mavis with a mischievous smile.

"Or even have the option of ordering," said Evelyn.

"So, what do you think?" June pressed on. "I thought it was beautifully done. Such a sad topic of course."

Mavis drew herself up. "Have the option? Stranger things have happened than a twenty-something dating a sixty-something. You would be surprised what some people are into."

"I think you should be satisfied with your fifty-something husband." Nora chuckled and shifted her round frame to a more comfortable position.

Evelyn nodded. "That was a good catch. Please don't say you're tired of him already."

"I'm not! Dave is gorgeous. I'm head over heels for him."

Nora laughed. "What a relief. It *has* been a whole six months since the wedding."

June sighed. "No one is listening."

"We are, June darling," Evelyn said, quickly. "I completely agree, beautiful writing. Very sad."

"I thought that too," said Nora.

"Absolutely." Mavis nodded.

June glared at them. "Y'all didn't read it, did you?"

"Did too!" said Evelyn.

Nora nodded. "I finished last night."

"Of course we did," Mavis sniffed.

"Liars," said June.

Nora glanced at the others, then admitted, "Well, I got half-way…"

Evelyn hung her head. "I watched the movie…"

"I didn't even try." Mavis shrugged.

"Why do I even bother." June shoved the book away.

"Because you love us." Nora patted her hand and laughed her big booming laugh that came out of her so freely. Evelyn smiled tenderly at her friend, her heart squeezing slightly at the thought of the near miss she had last year.

Nora had been having some heart trouble, something to do with the rhythm of it, and had been hospitalized for a few days. Their little group had held their breath, waiting to see if she would make it out. Since then she seemed fine, but they all started taking their health more seriously after that. It was the terrible reality of life on this side of sixty. Health things were rarely a minor issue. Evelyn couldn't imagine a world without Nora's laugh. She used to say that about Doug, though. Sometimes the unimaginable still happened, and one just had to learn how to cope. There was no other option, not for Evelyn, at least.

"Isn't it nice to just chat and catch up without an agenda?" Mavis said.

June scowled. "Of course it is, but we meet every week to chat. Just once a month I would like to have an intelligent discussion about literature instead of this nonsense about men or health or whatever else we always talk about. I don't think I am asking too much—"

"Next month we will do better, Junie. I promise,"

Mavis said. "You can even pick the book again. Right, ladies?"

Evelyn and Nora quickly nodded with a murmur of their assent.

"Now, speaking of love and men." Mavis turned to Evelyn, "I have something to run by you. Now, I know you're still recovering from Doug—obviously—but my brother Vince is coming for a visit and has been single since his divorce five years ago and—"

"Mavis, you cannot be serious," said June.

"What?"

"You want to set Evelyn up? Good Lord. What would she want a new romance at this stage of life for? And this soon after Doug! Have you lost your mind?"

"Um—" Evelyn said.

"Doug has been gone for a year, June. Evelyn has every right to move on. Just because you boarded everything up years ago doesn't mean the rest of us have."

June gasped.

"Ladies, please—" Evelyn tried.

"You are out-of-control, Mavis Stetson. Don't go projecting your ridiculous lifestyle choices on us," said June. "Evelyn is happy the way she is. She isn't going to get involved with someone, especially a man from Edmonton! What is she going to do? Move and leave her family and friends? Never see her great-grand baby again?"

"No one said anything about her moving, it would just be a date. Goodness June, it has nothing to do with you. Though maybe *you* are the one I should set up. Lord knows Albert isn't getting the job done, and you could definitely use a good—"

Evelyn quickly interjected, "There's actually something I'd like to tell you, regarding all this."

"Regarding what?" June said.

"Well, dating."

Nora gasped. "You're dating someone?"

"No," Evelyn said quickly. "Not really. We've chatted a few times over email, mostly. We video chatted twice this week, and that's as far as—"

June gasped. "You're *internet* dating? Evelyn Williamson! What on Earth are you thinking? He could be a serial killer!"

"I think it's wonderful," Mavis said. "That's how Dave and I met."

"It's not internet dating. It's someone from my past. From Cornwall."

Nora's eyes grew the size of saucers and her mouth fell open. "You're dating someone, from *England*?"

"Not dating—"

"Oh goodness," June said.

"Edmonton isn't looking so bad now, is it Junie?" Mavis smirked.

"Ladies, please. Let's not get carried away. We are just talking. But I thought you should know because I think I'm going to go visit him."

Nora held up her hand. "Sorry, can you slow down a little? When did all this start, exactly?"

"A couple weeks ago. Lena and I were—"

"Lena?" Mavis said. "Lena who?"

June frowned. "Not the Lena that Doug—"

"Yes, that Lena," Evelyn said. "We've been hanging out a bit and...what?" She stopped as her three friends gaped at her.

"Evelyn, honey..." June said. "Why are you

hanging out with her? How did that even…"

"Oh God, does she know?" Nora asked. "Did she track you down?"

Evelyn shook her head. "No, no, we just connected at the theater and—"

"She doesn't know?" said June. "About Doug and—"

"No, she doesn't." Evelyn's face colored. "It didn't seem like it mattered and—"

"Doesn't matter? Oh, honey, of course it matters," said June. "Especially if you're being friendly. You need to tell her."

"Why does she need to tell her?" said Mavis. "You're just making sure she is okay, right Evelyn? There's nothing wrong with that."

"Nothing wrong? Mavis come on," said June. "It's not right to keep this big of a secret. It's deceitful."

"Okay, enough," Evelyn said. "The point of all of this is I am going to be gone to England soon to see Edwin. I don't need any of your permission for that, or for Lena. Or for any other thing. I just wanted you all to know so that when I don't show up for coffee, you won't think I'm lying dead in my apartment. That is all."

Mavis, June, and Nora studied the table. Nora looked up and said tentatively, "Can I just ask…what is your plan? With Lena, I mean."

Evelyn huffed a sigh. Why was everyone so concerned with this? First her daughters, now her friends. She struggled, trying to find the words to explain. "It's just…there is no plan, really. I just know this is what Doug would have wanted. And as a matter of fact, she's been a great friend. I enjoy her company. She's a sweet girl."

"How often do you see her?" Nora asked.

"Just now and then," Evelyn lied. They'd been consistent meeting once a week for the past month. Usually it was at the movie theater, but this Tuesday Evelyn couldn't make it because one of her grandkids had a lacrosse game. They were planning to meet this evening, but her friends didn't need to know that.

"I just hope you're being wise, sweetie. You don't need any more heartache," said June.

Mavis came to her rescue. "Of course she is being wise. It's lovely what you are doing, Evelyn."

"Thank you."

"Now." Mavis clapped her hands. "I want to hear more about this Englishman. You're really going to England to see him?"

"I think so, yes. I'm due for a visit. Lord knows how many more I'll get in. I might pop over and see him while I'm there. I haven't been to St. Ives in forever. It will be fun to see it and—"

"What's he like?" Mavis said impatiently. "Age? Looks? Rich?"

"Mavis, really." June tutted. "Is that how you rank men?"

"Of course," Mavis said. "How else? Spill everything, Evie, darling."

Evelyn grinned, feeling oddly like a schoolgirl again. The whole thing was silly. It wasn't necessarily a romantic relationship, it was more like two lonely people enjoying having a reason not to feel so lonely anymore.

The first time they video chatted she'd seen he was as nervous as she was, which made her a bit giddy. Imagine, her making Edwin Peterson nervous! Her younger self never would have believed it. They had loads to talk about, so much so that two hours passed without her even realizing it. They set up a time to talk again the next day, and that time she baked cookies as they visited. When they hung up and the silence filled her little condo again, she realized how much she missed having someone there. Mavis held firmly to the belief a person was never too old for love. That might be true, but one thing was for certain, there was never an age limit for needing company to combat loneliness.

This made her think of Lena, and how young and heartbroken the girl was. Evelyn hoped Lena would find her footing soon. Her life (Lord willing) would stretch on for many years still. Evelyn hated to think of Lena going through it alone.

"There's not much to tell," Evelyn said to her friends, "but I promise, if I have something to report, I will."

"Will one of your kids or grands go with you to England?" Nora asked.

Evelyn shrugged. "I'm not sure yet. I only just decided last night."

"Well, try and take someone," Nora suggested. "England is very far away."

"She goes every year," Mavis said.

"And every year she gets older. What if something happens?"

"Like what?" Mavis asked. "She gets dementia overnight? She will be fine, stop your worrying."

"I'll think about it." Evelyn promised.

CHAPTER FIFTEEN

The slow, steady tick of the clock counted the wasted minutes Lena spent sitting behind her desk. Someone coughed, papers rustled. The sound of the low tapping of computer keys clicking away seeped through the thin walls—people typing stories, creating ads, sending emails. A florescent light flickered overhead, emanating a humming sound like a trapped bee.

Another hum drum day of the same old, same old. Lena twisted her chair back and forth, adding a little squeak to the sounds of the office. She stared at the phone, waiting for it to ring.

How did people do the same job for twenty, thirty years? Especially a job that involved most of the day sitting and staring at a computer screen. She couldn't imagine it, being in the same place, doing the same thing day in and day out—spending one's entire life in the same routine…Would that be her? A career newspaper receptionist, stretching two hours' worth of work over eight hours, five days a week. Forever being yelled at because a little kid didn't place the newspaper correctly on a front step, or an ad salesperson messed up on an invoice, or (as an especially aggressive woman pointed out to her today) a reporter misspelled a name…

Depressing.

Lena needed out of this cycle. She'd known it for a while now. It felt like something she would get to, eventually. She assumed deep down that she would not be here forever. One day she would look up other jobs, send out resumes, take charge. But the days kept slipping by, weeks turning into months and still, here she sat. Nothing changing.

It was like someone who says one day they would write a book, or travel the world, or start working out. Of course they would get to it one day. Then suddenly life is almost over and there's a long list of the "someday soon" that never got accomplished. Maybe that's how people ended up doing the same desk job for thirty years. They never get around to doing anything else.

That would be her, if she wasn't careful. She had that type of personality. Lena was a wisher, not a doer. A let-life-happen to her type.

Evelyn was a doer. Even though, one could argue, she hadn't exactly done much. She hadn't had a big career, didn't accomplish anything particularly grand—but Lena just knew, there's a woman who's lived and loved life.

Maybe that's enough of an accomplishment. It certainly would be for Lena.

She twirled her diamond ring around her finger thinking, then paused, considering it. It was pretty, she decided, not for the first time. Maybe not what she would have picked, but it still was a nice ring. If Lena had a say, she would have liked something a little simpler and more elegant. A yellow gold band with a single round diamond, perhaps. What she had was white gold, with three square diamonds, the middle one bigger than the sides. It used to belong to James' mom. It had been a very special gesture when he gave it to Lena. Though part of her wondered if it wasn't a tad unlucky, to wear the wedding ring of a divorced woman who died early of cancer. Maybe it *was* unlucky, which was why she was in this situation. It was all the ring's fault.

If that were the case, she should certainly stop wearing it.

She'd thought about it taking it off, but she never could quite muster up the energy to actually do it. She fiddled with it a little more, then slowly began to pull it off. The ring got stuck on her knuckle and she had to twist and pull, squishing all the blood in her finger up towards the tip. With a final yank it came free, her hands flew apart, and her elbow slammed into the desk. The resounding bang of bone connecting with wood caused a slight pause in the typing flow, then it continued again.

Lena bit her lip to keep from swearing, clutching her throbbing elbow. She let out a small whimper and twisted her arm to see the bruise forming. Bad luck indeed. She opened her palm and examined the ring—a little dirty. She hadn't taken it for a cleaning in a while. James had always reminded her to clean it every few months. Without his care, it had become neglected.

Lena placed it on the desktop. Her finger felt strange without it. Naked, almost. There was a white patch on her finger where the ring usually sat, like a brand. Every time she touched her ring or noticed it this last year, she felt like a fraud, like a woman masquerading as someone's wife. But when she'd imagined not wearing it, she had felt...almost guilty. Like she was lying to herself and others. She wasn't available per se. Not single and ready to mingle...She was stuck in this place between being married and not married. Single and taken. Committed and free.

What would she do with the ring anyway, if she

didn't wear it? Tuck it in a drawer somewhere? Pawn it? Give it to a cousin of James'? He would've been livid with any of those options. It was his most precious possession, the reminder of the mother he loved and lost. Maybe she should have buried it with him...She still could, she could dig a little hole by his grave now, tuck it in there, and pat the dirt back on top, right beside the headstone or something. That seemed wasteful though, but maybe that was how James would have wanted it.

No, James would have wanted her to wear it. To be his, even if he wasn't here. To have this glittering flag on her finger for the rest of eternity as a sign to any other man that she was still taken. That would be the option that would make him the happiest. He had been the jealous type in life, and she doubted very much that death would have changed that. It used to cause a few fights now and then. Especially at the beginning of their relationship when he would get angry at little, ordinary things. Like if she was studying at the library with a male classmate, or if she went to a bar without him...She sort of understood where he was coming from. He didn't have many relationships in his life. His main ones had been his mom and her. Of course he was protective of what they had...

Lena stared at the ring for a minute longer, then slipped it back on, pushing it over the knuckle and back to its usual place. It went on easier than taking it off.

That must be symbolic somehow.

Lena's phone went off with a text. She snatched it up, glad to have something to distract her. It was from Evelyn.

—*Don't forget, meeting after you're done work. Walking paths at Bower ponds.*—

Lena texted back that she remembered. Really, how would she forget? It was the only plan she had all week. Maybe during their walk she should ask Evelyn what she thought of wearing her wedding rings still. Lena had noticed Evelyn still wore hers.

A few seconds later, another text came in.

—*Good, have an idea to run by you. Bring hot drinks. London Fog for me*—

Lena snorted. Evelyn, she noticed, never asked, she always told. It was an odd trait for a woman to have. Slightly off-putting at first, but Lena supposed that's what doers did.

What 'idea' did Evelyn want to run by Lena? Something outlandish and inappropriate, most likely. A blind date? Maybe Evelyn had a grandson she wanted to fix up or something. Or maybe she had concocted a scheme to get Lena in a make-over program. That seemed like the sort of thing Evelyn would do. More than once Evelyn had subtly hinted Lena might need a wardrobe change or a more modern haircut.

Or perhaps it was about getting her to do some volunteer work—that wouldn't be so bad. It would probably be good for Lena to get involved in a few things, give her something to do with her free time. As long as it wasn't something that required a lot of *visiting*. Maybe she could be, like, the background person who did the organizing of things instead of the front-line person...

It was sad that guessing what Evelyn's intentions were was the most excitement Lena experienced all day. The office was especially dull today, probably because Jerry had left at noon for a dentist appointment. He wasn't buzzing around annoying everyone like usual. As frustrating as Jerry was as a boss, at least he kept things mildly interesting.

She sent a thumbs up to Evelyn, then leaned back and stretched.

One more hour.

Unfortunately, the stretch from four to five was the longest one. It was when the boredom threatened to completely overtake her and turn her mind to mush. She swore she lost brain cells sitting here day in and day out. Soon she wouldn't be able to form a coherent thought.

Her phone buzzed again.

A text from Sean.

Lena clicked her phone off without answering. Ever since their date, or whatever it was, on Saturday she had felt a bit off whenever his name popped up on her phone. Which was a lot.

Should she tell Evelyn about Sean tonight? Lena rolled the idea around.

Maybe not. Maybe she would see how Saturday went after they hung out again. She might have a better idea what exactly was going on between them after that.

CHAPTER SIXTEEN

Evelyn arrived early to the park.

It was her belief that on time was late, early was polite, and late was inexcusably rude. As a consequence, she spent much of her life waiting on others and having to silently forgive them when they finally turned up. It seemed most of the world ran on a clock that was at least ten minutes behind the actual clock, and those who lived in reality were the ones who were punished by having to accept the tardiness of everyone else.

It used to irk her to no end, but age had taught her there wasn't a benefit to getting upset over things she couldn't control. Plus, having a few minutes to herself before whatever might lay ahead proved to be quite beneficial. She was always mentally prepared and rarely felt flustered, whether it was for family gatherings, a volunteer function, or something unpleasant like an invasive doctor appointment. It always paid to be prepared.

Evelyn chose a picnic table to sit at as she waited for Lena to join her. She leaned forward over the rough wooden tabletop, folding her hands in front of her, breathing in the raw fall air. She had her leather gloves and her jacket with the big black buttons on today, it was mild enough she left her fur hat at home. The sun had been out all day with little competition in the deep blue sky to challenge its rays. Still, there was a bit of wind with that clear, fresh chill to it to keep things from getting too warm. It played with the fallen leaves, rolling them across the walking path, gently rustling those still clinging to the tree branches.

There were quite a few people at the park today—riding bikes, going for walks, letting their children climb all over the park playground. Evelyn enjoyed watching them go to and from and witnessing a brief flash of their lives. There was a pair of women fast-walking together, each wearing thick, skintight yoga pants, vests and wool headbands. They pumped their arms and chatted non-stop as they moved past. A cyclist went the other way—also in a skintight suit—head bent, his powerful, hairy legs moving up and down, up and down. A mom ran by, chasing down her toddler. She scooped him up and gave him a big kiss on his still baby-like chubby cheeks. She, too, was wearing tights. Evelyn noticed throughout the ages that fashion was getting more and more form fitting. Lord only knew what it would be like in another twenty years. Maybe people would give up clothing all together and just walk around in body paint. The look would be the same.

There were several parks in the city, but this was Evelyn's favorite one. It was in a dip, filled with trees and away from the major streets. It was easy to deceive herself that she wasn't in a city at all when she came here. There was a great big pond in the middle—people used it for kayaking or paddle boating in the summer and skating in the winter. Walking paths disappeared and emerged from the thick forest that created a boundary between the park and traffic, perfect for walking dogs or pedal-biking. Canadian geese, too used to humans, sat in clusters on the pond's edges, their long necks stretching and bobbing, wings fluttering and settling on their gray tinted backs. They would be gone soon, leaving in great waves across the skies to warmer places until they returned in the spring. Amazing creatures.

It astounded Evelyn that they mated for life. It seemed so strange that a bird would have such a deep attachment to another bird that they would stick together for their lifespan. That they were capable of that instinct, when so many humans were not.

Maybe it was easier for the geese. They didn't have so many complicated emotions—feelings that could be hurt, hormones that could betray. It was probably easier to be monogamous without all that.

She and Doug had made it. It was the accomplishment she was most proud of. It had taken a tremendous amount of work, daily efforts to forgive, and—sometimes—some much needed breathing space, but they had done it. Till death did they part.

Evelyn closed her eyes, a little smile on her face. She concentrated on the feeling of the sun on her exposed skin; the wind playing with her hair across her cheek. The sounds of laughter, feet slapping on the paved paths, geese honking. The underlying rumble of traffic in the distance. Just a few minutes of stillness…

"What are you doing?"

Evelyn snapped her eyes open and smiled up at Lena, who had appeared beside the picnic table. "Relaxing. It's quite good for you, you know, to just sit and stop moving and talking and thinking for a few minutes. I try to tell my grandkids this—whenever they have a second of downtime, they are looking at their phones. It's not healthy to always be entertained."

"Another wise opinion I'll be sure to take note of."

Lena placed a coffee cup in front of Evelyn and took a sip of her own.

"Such snark. Another good day at work?"

Lena shrugged. "The usual. Want to walk?"

"Yes, that would be good." Evelyn swung her feet from under the picnic table and stood up, grabbing her drink. "I imagine you're tired of sitting."

"A bit."

They set off, choosing to loop around the pond instead of taking a longer path through the trees. Evelyn snuck a look at Lena as they moved slowly. She was wearing a bright blue fall coat with a bit of puff to it, a small, neglected rip in the arm. Not fashionable at all. She needed a coat like Evelyn's—it was warm, yet stylish. Perhaps she would pick Lena one up, if Evelyn could do it in a way that wasn't overstepping.

"When is your birthday?" Evelyn asked.

"May. Why?"

"Oh, no reason. Just curious."

Drat. Too far away. Well, maybe she would still buy one and tell her it was an extra that she needed to be rid of…

"I've been thinking about taking my wedding ring off," Lena said.

"Oh? How come?" She took a sip of the London Fog, enjoying the milky sweet taste on her tongue.

Lena shrugged, her hand drifting up to her ring finger.

Her poor bare hands, Evelyn made a note to pick up some leather gloves for her as well. Leather gloves were never out of fashion, and they were wonderfully warm.

"Do you think about taking yours off?" Lena asked.

"Mine? Oh, no. I don't think so. There's little point,

really. I mean, they've been on my hand so long I might have to saw the whole finger off if I wanted to remove them." She laughed lightly. "You're in a different situation, though. When you feel ready, I think it's a good idea."

"Maybe." Lena let her hands fall back to her sides. "I just keep imagining what James would think. If I did."

"Surely, he would want you to be happy. To move on eventually, right?"

"Yeah..."

"What?"

"Nothing."

"You sure?"

Lena nodded. They walked in silence for a bit, sipping their drinks.

"I love this park," Evelyn said. "Doug and I would come walk here at least once a week. Even in the winter."

"I've only been here once or twice."

"Really? You should come more. It's one of the best things about this city. Doug and I actually went for a walk here on our last day together. It was lovely."

Lena stared at the ground. "James and I...we had a fight the night he died. One of those fights that start about something small and then turn into something big, you know? It started about laundry. He left angry. He did that sometimes, storm out in the middle of a fight and not come back for a couple hours."

So, James had a temper. Typical of an aggressive picky-eater. Evelyn was quiet, waiting for Lena to continue.

"I guess he went to a bar? A club or something. He was taking an Uber home when the crash happened. A police officer came to my door. They told me he was dead. It was so surreal." Lena shook her head. "I still can't believe it sometimes."

"I'm so sorry. That's a terrible way for it to…end." Evelyn felt sick. At least her last moment with Doug had been positive. If he'd died after they had a fight…that would've been hard.

"I replay it over and over," Lena said, her voice thick. "If I'd just done the damn laundry. You know? So stupid."

"Oh, honey." Evelyn stopped walking and gently grabbed Lena's arms, so they faced each other. "You cannot blame yourself. You hear me? It was an accident."

"I know." Lena wiped at her eyes. "I know it was. It just…sucks. I would have liked to say goodbye at least. Tell him I loved him."

Evelyn nodded. "I know."

"I mean, he just left as this alive, angry man. And then returned to me as a pile of ashes. What the hell is that? How is that fair?"

"You never saw the body?"

Lena shook her head.

Evelyn gave her shoulder a squeeze, then they continued walking. "I think it's a mistake when people don't view the body. It helps it become more real. My dad was Irish. Now they do a proper job of those things."

"Of death?"

Evelyn nodded. "It's less common now, of course. Growing up, though, I went to several wakes with my father. We didn't live in Ireland, but we visited lots and he always tried to make it back when someone died. It's a beautiful tradition. They really honor the deceased. They aren't afraid of death; they stare it right in the face.

The body laid out for people to touch and embrace, to say goodbye. It's a time of mourning and merriment. Nothing teaches you more about living than understanding dying."

"I don't know if I would have liked that, laying James out on display."

"You'd have to see a wake to truly understand. It's more…" Evelyn searched for the right word. "It's honoring. It's understanding that death is a natural part of life and celebrating who the person was. It's beautiful, really."

They walked along, each in their own thoughts. A high pitch squeal came from the playground they were passing. A young girl with long brown hair streaming behind her ran away laughing from a boy who was so blonde he looked almost bald. They couldn't have been more than four years old. Evelyn smiled. She loved watching little ones playing. They were so unencumbered with their easy laughter and energetic games. They lived completely in the moment they were in, an art that would be lost in a few short years. Sweet little things.

Growing up happened much too fast. It was too bad people couldn't hold on to the optimism of youth a little longer. Too bad that reality could be so harsh—heartbreak so potent.

"So, what is it?" Lena asked, breaking the companionable silence.

"What's what?"

"The thing you wanted to run by me? I've been on pins and needles trying to guess."

"Oh, yes." Evelyn brightened. "Well, as you know, I've been video chatting with Edwin."

"Don't tell me, he has a grandson you want to hook me up with?"

Evelyn laughed. "No, but that would be convenient, wouldn't it? Actually, I haven't asked him. I will though."

"Please don't."

"You are the one who brought it up. I think you secretly want me to 'hook you up' as you say."

"I don't."

"Uh-huh. Anyway, the video-chatting has been going quite well. So well in fact, I've decided I'd like to go see him in person."

Lena looked at her, surprised. "You're going to England?"

"I am. London first, then on to Cornwall. I decided yesterday."

"For how long?"

"At least a week, maybe more."

"Huh." Lena plucked a leaf from a branch as they walked and twirled it in her hand. "I think I might miss you, when you're gone."

Evelyn chuckled. "I'm sure you would. But the good news is you won't, because I've decided to invite you."

"Excuse me?"

"I'm inviting you to England. My friends suggested I bring someone. Normally I would think of asking one of my grands or kids, but they don't actually enjoy travelling with me. Plus, they have been so many times that it's not a thrill. Then I thought to myself this afternoon, Lena should come! It's perfect."

"You can't be serious."

"Why not?" Evelyn said. "It would be good for you. Get away and get some clarity on life. Lord, knows you need it."

"What does that mean?" Lena stopped.

"It just means, well, I know you are unhappy."

"Of course, I'm unhappy, Evelyn."

"There's a difference between grieving and being unhappy, Lena. I'd bet, even before James passed, you weren't happy."

"Why would you say that?" Lena's voice was hard. "You don't know anything about my life before."

Evelyn ignored her tone and pressed on. "I know you feel stuck in a job you hate. I know you feel you don't have much direction in life. Correct me if I'm wrong."

"I had direction when James was alive."

"Okay, but what about now? There's nothing like travelling to give you a little perspective. And you know what? I'll even pay for the flights."

"Don't be ridiculous."

"It's no trouble. I'm quite rich."

"Evelyn, I can't go to England with you."

"Why not?"

"Well, my job and—"

Evelyn waved her hand and started walking again. "You hate your job. If they won't give you the time off, then quit."

Lena shook her head. "You're a bad influence on me, you know that?"

"I am a terrific influence on you. Just think about it, alright? Let me know by, say, Monday. Have you ever been to England?"

"No, I haven't."

"Oh, you must come then. Everyone has to visit London at least once, and of course you can't walk this good Earth and never visit Cornwall. It's the perfect time of year too, not as many tourists in the fall. St. Ives in the summer is a nightmare, the locals call the tourists emits—meaning ants—because they literally overrun the place, but it won't be too busy now."

"I'll think about it, okay?"

"Yes, do, and let me know. We would have so much fun."

Lena looked at her, eyebrows raised.

"What?" Evelyn asked.

"You never slow down, do you?"

"I try not to. At my age you should speed up, not slow down. As long as my health and wealth allow, I will not waste the time I have left."

"Well, I hope when I'm your age I'll have half the amount of enthusiasm that you do."

"Don't wait until then, dear. You and I both know how fragile life can be."

CHAPTER SEVENTEEN

Lena couldn't remember why she stopped painting, but she remembered why she had started.

Even from a very young age she'd shown she had artistic talent. From the time she could hold a pencil, she began doodling on every scrap of paper available. By the time Lena was four she would draw tiny patterns across the page, in such fine detail that her mother wondered if she might be a little autistic. That and she'd always been a serious, quiet child. It wasn't until she was ten though, that she was first introduced to the world of painting. Her mom signed her up for an after-school art class, reasoning that if they couldn't stop her from drawing all over her math notes, then they should encourage her to at least draw well.

Lena had soaked in the classes. When they came to the lesson on oil paintings, her world was transformed. For a young girl who had trouble expressing her thoughts and emotions, twirling and twisting colors on a canvas felt like her soul was finally breaking out. Like the images she painted could express the words she couldn't force her lips to say. She'd finally found it—her way of speaking.

It was almost overwhelming. She painted with colors that were far brighter, more exciting than her surroundings. It was like she was finally seeing life in the vibrancy that it could be, the way other people seemed to see it. Her parents were astounded when they saw her paintings. Not that her work was particularly good back then, but that they could see it—all that the paintings expressed. They didn't know their quiet little girl had that in her.

She'd kept at it after the lessons ended, gaining confidence and skill as the years passed. Cheryl would lie on the couch snapping her bubblegum and reading comics while Lena worked on her latest piece, each content to be together and separate at the same time. The summer after Cheryl died and Sean left, Lena's paintings were slowly leeched of the bright colors that had excited her. She painted storms with dark gray swirling clouds, crashing ocean waves, rain-stained skies, dying old trees.

Her way of grieving.

Then in college, she studied art more than she practiced it. Her personal projects took months to complete, but there was no heart in them anymore. Then they just stopped. All together.

But she'd been fine, she filled the void with James. With his passions and interests, such as they were. She watched hockey games with him, something she had never done before. She let him pick the movies they watched and make the weekend plans. Decide when they would see her family, when they would go out to eat, where they would live and for how long. When they would have kids.

This had seemed natural. He was a leader, she a follower. She'd followed Cheryl her whole life, really. She was drawn to people of strong character. There was nothing wrong with that. It was easier, too, to join on his journey in life as opposed to forging her own way.

Then Evelyn entered. This spunky elderly lady who

had more passion and enthusiasm in her right hand than Lena did in her entire being. Who blew apart her carefully dulled life with baking and questions and a weird obsession with Lena's sex life.

"What do you do for fun?" Evelyn had asked near the end of their walk yesterday. "You must do something other than watch movies."

"Why must I?" Lena had responded. "Why must I be driven and passionate and all those exhausting things? Why can't I get through life, just exist?"

"Because that isn't living," Evelyn had answered sternly. "Life is a gift, don't waste it. You don't want to be one of those people who float through life, wasting away the hours in a day. Having no passion or zeal for life. Waiting until they can retire and golf. That's not living, that's dying slowly."

Lena's lack of hobbies wasn't the only thing under a microscope as of late.

Lately as she sat alone in her condo, the silence thicker than usual, she couldn't stop playing back memories of James. It was like taking off sunglasses and realizing the sunset was actually a completely different color then she'd first thought it was. The small remarks from her family, the purse of Evelyn's lips when she talked about him...it all began to make her wonder if what she and James had wasn't normal after all.

Almost always, she shut down those thoughts. Banished them to the back of her mind again. They felt dangerous—shaky. Like going down that path had the potential to explode the last stable ground she stood on.

No matter how hard she fought it, they kept resurfacing.

Like now, as she tried to relax in the bath she was

marinating in. She replayed a time when James had been furious at her in the parking lot at the grocery store. She'd accidentally dropped a carton of eggs and they had cracked and splatted on the pavement. She stumbled through her apology as his face twisted. "What is wrong with you?" he had said, grabbing her arm and yanking open the car door. "Just sit. I'll load the groceries. Fuck, Lena!"

How many times did he say that to her over the years? *What is wrong with you.* She could hear his voice so clearly, the tone he would use, the disgust so obvious. She could feel it still, the words coming off his tongue and slamming into her. He even said it on the eve of their wedding day. What did she do again? Something at the rehearsal dinner...spilt her drink, maybe? Yes, that was it. She had spilt it and gotten his pants wet.

That was almost four years ago. Next week would have been their anniversary.

Lena reached over the edge of the bath and grabbed her wineglass. She lightly swirled the red liquid as her thoughts continued tumbling.

That wasn't the worst thing he had said to her, if she was being honest. He could get mad. His temper was always sizzling beneath the surface. When he got angry, he would say things he didn't mean. *Pathetic, idiot, crazy*...words that Lena sat with and absorbed until he was done.

But he could be so kind, too. She had to remember that. He used to make her laugh so hard she would get a stitch in her side. He would cuddle her at night, gently pulling her close to kiss her ear. He often would bring home gifts for her for no reason. Her favorite ice-cream, a new sweater, a candle, bubble bath...Plus he'd almost always apologize for the things he said.

She tried to focus on that now, the good times, but unbidden another memory surfaced of a time James was furious at her. She'd gotten home late from work and didn't text him. He was so mad that he stormed out and disappeared for three hours. Then he came home like nothing happened. Lena had been racked with guilt. Worried he was going to leave her…

Huh.

Come to think of it, so far she'd experienced two loves in her life, and both times, she'd been worried they were going to leave her for something better. Where did that insecurity come from? Maybe she should go back to therapy, talk through her childhood, figure out why she was so insecure with men…

Although, Lena thought, it had more to do with the nature of men than it did with her. She didn't want to be a skeptic, but really, men could be so fickle. So hard to please. They were so enamored with outside appearances. With unattainable beauty, the idea of something instead of the reality. To be fair, though, most of society was pretty obsessed with looks.

Recently when she was on Facebook, aimlessly scrolling, she came across one of the clickbait articles about celebrities who used body doubles for nude scenes. The list was vast, full of gorgeous actresses getting other gorgeous women to substitute in their legs or butts. It felt like a slap in the face. Here she was, thinking these women just had it all, when actually no one had it all, and Hollywood just frankensteined women together to make this ridiculous fantasy for men and a torturous standard for women.

It was impossible to live up to. She'd constantly felt

she was letting them down, both Sean and James. It was the way she knew they were hyper aware of other women. The way they subtly asked her to change. Sean wanted her to be more adventurous—more like Cheryl, really. James wanted her to be less independent, he wanted her to revolve around him, like a cliché 1950s housewife. Like his mother, she suspected.

She tried to please both of them but always felt like she fell short. Maybe it was unachievable. Maybe there was no such thing as a man who truly loved a woman the way the stories say they did. With the totally dedicated, lifelong pining, no-other-can-compare, I-have-eyes-only-for-you kind of love. Did any old men still stare at their old wives with admiration? Or were they too busy checking out the girls who were the same age as their granddaughters…

Did honest-to-goodness Happily Ever After love truly exist? Or did even the best real-life romances with even the most attractive of women have hard doses of reality break through the fairytale with disappointed expectations.

Maybe it *was* her. Maybe she was the problem after all. Because, before James, before Sean, there was Cheryl. Lena had been so desperate to be her friend, to have a friend, way back in grade one. Lena was the kid who cried on the first day of school, who clung to her mother's legs, terrified to let go.

In Kindergarten she always seemed to be on her own, her chair just a tad farther away from the others. It's not that she wasn't likeable. The other kids tried now and then to get her to come play. She just didn't know what to do when they did.

So when Cheryl came the next year and paid special

attention to Lena of all people, she was sure not to mess it up. She tried to be careful, to say things Cheryl liked, to dress similar, to ask her mom to pack the same sort of lunch Cheryl brought. Cheryl ate up the attention. She loved having someone to boss around. She was the center of their games, the one with all the ideas, and Lena did everything she wanted. So maybe it all did have less to do with the nature of men, and more to do with her own follower tendencies.

All of them—James, Cheryl, Sean—said they loved her, but *love* and *like* were not the same thing, were they? Lena gripped her wine glass tight. Old hurt and anger brewed in her chest. They had never built her up. They'd just taken some parts of her and then tried to mold those into something different...And now, Lena wasn't sure what she had left to work with.

Oh god, she was the pathetic mousy girl, wasn't she? The one in the TV shows who made the person watching want to yell, buck up! Stand up for yourself! Do something! Instead of wallowing away in too conservative gray clothes and hair pulled back in a lack-luster ponytail.

All this self-reflection was not good for her. If she wasn't careful, Lena would trigger another panic attack. She'd been doing well keeping those under control since the one at the movie theater last month.

Lena took a sip of her wine. A little dribbled down her chin and hit her chest, the cold startling her a little. She set the glass beside the tub and hunched down in the water, gathering the bubbles so it covered her up to her neck. They quietly popped around her, sounding like a bowl of Rice Krispies cereal as the sweet smell of tangerine oranges and vanilla wafted around her. A combination she didn't think would work together—but turned out it did.

Think of nothing. Think of nothing. Lena chanted in her mind. Did people who practiced mediation actually empty their minds and think of nothing at all? Was that even possible? She would like that, to think of nothing on demand. Maybe she should take up yoga. She could go to the mall and get some of those tight pants. James didn't like her to wear those in public, so she didn't own any…Oh, here she went again. Down the thinking rabbit hole. *Focus Lena. Empty your mind.*

In her peripheral vision, she saw her phone on the lid of the toilet seat light up with a text. Giving up on her attempt to be zen, Lena pushed herself up, dried her hands, and grabbed it.

Sean. Asking her if she was still up for hanging out tomorrow night.

She was about to text back yes, when she checked the time. Eight o'clock on a Friday night and all she planned after this bath was counting down the hours till she could fall asleep. She hesitated only a second longer, then typed and sent:

—*How about tonight?*—

The yes response came immediately.

She set the phone down and hauled herself out of the water.

She didn't want to be alone overthinking everything again tonight. Besides, some male attention was good for the ego, and she could use a boost. Sean was better than sitting around at a bar waiting for some stranger to hit on her.

Better the devil she knew then the devil she didn't, as they say.

CHAPTER EIGHTEEN

"Tickets are officially booked," Evelyn said hitting the confirm button.

"Brilliant." Edwin's voice came from behind the AirCanada web page. She minimized it so she could see him sitting at his desk, a mug of tea in hand, his dark silver hair carefully combed. There was a slight delay in the connection now and then, otherwise the picture was astonishingly clear. Modern technology never ceased to amaze Evelyn. When she had first moved to Canada, she could only afford one long-distance phone call a month, usually reserved for her mother or father and only for a few minutes. Other than that, the only way to communicate with the friends she left behind was by letters. She couldn't imagine today if one of her family members moved away, and they could only communicate by sporadic letters. That would be very hard. Then again, these days she couldn't imagine driving across the city without her cell phone. What if she had car trouble? Witnessed an accident? Needed directions? She was hopelessly and unashamedly dependent on her plus-size smartphone device.

She didn't understand other elderly people who resisted the convenience of communication (June still refused to buy a cell phone and it made planning things with her a real pain in the arse). It wasn't that hard to get the hang of. Evelyn knew there were pros and cons to technology and the massive role it was taking in society, but she was firmly in the camp of the pros. Look at her now! Staring at Edwin's face as she booked airplane tickets while he sat somewhere in Cornwall. In another twenty or so years she could probably beam there. She already decided if the time came she would volunteer to be a guinea pig for such an experiment. It would be a win/win situation—either she would go down in the history books as the first person to be teleported, or it would quickly finish her off. It would be a good way to go, far better than sitting around waiting for pneumonia or cancer or something equally nasty to do the deed.

"So your friend—what was her name again?" Edwin asked in a lilted Cornish accent that made Evelyn homesick with every syllable. She'd lost much of her accent over the years, but the more they talked, the more she heard it slipping back into her speech.

"Lena."

"Aye, right. She said she's comin' then?"

"Not yet. She will, though."

"Well, that will be nice." He leaned closer to the screen. "Can't wait to meet her and finally see you. In person, I mean."

Evelyn's smile widened. She busied herself tidying up the kitchen to keep from showing how much his words pleased her. "What time is it there, anyway? It must be very late."

"It's…" He consulted his wristwatch. "One."

"In the morning?"

He shrugged.

"Goodness! What are you doing up?"

"I couldn't sleep. Thought I'd have a chat with you instead of tossing and turning."

"Do you often struggle to sleep?"

He shrugged again. "Yeah, I suppose so. My brother is the same way, and my eldest son. Sort of runs in the family."

"Your brother…" Evelyn cast her mind back. "He was younger, right? Red hair? Tim, wasn't it?"

"Aye, yeah. Ten years younger."

"He was quite an energetic kid, if I remember correctly. What did he end up doing with his life?"

"He's a bobby. In London."

"Really?" Evelyn was intrigued. She always been fascinated with law enforcement jobs. It seemed so exciting. She would have made a good detective, she decided. She had excellent instincts and performed well under pressure.

"Yeah, he's pretty high up now. Might retire in the next year or so, though. I'm trying to get him to move out here when he does."

"That's lovely—that you two are so close."

"Well, family is family, you know? That's all you got in the end, isn't it?"

"Quite right." Evelyn folded her damp dish cloth and placed it in the sink. Just then, a succession of loud knocking on her front door made her jump. "Goodness, who would that be?" Her hand rested on her chest.

"Want me to stay on while you answer? Just in case?"

Evelyn smiled at his chivalrous gesture. "No, that's alright. You better get some sleep anyhow. I'll call you tomorrow."

"Righto. Night, Evie."

Evelyn grinned at the familiar way he said her name as she clicked the end button on their call. The knocking sounded again. In a few quick strides, she was at the door. She squinted through the peephole, then flung the door open.

"Sarah! What on earth are you doing? My goodness, did you walk here?" Sarah stood in the doorway in a big winter coat, cheeks and nose a cherry red and her blonde hair windswept. She lived a good thirty-minute walk from here. What on earth was she thinking? She was sure to catch a cold.

"Nice to see you too, mom," Sarah said. "Can I come in?"

"Right, yes, of course." Evelyn moved so her daughter could come in and shut the door behind her. She didn't sound right. Her voice was flat, robotic like. Deep bags circled under her eyes. Her skin looked pale. All quite worrying signs. "Did we have plans I forgot about?" Evelyn tried to sound casual, tried not to stare and analyze as Sarah shrugged out of her jacket and slipped her boots off.

"No, we didn't. Sorry to drop in like this. Do you have company?" Sarah looked around the condo.

"No, it's just me, as usual." She let out a forced little laugh.

"I thought I heard you talking to someone."

"Oh. Yes, I was video-chatting with a friend, actually."

"Who?"

"No one you know. Come to the kitchen, I'll get you a cuppa."

"That's alright mom," Sarah said, following her into the kitchen.

"You need one. You look chilled. I was just about to have one myself." Evelyn went about getting the water heated and a plate of some peanut butter cookies she made that afternoon. She kept her hands busy, selecting the tea, filling the mugs, arranging the cookies, trying to determine how bad it was. Should she cancel her trip? Book Sarah into a facility? She needed to call Cam. He would know how bad things actually were…

Evelyn set the cookies in front of Sarah and placed a steaming mug of tea beside it. "Now then," she said, studying her carefully blank face. "What's this all about?" Then she braced herself.

Sarah wrapped her hands around the mug. The slope of her shoulders and angle of her chin so familiar to Doug it broke Evelyn's heart. "It's…not an episode." Sarah turned her gaze up. "That's been…fine. I've started taking some new pills that have helped."

"You have? When? You said you were off them—"

"I went on last week."

"Why? Have you been struggling again?"

"As I said, that part is fine." A hint of annoyance rose in Sarah's voice.

That was good. Anger was better than getting little to no response out of her, as tended to happen when she spiraled down. Evelyn straightened. "Then what is it? You look terrible, dear. Are you not sleeping?"

"I'm not much, no. On account of all the fighting."

"Fighting?"

She could see Sarah tighten her grip on the mug. "The thing is mom…Cam and I aren't working."

Evelyn stared.

"It's…it's over, mom. We are done trying. There just isn't much holding us together anymore."

There was a beat, then Evelyn responded, "Not much to hold you together?" Her voice was a little harder than she intended. "What about the vows you made before God? What about twenty years of marriage? Your two children—one who is still living at home, by the way. Is that not enough to 'hold you together'?"

"We wanted to wait until Ashley was in college but—"

"You are *not* getting a divorce."

"Excuse me?"

"You are not. I won't allow it. Bloody hell, Sarah, don't be ridiculous."

Color rose in Sarah's cheeks. "I am not being ridiculous. This was a long time co—"

"You and Cam have always had your ups and downs. This will pass, just like the other times." Evelyn said firmly.

"That's just the problem, mom. The ups and the downs. The fights, the make-ups. It's constant, and I can't take it anymore. I can barely keep myself steady—" She paused, her voice catching. She cleared her throat and started again. "It's not healthy. For me, for him, for the kids. I know you like Cam and this will be hard for you—"

"Like Cam?" Evelyn snapped. "Of course, I like Cam. He is my son-in-law. Part of my family. This affects everyone, Sarah, not just the two of you."

"I *know* that. I know it sucks, but people get divorced, mom. It happens. We will have to find a way forward."

"*People* might get divorced, but *Williamson*'s do not." Evelyn said, her hands shaking. "What would your father think of this? He would be rolling in his grave right now if he knew." The words slid out, weapons she promised herself she wouldn't ever use against her girls, but there it was.

Sarah looked as if Evelyn had reached over and slapped her. She stood up, proper tears pooling in her eyes. "I know what dad would think," she whispered. "I know this is hard, this doesn't follow your perfect family plan. I'm sorry to let you down, but I have to do what is best for me and for my family."

"You think this is what's best? Tearing everyone a part?"

"I know it is." Sarah turned and went to the door.

Evelyn followed her. "Where are you going? We need to talk about this."

Sarah grabbed her jacket and stuffed her arms through. "I think I'm done talking."

"At least let me drive you home," Evelyn said, reaching for her own jacket. "It's too chilly to walk. You'll catch a cold."

"I want to walk." Sarah twisted the doorknob, then paused. "I am sorry, mom." Then she left, gently closing the door behind her.

Evelyn stood there for several minutes. She took a deep breath. This was just a slight hiccup, nothing she couldn't handle. Evelyn just needed some time. She would figure out a plan. She would text Cam, get his side of things. Surely it was Sarah driving all this. It couldn't be mutual. Cam wouldn't do this to his kids—to her. Maybe she would even call their marital counsellor and see if she could get them in for an emergency meeting. A marriage retreat! She would google some upcoming marriage retreats and sign them up. She wouldn't lose another member of this family. It would not happen.

Evelyn went back to the kitchen to grab her laptop, but as she reached for it, she suddenly felt exhausted.

Maybe tomorrow. She would begin her quest tomorrow.

Instead, she went to the bathroom and ran a tub, selecting one of her bath bombs to fizzle and disintegrate in the warm water. She undressed and eased herself in, leaning back with a sigh. She closed her eyes and listened to the silence of the condo as the terrible conversation with Sarah replayed over again in her mind. Evelyn wished she hadn't brought Doug into it. She wished even more that Doug were here to debrief with.

It hit her then, that this was the first thing with one of the girls that she had to deal with without him— besides his death, of course. They'd always been a team, leaning on one another, calming each other, helping each other act reasonably to whatever it was the girls were throwing at them. She never thought at seventy she would still be parenting, still be dealing with her children's dramas and feelings and lives. Still being hurt by them and hurting them back too. Family was complicated.

She missed Doug.

Evelyn sunk down deeper into the comforting warmth of the swirling purple water, wondering how many more times her poor heart was going to be broken—how much more she was going to have to take until life was finally through with her.

CHAPTER NINETEEN

This time Lena let Sean pick her up, but she made sure to be ready and waiting for him in the parking lot when he arrived.

He rolled down the window and gave her an up-down with his eyes. "Nuh-uh."

"Excuse me?" Lena said.

"Not going to work," said Sean. "This isn't going to be a jeans and hoodie kinda night. Go put on something short and tight."

Lena put her hands on her hips. "Really, Sean?"

"C'mon! It's Friday night and we are young and hot, lets act like it."

"What are we gonna do?"

"I'm taking you out on the town. Drinks, clubbing, and—"

"Clubbing? Aren't we a little old to be going clubbing?"

"We're twenty-seven. That's hardly old. Besides, I bet you haven't stepped foot in a club before."

"It's not really my scene."

"Go get changed and I'll show you what you've been missing."

"It's freezing out. I'm not wearing something short."

"It will be warm in the club. Come on, don't be a killjoy."

Lena shook her head but found herself going back

up to her condo. A few minutes later she emerged, with her hair down and wearing a short black romper with a deep V-neck, the kind that a bra didn't work with. A long gold necklace looped low between her breasts, and a matching black clutch purse completed the look. The romper was a gift from her sister-in-law—of course—which had never seen the outside of her closet. She did a little twirl for Sean, then put on her leather going out jacket, zipping it firmly up.

Sean grinned as she slid in. "Now, that's more like it."

"Just drive." Lena felt her face flush, but she was pleased.

They went for drinks first. Sitting at the bar, Lena let Sean order her whatever he wanted. She copied him, shot for shot. As the alcohol worked its way into her system, her laugh became louder and her posture looser. She let Sean sit close to her and run his fingers up and down her thigh, enjoying the obvious attraction he felt for her and feeling attracted back.

She finished another drink and signaled for the next. No more wimpy mousy girl—not tonight at least. Tonight she was going to stop being so stiff and just have some fun. Who knew, she actually might have something of interest to report to Evelyn next time they met.

The bartender—who did not look much like a bartender should with his hipster glasses, V-neck black shirt, and toque carefully pulled back, pinning some hair to his forehead—set another shot in front of her then wandered over to the other side to help some other good paying customers get plastered. He looked more like he belonged in a coffee shop than a bar, she decided, but who was she to judge? Hipsters could be bartenders just as big burly men with tattoos up their arms could serve people their morning lattes. It was a free country.

"I bet he snowboards," Lena said to Sean.

"What?"

"The bartender, he looks like he snowboards." This seemed funny for some reason. She heard a high girly laugh and a second later realized it came from her. That made her laugh more.

Sean raised his eyebrows. "Doing alright there, Len?"

She nodded, gasping a little. She threw another shot to the back of her throat, swallowed hard, and slammed it down like she was in an old western. "Okay, Sean." His name sounded funny on her tongue, like she was shushing a baby. Sssshhhean. She swallowed, trying to concentrate. "You have to tell me. Why didn't you date Cheryl?"

"Lena," Sean groaned.

She held her hands up. "What? It's not a big deal. I just want to know."

He sighed.

"It's just, you guys were so close. It always seemed like maybe there was something?"

"We were kids, Lena."

"I know, so it doesn't matter anymore." Lena tried to smile coyly. As coyly as she could while trying not to fall off the barstool.

Sean studied her. "You want to know?"

She nodded, her vision shifting with the movement.

"I asked her out."

"What?"

"She turned me down. Then I asked you."

Lena blinked. "Oh."

They were kids. It was a long time ago. So why did that sting?

"She never told me," Lena said. Then she asked the awful question that she never had the guts to before. "Did the two of you, while you and I…?"

Sean shrugged.

Answer enough. Lena felt something in her splinter. Her friend, her best friend, had messed around with Sean. Lena had known, hadn't she? A part of her always knew. Confirming it now, though…it was like getting hit with a sucker punch. It was a typical, cliché high school love triangle, and she had played the fool.

"I'm not that guy anymore, Lena. I was young and stupid. But, I did love you," Sean said. "Hey, look at me." He tilted her chin up. She looked at him, feeling numb. "We are starting fresh, right?"

Lena found herself nodding.

Sean grinned. "Good. We've both been through enough shit. One more drink and it's dancing time." He waved over the hippy bartender again.

As soon as it was poured Lena grabbed the shot and slammed it back, then she stood up unsteadily and followed Sean out.

They walked across the street to the club. As soon as they entered the building, the music assaulted her ears. She blinked, a little taken aback at the noise, the heat, the bodies pressed together with the flashing lights drumming to the bass. Sean grabbed her hand and led her into the thick of it. Her romper was right on par with this crowd. If anything, it was a little modest. Lena tried not to stare at the girls doing impossibly sexy moves and at the guys grabbing their hips. This was hardly considered dancing. This was like making love with clothes on. And way, way out of her league, even if she had a little liquid courage lighting her veins. She yanked on Sean's arm trying to get his attention, but he pulled her to him, laughing.

He crushed her against his chest, his mouth against her ear. "It's easy, Len!" he said, feeling her stiffen in his arms.

He put his hands on her hips and moved her body to the music. Lena took a breath. She could do this. *Cheryl* would do this. Sean preferred Cheryl. Everyone did.

Lena leaned into the dizzy feeling the alcohol provided and let it guide her senses—let it release her and push away old feelings of hurt and grief and confusion. Cheryl was dead. Lena was alive and dammit, she was going to feel like it.

She moved to the music, letting the crowd, the beat, and the drinks turn her into someone else. Sean's hands were electric, sliding down over her backside and cupping her. His fingers under the bottom of her romper and on her skin. She pushed into him, encouraging him, knowing that she was toeing a line that if crossed she would regret.

Who cares.

The thought pounded across her mind. Who cared if she was being irresponsible. If she was out of control. Who. The. Hell. Cared. She threw her head back, whipping her hair, then grabbed the back of Sean's neck, and yanked him down. Their lips smashed together. His tongue was in her mouth. She kissed him back urgently.

Alive. Alive. Alive.

It was a chant within her. Like she needed to prove it, because she was still here. Cheryl was not. James was not. But she was. Alive and moving, sweating and living.

She broke off the kiss and turned so he was behind her. Her chest was heaving. She felt his breath on her cheek, his groin hard, pressed against her. As they moved, his hand slid up her side then across to the exposed skin between her breasts, his fingers tangling with the gold chain. His hand moved sideways and under the fabric of her romper, cupping her bare breast.

His boldness startled her and broke her brief feeling of rebellion.

This wasn't dancing. This was so not dancing. This was foreplay in the middle of a crowd, and it was too much, too fast. She twisted so she faced him, perched on her tiptoes and yelled in his ear that she wanted to leave.

He nodded and grabbed her hand, leading her out of the crowd, across the sticky cement floor, to the cigarette infused air outside. The cold slap of air was at first a relief from the hot, sweaty club, but a second later she shivered. Where was her coat? The bar, maybe. The thought of trying to track it down felt like too much effort with the way her head was feeling. At least she'd left her clutch in the car.

"Home?" he asked, his voice tight.

Lena nodded, her ears still ringing. They walked across the parking lot to the car. Lena paused at the door as Sean fumbled the keys out of his pocket. "Should you be driving?"

"I'm fine."

If he was feeling a fraction the way Lena was, then no, he wasn't fine. All those Don't Drink & Drive radio commercials played through her mind as she got in and buckled herself up. She should say something, refuse to get in with him. But she didn't. She sat back and gripped the door handle, as if ready to spring out if she needed to.

Too polite. Too timid.

The words that would be etched on her tombstone one day.

They drove mostly in silence back to her condo. Her head was still pounding with the residue of the obnoxious club music.

"So," Lena said. "That was clubbing."

Sean smiled a little but said nothing. He pulled into her complex and parked.

She unbuckled, relieved they got here without killing anyone. "Well, thanks for—" Her words were cut-off by Sean leaning over and kissing her hard, his hand on the back of her neck, trapping her to him.

She tried to pull back, "Sean—". He kept kissing her, moving down her neck. "Sean, wait a minute."

"What? You want to go inside first?"

"No, I—" Lena couldn't finish her thought. Suddenly, Sean was over the console, pulling the seat lever so they slammed back. Then he was on top of her, crushing her.

"Stop…please." Lena tried to sound firm, but her voice was weak.

"Little harder to do it in here then when we were teens." Sean chuckled. He played with the gold necklace, wrapping it around his hand and tugging on it playfully. "Why don't we go inside and—"

"Just slow down, okay? I don't want to have sex."

"What?" Sean froze.

"Not—not tonight, okay?" Lena squirmed, but his weight pinned her to the seat. He was so heavy. So strong. He could do whatever he wanted, and she couldn't stop him. The thought was terrifying. How did she get herself in this position? She was smarter than this.

"Why?" His voice was hard.

"I'm not ready for that ye—"

"Not ready? You're not exactly a virgin, Len." His grip on her necklace tightened. She could feel the chain digging into her skin.

Keep calm. Lena tried to focus on those words and tame the hysteria rising in her throat. She just needed him to get off so she could get out of the car and make it to her condo. "M-maybe next time? Okay? Th-that would be f-fun. Okay?"

He stared at her, his face twisting into disgust. She couldn't ignore the pain of the necklace now. She grabbed his hand. "Sean, you're hurting me."

He didn't move. If anything, the chain dug harder into her.

"S-Sean?"

His chest labored as he stared unblinkingly down.

Paralyzing fear built into a silent scream within her. She wanted to scratch at his arms and force him to let go, but the look on his face froze her in place.

Then suddenly, the spell broke. "Yeah, course." Sean released his grip and moved off of her, back over to the driver's side.

Lena stared up at the car roof. Her heart hammered in her ears.

"I'll walk you to your door," Sean said, getting out.

Lena fumbled with the lever to make the seat upright again. Sean opened her door as she shakily got to her feet. "You don't need to w-walk me."

Sean smiled at her, his voice light. "What kind of gentleman would I be if I didn't?"

Lena tried to smile but couldn't. She walked as quickly as she could to her door, pulling her keys from her clutch. She unlocked the door and slipped inside, "Goodnigh—"

"Wait," Sean said, stopping the door from shutting.

Lena's body tingled with panic.

"Don't I get a kiss goodnight?" He opened the door wider and leaned down. His lips touched hers gently. "Next time will be fun," he whispered. Then he smiled and shut the door.

Lena heard him walk away. She didn't move, her breath hitched in her chest. Then, with shaking hands, she locked all three locks on the door and scrambled up the stairs. She kicked her shoes off, pulled the necklace over her head and flung it away. She went to the bedroom and without undressing climbed in bed and pulled the covers over herself.

She was trembling.

What was that? What just happened? The look on his face…She had, for a moment, thought he was going to do more than force himself on her. She thought he was going to…she couldn't even think it.

She pulled the covers tighter.

Surely not. She was just scared and drunk and exaggerating everything. And Sean was drunk too. She'd given him mixed signals. He was disappointed, that's all. Nothing really happened.

Lena's hand drifted to her neck. She could still feel the bite of the chain on her skin, the heavy weight of him pinning her down. The cold look on his face looming above her…

No.
Stop.
It was too many drinks. That's all.
Nothing happened.

CHAPTER TWENTY

Evelyn loved airports.

Just walking inside the building made her arms tingle and the blood rush in her veins. It was the air—she could practically smell adventure rolling off people. It radiated off those who were arriving home exhausted from the journey, their suitcases weighed down with trinkets and souvenirs. It spilt from the travelers leaving, walking with a perky spring in their step, anticipating the new that awaited them. It came from the people who were waiting anxiously for a plane to arrive, clutching signs and flowers to welcome their loved ones.

There were all kinds of people here—the well-seasoned travelers walking with purpose towards their gates, to the nervous first-timers clutching their passports to their chests like lifelines. So many languages, so many people from different walks of life. The greatest sample of humanity all milling together before they jetted off around the world.

It never got old.

It was infusing Lena too. Evelyn could see it in the way Lena walked a little faster than normal. Her shoulders back and her face alert, taking in their surroundings. It was just the thing she needed. This past week Lena called to say she would accompany Evelyn on the trip but cancelled getting together that Tuesday. They hadn't really talked in the lead up to leaving, just a few texts to clarify travel plans.

Evelyn's trusty maternal instincts were telling her something was off. Maybe it was a work thing, or a family issue? Or maybe, perhaps, it was boy troubles? Evelyn suspected Lena might be seeing someone but was too reserved to tell Evelyn about it. She caught a text now and then on Lena's phone from someone named Sean (not that she was intentionally snooping—it was in plain view on Lena's phone. It's not like she attempted to hide it…) Well, in any case, this trip would be good for the girl. Lena told her it was only her second time leaving North America. She'd honeymooned at a resort in Mexico, but other than that had not gone anywhere.

Evelyn remembered her first time leaving the UK. She had been a bundle of nerves, made worse by having to manage a tantrum throwing two-year-old while five-months pregnant with Sarah. Not only was she irrationally terrified of giving birth on the plane, but she was leaving behind all the friends and family she'd ever known for a new home across a very big ocean. She hadn't known much about Canada. In her mind Canada and the US melded together, so most of what she imagined she assumed from movies she'd seen about America. She knew a few things though: that Canada had a reputation for being friendly, had Mounties, and the famous maple syrup. She also knew it would be snowier in the winters than England, but hotter in the summers. And she was aware that Canada had more land mass and fewer people. Nothing could have prepared her for the reality of that last statement, though.

She couldn't believe the amount of space there was in this country. The roads were huge and straight, nothing like the windy narrow roads in Cornwall, where one car would frequently have to pull into the hedges so an approaching car could squeeze by. The ditches in Canada themselves were big enough for farmers to utilize, and houses were spaced out so far it would take hours to walk from one to the other.

It was amazing.

While the cities were quite underwhelming compared to London, Evelyn easily fell in love with her new home. It was a young country full of young energy. Young, of course, in the sense that Canada only became a country a hundred years ago. She was well aware that the land itself and the First Nations who lived here long before the European explorers first set foot had a vast and beautiful history that was not properly acknowledged (she prided herself on being culturally aware and appropriate, something she knew her generation was accused of not being). But when it came to Canada being—for a lack of a better term—settled, it was very young. It was a country that was maturing and developing before her eyes, and it was exciting to be a part of it, to make her little mark with their restaurant franchise.

Still, she missed England—the history and the rich culture were hard to replicate. She found her heart started yearning for her old home country now and then, more and more now that she was getting older.

After they got their baggage checked in, Evelyn took charge right away and got them through security in record time. They ate breakfast at a restaurant near their gate, then relaxed with their coffees and books until it was time to board.

"Nine hours and we are there." Evelyn said, buckling herself in. "You are going to love London.

There is so much we need to do. Westminster Abbey, of course. The Tower of London and Buckingham palace—oh, yes—we should go to the theater. Have you been to a live play before? It's the most magical thing. Especially the West End in London. This is going to be so much fun. I am so glad you decided to come."

"So you have said about ten times this morning." Lena grinned. "I'm excited, I've always wanted to see—" Her phone buzzed with a text, distracting her. She glanced at it, her smile melting off her face before she switched her phone to airplane mode and put it in her purse. But not before Evelyn saw the name that popped up. This Sean character again.

"Who was that?" Evelyn asked, as casual as possible.

"No one."

Evelyn cocked her eyebrow. "It was someone."

"Evelyn."

"Right, sorry. Too nosey." Evelyn tapped her finger on her thigh and tried a different approach. "Oh, I didn't even ask about your work. They were fine with such a short notice? Everything good there?"

Lena shrugged. "Yeah, he was fine. I wore something low cut and made it sound like he would be my biggest hero for approving my vacation."

Evelyn frowned. "Aren't you ladies past the point of needing to use your bodies to get things from your bosses nowadays?"

"Are men past the point of being narcissistic assholes?"

"You are far too young to be sounding so bitter against men."

Lena didn't answer. She grabbed the safety

pamphlet and flipped through it.

Evelyn sighed and let it drop. She stared out the window at the runway, eager to get going. All week she'd been filled with a nervous sort of energy waiting for this trip. She had repacked her bag three times, scheduled then cancelled a hair appointment, and baked so many muffins, lemon loafs and zucchini bread, that she filled all her grandkids' freezers. It felt good to finally be done the waiting and actually going. It was ridiculous, the nerves she felt for seeing Edwin face to face. She kept reminding herself that she was much too old for a whirlwind romance (no matter what Mavis said) and it couldn't possibly amount to anything. Even so, it wouldn't hurt to have a bit of fun, would it? She couldn't let her teenage-self down, who'd spent countless hours mooning over the famous Edwin Peterson. Evelyn chuckled. If good things come to those who wait, then she had sixty years' worth of goodness heading her way.

She snuck a look at Lena, who was still pretending to read the pamphlet. Evelyn hadn't told anyone that Lena was accompanying her, besides Edwin, who knew nothing besides Lena's name. Evelyn didn't want to cause a fuss before she left, and besides, after this trip there might be nothing to fuss about. Travelling did one of two things to friendships—it either solidified it with shared memories and good experiences, or it made one realize they absolutely cannot stand the other and stopped it dead. Honestly, it could go either way for them. Her girls had flat out said they hated travelling with her, and her grandkids had hinted the same. She was too controlling and talked too much, apparently. A trait they were all unaware they themselves had inherited, but whatever.

Besides, it wasn't *controlling* to have a plan. They only had a short window in England, and it could not be wasted wandering around debating what to do next. Evelyn had everything figured out. She decided they would spend the first few days in London. They needed time to adjust to the time change and Lena couldn't go to England and not experience London. Plus, Evelyn wanted to get her footing under her before going to see Edwin. After that they would go to St. Ives and stay in a cute bed-and-breakfast just a few blocks from her childhood home, right by the beach.

That was something she missed dearly. Alberta had some beaches, but the often murky, freezing man-made waters with coarse dirt that passed as sand were not the same as breathing in the sea, hearing the gentle slapping of the waves against the rocks and seeing the sky and water mixing in the horizon.

Finally, all the passengers seemed to be seated. The flight attendants stood in their designated spots throughout the plane for the safety demonstration—smiles as fake as plastic on their faces as they pleasantly showed what to do, should they all begin falling to their doom. Evelyn politely watched the nearest one, a curvy, heavily make-upped woman with a bird-nest bun at the base of her neck. Poor thing, that bronzer was not doing her any favors.

The plane started rumbling down the runway just as they finished up. Soon they were pinned to their seats as the great big machine they were strapped to ascended into the air, the land beneath them quickly reduced to little squares varying in shades of green, brown and gold. As the plane leveled out there was a collected release of pent up breath around the cabin as the people shifted and adjusted for the long flight ahead. So much build up—getting to the airport, boarding, take off—only to be stalled by hours of being squashed together in suspended boredom and discomfort. Except for those in first class, stretched out like the Queen of Sheba in their little pods up there with their fluffy pillows and soft blankets. Evelyn really should consider joining them, it's not like she couldn't afford it. It just felt like such an extravagance…

"So, are you nervous?" Lena asked.

"Nervous? For?"

"Seeing handsome Edwin in the flesh."

"Oh." A thrill shot through her, and she laughed a little. "Well, yes. I think I am."

"You keep wringing your hands," said Lena.

Evelyn looked down at her lap where her hands were clasped tight. She tried to relax them. "I can't remember the last time I was this anxious. It's kind of fun."

"You *would* think feeling anxious is fun." Lena folded her arms. Her eyebrows were drawn together in a slight frown that Evelyn was worried was becoming too habitual for a girl so young. Time to get to the bottom of whatever was bugging her. A direct approach might be needed.

"You doing alright? You seem on edge this morning."

Lena shrugged. "Just tired."

"You sure?"

Lena gave her a look that eerily resembled the teenage disdain her daughters had used (and still did sometimes) when Evelyn was pushing too much.

"Okay, okay." Evelyn let the conversation slip into silence again. Clearly, Lena wasn't in the mood for discussing anything. Evelyn was just about to select a movie on the tiny screen in front of her when Lena spoke up again.

"It was our anniversary on Wednesday. Would have been four years."

Oh. That explained it.

"Oh, I'm sorry. Did you do anything to mark it?"

Lena shook her head. "Should I have? Did you?"

"Nothing official. I just stayed in and was extra sad. That was in the summer."

"I would have liked a summer wedding."

Evelyn smiled. "It was beautiful. We had it outdoors, which was risky for that time of year—July can be quite wet in England—but I wanted to be surrounded by nature when we said, 'I will'. I might have a bit of a hippy in me, I'm not sure. Anyway, it turned out to be a beautiful day. A little chilly in the evening, but I had this wonderful shawl that looked quite pretty."

It was cliché to say, but it had been one of the best days of Evelyn's life. She'd just been so happy. Her face had hurt from smiling all day. When they finally left the reception, they were both giggly and hungry—somehow, they consumed more champagne than food. Before they went to the hotel, they stopped at a pub and got some fish and chips, still in their wedding outfits which attracted curious stares and some congratulations. The deep-fried salmon and tartar sauce clung to their breath as they made love as husband and wife that night. Not the most romantic smell, but it still brought her back to that moment and made her smile all these years later.

"It rained on our wedding," Lena said. "Poured. With thunder and lightning and everything. Isn't that odd? Heavy rain in October? James was in a foul mood all day because of it. He said everything was ruined. It was supposed to be outside. We had to quickly move everything indoors. I wasn't sure anyway about having an outdoor wedding in the fall. It was almost guaranteed to be cold, but that's what his parents had done, and he wanted to replicate it."

"Well," Evelyn struggled to say something, "rain on a wedding day is good luck in some cultures. It means long lasting and fertility, or something."

"I think it was bad luck." said Lena. "Or a warning."

A warning of what? The early end to the marriage? Or did she mean something else…

Evelyn studied her young friend's face, her down-turned mouth, the dark bags under her eyes and pale skin making the freckles on her nose stand out. She looked sad, defeated almost. What was going on with her today? Something must have happened.

Well, Evelyn had time to figure it out.

After the first round of snacks and drinks came along, Evelyn cast a sideways look at Lena as she sipped on her plastic cup of water. "So, have you thought much about dating?"

Lena groaned and leaned back. "Evelyn."

"I'm just asking."

"If I am going to be strapped beside you for the next eight hours, then we need to lay down some ground rules."

"Such as?"

"How about, no questions. Period. Let's have a question free flight."

"Fine." Evelyn took a sip of her water. "It will be quite boring, though."

"I'm fine with that."

Evelyn ripped open her little package of cookies. She crunched on a few then said, "There's something sexy about the name Sean."

Lena whipped her head around. "Evelyn!"

"What? It wasn't a question."

"How do you know about Sean?"

"*That* is a question."

"Evelyn."

Evelyn chuckled. "I saw him texting you. Why didn't you tell me you started seeing someone?"

"Because. I'm not. Not really…Sean's my ex from high school."

"Oh? Ex's can be a good place to start sometimes."

"Stop it."

"What?"

"It's not like that." Lena folded her arms over herself. "He just moved back to Alberta. I haven't talked to him since…since our friend Cheryl died. It's complicated."

"How so?"

Lena clamped her mouth shut.

"Lena, honey. You shouldn't keep things so bottled up. It's good to talk to people about things. It will keep you from turning into a depressed old lady." Seeing no change in her face, Evelyn sighed. "You are stubborn, you know that?"

"I'm not the stubborn one here."

"Whatever you say." Evelyn made a show of getting her book out of her bag. She flipped it open and stared at it pointedly.

Lena was quiet, watching her. Then she finally said, "Okay. I'll tell you."

"Excellent." Evelyn snapped the book shut. "Fire

away."

Lena exhaled. "It's…complicated because Sean was the first guy I really liked. But him and Cheryl, they had a thing going too. He was there the night she died."

"The night she drowned." Evelyn interjected.

Lena looked startled.

"You told me she drowned. In the river."

"Oh. Yes. The night she drowned. It was graduation night. We'd been drinking, and…and we were stoned. The three of us went down to the river and…I don't remember what happened. But they—I—found her in the morning. They think she passed out, landed in the water and…drowned."

"I'm so sorry." Evelyn put her hand on Lena's arm. "That must have been awful."

"It was. I always wondered if Sean knew more about what happened. But he won't talk about it. I get why, though. He…loved her too. Anyway, he wasn't the most stand-up guy back then. I don't think he is now either."

"What do you mean?"

Lena shrugged. "He always felt a bit, dangerous maybe? Always pushing the limits. Like Cheryl. Sean and I went out the other night and I don't think much has changed. We ended up drinking a lot and he…"

Evelyn felt a shot of fear go through her. She had a terrible vision of what a drunk, dangerous man might have done. "He what?"

"He just…I don't know. He…I thought he might…" Lena shook her head. "I don't know. I was pretty drunk too. Never mind."

"Did he hurt you?"

"No, not really."

"Not really is not no, Lena. What happened?"

"No, I mean, he scared me a little. That's all. But I probably read the situation wrong. Let's drop it, okay? I told you it's complicated. I'm not planning on dating him, anyway."

Evelyn opened her mouth to say something more, but Lena turned pointedly away. Evelyn watched her, then shifted in her seat, trying to banish the disturbing images filtering through her mind. Whatever happened was not okay, this Sean person better stay the hell away from Lena.

Evelyn shot her another side-eye look. Poor girl. No one should have to go through as much as Lena had. Dead best friend, psycho ex-boyfriend, dead husband…it was too much.

Well, her luck was about to change, Evelyn would make sure of that.

"Things will start looking up." She patted Lena's hand. "Travelling does wonders for the soul, you'll see. I myself am looking forward to having a break from reality. My daughter informed me she intends to get a divorce from her wonderful, loving husband."

"Oh. I'm sorry, that must be tough."

"Yes." Evelyn agreed. "I'm working on it though."

Lena frowned. "Working on it? What do you mean?"

"Well, it won't happen. I've sent them some excellent material on relationships and links to some marriage retreats. They just need a bit of support to get past this rough patch. What?" Evelyn said, noticing the look on Lena's face.

"Isn't your daughter, like, fifty?"

"Forty-six."

"Does she mind? You being this involved in her

stuff?"

"Of course not. I'm her mum," Evelyn said, "and she needs help right now."

"Does she want your help?"

"Does that matter?"

"Sort of. You know, Evelyn, you can't fix everyone and everything."

"Watch me."

Lena's eyebrow rose. "I think you might have some control issues."

"That's not the first time I've heard that," Evelyn said breezily. "Now, what movie shall we start with? Something funny, I think."

CHAPTER TWENTY-ONE

Lena willed her feet to keep moving. Just a few more blocks. Surely, they were almost there…Every step brought pain from the soles of her feet up to her calves. She bit back a moan.

How was Evelyn still moving so quickly? Lena looked desperately at Evelyn's back a few feet ahead. Her long silver hair bounced lightly as she chatted away over her shoulder about the things they'd seen, giving more facts and information that she hadn't thought to say before.

Evelyn's theory about being invincible was correct. There was no doubt now in Lena's mind.

Evelyn turned just then with a frown. "Keep up, Lena! We're almost there."

Lena didn't reply, she had no energy or strength to. Three days of rushing around London left her completely depleted. This was the most walking she'd ever done in her entire life. Evelyn's schedule was tight, every minute accounted for. There were small respites when they stopped to eat, but the second they started moving again, the aching returned to Lena's legs.

By the end of her first day Lena had stood where Anne Boleyn was beheaded, rode the London Eye, walked down Baker Street, visited Covent Garden— where they had a delicious cream tea with clotted cream spread over warm scones and smothered with sticky sweet jam—stood outside Buckingham Palace, and watched the guards in their tall furry hats parade around in utter seriousness. Then they saw Les Misérables in the West End.

London was magnificent, a wonderful mix of modern and ancient, familiar yet completely alien. There were sky-high buildings that no city in Alberta could boast of, big screens flashing advertisements, stores crammed on every corner, and the endless hustle of people coming in all directions. It was incredible— almost overwhelming—how much more life existed outside her own little bubble back in Alberta.

It was all quite orderly, but busy. People waited patiently for the subway trains in the efficiently run Underground. She'd felt a bit like livestock as she joined the crowds being shuffled back and forth with an automated voice directing them. Doors opened and closed, people filed in and out. The automated voice in a wonderful British accent would politely remind them to, "Please mind the gap" as they boarded.

The great mounds of people all walked on the same side when going the same direction, and they stood on one side of the escalator so people could move past them. All the order struck Lena as odd, almost comical. She was not used to seeing the masses act in such uniformed and sensible conduct in day-to-day life—it seemed to fit perfectly with the English stereotype. The only exception seemed to be how people parked. There were cars facing either direction on both sides of the street, like the drivers pulled up and jammed their cars in wherever they might fit.

Evelyn was in her element, confidently guiding them through the underground maze, leaping off this train to catch that one, so they could pop up like moles all around the city. By the time they had returned to their little hotel at the end of day, Lena would collapse on her bed and fall instantly asleep.

Little was the correct describer for their lodgings. It didn't look a thing like any hotel she'd stayed at before. She actually thought it was just another house when they first approached it. It was nice enough with freshly painted white walls and blue trim around the doors and windows. They had their own rooms, which were about half the size of her den at home, with a single bed and a nightstand crammed in the corner. There was one bathroom down the hall to be shared by occupants on both floors.

It felt as if everything in England was small. The cars, the homes, the streets, sidewalks, roads, and stores...All squished and condensed to take up the least amount of space possible. She felt like she'd wandered into a land where everything had been shrunk.

Her favorite so far had been visiting Westminster Abbey today. They were given headsets that explained the history of the memorials as they walked around. The amount of famous people who were laid to rest or commemorated in the church was staggering. Impossibly impressive coffins were on display, names of other notable people were etched in the floor and walls: William Wilberforce, Charles Darwin, Isaac Newton, Queen Elizabeth the first buried beside her rival and her sister Queen Mary, Jane Austen, Charles Dickens...the list of the dead was endless.

Lena walked around in slow fascination. So many people who had done so many notable world changing things, good and bad, whom she'd learnt about and heard of her whole life were all around her. It was an astounding realization that the people from her history books used to be real, breathing, living people who had thoughts and feelings—whose bodies now lay as a pile of bones and dust beneath her feet. No matter how rich, powerful, smart, and driven, death claimed them all. As it would every single person walking around learning about them. It was an overwhelming and humbling feeling. It also stirred something in her, looking at all these people remembered for something. What would she be remembered for? A reluctant newspaper receptionist from Alberta, Canada. What dent could she possibly leave on this earth? It was an inspiring, beautiful, sad place.

Though all inspiring, life-changing thoughts were driven from her mind now as she tried her best not to collapse into an exhausted heap on the sidewalk.

Really, how could Evelyn keep up this pace? She was seventy. Seventy! Shouldn't her knee hurt or hip or something? Shouldn't Lena be the one telling Evelyn she could make it, just one more place and then they would rest…? This was ridiculous.

It was official—she was going to join a gym when she got home.

"Here we are." Evelyn announced, pausing. "The National Gallery."

Lena stared dazed at the sights around her. She'd been walking with her head down concentrating on moving forward, so she hadn't notice that they'd walked into a courtyard type thing with fountains on either side and in the middle, a large column with four lion statues on each corner. Ahead up a few rows of stairs a large white building with a circular top stood with a line of tall white columns. People were milling about, going in and out, some leaning tiredly against the walls at the base of the staircases, others took photos beside the lion statues. It looked like a government building, or perhaps another royal residence, not a museum. Lena mutely followed Evelyn up the stairs and inside.

Instantly, Lena's tiredness vanished. The sounds around her dulled as they started walking along the passages. Evelyn, for once, was quiet, walking her own way around the gallery which was just as well because Lena needed a few moments to herself to collect her emotions. It was just so breathtaking. Famous paintings from artists that she'd studied in school, whose work she had admired and analyzed, were hanging in front of her.

Incredible.

Here was the actual canvas' the artists labored over—that they breathed on and stepped back from to squint at to decide if it was finished or if it needed something more. The actual products of endless sketches and imagination, of trial and errors. Paintings sold often to support a starving artist lifestyle. Most of them probably never would have imagined the fame they would accumulate centuries later from their artwork. They would surely be pleased, though. It was, after all, the secret goal of all artists to leave a legacy that would echo through the generations. Not necessarily the wealth or prestige that sometimes (but rarely) came in their lifetime, but something they could leave behind that actually mattered, that made a ripple across history. Proof that they had once been here and done something. It was sad to think most artists never saw this dream to fruition.

It seemed in most cases fame for any kind of artist

usually was gifted after the person died thinking they were inconsequential. She'd written a paper in university about this very thing—the list was long. There was Vincent Van Gogh, who only sold one painting in his lifetime. Johannes Vermeer was able to scrape a living together with his paintings, but finances were a constant stress. He died in 1675 but became famous in the 19th century. Oscar Wilde was completely bankrupt at the time of his death from paying legal fees after being arrested for homosexuality, only to become one of London's most popular playwrights posthumously. Claude Monet, one of her favorites, received much scorn and criticism over his lifetime for his art and didn't become properly famous until he was deceased. Herman Melville who was the author of Moby Dick, now considered a great American novel, died as a forgotten author whose work was a flop.

Apparently, death made one relevant. It certainly was that way when Cheryl died. Suddenly everyone had been her best friend. Kids from their class who barely spoke to her were sobbing in Lena's arms at the funeral. Suddenly, Cheryl wasn't the troublemaker who was going to amount to nothing. She was a beautiful young woman whose talent would never been recognized. Words like 'spirited' replaced 'obnoxious' and "need-for-attention" became "natural star of the show." The school Cheryl had almost been expelled from multiple times hung a picture of her on the wall.

Forever remembered.

Forever famous.

The first girl to drown in the river.

Lena supposed it was easier to celebrate people after they were gone because of humanity's natural inclination towards jealously. It was hard watching the living succeed, but the dead? They couldn't gloat or strut about or enjoy the splendor of their work or their fortunate good looks. Why not then let them shine?

Lena moved slowly around the gallery, stopping and examining the paintings for several minutes before moving on, trying to recall everything she could think of about the artist and their work. She felt like she was in a bit of a trance as she went deeper into the museum. The art was so impossibly beautiful. The colors so vivid and fresh looking as if they were painted weeks ago, not centuries. Some were shockingly small; others took up most of the wall.

She stopped in front of a painting by an artist known as William Turner. She loved his work. He painted vivid landscapes, ships at sea, turbulent clouds, and violent ocean waves. He had been known as a difficult, eccentric man. He never married, but fathered two children, two girls with a woman who was thought to be his housekeeper or an older widow (maybe it was both, she couldn't remember exactly). He travelled Europe, opened his own gallery, and was a professor at the academy. After his father died his life took a turn. He reportedly became more pessimistic and depressed. The latter part of his life was spent in poor health and poverty.

Well, grief could do that to a person, if they let it. She knew that better than anyone.

She thought she could see it when she studied his work—the intense emotions he felt, the war within raging on the canvas. How he used the natural elements of rain, water, fog, and sky to convey so much—to create such breathtaking paintings.

She stood now, staring at a painting of sailors caught

in a storm, being tossed around by the wind and waves as dark clouds circled above. In the foreground people were huddled on the pier, clinging to the sides, clearly terrified of the power of the storm raging around them. The boats, too, were full of people trying to ride out the storm, clinging to paddles, yelling instructions. It was almost as if she could hear the sounds of the sea spraying, the wind whistling, the screams of the sailors as they battled the impossible. Jolted about, out of control, crying for help. Just trying to survive.

Lena felt her breath hitch, her chest tighten. She crossed her arms over her breasts, trying to steady herself. She couldn't look away from the painting. She could *feel* it, the panic those people felt. Soaked to the bone with sea water. Just trying to hold on. It was a picture of fear, but also of beauty. That was the artist's talent—turning fear and chaos into beauty. Her eyes flickered up to where Turner painted in the middle of the darkened clouds a spot of blue. Blue sky amid the storm, the small promise of coming peace—that the turmoil would end. The people though, in the boats and on the pier, they couldn't see it. All they could focus on was the danger they were in. In the thick of it, that's all anyone could see, it's all they knew.

It's all she'd known.

The thought hit her like a thunderclap.

The strange control, the slow dying of herself. The need for protection. The verbal abuse that slowly grated away at her soul. The confusing feelings of love and rejection.

Not seeing, not noticing that it wasn't okay. It wasn't normal.

The loss and grief that had consumed her—

paralyzed her. She'd been in survival mode for so long, clinging to whatever was near to keep her afloat—not realizing it wasn't saving her, but drowning her slower. Then another wave had hit.

And deep down—underneath the pain, the grief, the heavy burden of sudden loss—underneath all of that, if she could be truly honest with herself, as she stood beside James' grave staring at the fresh earth, was the small feeling of relief.

"Lena?" Evelyn's gentle voice snapped her out of her trance.

She turned to Evelyn, shaking, surprised to feel tears wetting her cheeks.

"Are you okay, love?"

She nodded but couldn't speak. Her chest rose and fell rapidly as pain built and spread through her.

"Okay, come here, hon. It's okay…" Evelyn put her arm around Lena and gently led her out of the exhibit. They made their way out of the building, back to the brisk air outside. As soon as they were down the steps and around the corner, Lena collapsed on the ground with her back against the wall. She let it come, the tears, the memories. The good and the bad feelings swirled inside her, spilling out until she had nothing left but small hiccupping sobs.

Evelyn waited beside her, letting her cry until she was done.

****

"It wasn't all bad." Lena stared down at the foamy top of the flat pint of dark brew Evelyn had ordered them. They sat close together at the bar, the pub mostly empty except for a few older men intently watching the soccer game on the TV. Evelyn leaned her head on one hand, watching Lena.

"It wasn't. I loved him. I really did. I was happy…most of the time I think I was happy." Evelyn was quiet. Lena pressed on, needing her to understand. "No one is perfect, you know? You said, no man is the lottery. Every guy has flaws—"

"There's a difference between having flaws, and just being an asshole."

"You didn't know him. You don't get it. He—"

"I didn't have to know him. It's enough knowing what you've told me. He didn't treat you right." She said it gently, but it still stung.

Lena stared miserably down.

"It doesn't mean he didn't love you. Or that you didn't love him."

"No marriage is perfect…"

"Definitely. But at the very least, your husband should build you up. He should help you become the best version of yourself. He shouldn't push you down, try to change who you are to suit himself."

"I know." Lena's voice was small. She took a sip of her beer and grimaced, the bitter taste too strong for her.

The other thing she knew, but felt too ashamed to say out loud, was that she knew she'd let it happen. It had felt easier that way, especially when she was hurting so badly after losing Cheryl—after the way Lena lost her. Knowing on some level that it was her fault. She'd been there. She should have stopped it, or at least remembered how it happened.

All that guilt and grief suffocating her…James took the load off her shoulders. She hadn't needed to do much thinking with him. It had been nice in a way—except for the times when he made her feel worse. When he made her feel small and trapped…when it became a different kind of suffocating.

But that was okay too, wasn't it? Because it wouldn't have been fair for her to be too happy. Not when Cheryl's life ended the way it had, and Lena got to go on living. Maybe that's why she'd stayed with James, why she'd married him. She knew he would keep the score more even.

What a twisted thought.

"What are you thinking?" Evelyn asked.

"I don't know." Lena paused, trying to formulate her thoughts. "Do you think…maybe him losing his mom influenced why he acted that way? She was all he had…I think being so out of control there, maybe it made him need to control me? The other woman in his life?"

Evelyn shrugged. "Maybe, but there isn't really an excuse for it. Everyone has problems. No one gets through life unscathed, that doesn't give you a license to hurt others. You said he wasn't physically abusive?"

"No, no, of course not." Lena answered, hastily.

Then an image came to her mind, not of James, but of Sean. The look on his face as he stared down at her, the gold chain digging into her skin. The feeling of terror taking over her senses. She felt sick and swallowed hard, pushing the memory away. "J-James would never do that. It was just mainly…he said things. And he dictated a lot of things…it sounds silly saying it out loud. I don't even know the point of talking about it now." She took another long sip and wiped her mouth.

"Verbal abuse is still abuse." Evelyn said firmly. "And the point is because clearly it's still affecting you. He still has a power over you."

"I don't think that's true."

"No?"

Lena paused. Was it? Was that why the condo still looked how James wanted it to look? Why she still didn't have friends, why she still didn't go for drinks with co-workers. And didn't paint. And only dressed in the clothes he had approved of?

Evelyn patted her hand. "This is an excellent step. Admitting out loud that things weren't all roses. It's the first step to forgiveness."

"Forgiveness?"

Evelyn nodded. "In order to let it go, to truly move on, you need to forgive him. Or he will haunt you forever. Forgiveness is more about the person who was wronged, then the one who did the wronging."

Lena bit her lip. "I still miss him. I wish he didn't have to die…we could have fixed things, I think."

"Maybe you could have. You should know, though, it can be better than that. Marriage, I mean. It can be better than what you had."

"You and Doug had it pretty good, eh?"

Evelyn smiled. "We did. Though I did do my fair share of forgiving, that's for sure."

"Like for what?"

Evelyn's smile melted. "Well, for leaving me for one. For dying on me. I had to forgive him for that."

CHAPTER TWENTY-TWO

The first thing Evelyn planned to do after they settled in their lodgings in St. Ives was take Lena to eat a traditional Cornish pasty. Filled with a variety of ingredients, but most well-known for beef, potatoes, rutabaga, onions, salt, and pepper baked to perfection: the Cornish Pasty was a mouthwatering delicacy, and it only ever tasted right when eaten in Cornwall.

They took the train most of the way from London. It took just under six hours to travel from the bustling city to the small seaside town on the very tip of Cornwall. Lena had slept most of the way.

Evelyn had tried, but she couldn't empty her mind enough to sleep. Her thoughts kept swirling around—memories of St. Ives, her conversations with Edwin, memories of Doug, Lena tearfully talking about James, her standing there looking at that painting seeming so lost and afraid. St. Ives again. On and on it went. It was a relief when they finally arrived at St. Erth's. They switched for the short train ride to St. Ives, then took a cab to the bed-and-breakfast.

Evelyn now stood by the window in her room looking out over the rocks to the sandy beach with the blue green sea gently hitting the shore while Lena freshened up.

Home.

Evelyn was home again.

It felt so good, and so strange. The last time she came home was on a trip with Doug. They stayed for three days in this same bed-and-breakfast. He'd only been to St. Ives a handful of times before with her. Every time Evelyn visited, she wondered why she didn't visit more. It always felt like a great sigh of relief coming back. Like she had been holding her breath until the next visit, which was funny because it's not like her childhood held a lot of great memories. Still, outside of that she did love this town—loved the sea, the shops, the people. There was a part of her that would always belong here.

She had wanted Doug to love it here too. She had always watched his face for clues that he felt the way she did as they visited the stores or walked along the beach.

"It's beautiful here, isn't it?" She'd pressed.

"Gorgeous!" He had said, but she felt he was just humoring her. He hadn't thought it was any more special than any other place. It had saddened her, like the times she would get all dressed up and he wouldn't give her a compliment until she hinted so heavily the compliment meant nothing when it finally came.

Evelyn turned away from the window and grabbed her phone. She sent a quick text to Edwin saying they'd made it and were going for pasties. He responded immediately, suggesting a place and told them he would meet them there.

—*I can't wait to see you.*—

She stared at his last text, then put the phone in her bag. Thinking of Doug one minute, then texting Edwin to meet up the next...it felt strange. Like she was doing something wrong.

Lena knocked on her door, then entered. Her ripped blue jacket was zipped up and her hair stuffed underneath her toque. "Ready?"

"Do you think this is all too odd?"

Lena sat on the edge of the bed. "Meeting up with Edwin?"

Evelyn nodded.

"No, it's not odd."

"It's strange though, isn't it? I keep telling myself that it's just meeting up with an old friend. Except we aren't old friends. And our conversations—they have felt more…intimate then just a friendly conversation. What if it's awkward in person? What if we expect different…" She trailed off, then laughed a little. "Listen to me go on and on. So silly, getting all worked up over all this. I mean, I'm seventy! What am I thinking is going to happen? Never mind, let's go."

"Don't do that, Evelyn."

"Do what?"

"Downplay your feelings. Hide behind your age. You are the most youthful seventy-year-old that I know. You have every right to have a whirlwind romance, even if you were bedridden in your nineties."

Evelyn looked down at her gripped hands. "It just feels so…insane."

"Which is why it's absolutely perfect for you."

Evelyn laughed and gathered her purse. Nothing to do but move forward anyway. She had already crossed an ocean to be here. She did up her jacket, slipped on her gloves, and followed Lena out of the room.

They left the B&B and made their way through the winding side streets to Main Street. It was cool today. The sky was covered in dark gray clouds. Overhead, the seagulls circled and squawked loudly. Evelyn hunched her shoulders to her ears. She should have worn something to cover her head, but vainly, she did not want to ruin her hair.

Main Street was just the same as it always was— shops lined either side with streams of people coming and going. Even on the off season, there was a decent amount of business. The sound of the ocean played gently in the background as groups of tourists walked by, laughing, with cameras hanging around their necks. Evelyn and Lena walked slowly, their feet clipping down the cobblestone as they breathed in the salty air. London was all about hurry—always somewhere to be, something to see. But here it was about lingering, admiring the sights, taking in the smells, letting the sound of the ocean seep into her skin as she inhaled and exhaled.

"So, this is where you grew up." Lena looked around. "I feel like I'm in a storybook. This is exactly how I would picture a seaside town."

"It feels pretty idyllic, doesn't it? It's been awarded Best UK Seaside Town a few times, actually."

"I can see why."

"It used to be quite the hotspot for artists. Back in the day it was as exciting as Paris, in fact, and more progressive than London. They say some of the most exhilarating art of the twentieth century came from artists in St. Ives."

"I think I knew that, somewhere in my brain." Lena studied the shops as they passed.

"You know about art, don't you? I saw it on your face when we were in the museum."

Lena shrugged. "I studied art in university." She hesitated, then added, "I used to paint a bit."

It was the casual way she said it, with her eyes on

the ground, and the slight tension on her face that made it so obvious. *Ah*, Evelyn looked at her with fresh eyes. *That's who you are*. A painter, the way she herself was a baker. That suited Lena perfectly, artists could be temperamental little things. Too retrospective for their own good, too weighed down by things they couldn't understand.

"You should paint again," Evelyn said.

"I might. Is this it?" Lena stopped in front of a large window stuffed full of different baked goods.

Evelyn felt a jolt bolt through her stomach and her fingers tingle. She immediately patted her hair and tucked the piece that always stuck out behind her ear. "Yes, this is it. I guess we should go inside and—"

"Evelyn Webb, look at you!" The deep voice rang out behind her.

Evelyn turned to see Edwin grinning, walking briskly towards them. He was wearing a brown leather jacket over dark jeans, and one of those caps all Cornishmen seemed to gravitate towards in their old age. She was just able to register the fact that he looked fabulous before he swooped in for a hug, taking her off-guard. She awkwardly patted his back, breathing in the scent of his cologne, then stood a little shell-shocked as he turned to Lena.

"Are you Evelyn's friend? Lena?"

Lena nodded and shook his outstretched hand. "You must be Edwin."

"Guilty. I must say, when Evelyn said she was bringing a friend, I imagined someone a little older. You aren't her granddaughter, are you?"

Lena laughed. "No, just her friend. I'd say I keep her young, but it's really the other way around."

Edwin laughed a deep masculine laugh and gestured to the bakery. "Shall we?"

They ordered their Cornish pasties, then took them outside to eat as they walked. Edwin chatted easily with both of them, telling Lena which stores she should visit, then switching to reminiscing about school days with Evelyn. She let him steer the conversation, feeling light on her feet, watching him gesture with his hands. He had the same charisma that she remembered him having in their youth. The easy-going, I-got-this confidence men who had been handsome and successful their entire lives naturally gave off.

He walked them back to the B&B just as it started to lightly sprinkle. "Sure you don't want a proper dinner before you turn in?" he asked.

"Quite sure. I think we both need an early night," Evelyn said. Lena nodded.

"Tomorrow then, I'll meet you here in the morning." He gave her a quick hug goodbye and a good-natured wave to Lena.

She felt Lena staring at her as they let themselves in. "What?"

"Nothing. You're just smiling a lot."

"Am not." But she could feel the smile tugging at her lips.

Lena grinned. "You like him, don't you? I don't blame you, he has a certain swagger, doesn't he?"

"He's always been like that."

"He likes you too."

"Oh, stop it."

"He does. He kept glancing at you every two seconds."

"Don't be ridiculous," Evelyn said, but her smile

widened.

On their third day in St. Ives, Evelyn and Edwin were walking through her old neighborhood. The last few days were all she'd hoped for and more. They spent most of their time together, eating at different places, and going for walks on the beach or along the rocky cliff edges. Sometimes Lena went with them, other times she explored on her own and it was just the two of them, laughing hard at each other's stories, visiting their old stomping grounds, reminiscing about days past.

"Here it is," Evelyn said. They stopped in front of a little brick house with a green garage door and a small rectangle patch of yard out front.

"This is the place? I lived just two streets down."

"I know." Evelyn flushed. "I mean, I wasn't a stalker or anything. I just…knew that." Actually, she'd been a bit of a stalker—walking out of her way to pass his house on the way to school, going by on weekends, hoping for a "chance" run in. But what love-struck teenager didn't do a little stalking now and then?

She cleared her throat, pushing past the awkward moment. "I always come by here when I come for a visit. Just to remember what life used to be like. It's always a little surreal. Like no time has passed but also an eternity has."

Edwin stared up at the house, his hands on his hips. "You ever go inside?"

"Oh no, no, I just look. Come on, let's get some lunch. You're finally showing me the pub you and your son own today, right?"

"Now hold on, don't you want to see inside? You've come all this way."

Evelyn shook her head. "It's fine. Really."

But in true masculine fashion, Edwin didn't listen. He marched up to the door and knocked firmly.

"Edwin!" Evelyn said, but she went up beside him.

The door opened to reveal a young, blonde woman in a green sweater, a one-year-old baby balanced on her hip. "Yes?"

Edwin gave her a winning smile. "Hi Miss, this might sound strange, but my friend here used to live here. Mind if she comes in for a quick look around?"

The woman shifted her eyes to Evelyn, who tried to look as nonthreatening as possible. "We won't be long, I promise." She clenched her hands, suddenly keen to be let in.

"Sure." She finally said, opening the door a little wider. She hitched the baby up higher on her hip and moved to let them inside. "My husband will be home any minute." She added, a little nervously, Evelyn thought. Not that she blamed her. It would be a little disconcerting having two strangers randomly show up on your doorstep.

Evelyn stepped over the threshold with Edwin close behind, half expecting to see her parents there waiting, sitting in opposite ends of the living room with the silence thick between them. She paused, trying to let her brain catch up with her eyes. It was the same place, but also, it wasn't. It seemed smaller...and cleaner, obviously. The colors and smell had changed, but it still felt so familiar it took her breath away. She could easily picture how it once was, the stacks of junk spread out everywhere, her father's bookshelf in the corner, dirty dishes overflowing in the sink, cracked eggshells piled on banana peels, and used napkins stuffed in the corner on the kitchen counter...

She went up the old, creaking stairs to the sloped roof bedroom where she used to retreat to. There was a crib where her bed used to be, where she used to lay sprawled out dreaming of the man who was now walking next to her. She said nothing as she moved through the house. He was silent too, letting her memories take reign.

Evelyn felt almost choked with an emotion she couldn't quite name. It was a bit of a shock when she realized it was longing. Longing for how life could have been. This *should* have been the way the house was when she was a little girl. It should have been orderly, peaceful, clean. She should have wanted to come home every day, knowing it was a place of safety. She should have been able to invite friends over without feeling embarrassed, her mum should have baked cookies for an after-school snack and wiped down the table when they were done. She should have told Evelyn to do the dishes, clean her room. Normal mum things that kept a household together.

If she could just go back, do it all over again, she could make it that way. She could enjoy her youth, drink her fill of the simpleness of life back then.

She missed it, like it was an actual reality somewhere in her past, the life she could have had. How different would she be now? Where would she have ended up? It was impossible to know.

Evelyn thanked the young mum on their way out, and let Edwin guide them to the harbor, too lost in her own thoughts to pay attention until they stood outside a beautiful stone building right off the water.

Edwin opened the door for her with unmistakable pride. He led her to the bar where he introduced his son, Seth, who looked like an exact younger version of his father, down to the dark hair already threading with gray and sharp nose between dark blue eyes. Seth cheerfully made small talk as he poured two pints for them. They caught the lull that comes after the lunch rush hour and before the dinner time surge, so they had their pick of spots. They took their drinks and sat by the window with a perfect view of the sea. To the left of them there was a large fireplace that crackled with burning wood and radiated enough heat to warm the entire room.

"What a beautiful place," Evelyn said, looking around.

"Not bad, is it? The lad we bought it off of did all the hard work, making it look nice. Nearly bankrupted himself and had to sell, poor bugger. Good thing though, because I'm shite with handiwork. There're actually a few rooms upstairs he was going to use as an inn. We didn't want to take that on though. There's where I'm staying now."

"Really? You live here?"

Edwin nodded. "It started out as temporary when we were getting the place going. Then I found I didn't mind it. It's simple. Peaceful. Two things my life hadn't been. We opened eight years ago, and I can't remember another time in my life when I felt this content."

Evelyn took a sip of her drink as she digested what he said. "Why weren't you content before?"

He shrugged. "I was in a high-stress job. Making buckets of money, but I spent all my time working, so it didn't matter. I couldn't enjoy it. After I finally retired, I've actually been able to spend time with my kids and grandkids."

Edwin stared into his beer; a frown etched between his eyebrows. "I always thought when I was working that

I would get to a place in my life where I would finally have time to focus on things that mattered. Then suddenly I looked in the mirror and I was over sixty, divorced with no family around. What kind of life was that? I wish I thought about it sooner." He laughed a bit. "I spend a lot of my time regretting stuff now. I used to always look forward, you know? I didn't re-live the glory days over and over. I was always ready for what was next. But now...now all I do is look back. Because looking forward, bloody hell, it scares me, because what's forward? It's the end, isn't it? We are at the tail end of life and suddenly there just isn't enough time."

Evelyn nodded. "I know exactly what you mean. Especially since turning seventy. That's old, isn't it? People die in their seventies and its yesterday's news. When my mum passed away—just a few years ago—she was in her nineties and got quite sick in the end. I thought, Lord, she must be ready to go. But when I visited her, I could see she was frightened, even though she had faith that there was life beyond death."

Evelyn paused, remembering the sight of her mum, looking so impossibly old and depleted. Her body and mind giving out. She was so lonely in the end in her little hospital room. Evelyn was sure her mum had no other visitors who weren't paid to be there. A sad way to end one's life. Evelyn had gripped her mum's hand as she sat beside her bed. She had been scared to hold on too hard in case her mother's bones snapped beneath her pale skin. Growing old was a blessing, but it could also be a curse. To watch one's life slowly be sapped away while the ghost of days past constantly replayed...

She shivered, then continued. "It really hit me, seeing my mum like that. Even when you get older and you know it's around the bend. Even when you have lived a good long life and have no reason to not be ready, you believe with all your heart in heaven—there's still some fear. How can you be ready for everything you know to end? And it's not so much death I fear, because I do have faith too, it's…not living. I feel like I still got a lot of living left in me. And of course all the people who would be sad when I pass. I hate to think of my children and my grands being sad."

"I feel like I just started living, in a sense. Better late than never, I guess," Edwin said. "I miss being a kid and not thinking about death all the time. Was it weird seeing your home today?"

Evelyn nodded. "It was. I kept wondering what the version of me who used to live there would think, seeing the old lady I've become."

"I think she would be pleased she aged so well." He looked steadily at her when he said it, his eyes tracing her face.

Evelyn grinned and looked down.

"I love your hair," he said. "Most women cut their hair short at our age."

Evelyn automatically reached up and fiddled with the end of it. "Doug liked it long."

"He sounds like a good fellow."

"As good as they come." Evelyn took another sip. "What about you? You never met someone after your divorce?"

Edwin shrugged. "I saw someone for a few years after. She was at a different stage of life than myself."

"So, she was younger than you." She had a hard time keeping her voice neutral.

Course, he would go for a younger woman after his

divorce. He would've had his pick, so naturally he would look for someone younger. The cliché of it was disappointing, even though Mavis did the same with her younger husbands. Somehow that seemed fine, even empowering, but when men went for someone younger, it made Evelyn's lips pinch. She was well aware of the double-standard, but it couldn't be helped.

Edwin gave her a sheepish grin. "Aye, she was. But don't look at me like that, you'll be pleased to know it was a bad idea from the start. We were together a few years. Then I got my priorities straight, spent more time with m'boys, moved home, opened this pub. It fizzled out when I left London. I was busy after that and enjoying the peace of my new life. I was just starting to wonder if I might be a bit lonely when I got your email."

"I wasn't entirely sober when I sent it." Evelyn confessed.

Edwin laughed. "I wondered. I couldn't believe my eyes when I saw it was you. The pretty shy girl from school who sat behind me in class. I sure have enjoyed talking to you though. You're easy to talk to."

Evelyn held his gaze. "I've enjoyed talking to you, too." They stared at each other, silence lapsing between them, broken only by the clink of glasses at the bar.

Edwin cleared his throat. "So, what's the full story with Lena?"

"Story?" Evelyn's hands came together in a clench. "No story."

"Course there's a story."

"I told you. She's a widow too and—"

Edwin held up his hand. "I know what you've told me. But you always get this look on your face. There's something more, isn't there?"

Evelyn stared, then said, "Alright, yes. There's something more. But she doesn't know." She told him then, told him everything. His face remained unchanged until she finished.

He took a long sip from his pint then said, "Well, you got to tell her."

"Why?"

"She's your friend, isn't she? You wouldn't keep this from a friend."

CHAPTER TWENTY-THREE

The sound of seagulls floated gently with a light breeze into the room as Lena stretched and opened her eyes. She rolled from her belly to her back and closed her eyes again, enjoying the warmth of the silk sheets wrapped around her body in the morning's stillness. She was in that wonderful state of waking slowly, the relaxing edges of rest still clinging to her body as energy slowly infused her blood. She'd forgotten how luxurious a good night's sleep was. She could have stayed this way for an hour more, maybe even drifted off again, but her phone dinged and with it her eyes opened.

She flung her arm out and felt around the nightstand until she located the phone, then brought it in front of her face. Ten in the morning already. She'd been sleeping in every day since they had arrived in St. Ives and waking with a sense of displacement, but the wonderful kind. Like she was in someone else's body, living some stranger's life in this storybook town.

For the first time in maybe forever, Lena felt something very close to light. There *was* something about travelling that was good for the soul. Something about stepping outside of normal routines that refreshed and rejuvenated.

On her phone there was a text Evelyn sent two hours ago saying she was going for breakfast with Edwin, and they would meet up later. The new text that had burst her sleep-fused bubble was from Sean.

—How's your trip, babe? Missing you.—

Lena frowned, her new peaceful mood challenged.

*—What are you doing up?—*She texted back.

The reply came right away.

—Thinking of you—

Then another;

—send pic?—

Lena rolled her eyes. It was three in the morning back home. He must be drunk.

—No—

Then she tapped out another message.

—Turning my phone off for the day. Talk to you later.—

Without waiting for a reply, she tossed the phone to the edge of the bed and fell back against the feather pillow. Sean had been persistent in texting her throughout the trip, ignoring her curt one-word answers, acting like everything was fine.

Maybe things were fine. Lena chewed her lip. The memory of their last night together wasn't as clear in her mind as it used to be. Maybe she'd just imagined the tension? Maybe it felt overblown because they both had been drinking…It could just be a misunderstanding. Sean probably didn't even realize he'd upset her. Maybe she was mostly disturbed because it was the first time she had done something with a man since James—it was a lot to take in…

Lena sat up and swung her feet over the edge of the bed. She didn't want to think about Sean today. Or James. This was her last full day in St. Ives. Tomorrow after lunch they would head to Heathrow Airport to catch the flight home.

She wished she had more time here.

Lena wished she *lived* here. The thought stilled her on her way to the bathroom. She could move here, couldn't she? Nothing was holding her back, well besides her mom. Her mom would miss her. But they could video chat…The thought danced around in her mind as she combed her hair and brushed her teeth. What if she could walk down to the beach every day. What if she worked in one of those tiny shops on Main Street, ate Cornish pasties and cream teas, let the cold sea waves hit her knees and sat on the rocky cliffs staring into the horizon every night.

She could start over here. Start completely fresh. Sleep well every night. Permanently become this person who she felt like right now…She spat in the sink and wiped her mouth. It felt too good to be an actual option. This wasn't reality, this was just a break from reality. She couldn't just pack up and start over again…Could she?

Lena stared at herself in the mirror…then snapped her gaze away and placed her toothbrush back. No. It didn't work like that. Problems didn't go away because of a new location, or hairstyle, or job. Even here in this peaceful town so different from home, there would be no escaping her past.

Lena pulled her nightgown up over her head, got dressed in jeans and a sweater, and pulled on the new coat she purchased the other day. It was deep red with big buttons and went to the middle of her thigh. She'd seen it on a mannequin in a shop window when she was slowly pursuing by. She had stopped and stared at it, loving the bright color and the way it matched the artsy mood of the town. It belonged perfectly in a shop window in St. Ives.

She'd looked down at her own less than thrilling old blue coat and on a whim bought it, along with a couple of colorful scarves. Evelyn had been less-than-subtly hinting Lena needed a new jacket, anyway. Now, she buttoned up the buttons, running her fingers along the soft, warm fabric, and tightened the belt that cinched around her waist. She fixed a red, white, and black plaid scarf around her neck and pulled her hair forward over her shoulders. She studied herself in the mirror, turning this way and that. She felt a bit like a little girl playing dress up. All bright and put together, like the focus of a photograph instead of the background.

"Well…" she said, smoothing her hands down her sides. "Last day." Might as well keep playing the part of the stranger.

After buying a muffin and a tea for breakfast at one of the cafes, Lena decided to go for a walk along the harbor. It was the nicest day yet since they had arrived—the skies were clear, and the sun was out, making her almost too hot in her new coat. She loved the harbor. She liked how foreign it felt, the flow of people moving this way and that on the walkway. The unfamiliar accents clashing with the soft slapping of the water against the stone wall. The boat's hulls nodding with the waves as they gently pulled on the ropes tethering them to the docks. She wanted to take one of the boats and let it loose, let it glide her away until she was surrounded by nothing at all. Just quiet and stillness.

As she walked, she felt hyper aware of herself—the slap of her feet against the stones, the sway of her hips, the feel of her skin against the fabric of her shirt, and the way others were looking at her. She could feel it, the eyes of women following her, and the gaze of men looking at her in that mildly appreciative way of theirs. It was the color, she thought, the bright, confident red, and the stranger's skin she wore. She was walking with a confidence she didn't have, with a lightness that didn't belong to her.

Lena's walk slowed as her eyes slid and settled on a woman who was sitting on a stool with an easel and canvas in front of her. The woman was facing the dock, a paintbrush in hand. She had blonde curly hair pulled up into a bun, a bright yellow sweater rolled up to her elbows, light colored jeans with smatterings of paint splatter on them. Her tongue slightly stuck out as she concentrated on her work.

Lena watched mesmerized as the woman's hand moved in easy strokes back and forth across the page. Her body was relaxed, her hand gliding up and down, up and down, like a dance. She seemed out of place amongst the surrounding hustle, like a stone in a river, letting the water rush around its smooth edges.

Lena was so enthralled watching she didn't notice how close she'd gotten until the woman glanced up, a question etched in her brow. The spell snapped.

"Alright?" She asked in a thick Scottish accent. "You're blockin' the light."

Lena jumped and blinked down at her. "Sorry, so sorry. I was just…your painting looks beautiful. Sorry, I didn't mean to bother you."

"Thanks." The woman eyed her. "You American?"

"Canadian."

"Ah. That's why you're apologizing so much." She grinned as Lena flushed.

"Sorry."

The girl laughed. "There ya go again. What's your

name?"

"Lena."

"I'm Maisie." Maisie eyed her with interest. "You on holiday?"

"Yes," Lena said. She enjoyed listening to this woman talk, her rolling speech sounded like a melody. "Leaving tomorrow, actually. You?"

"I'm taking a course at the school."

"School?"

"The art school. You know, St. Ives School of Painting?"

"Oh." Lena shifted. "Well, it's lovely. Your painting, I mean. I used to paint." Lena felt herself turn red again. She didn't know what possessed her to say that.

Maisie cocked her head. "Used to?"

"I haven't tried in a while. Life, you know...Anyway, I won't bother you anymore. Have a good day." Lena went to move past her, but Maisie shifted in front.

"Do you want to try now? I have an extra canvas here."

"Oh no, no, I couldn't use that. That's alright."

"Come on." Maisie said. She stood and reached behind her easel and picked up a canvas that was leaning against the wooden legs. "You're not admiring my painting. You're hungering after it. I know the feeling. I get it too when I don't pick up a brush enough. Sit your arse down."

Lena took her place on the stool and watched, a little stunned, as Maisie placed the fresh canvas in front of her. "But, what about you?"

"I need some lunch," Maisie said. "I'll be back. Get

to work now."

Lena watched Maisie walk into the crowd, then turned to the blank slate in front of her. She should just get up and leave. She would never see that strange, forward Maisie woman again anyway. She had no business using a stranger's paints and canvas…But even as the thoughts were making their way across her mind, Lena shrugged out of her jacket and reached for the brush.

It was as if her hands had developed a will of their own. She watched a bit fascinated as they began, tentatively at first, but then gaining confidence to develop a picture right before her eyes. She felt it, the old familiar feeling of release that had helped her express and be calm and keep sane all those years ago. The world quieted, but her soul lit up, communicating with her hands as they moved with purpose, knowing exactly what they wanted to say and how to say it.

She was unaware of time going by. Suddenly Maisie was back by her side, silently watching. Lena jerked backwards, and the brush fell from her hand leaving a streak of black on her knee. "How long have you been there?" she asked, her hand on her heart.

"A bit," Maisie leaned forward, peering at the painting.

"It's not done," Lena said, rubbing at the paint blotch, making it worse. "I haven't painted in a long time, I'm really out of practice. It's just the sky right now. If I had time I would add the waves and a boat and—"

"Hush girl."

Lena shut her mouth and stared at her knees. Unable to watch Maisie scrutinizing her work.

"The sky…" Maisie said softly. "You painted a storm. Just before a storm, I mean. It's brewing. Or maybe…maybe it's quieting." Maisie looked up beyond the canvas and back down again. "It's this harbor isn't it? But not sunny and peaceful like now. You didn't paint what you see."

"I never paint what I see." Lena looked up and stared at the torrent of colors swirling on the canvas. "It's what I…" Her words choked in her throat.

Maisie put her hand on her shoulder, her touch light like a butterfly landing. "I know. I know exactly."

****

"There you are."

"Sorry, I know I'm late." Lena plunked down in the chair opposite of Evelyn. "I got a bit distracted and then had to run and change before coming." She looked around. "Where is Edwin? I thought we were having supper with him."

"He's not coming. I thought it would be nice to be just us since it's our last night." Evelyn stared at her. "I *love* your jacket."

"Thanks. You didn't have to tell him not to come, it's just us all the time at home." Lena looked around the small restaurant. It could only seat maybe thirty people at once. The tables were wedged so close the servers had to turn sideways to get through. Local art adorned the walls, and a simple double-sided menu was laid before them. A tea candle flickered and burned in a round candle holder with flowers etched on the sides in the center of the table. It was just at the beginning of an acceptable time to have supper, so there were only two other tables taken. At home this restaurant probably wouldn't have stood out to her, but here everything felt more interesting, more exotic. She missed it already. Even though she was still here, she already missed St. Ives.

"Cozy in here," she remarked.

"Edwin suggested it. This used to be a tea house when I was young." Evelyn leaned forward. Her gaze was so intense that Lena felt herself tilt back in response. "How was your day then? Do anything interesting?"

"Sort of yeah. I made a friend, it's official on Facebook and everything."

"Exciting." Evelyn's knee jiggled up and down, making the wax in the candle quiver.

Lena studied her, unsure what to make of Evelyn's jittery mood. A long silver strand had escaped her braid and fell unnoticed down her shoulder.

"Are you alright? You don't seem yourself."

"What? Oh, I'm fine, love. Too much caffeine is all." She stopped shaking her leg. "Where is that waiter?" She half stood, as if to find him.

"I'm sure he will be here soon. Did something happen with Edwin?"

"No, no. We had a lovely day."

"Well, what is it? I can tell something's up."

Evelyn sighed. Her shoulders drooped. She stared down at her clasped hands.

"Evelyn," Lena lightly covered Evelyn's hands with her own. "What's going on? You can tell me."

She's sick. She's dying of cancer. The thought stilled Lena with cold fear.

Oh no, no, please. Not another one. What would she do if Evelyn died? It was too horrible to consider. Her friend, the only real friend she had. It couldn't be that, could it?

She swallowed hard. "Evelyn…you're not, dying, are you?"

Evelyn looked up sharply. "Dying?"

"Cancer or something? Is that what you won't say?" Lena blinked hard.

"Oh, heaven's…no, no, of course not. I mean, not that I know of. Of course you would jump to that, though. Old woman has something important to say so she must be dying!"

Lena pulled back. "What is it then? For Pete's sake, just tell me!"

"Alright." Evelyn squared her shoulders. "First though, I ask that you try not to react right away. Just let it sink in, okay? It's going to sound strange."

"The suspense is truly killing me."

Evelyn took a deep breath, then launched ahead. "You know how we met, that night, at the movies?"

"Yes…"

"That wasn't the first time I saw you."

"What do you mean?"

"I knew who you were, when I saw you there. I mean, before I ever saw you at the movies, I knew who you were."

Lena blinked.

"I knew you," Evelyn pressed on, "From James' funeral."

Whatever Lena thought was coming next, it wasn't that. "You…you were at his funeral? Why?"

"I felt obligated to go. Because, you see…Doug was the reason he died. Doug was the driver who crashed into the guardrail and killed him."

Ice flooded Lena's chest.

"What? What did you just say?"

Lena must not be understanding, Doug died from…from something. What was it? She was sure Evelyn told her…hadn't she?

"I'm so sorry, Lena. It was my husband's fault that you lost yours."

"Sorry…what do you mean? He was the driver? What was he doing driving an Uber?" None of this was making sense. Doug was rich, he wouldn't be driving people around in the late hours of the night.

"He did it sometimes, to keep busy. He liked it—liked talking to people. I know this is a lot to take in, Lena. I should have told you sooner, I just didn't know how. When I saw you at the theater, I wanted to make sure you were okay. Doug would have wanted me too—"

Lena's chair scraped back as she stood. She stared down at Evelyn. "Okay?" The word came out as a whisper. "You wanted to see if I was okay?"

It was so absurd. This whole thing. Soap-opera level absurd. There had to be a misunderstanding…But as Lena took in Evelyn's devastated face, she suddenly knew. It was like she could see it. The faceless driver Lena always imagined suddenly had the features of the man in the pictures at Evelyn's house. She saw him driving the car, James in the back. The dark night around them, something soft on the radio. Then the crash. Metal scraping against bone and muscles as they were crushed together. The sound of sirens. Their bodies laid out, battered, bloody, and already cold.

Dead.

Doug had been driving.

Doug killed James.

And Evelyn had known.

Lena couldn't form another sentence. She felt the tightness coming on, breath leaving her lungs and struggling to return.

Out.

She needed to get out of here right now.

She turned away and smacked into the waiter who was standing shock-still, obviously listening. He fell over and crashed into the neighboring table, but Lena didn't stop. She headed straight for the door, ignoring Evelyn calling out after her. She made it around the corner before she crouched down. Holding her sides, she rocked back and forth as the panic attack seized full control of her body. She gasped as the world swayed, pain building and spreading from her chest to the rest of her.

Evelyn had known.

CHAPTER TWENTY-FOUR

It was an unmitigated disaster.

That was how Evelyn described it to Edwin, and then again to the ladies when they met for their first chat in the food court mall after Evelyn's return.

"Well, what did you expect would happen?" June said. "You never should have started up with that girl. It was an odd choice, Evelyn, even for you."

"I told you not to tell her. Didn't I say that? I said to never tell her. Now look." Mavis contributed with a knowing shake of her head.

June tutted. "Of course, she needed to tell her. I'm just not surprised how it went. I would be livid if I was her."

"Junie, maybe be a bit more sympathetic," said Nora, "can't you see she's upset? It's alright, Evelyn. You were doing what you thought was best."

Evelyn fiddled with the paper edge of her coffee cup. "She won't take my calls or return my texts. I'm barely sleeping. I can't think of anything else."

"Keep trying, darling. She won't shut you out forever. Now, what happened with the charming Edwin?" Mavis leaned forward eagerly. "Don't spare any details. Do all his parts still work?"

"Mavis!" Nora scowled. "She just said she can't think of anything else. Don't change the subject. She's clearly distraught."

"I'm trying to cheer her up!"

If Mavis was trying to cheer Evelyn, that was not the way to go. Edwin was another problem that made her feel a bit sick. Not that he had done anything, in fact, he had been wonderful. It was just…their time together had been far more intense than she had expected.

They talked every day since her return, and she was starting to feel very off balance about everything. She convinced herself at the beginning it was just for fun, just two people who were looking for someone to fill the silence with. But she knew herself better than that. She was developing feelings for him. Which would lead to where? The answer was nowhere. She was getting emotionally invested in someone unattainable and she was too old for that sort of heartache.

That was a problem for another day, though. Right now, her mind was full of how to fix things between her and Lena.

Nora turned to Evelyn, "Have you discussed it with your kids? What do they think?"

"I haven't and I don't want to just yet. Not until I can fix things…"

"Don't you dare keep bothering that girl," June said. "You've put her through enough. I told you to leave her be."

"June." Nora shot her a look.

"It's alright." Evelyn bit her lip. She deserved every bit of criticism that June wanted to give. The look on Lena's face when Evelyn had finally told her…it was like Evelyn had reached over and slapped the girl. She expected Lena to be upset, of course, but Evelyn hadn't expected her to dash out of the restaurant, nor that she would be gone by the time Evelyn returned to their rooms. The only communication she'd received from Lena was a text saying she took the bus to Heathrow and was catching the first flight she could get home. Evelyn had tried calling, but it went right to voicemail.

"I have to make it right." Evelyn lifted her eyes to June's narrowed ones. "I can't leave things like this."

"If she doesn't want to talk to you, you can't force her." Nora said, gently.

"I can try…"

June snorted. "What are you going to do, track her down? Stalk her until she speaks to you?"

"She'll come around when she's ready, Evie, dear." Mavis patted her shoulder. "Now, I don't want to be insensitive, but I have been absolutely dying to tell you about the fight Dave and I had. It was rather spectacular, I wouldn't be surprised if it was the catalyst to our divorce, to be honest. So, he comes home and is just in the worst mood—"

Evelyn let Mavis' elaborate lover's spat story wash over her. She was still quite tired from jet lag—plus all the worrying was giving her a terrible headache. It could also be the amount of coffee she was consuming to get back to her regular schedule. She'd always been one of those people who could feel caffeine the moment it entered her bloodstream. She usually passed coffee over for tea, but after returning from a trip overseas—which always seemed harder on her sleep cycle than going—she consumed horrible amounts of coffee, leaving her jittery and feeling sick, but semi-awake.

How was Lena adjusting to being back? How was returning to work? How was she processing everything? There were so many questions Evelyn wanted to know the answers to. If only Lena would answer her phone.

Evelyn stood up, abruptly cutting off Mavis. "Sorry, ladies, I'm not feeling all that well. I'll catch up with you next week." Without waiting for a reply, Evelyn gathered her purse and headed away from the table.

She'd parked where she usually did, on the other side of the mall, so she had to walk through it. But not even shopping for little knickknacks could distract her now. She walked past the stores with her eyes trained on the floor, trying to ignore the sick sensation at the bottom of her stomach. It had been a while since she felt this way. It was similar to the feeling she got when she spoke too loud about someone who happened to be standing behind her. That sick, embarrassed, there's-no-coming-back-from-this-one pounding dread.

Evelyn drove in silence to her condo. By the time she got inside and sat heavily on the couch, her phone had dinged several times with texts. She didn't expect to see Lena's name attached to any of them, but still felt a bit of hope. She thumbed through the messages, not feeling inclined to answer any of them.

Five texts from Alice and one missed call. Three texts from Sarah. At least Sarah was speaking to her again. She'd given nothing but icy silence this past week.

Evelyn knew why they were bombarding her right now. Usually after returning from a trip they would all get together so Evelyn could debrief about the vacation and hand out the presents she brought home. She didn't want to see any of her family just yet, though. She couldn't bear to tell them of what happened, they were already so unsupportive of her relationship with Lena. To see their told-you-so faces when Evelyn confessed what happened, how Lena reacted upon finding out…She just couldn't do it yet.

Evelyn tossed her phone aside. She tried to concentrate on a novel for a while, then set it down with an impatient huff. She turned the TV on and tried to watch some idiotic sitcom which immediately annoyed her. She turned it off and went to the kitchen, clicked on the kettle, and stared at her warped reflection in the shiny exterior while the water slowly boiled into an obnoxious whistle. After fixing herself a cuppa, she went back to the couch. The swirling steam played against her face as she held it up under her chin, breathing in the bittersweet scent of the brewing leaves. She took a little sip, swishing the hot liquid around her tongue as she leaned back against the couch cushion.

The quiet in the condo felt heavy, just her own slow breathing in and out, in and out to fill the ever-present silence.

I wish Doug was here.

The thought sent a longing trembling through her body. Her eyes burned a little.

Doug would fix things. He'd always known how to comfort her when she was feeling low. He could make her laugh, no matter how awful she felt. She missed him. His scent, his voice, his hands. The easy way he would put an arm around her, bringing her tea and asking what she was reading.

Course, if Doug were here, she wouldn't be in this predicament. She probably wouldn't even know who Lena was.

"This is your mess, Doug," she said out loud. Then felt guilty.

It was an accident.

It wasn't really his fault. At least, she hoped not. No one knew why the car swerved into the guardrail. Maybe he'd been fiddling with the radio. Or texting on his phone, though she couldn't imagine him doing that while being responsible for a stranger in the backseat. What had he been doing then? Over the months she had tried to understand, to imagine what happened that night, but she just couldn't think of what caused her capable, responsible husband to lose focus enough to cause the crash. She'd wondered if something medical had happened, a heart attack maybe, or an aneurysm, but the autopsy showed no irregular findings.

She could remember that night so clearly. Watching Doug shrug on his leather jacket, chatting about something he saw on the news that morning. Evelyn had asked him to please not be out late. She thought the whole Uber driving thing was an odd pastime, but she understood why he did it. He liked to keep busy, and he enjoyed chatting with people. Uber driving was right up his alley, and it made him happy. She had told him when he started she wasn't comfortable with him driving late, so he rarely did it.

But that night Evelyn had her youngest granddaughter for a sleepover, and he wanted to be out of their way.

There was no weird sensation watching him leave, no warning in her gut that his quick peck on her cheek would be the last touch she would ever receive from him. She'd always thought she would *know*, that she would have some sort of intuition if something terrible was going to happen. But she hadn't known. She didn't even sense it when his spirit left his body close to midnight. She'd been sleeping soundly, dreaming some nonsense dream.

It wasn't until Evelyn stood in her housecoat staring

at two young officers in her doorway nervously asking to come in that she'd known. It was like a cold gust of air blasting her insides, the sudden knowing that he was gone.

He was dead, as was the young man he had been driving. Doug would have been crushed, knowing he was responsible for ending a young man's life, leaving behind a young grieving wife. Evelyn felt crushed for him. She had taken the responsibility Doug would have carried.

She couldn't stop thinking about that young man— she learned everything she could about him, stared for hours at his picture on the real estate website before they took it down. She attended his funeral, quietly slipping into the back row. She could hardly look as Lena came down the aisle, flanked by her family. Evelyn even went through the receiving line—she'd planned to say something then. She had a little speech prepared. She was going to say, "I'm so sorry for your loss, it was my husband who was driving. I'm so, so sorry." Simple, to the point. That was the plan. But when she got to Lena, and saw her pale face and sad blue eyes, saw her resemblance to a young Alice, Evelyn couldn't get the words out. She just gave Lena a quick hug and then left to go cry in her car.

Then Evelyn saw her months later at the theater, looking so sad and alone. Over and over again Evelyn saw her. It was fate, giving her a second chance to right the hurt Doug caused. She owed it to him, and she owed it to Lena. Except she'd messed it up terribly.

But Evelyn could still fix it.

She just needed to talk to Lena again—in person. Lena would be more understanding now that she'd had some time to process. Evelyn was sure of it.

Her phone dinged just then with a message. Evelyn seized it then deflated a little, seeing it was Edwin again. She needed to get on top of this, get on top of all of this. Everything was spinning out of control, and it was making her feel physically ill. Without reading what he wrote, Evelyn quickly typed out a message.

Edwin,

I've been doing a lot of thinking, and I am sorry to do this, but I don't think we should keep talking. I don't know where you are at, but I am getting too emotionally invested in this relationship and I don't see it leading anywhere productive. I hope you have a good life. Our time together meant a lot.

Evelyn

She sent it, feeling absolutely horrible, but tried to push down her doubt. It was the right thing to do. She knew it was.

Now on to the next.

Evelyn checked the time, then got to her feet and grabbed her purse, gloves, and jacket. Lena would be done work in a couple hours, Evelyn decided she would wait for her and simply force her to talk. Enough of this waiting around feeling glum.

She stopped at a coffee shop on her way to pick up provisions, then she drove to the newspaper building and parked close to Lena's car. She turned the engine off so as not to kill the environment in her quest and cracked the windows to let in some fresh air. Keeping a careful eye on the front door, she slowly chewed chunks of donut between sips of chemically flavored coffee. All she needed was a partner to trade lines with and a pair of binoculars. Maybe some aviators too. She should have dressed more for the occasion, in all black with a headscarf or something…

As it turned out, staking out a place was a very boring event. Evelyn shifted her position and huffed. She really should have timed this better. Maybe she had time to go get groceries and then come back…She was just about to start the ignition when Lena suddenly burst out of the newspaper's door. She looked angry: her face a deep red Evelyn could see from her position. Lena walked quickly towards the parked cars. Evelyn hunched down, suddenly very unsure of pursuing her plan.

Lena paused at her car door and started fishing around in her purse. She pulled out her ringing phone, put it to her ear and snapped, "What!"

Goodness. Evelyn slithered lower. Definitely not a good time for her whole 'cornering and forcing to talk' plan.

"Sorry." Lena said into the phone, her voice still hard. "I just quit my job…No. No, I'm fine. Sean, really, I'm…actually…what the hell. You have booze?" Lena snorted. "Yeah, course you do. I'll come over. Okay. See you soon." She hung up and yanked her car door open.

Evelyn chewed her lip. She should get out and say something now. Lena just quit her job! And judging by her angry face, not on good terms. Now she was going to meet up with Sean? As in the complicated ex who did whatever it was last time they had hung out that scared her, *that* Sean? With booze? While she was angry and hurt…this wasn't a good idea.

Evelyn grabbed the door handle, but suddenly Lena was reversing and spinning her car to exit. Not sure what possessed her, Evelyn turned her car on and eased out to follow her.

"What am I doing? What. Am. I. Doing," Evelyn said under her breath as she followed Lena into traffic. She'd gone from a stakeout to stalking. This was a bit much. She should turn around and go home. Or honk and make Lena pull over. Something!

Still, Evelyn did nothing, just kept following Lena until they were out of the city, heading down the highway. Goodness. Where on earth did Sean live? This was getting harder and harder to explain should Lena catch her.

"I'll just make sure it all looks okay," Evelyn said, reasoning with herself. Her voice sounded nervous.

She cleared her throat and gripped the steering wheel. Yes, she would just make sure it looked okay and then she would leave. Lena was in a vulnerable place right now, and she was going to hang out with some guy that she admitted was bad news and drink alcohol. Anyone who had watched any amount of TV knew this was a recipe for disaster.

Soon they reached a town called Redwood. She signaled after Lena and turned in. They drove through the town to a residential area where Lena finally stopped and parked in a driveway. Evelyn parked across the street and waited.

Lena got out of her car. Before she reached the front door of the house, it swung open, revealing a young guy with short blonde hair in a plain white t-shirt. He was holding a bottle of vodka and grinning. Evelyn felt a thrill go through her as she watched. She did not like the looks of him. He had a predator grin—she was sure of it. She watched Lena disappear into the house and sat back, wringing her hands. What was she to do now?

Leave, of course. Evelyn should leave and go home.

Lena was a big girl. She could take care of herself. Evelyn had zero business being here. She checked the time. It was close to five o'clock. It would start getting dark in an hour, and Evelyn didn't particularly like driving on the highway in the dark.

"Time to head home," Evelyn said, but she didn't make a move to go. She couldn't shake this uneasy feeling sitting on her chest. What if something happened? What if Evelyn drove away and found out later that something horrible occurred? She would never forgive herself. Why, oh why did Lena come see Sean?

She tapped the steering wheel, thinking. She would wait. Just for a little while. Not that she could tell a great deal from sitting in the car while they were inside, but she would wait and maybe call Lena in a few minutes. She would call and call until she answered. If she sounded fine, Evelyn would go.

And if she didn't sound fine?

Evelyn bit her lip.

She would cross that bridge if she came to it.

CHAPTER TWENTY-FIVE

"So, why'd you quit?"

Lena took the offered glass of vodka cranberry. She took a sip and grimaced. More vodka than cranberry—in typical Sean fashion. It was good though. She needed it right now. She felt jittery, her heart still madly racing since the altercation at work. Since the bomb from Evelyn, really. Now, here she was with Sean—the first time they were face to face since going out that other night.

When he opened the door with that grin, Lena had a flash of that moment in the car and her hands shook. She'd stuffed them in her pocket before he saw and followed him inside. The whole drive up she had a nagging feeling that she shouldn't be doing this. She was in a reckless mood and was bound to do something she regretted, but anger made her push the gas pedal harder. Anger at her boss for his obvious come on that made her fly off the handle and quit. Anger at Doug for driving James into that guardrail. Anger at Evelyn for keeping it a secret. For knowing this intimate detail and not telling Lena.

She was at James' funeral. That thought kept coming back, feeding the heat burning her insides. It tilted everything into this weird alternate universe. One where they hadn't met at the movies and become spontaneous friends, linked by their mutual grief. Evelyn had planned it, had deliberately found Lena and forced their friendship to happen because Evelyn was trying to…What? Make amends? There was no making amends for something like this.

Had Evelyn been relieved when Lena confided in her that James might not have been the picture-perfect husband? Did that take a load off Evelyn's guilt? *Oh, well, it's better for Lena that her controlling husband was offed. I'll just bake her some cookies and we will call it square.* The thought pulsed anger through her again and again. Terrible, righteous anger that Evelyn might've thought there was a positive to be found in James' death.

"It was stupid." Lena gripped the glass hard. "My boss is an ass, and I got fed up."

"What he do?"

"Made some dumb sexual comment." It had been nothing new, or even that bad. He had said something about her clothes, how she knew how to dress to compliment her body. She was wearing a red long-sleeve sweater dress with tights. It had a scoop neck that completely covered her cleavage, but fit slim. It was the way he said it, his eyes trained on her breasts. She'd been done. Done with him, with the stupid job she hated, with all the cards life had dealt her. She'd stood up, said *I quit!* Like in a movie, gathered her crap, and left, face flaming while he stared opened mouthed after her.

"Bit dramatic to up and quit over that, isn't it?"

"Maybe." She gulped down the rest of the drink, nearly gagging. She coughed. "Another?"

Sean took it and made them both a second drink. He handed it to her, then sat on the couch opposite of her.

"Why were you calling me, anyway?" Lena asked.

Sean shrugged. "Was bored. You weren't texting me back."

"Why aren't you working?"

"I'm part-time right now."

"Oh."

Sean's phone vibrated. He took it from his pocket and looked at it. A flash of anger crossed his face as he stared at the screen.

"Everything ok?"

"Fine. Just my…old landlord. Bugging me about stupid stuff. Every time she gets drunk she starts spamming me." He placed the phone face down on the coffee table.

She was pretty sure he just lied to her, but what did she care about his personal business? It was probably something shady she didn't want to know about. She pushed down the unease building in her stomach and swished her drink around the cup.

Sean leaned back, watching her lazily. "It's nice to see you again."

Lena took a sip to hide her discomfort. She didn't like the way he was looking at her. Knowingly, hungrily almost.

Relax, Lena. She was probably imagining it. She was just hyper aware of him because she knew that if she wanted it, something could happen between them. He would be game, if she initiated. She could feel it between them, like a large question mark. She felt the imprint even now of his hand on her breast. His lips on her throat.

She felt her face heating and threw back the drink, starting to feel the pleasant tipsiness she was here for.

"What are you thinking?" Sean asked, a slight smile on his lips.

"Nothing." Lena murmured. She looked around for a distraction. "I like what you've done with the place."

Sean laughed. "Yeah? You like the bare walls and second-hand furniture?"

Lena shrugged.

"Not as homey as when you lived here. You should help me decorate it."

"I'm not very good at that." Lena got up to get another drink. "Want another?"

"You're hitting them pretty fast."

"So?"

Sean shrugged. "Sure." He got up and came over to the counter.

She poured them more.

"I know what you need," Sean said. "Something to relax you." He leaned over her; Lena stiffened. His hand slid past her, opened a drawer, and pulled something out.

Lena blinked at the plastic bag. "You keep joints in your kitchen drawer?"

"Where else would I keep them?"

"I'm not doing that."

"Why not? It will take the edge off."

How many times had she heard that coming from him? She shook her head. "I haven't done that since...since that night."

Sean sighed. "Why do you keep bringing that up?" He slipped a joint out of the plastic bag and put it between his lips.

"You said we could talk about it."

"Now? You want to talk about it now?"

Lena shifted, suddenly unsure. "Maybe...not now. I just want to drink right now."

Sean grinned, the joint between his teeth. "I like that

plan."

He lit up as Lena drank. The sweet smell of pot seeped into the room, filling her with sick uneasiness, as it did any time she smelled pot since graduation night. If her parents could see their house now, filled with pot smoke…They hated when she'd done it in high school. They used to ground her when they could smell it on her clothes, threaten to take her out of school and homeschool her if she didn't dump Sean. Nothing worked. No amount of threats could peel her away. Eventually they stopped threatening and just looked sad, watching her leave with Sean and Cheryl. She hated disappointing them, but she hated being alone more.

Sean took a deep inhale, the smoke curling out of his lips. "You sure you don't want some?"

She shook her head, her vision going out of focus and back.

"I don't do it all the time. You probably think I do."

"I don't care if you do."

"Well, I don't."

"Okay." Lena tipped back the rest of her drink. How many was that now? She'd no idea. Her hands felt numb. That probably wasn't a good sign. "You know, you aren't very good for me. This is twice I've drank too much hanging out with you."

"You're the one who wanted to drink tonight."

"You've never been good for me." Lena went on. "You got us in so much trouble in high school."

"I don't think you can put all the blame on me."

"You guys liked doing that, didn't you? Getting me in trouble? I was like some sort of pet to you both."

"No, you weren't."

"Poor little quiet Lena, let's see what stupid things

we can make her do."

"It wasn't like that, Len."

"I feel like a kid again." Lena slumped back and stared at the ceiling. "Like my parents are going to come and bust us any second."

Sean chuckled. "I'm still scared of your dad. He barely said two words to me when I saw him."

"Remember how we used to sneak out to the river, all three of us. Hang out by the water with our stolen booze. We were real badasses back then." Lena could picture it, them lying there on the damp grass, stars overhead. Feeling invincible and daring—better than their classmates, better than the whole town when they were just typical rebellious teenagers doing what everyone else was doing. She could see Cheryl dancing in the moonlight, swaying her hips, her blonde hair wild, eyes bright, hollering at her, *Come on, Lena! Dance with me!* Lena always shook her head no. Cheryl was dancing for Sean, and Lena hadn't wanted to be part of the show. Sean's arm would be around her, but his eyes would be watching Cheryl move. How stupid and blind had she been back then? How desperate to be part of something—to be loved by someone, only to be used by both.

Her insides boiled again. The alcohol that had numbed now turned to fuel. She was about to say something, but her ringing phone stopped her thoughts. She fumbled around her purse until she pulled out it out.

Evelyn.

Again.

She hit ignore. Almost immediately the phone rang again. Then again. Lena jabbed at the answer button. "Leave. Me. Alone." She disconnected before Evelyn could answer.

"Wow, who pissed you off?"

She jolted to her feet, grabbing the couch to steady herself.

"Where you going?" Sean blinked at her.

"Let's go."

"Where?"

"Where we always go. That's what we do, right? Get high, get drunk, screw best friends."

"Why are you so pissed?"

"Come on." Lena left her purse on the coffee table but tucked her phone in her back pocket. She moved to the door. Sean hesitated, then came after her, grabbing the rest of the vodka on his way.

The air was rapidly cooling as they crossed the road and entered the park. The sun stared at them as they walked—an orange ball, shrinking with every passing minute, splurging out pink and purple across the sky at a last vain attempt to leave an impression.

Lena stumbled once and Sean grabbed her. He held on to her arm after that as they walked.

Under their feet the leaves crunched, the dying unkept grass grabbed at their shins as they moved through. They reached the small clump of trees on the other side, then followed the well-worn path to where the river was waiting.

Lena collapsed when they finally reached it. She could feel the soft edges of the earth seep into her leggings as she stretched out. The air had a blue tinge of night now, but she could easily see the muddy water with its slow trickle forward just feet ahead of where she sat.

Cheryl died here.

Was there a part of her that remained still? Lingering

along the muddy banks? Watching them now? Lena imagined her ghostly form walking along the banks, holding up the edges of her grad dress, face pale, hair wet. It made her want to vomit.

"You think she can see us?" Lena asked as Sean sat beside her. "You think she's mad she died, and we went on living?"

"No." Sean took a swig of the vodka, then set it between them. "There's nothing after death."

"How do you know?"

He shrugged. "It's just what I think."

Lena dug her heel into the ground. "I'd like to think they are out there somewhere. James and Cheryl." A rush of emotion made her swallow hard.

"They're not."

"What?"

"They aren't out there, watching over us or any of that shit. When you're dead, you're dead."

"That's not an overly hopeful thought."

"Yeah well, life's a bitch." Sean looked around. "Why did you want to come here?"

"I don't know." Lena studied the river. "I haven't been back since she died. It's weird, isn't it, being here again?'

"Yes."

There was something in his voice. A tightness as he stared at the water. Lena flicked her gaze to him. "You remember something, don't you?"

"I was wasted like you, Len, and I left early. Why do you care? She was drunk, she slipped, she drowned."

"We were here, though. Why didn't we do something?"

"You were passed out. In like, twenty minutes after

getting to the river, you were out of it."

"I remember…a fight? I remember yelling…"

Sean turned to look at her. "What?"

"It's blurry, but I remember hearing yelling…" Lena closed her eyes, willing her mind to go back. The smell of pot, the sound of the water, her grad dress bunched around her…

Think.

She'd been laying on her back—her face to the side, drifting in and out. She'd been cold, she wanted to move—to get off the ground but everything was tilted and hazy. She could see Sean and Cheryl, standing by the water's edge. Voices raised.

"You guys were fighting, right? What were you fighting about?"

"You don't remember anything. That's what you told the cops."

"I know. I was in shock after. I couldn't even get out of bed. But now…I think some pieces have come back. Sometimes I think I remember hearing…"

Sean got up and strolled to the edge of the muddy bank.

"Sean?" She stood up, her head swimming. "What?"

"What else?" Sean turned to her. His face was hard. "You remember anything else?"

"What?" She blinked. "No—I don't think so…That's why I want to know what you—"

"Let it fuckin' go, Lena. You want to know what I remember? Cheryl was a selfish whore. She'd screw me whenever your back was turned."

Lena's mouth fell open.

"She played both of us all the time. She got off on it."

"What the hell are you talking about."

"Cheryl! She was a psychopath. Throwing herself at me, then icing me out, just to mess with me. Just to keep me wanting her instead of wanting you. It's better off she's dead. She was messed up."

Lena felt numb. His words hit her like rocks smacking a glass window, spiderweb cracks formed in the protected shield she'd surrounded herself with. She could see it—see them—red-faced, Sean grabbing Cheryl's arm, their voices loud.

"You…you were hitting on her when you thought I was passed out," she said, slowly. "Cheryl rejected you…you got angry."

"Shut up. Shut up, Len."

"You pushed her…"

"I said, shut up!" Sean lunged, in two steps he was in front of her, his arm back. Then his fist connected with her face.

Lena reeled. She fell to the ground.

Looking up, terrified, she touched her cheek.

"You never knew when to fuckin' quit!"

She scrambled backwards. "S-Sean—"

His eyes were wild as he came after her. He grabbed her ankle, yanking her towards him. Rocks and mud dug into her back as she slid across the ground. Suddenly, he was on top of her, his face distorted, hands around her throat. Lena clawed at his hand. She made terrible gurgling noises as he squeezed her throat closed. Black spots took over her vision as wild panic seized her.

This was it.

This was the end.

She was going to die.

"You fuckin' bitches all die the same. You know

that? Fuckin' pathet—"

There was a sick thwack sound and the grip around her neck eased. Sean sat on top of her, eyes wide. Something wet dripped off his head and splashed on her cheek, then he slumped over.

For a split-second Lena laid there, frozen. Then she shoved him off her and squirmed away. She rolled to her side, gasping and retching, clawing at her throat—still feeling his fingers wrapped tight around it.

"You're okay. You're okay, Lena."

She looked up, heaving. "E-Evelyn?" She rasped.

Evelyn made to move towards her, but by her feet, Sean stirred. He started to sit up. Evelyn jerked and raised her hand, but Lena was faster. She lunged forward, grabbed the vodka bottle and swung it hard downwards against his head. It made a horrible cracking thunk sound and Sean went down, twitched, and laid still.

Lena stared, not quite registering what she was seeing. Sean was lying on his side, his eyes wide and mouth open. Blood was pouring out a gash on the back of his head. On the side where she struck him, there was another terrible bloody laceration.

With a gasp, she scrambled backwards away from him. "Oh. My. God. Oh, my god." The words came out like a scratchy whisper.

Evelyn stared down, transfixed as a pool of blood spread impossibly fast from Sean's head. A large rock dangled in her hand.

Then Lena bent over and threw up vodka cranberry all over the grass.

CHAPTER TWENTY-SIX

The blood was different then Evelyn would have imagined. It wasn't bright red like when someone scraped an elbow. It was dark, almost black looking. But that could've been because there wasn't much light.

And there was so much of it, that was another shock. It oozed out and spread across the ground like a dam broke. For an absurd moment, she wanted to reach out and touch it. It looked thick and sticky, like molasses. A roaring filled her ears, the world narrowed to the body sprawled out before her. In her hand she still held the rock, it dangled innocently by her side.

She looked down at it and blinked. *I think I'm a murderer*. The thought drifted abstractly across her mind. A murderer? Her? Interesting. She never would have pegged herself as one. Never thought she had it in her. But there was no denying it. There was the body, for one thing.

And the blood.

All that blood.

Get rid of the evidence. That seemed logical, that's what murderers did. They got rid of the evidence. Thank goodness she watched so much television.

She jolted into action then, throwing the rock as far as she could into the river.

A panicked voice shouted behind her, "What are you doing? What did you just do? Oh god."

Evelyn looked at Lena, hunched over the vomit she'd just unloaded from her stomach. They made eye contact, then Lena started retching again.

Evelyn blocked out the disgusting noise, her mind whirling, trying to register what just happened. Just a few moments ago she'd been standing on the edge of the woods, shifting from one foot to the other, knowing she was crazy for spying and that she should leave.

She hadn't planned on following them. She was about to leave after Lena harshly hung up on her, but when she saw them come out of the house—clearly intoxicated—Evelyn stayed and watched them walk past. Then Sean had reached out and steadied Lena when she stumbled, and a warning flare shot through Evelyn. The way he held his grip on her, the story Lena had told her...it sent tremors down Evelyn's spine. What were they doing, trudging off at dusk? She couldn't just drive away. Before even fully deciding on it, she had gotten out of her car and quietly as she could, she followed.

Evelyn had felt terribly exposed crossing the field as she carefully stepped through the tall grass, watching the shape of their backs up ahead. At any moment they could've turned and seen her trailing behind. She wasn't sure what would've happened then, but she assumed it would've been awkward.

By the time she reached the river, they were already sitting down talking. Evelyn could hear them from where she had stopped at the edge of the trees. She stood uncertain, feeling as jumpy as a wild rabbit, every rise in their voices making her want to dart back into the shadows.

Then suddenly things in the air shifted. Sean's body and voice hardened—his anger pulsed like an electrical current. Evelyn had felt adrenaline laced with fear kick into high gear and thump through her blood. Something was going to happen. She needed to get Lena out of there.

Before she could move forward, things escalated. Sean hit Lena, hard. Then he was pulling her towards him, and he was on top of her, with his hands on her throat. Evelyn had gasped in shock for a moment, then her body reacted.

She was barely aware of grasping the heavy jagged rock. It was like someone else took over her body. One moment she was emerging from the trees, the next she was bringing the rock down on Sean's head, harder and heavier than she ever could have imagined hitting someone. The blood began to trickle instantly, before he even hit the ground.

Now she stood above his body—after Lena gave him another good smack—the bloody rock at the bottom of the river.

Lena finally stopped throwing up and proceeded to freaking out, the blood-tipped vodka bottle still in her hand.

Evelyn turned to her and blinked. She felt the words leave her mouth, "We need to get rid of the evidence. We can't get caught."

"W-what are you talking about?" Lena was visibly shaking, her skin as pale as the body at Evelyn's feet. "We need to call for h-help. We need an ambulance."

"And tell them what, exactly? Come pick up the guy whose head we just bashed in? He's dead, Lena. Clearly, he is dead." Evelyn looked again at the body. So much blood. Would it stop coming out soon? How much blood could possibly be in the human head?

Her hands shook, she grabbed them firmly. *Don't*

freak out, think. She needed to keep it together, she needed to solve this problem. That's all this was: another problem for her to fix. She was good at that. She could fix anything.

Still, even with her pep-talk, she felt her heart throbbing madly and her arms tingling.

This was bad.

This was so, so bad.

"You don't know he's dead!" Lena said. "W-we need to check."

"We don't need to check, Lena, Look at him. I can practically see his brain."

Lena rocked back and forth on her toes, "Oh, my god. Oh god. Evelyn! What did we do? Are you sure? Are you sure he is dead? Maybe he isn't dead!"

"Shh!" Evelyn hissed. "Keep your voice down. I'll check, alright? Just wait." She gingerly stepped around the blood to move in front of the body. She had no idea how to find a pulse, but in the movies they pressed two fingers to the throat so that's what she did, but she jerked back as soon as her fingers touched his already cooling skin.

Lena screamed. "Did he move? Did he just move?"

"Bloody hell, he didn't move, Lena! He's dead alright? His soul's departed—left this earth. He's gone."

"We killed him. Oh my god, we killed Sean." Lena's voice began to climb.

"Calm down, Lena!"

"You calm down! What are you even doing here?"

"Saving your life apparently!"

"How did you get here? I don't understand—"

"That's not important right now. Let's figure this out first, okay? Now listen..." Evelyn scrambled, trying to work out a plan. "I think we need to dump the body into the water."

Lena gasped. "What? What are you talking about? We need to call the police!"

"The water will help get rid of some of the evidence...right? Like, wash the DNA away? Or at least we can sink the body...yes, we can fill his pockets with stones! Or something...no one will find him..." Evelyn wrung her hands.

"You're insane. That's not going to work, Evelyn! This water is like, knee deep. And don't you think the massive amounts of blood on the ground might give something away? What we need to do is call the freaking police."

"We aren't calling the police, Lena! This is bad, very bad. They will arrest us and throw us in jail! You are too young to go to jail, and I am too old, so we need to take care of this."

"Oh, and what exactly is the prime age for going to jail? Forties? This is insane."

"We are taking too long. Someone could be coming." Evelyn glanced over her shoulder.

Lena stared at the body. "It was self-defense, though, right? It's not m-murder if it's self-defense. We will be fine..."

"Get your head out of your arse, Lena! Murder is murder. We have no witnesses. We can't prove anything!" Evelyn pinched the bridge of her nose, trying to force clear thoughts to enter her mind. She actually didn't know if what she was saying was true. All she knew was that being found with a corpse, with a bashed in head, that she happened to have bashed, wasn't good.

"I don't think we should move him—"

Evelyn held up her hand, cutting her off—did a twig just snap? Was someone coming?

"What?" Lena whispered, panicked. "Did you hear something? What?"

She strained her ears, but all she could hear was the pounding of her own heart. "We need to get out of here. Now."

"We can't just leave him!"

"We are going to move him, then leave him." The water still seemed like a good idea, it had to do something, right? Get rid of some evidence?

"What? No, Evelyn! Stop! What are you—"

Evelyn wasn't listening. She went around and grabbed his legs and pulled with all her might. He slid a few inches down. "Come on. Help me!" She gasped as the ice-cold water started sinking into her boots. Lena stood with her mouth open, staring at the streak of blood smeared on the muddy bank as Evelyn pulled. He was incredibly heavy. With a grunt she pulled again, lost her grip, and stumbled backwards, falling on her backside. The shock of the cold water covering her legs made her shriek.

"Evelyn!" Lena lunged forward into the water and helped Evelyn to her feet. They stood together, listening with bated breath to see if anyone was going to emerge from the bushes.

Evelyn's body felt like ice, the cold air immediately stuck to the wet parts of her, making her shiver violently. She looked at the body, half in the water, a long smear of blood behind him, his eyes still open. She felt sick.

"Let's go." She couldn't touch that body again.

"We can't—"

Evelyn looked down at the bottle still clutched in

Lena's hand. "We need to get rid of that. Throw it in the water. Or wait, will it float? No, it wouldn't, right? I don't know, just bring it."

"We can't—"

"Move, Lena. Now!" Evelyn dragged Lena up out of the water on to the bank and back towards the trees. Evelyn kept a grip on her arm as they went. Lena sobbed as they moved through the trees and crossed the field. Their soaked feet squished sickly as they walked.

"Almost there," Evelyn said, trying to reassure herself as much as Lena. She wished in this moment that she'd changed into darker clothes before beginning her initial stake out, though she didn't think anyone looking could properly see them walking in this light. The sun had properly set now, and the streetlights lit up the road. Across from where she parked, the windows of houses glowed as their occupants moved through them. A car drove down the street and parked at a nearby house. Evelyn slowed their pace, wanting the occupants of the car to get inside before she and Lena emerged onto the sidewalk. She heard a door slam and quickened her step, finally reaching her car.

"Get in." Evelyn opened the car door for Lena and then circled around. She slid into the driver's side and twisted the key. The roar of the engine made her jump. She eased out onto the street and willed herself not to speed.

Act casual. Act casual.

She glanced at Lena's lap where she gripped the bottle. Hard to act casual with a murder weapon in plain sight—and with Lena sobbing her eyes out.

"We need to get rid of that. Lena, do you hear me? I need you to focus."

Lena took a deep, hiccupping breath. "This is so messed up."

"I know it is."

"How can you be so calm?" Lena demanded. "Is serial killer another secret you've been keeping?"

"Don't be ridiculous." Evelyn turned down a random street.

"Where are you going? The highway is that way."

"I'm making sure we aren't being followed."

"Who the hell would follow us?" Lena said, a hysteric note in her voice.

"I don't know! Okay? I'm just being cautious."

"Don't you think a car cruising around is more suspicious than one just leaving town?"

"Fine! We will go, okay? We need to get rid of that." Evelyn repeated, glancing again at the bottle. "Don't get blood anywhere in the car." It was unnerving having the bottle there, like a big red blinking light saying, *they did it! Look! They did it using this!*

They finally got on the highway. She gripped the steering wheel so tight her hands hurt. Once they got back to the city, then what? What was the plan? They drove in silence for a while, the air thick between them.

"Evelyn…"

"What?"

"What are we going to do."

Evelyn looked over at Lena. She was staring straight ahead, no longer crying. Her eyes wide and her mouth trembled.

"We just killed someone," Lena's voice was a whisper. "We killed Sean and left him there. What are we going to do?"

Evelyn was quiet, then said. "You know he would

have killed you, right? He was going to kill you, Lena. We did what we had to."

Lena was silent.

Evelyn cleared her throat as she cast her mind for something to talk about to keep Lena calm. To keep them both calm. "S-so…you quit your job. Good for you, you shouldn't work a job you hate."

Lena twisted to look at her. "How did you know I quit?"

"What? Oh…well, I heard you, in the, um—the parking lot…"

"What?"

"I was waiting for you to be off work so we could talk. You weren't answering my calls or texts. Then I heard you on the phone with…" Evelyn stumbled there. It didn't feel right to say the name of the man they had just left lying in a pool of his own blood. "With—erm— him. I was concerned, so I followed you and—"

"You *followed* me?"

"Just a little bit."

"Oh my gosh, Evelyn. You're insane."

Evelyn bristled. "Well, it's a good thing I did, isn't it? Tonight could have had a very sad ending if I didn't."

"Murdering someone isn't a sad enough ending?"

"Not as sad as it would have been if it was *you* who got murdered." Evelyn blinked hard. Her voice caught. "I never would have forgiven myself."

Lena didn't answer.

Evelyn pressed on. "I'm so sorry, Lena. For everything. For Doug and for James. For hurting you…"

Lena shook her head. "We have much bigger problems than that now."

"I know…but I want you to know that I am truly,

deeply sorry. I consider you a friend, a good friend. I hate that I hurt you."

Lena stared out the window. Ahead, the city lights grew closer and closer. She cleared her throat then said quietly, "I consider you a friend too."

Too soon they were in the city. Evelyn tensed up again. Where to go, what to do? Her mind raced. "We need to get cleaned up. I think we should—" Her cellphone rang just then, coming in loud through the Bluetooth, making them both jump. The screen announced it was Alice calling.

"Should you answer?" Lena said.

"No, no. Let it go to voicemail." She couldn't talk to her daughter right now. Alice would immediately know something was wrong.

"You have seven missed calls, and like twenty texts." Lena said, looking at her phone.

"Oh, bollocks. Okay, call her back." Evelyn tried to steady her breath.

Alice picked up on the first ring, her panicked voice filled the car. "Mom? What the hell! We haven't heard from you in hours. Are you okay?"

"I'm fine, sweetheart." Did her voice sound higher than normal? She tried to lower it. "I was at the movies, darling. I forgot to turn my phone back on when I left."

"The movies? You never go on Thursday to the movies."

Damn her predictable schedule. Evelyn exchanged a panicked look with Lena. "Oh, yes, I know. But there was one I really wanted to see, anyway I'm just having a late supper. I'll call you tomorrow, honey, okay? Text your sister for me, will you?"

"Okay…you sure everything is okay? You sound

kind of funny."

"Yes, yes, of course. Still tired from the trip is all. I've got to go, chat later." Evelyn pressed the disconnect button and let out a pent-up breath. How was she ever going to face her family again after tonight? How was she to sit across from her grandkids and ask about their day. Or hold her sweet great-grand baby, stroking his little face with the same hand that raised that rock...

Don't go there.

Right. Stay focused. She would have to save all moral dilemmas for another night. They needed to get cleaned up, make a plan, and figure out what their next move should be. It was easier to think now that they weren't staring down at the poor man's body.

Not poor man. He tried to hurt Lena. He would have killed her. The *bastard's* body. That was more like it. Except she felt bad calling him that. The man was dead after all, and at such a young age...maybe he would have changed. He could have lived a long, better life with some intervention. Some therapy maybe...

"Evelyn? You okay?"

"Sorry." She shook her head. "I was spiraling a bit. We're almost there." Soon they pulled into her parking lot. Evelyn popped the trunk and grabbed one of her reusable grocery bags. She handed it to Lena, who placed the Vodka bottle in it and grimly flung it over her shoulder. She stared at Evelyn.

"What?"

"You have some...splatter on you."

Evelyn looked down. "Good lord." She examined Lena. "You do too. There's some...on your face."

Lena's hands flew up to her face. "On my face?"

"Never mind. Let's just get up to the apartment."

"What if someone sees us?"

"It's nearly eight p.m. in a sixty plus building. The chances of seeing someone are very slim." Evelyn tried to sound more confident than she felt. It *was* a safe bet. She rarely ran into her neighbors as it was, but still if they did see someone…Maybe it didn't look like blood? Maybe they could say it was mud? And what about being soaking wet? That was a little harder to make an excuse for…Whatever—she would think of something. They couldn't stand here all night.

They reached the elevator and rode in silence up to her floor. When the doors opened, they practically ran to her apartment door. She closed it behind them with a relieved sigh.

"Alright. Go have a shower. Don't get dressed in those clothes again. I'll get you something."

Evelyn hurried to her room and located some spare pajamas. While there, she stripped out of her own soaked clothes and put on a robe. She came back to the kitchen and stopped. It was the first time she properly looked at Lena in good light, and now she could truly see the marks left around Lena's neck and the bruise forming on her cheek from where he struck her.

Bastard. No question.

"Oh, Lena." Evelyn moved closer and gently pulled Lena's shirt away to better see. There were already purple and black marks around her neck. Scratch marks too, from Lena's own fingers.

Lena was shaking. "I think—um—we should take a picture. If things—if we need to prove something…"

Evelyn swallowed and nodded. "Yes, yes, you are right." She grabbed her phone. Feeling sick to her stomach, she leaned close and snapped a few pictures. It looked worse somehow, looking at it through the lens of her phone—the image imprinted there reduced Lena from the woman she was into just another victim. Another woman traumatized by another man. Sick fury rose in Evelyn. Fury that this happened, that it was so common, that their lives would be forever marred by this experience, because of a loser man who thoughtlessly attacked a woman.

Without a word Lena took the offered pajamas and went to the bathroom.

Once the door clicked shut, Evelyn breathed out a shaky breath, then took the vodka bottle out of the bag and went to the kitchen sink. She wondered if she should google how to remove blood from glass, but then decided it was best not to have any history on her phone of the search. She would just have to guess. She ran it under cold water, scrubbing at the dried blood. She used some bleach as well, which seemed to be a thing to do. Then she dried it with a towel, and careful not to touch the glass again, slipped it into her recycling bin.

There, best she could do.

She was just finishing wiping down the sink with bleach when Lena emerged, her wet hair down her back. There was more color in her cheeks from the hot water, but she still wasn't looking very good.

"Make us some tea, will you? I'll be just a sec." Evelyn hurried to have her own shower. She didn't want to leave Lena alone for long.

She scrubbed every inch of her skin, turning the water as hot as she could stand. It was there she finally allowed herself to cry and tremble, but only for a few minutes. Then she twisted off the tap and stepped out into the steaming bathroom. She toweled off and got dressed quickly. Then with practiced hands she combed and braided her hair. Gathering her and Lena's discarded clothes, she went back to the kitchen.

Lena was sitting at the island staring into an untouched cup of tea.

"Right." Evelyn said, stuffing the clothes, their jackets and her leather gloves into a garbage bag. "We will need to solidify our alibis. That's going to be very important. Did anyone see you go into his house?"

"How would I know?" Lena said, still looking into the teacup. "I didn't even realize I was being stalked by a crazy lady."

"Right. Well, let's hope that—"

"Evelyn."

"Yes?"

"This is…insane." Lena looked at her. "We have to tell the police what happened. I think it will be okay…it was self-defense. There is no way we can cover something like this up. This whole thing is just…" Lena shook her head, her eyes filling again. "I mean Sean is…we…"

"I know." Evelyn wrapped her arms around Lena and let her cry. "I know. It's all going to be alright though. I promise."

"H-how? You can't fix everything, Evelyn. Sometimes things are out of your control. Sometimes there is no solution."

Evelyn stiffened. She folded her arms to hide the fact her hands were shaking—to hide how much Lena's words terrified her. "It will be okay," she said as firmly as she could. "I'll make sure of it. I'll take care of you, Lena."

CHAPTER TWENTY-SEVEN

It was the second time Lena woke on the futon in Evelyn's apartment feeling groggy and disoriented. She cracked opened her eyes then shut them again, trying to shut out the flood of thoughts pounding the sides of her head and the sound of Evelyn rummaging around in the kitchen. Evelyn supplied both of them with strong sleeping pills the night before. They had done their job, knocking Lena out into a dreamless sleep for most of the night, but they left her head feeling like it turned to stone.

Of course, that could have been from all the vodka cranberries she had consumed, though most of that had emptied from her stomach onto the banks of the river.

With Sean.

Who was now dead.

The image of his bloodied head filled her vision. Bile rose in her throat. For a moment she thought she was going to be sick. How did they get into such a horrible predicament?

Did this happen to other people? Did normal citizens ever wake up and suddenly realize they were now the feature of those horrible stories on the news? How many of the convicted murderers and criminals she used to judge and dismiss were ordinary people who just got in way over their heads—who looked at their life one day and wondered how the hell they got there.

How the hell *did* she get here? She gingerly touched

her throat, still sore from last night when Sean wrapped his fingers around her windpipe in a death hold. The same fingers that used to caress her skin, give her goosebumps and send lightning bolts through her chest.

You fuckin' bitches all die the same. You know that? Fuckin' pathetic.

His snarl reverberated against her skull. The last words he would ever speak.

That was it, wasn't it? That was his confession—he killed Cheryl. He must have. Why else had he turned like that when she questioned him?

It hit her like an electric shock last night. She remembered more. Sean and Cheryl had been fighting. Probably because Sean was angry Cheryl didn't want to hook up beside a passed out Lena on the ground. Did he push Cheryl down and choke her too? Did she struggle to breathe, claw at his hands, watch his face distort till there was only blackness? No—the police would have found marks on Cheryl's body, wouldn't they have? They would have known if she'd been strangled. Did he just drown her then? Push her out of anger into the river and hold her there until she stopped moving? The image of Sean bent over Cheryl, holding her head in the water as she flailed made Lena want to be sick all over again. Yet, it clicked somewhere inside her. It was the answer to the foggy question that haunted her since that night. That's how it happened. She was so sure of it.

She would never know, of course. The only person who could truly tell her was lying cracked open on that very riverbank.

Someone would find the body today.

The thought made her eyes fly open. She grabbed her phone and immediately checked the local news site, half expecting to see her picture with a wanted sign, but there was no mention of a body found in Redwood. Well, that would've been pretty quick, but it was going to happen.

It was only a matter of time until they found him. People went walking by the river all the time.

Then what?

The loud bang of a cupboard door slamming made Lena jolt. She turned her head to see Evelyn flitting around the kitchen, an apron tied around her waist, her silver hair falling out of the braid she slept in. Judging by the mix of smells in the air, Evelyn was baking up a storm.

Lena forced herself to sit up. After taking a moment to steady herself, she padded over to the kitchen, running her hands through her tangled mess of hair. Evelyn barely glanced up from the dough she was pounding as Lena slid onto a stool at the island. Evelyn's eyes looked bruised against her pale skin. Blueberry muffins littered the counter, along with a banana loaf, and two kinds of cookies. Chocolate and peanut butter, by the looks of them. Bowls, spatulas, and measuring cups filled the sink and spilled over on the flour dusted counter. Cracked eggshells sat in clumps beside empty butter dishes and an open sugar container. It looked like a bakery exploded.

Lena looked around with wide eyes. "Holy hell, Evelyn. Have you been baking all night?"

"I slept a bit," she said. She wiped at her cheek, leaving a smear of flour.

By the state of the kitchen, Lena doubted that very much. Maybe Evelyn hadn't taken her own advice with the sleeping pills after all. She should have, she looked terrible. Lena watched as Evelyn worked the dough, her hands kneading and pressing with aggressive enthusiasm. Her old, wrinkled, innocent looking hands.

That lifted a rock and brought it down on a man's head just last night.

How did this little old woman have the strength to crack open a human skull? It must have been one of those adrenaline moments, like when parents lifted vehicles to rescue their kids. Hysterical strength, they called it. The same strength that had coursed through her when she used the vodka bottle as a club...

"I'm making cinnamon buns," Evelyn announced. "They won't be ready for a while. Muffin? Do you want a muffin? There's blueberry. Help yourself."

"Thanks." Lena blinked. "Um, Evelyn. Are you alright?"

"As alright as I can be, I suppose," Evelyn said. Her phone buzzed on the counter beside Lena. "Can you check that?"

Lena looked at it. "A text from Mavis saying, 'call me'."

"She can wait." Evelyn slapped the dough into a big bowl. She ripped off a piece of cling wrap and pulled it tight over the top. "There. What next? Brownies? I could use a nice brownie." She bent to grab another dish.

"I think that's enough baking for a little...Don't you?"

"Oh, you never can have enough baking."

"Can't you?" Lena looked around the kitchen with her eyebrow raised.

"I think it's important we act as normal as possible."

"This is normal?"

"It helps me think."

"You should rest…"

Evelyn slammed the bowl down and stared at Lena. "You know life as we know it is over, right? We are either going to get caught, or, lie to our loved ones the rest of our lives."

Clearly, Evelyn had spent the night spiraling instead of sleeping. Lena didn't know what to say. It was true, wasn't it? They were damned either way. Unless they came clean. Maybe there would still be hope if they just confessed what happened…

"I know what you are thinking."

Lena looked up. "Huh?"

"You want to confess." Evelyn folded her arms.

"It might be the best option…" It was self-defense. Lena clung to that. Surely, they wouldn't get in too much trouble for self-defense? She had the markings on her neck as proof. She and Evelyn didn't have any priors. Though, maybe she should clarify that with Evelyn— Lord only knew what skeletons that woman had in her closet. Right now, nothing would surprise Lena.

Evelyn stood still, then rubbed her face hard. "Maybe. I just need to think…give me the day, okay? I need to find out what we are up against…"

Lena clenched her fists. "Okay," she said, finally. "One day. You don't have any priors, do you?"

"What?"

"Like, have you been arrested before?"

"Of course not!"

"Well, how should I know that? You're pretty good at keeping secrets. You did club a man with a rock."

Evelyn glared. "First off, that was to save you. It's not like I go around hitting people with rocks willy-nilly. And I seem to recall you doing some of the clubbing yourself. Secondly, I thought we were past the secret keeping thing."

"We are," said Lena. But a part of her wasn't. A part of her felt like she'd fallen off a cliff away from reality into this topsy-turvy universe, and it all started with the realization that Evelyn's husband killed hers.

Lena must be cursed or something. Dead husband, killed by new friend's husband. Dead best friend, killed by crazy ex-boyfriend, who was now dead because of said friend and herself—and more disfunction than she would care to admit laced through all those relationships.

Whatever therapist landed her was going to have a hell of a job unpacking all that.

"Good," Evelyn said. "In the meantime, we need to act as normal as possible. What would you normally be doing today?"

"Well, seeing as how I quit my job yesterday, I guess I would lie on the couch and spiral into depression."

"You're on track then."

Lena's phone buzzed. She looked at it and grimaced. "Oh, shit. I forgot I told my mom we could meet today. I texted her after I quit."

"Can you handle that?"

"I don't know…No, I shouldn't go, should I? She'll know something is up…"

Evelyn's phone went off. She grabbed it. "Oh dear. My daughters want to get together this morning…" She tapped her fingers against the counter, then said, "Go. You should go meet your mom. Try to relax. Don't think about anything. I'll be in touch later with a plan."

"I should help you—"

"No, no, we must not give the people in our lives

reasons to suspect anything. Especially you. When news comes out about…them finding him…it's just best we try to carry on normally until then. Alright?" Evelyn untied the apron from her waist. "Come, let's find you something to wear." She hesitated, then added, "And some make up for the—the bruises. I think I have a scarf that will work, but you're going to have to explain the one on your cheek…"

"Oh. My. God."

"What?"

Lena felt the room shrink. She stared at Evelyn.

"What? What is it?"

"My…my car. Evelyn. We left my car parked outside Sean's house. My purse and keys are on his coffee table."

Evelyn froze.

Lena clamped her hand over her mouth.

"Bloody, bloody hell."

****

They were so not going to get away with this. They were too freaking stupid. How could Lena completely forget about her car, parked like a billboard sign with a signed confession plastered on it outside of Sean's house? They might as well have left a note for the police to come straight to Lena's house to pick her up for questioning.

She pulled at the pink knitted sweater of Evelyn's and adjusted the scarf slung around her neck, feeling sweat dampening her back. She twisted the heat all the way to cold and pulled the seatbelt away from her chest. "This is so stupid, Evelyn. We should just go right to the police," she said, for what felt like the umpteenth time.

"I told you. I just need the day. I need to figure out

how much trouble we are in."

"Pretty sure the answer is a lot. We are in a lot of trouble!"

Evelyn shot her a look. "Don't be snarky. Maybe this is our chance, to go back and move the body and—"

"Are you insane? Move the body where, Evelyn? Across the field in broad daylight? Why are you so intent on covering this up? It's the stupidest option!"

Why did she listen to Evelyn last night? She was clearly out of her mind. They should have called the police immediately. This nightmare would be over, or at least would be dealt with. They could have been home right now knowing they did all they could instead of feeling like a French nobleman kneeling at the guillotine waiting for the inevitable drop.

"Let's stop going in circles. We will get your car, go about our day, and go from there. Alright?" Evelyn glanced over at her. "And we must—above all else—stay calm."

"I suppose we should just 'keep calm and carry on'," Lena said in a terrible British accent.

"Quite right."

Lena snorted, her chest heaving. She didn't feel one ounce of calm. She felt like a panic attack was just one breath away. She closed her eyes and tried to focus on her breathing.

In.
Out.
In.
Out.
"We're here."
Fuck.

Lena opened her eyes. There her car was, sitting outside Sean's house. No swarming police yet, at least.

"Just go get your purse, then walk casually to your car. Get in and drive off. It's going to be fine," Evelyn said, but she sounded nervous. Both her hands were clutching the steering wheel.

"Right. Okay." Lena unbuckled her seatbelt and clutched the door handle.

"And Lena."

She turned.

"You promised, remember. Give me today and I'll come up with a plan. Maybe turning ourselves in is best, but we have to know it is before we do. Okay?"

Lena could see it just then—Evelyn's age. The dark circles under her eyes from not sleeping, the wrinkles on her face. She looked old and frail. And scared. Evelyn was just trying to do what was best, in the worst situation she'd ever been in.

"Okay." Lena whispered. She opened the door and propelled herself out.

She hitched up the pair of jeans she'd borrowed from Evelyn, which were much too big around the waist, and took long strides across the street, feeling as nonchalant as a mouse in a crowd of cats. She hesitated just for a second at the door, before twisting the knob and letting herself in.

The house was quiet. Of course it was quiet. No one lived here anymore. There was a faint smell of pot still lingering in the air. The glasses they'd been drinking from were sitting on the coffee table with her purse and Sean's phone. She stared at the two cups. Should she do something about that? If a cop walked in here, they could easily deduce that Sean had someone over for drinks…would that even matter? It's not like they had her DNA sample…But maybe that would lead them to ask the neighbors about who'd been over recently? Of course they would do that anyway probably…

Ah, piss it.

Lena grabbed the two cups and moved to the sink. She washed them both quickly and put them still wet back in the cupboard. Heart pounding, Lena went back to the living room and grabbed her purse. She flung the strap over her shoulder than stopped, staring at Sean's phone.

There would be texts on there from Lena dating back a few months. A phone call between them right before she came over last night.

She hesitated for the briefest moment before grabbing the phone and stuffing it in her purse. She left quickly, shutting the door firmly behind her. Grabbing her keys, she jammed the unlock button and was just reaching for the handle when the booming voice of Mr. Wright made her jump and slam into the door.

"Ms. Wilson! Didn't think I'd see you here again." He stood on the other side of his precious hedge in a bathrobe, thin gray hair slightly swaying in the wind.

Lena turned, fully aware of her cheeks glowing. "Morning, Mr. Wright. I was just picking up something I forgot…to pack. When we moved. When my parents moved, I mean. Something they forgot."

"Quite the bruise you got there."

Lena's hand fluttered to the scarf around her neck, then she remembered her cheek and her hand flew to it. "Oh, it's nothing, I, uh, fell off my bike."

Stupid! Why didn't she come up with an excuse for the bruise?

Mr. Wright folded his massive arms across his chest, a frown on his face. "Uh-huh. I noticed your car was here last night. You're not involved with that boy again, are ya?"

Shit. Shit. Shit.

"N-no. No. That wasn't me. My car. I just grabbed something. Sean isn't home."

Stop talking! Lena clamped her mouth shut. Heat throbbed off her face, which she was sure was as crimson as ever.

"Well, I sure hope you aren't. You can do better than that, Ms. Wilson. I know your parents would agree."

"No—yes. I'm not. No worries there."

Mr. Wright raised his eyebrow.

"Right, well. Have a good day." Lena yanked the door open.

"We sure miss having your parents live next door," Mr. Wright said. "They were good neighbors. How are they enjoying the city?"

"Oh, good. I think. They like it good."

"Good, good. Tell them I say hi will you?"

"Sure. See ya, Mr. Wright."

"Not too soon, I hope," he said, pointedly.

Lena let out a shrill laugh, then got in the car. She backed out, not daring to look at Evelyn as she flew past and down the street.

That was horrible.

Mr. Wright definitely thought she was dating Sean. He saw her car there last night. Saw her now acting like a nervous wreck. The cops would question him when the body got discovered and he would immediately give them Lena's name. She could hear it now. *Yeah, the Wilson's girl. She seemed mighty jumpy this morning.*

Her car was parked there all night too. She tried to lie about it and about this bruise on her cheek…

And now, of course, she had Sean's phone.

Stupid, stupid, stupid.

Things were getting steadily worse.

Lena's phone rang. She pushed the Bluetooth answer button. "That was horrible. I definitely made everything worse."

"Lena?"

Not Evelyn.

"Mom! Hi! Sorry, I thought someone else was calling." Lena scrambled. "What's up?"

"Is everything okay? What was horrible? What is worse?"

"Nothing, nothing. Just—uh—work. I'll tell you about it when we meet, at eleven, right?"

"Okay…" Her mom sounded suspicious. "I was just calling to see if I should pick up something for an early lunch?"

Lena's phone beeped with another call.

"Sure, great, mom. Anything is fine. See you soon!" Lena hung up and answered. "Evelyn?"

"Lena! What did you say to that man? I told you not to talk to anyone."

"I couldn't just ignore him!"

"Was it bad?"

"Very bad. He knows my car was there all night. Evelyn, we are in deep shit."

Evelyn was quiet, then said, "Okay. Don't panic. I'll be in touch later." Then hung up.

Don't panic. How was she not supposed to panic! Lena breathed in deep through her nose, out through her mouth in several rapid successions like a woman giving birth.

Evelyn frickn' better make good on her promise to come up with a plan today, or Lena was going to be the next body discovered, having imploded from sheer stress.

CHAPTER TWENTY-EIGHT

Evelyn was going to come up with a plan.

She always did.

Not necessarily to cover up a murder—but really—problem solving was problem solving whether it was for the library board, her children's marriages, or a dead body on the banks of the river.

Whether they should have called the police last night or not was irrelevant. What was done was done. She now had to figure out how much trouble they would be in if they turned themselves in now. Or how to convince the police that Lena's car there overnight had nothing to do with what happened—which felt like a long shot, but Evelyn had promised Lena she would take care of her, and she would.

It would be an easier task to accomplish if Evelyn could get rid of the pounding headache that made her forehead feel as if it was made of cement. It would also be easier if she didn't feel like there was this pressure building and building that was going to crush her at any moment.

She should have taken the sleeping pill to get some rest last night. She had intended too, but she couldn't quiet her mind enough to want sleep. Then she found herself watching crime TV on her smart phone, which certainly did not help anything—in fact, it might have made things worse. She'd finally gotten up to get a glass of water and then next thing she knew she was bringing out the flour and tying an apron around her waist.

Oh well.

Now, Evelyn was sitting on a bench downtown waiting for her daughters to show up. She tried to get out of meeting them, but they were insistent, saying if she wouldn't come meet them then they would show up at her door. Not willing to face her daughters in her disaster of a kitchen, Evelyn drove straight from Redwood to downtown Red Deer. Her foot jiggled up and down as she scanned the sidewalk for her daughters.

She really didn't have time for this.

There were a few people walking downtown this morning: some dressed in suits moving with determined purpose to their important jobs, others leisurely popping in and out of stores laden with shopping bags full of things they likely didn't need. She watched them as they walked past, their lives feeling so distant from hers now. She used to be one of those normal people, with normal worries and fears. Now she was separate. Separate from society, damaged and haunted by an action that was unforgivable.

But it was unavoidable, we had to. Wasn't it? The details seemed foggy now. Whenever she thought back to last night, all she saw was the boy's face, his blank eyes, and all that blood...

She shivered and fumbled with the top button of her back-up fall overcoat, then rubbed her hands together—missing her leather gloves. There was a chill this morning, nothing compared to how the weather would be in a month from now when waiting outside would be unthinkable, but she was certain her shivering body had little to do with the temperature and more to do with the panic building on her insides.

She was itching to google something that might give her some sort of direction, but she felt certain it would be a bad idea to have her phone connected to that type of history. They could find that, couldn't they? Even if she deleted it? She was sure she'd seen a crime TV episode where the search history on the suspect's phone had been crucial to the case. So it must be possible to get that type of thing off a phone…And if it came to them needing to keep covering it up, she didn't want to make it too easy for them to piece together what happened…

"Mom, there you are. We were waiting by the bench across the way."

Evelyn startled as Alice and Sarah approached, each wearing their own overcoat. Sarah's black and Alice's gray. Alice had her hair swept up in a clip, Sarah's short blonde hair was the same as ever. They each wore a pair of leather gloves that she had bought them. It was funny that under all this stress, her brain still registered and— if she were honest—judged what her daughters were wearing. She supposed some instincts were harder to suppress than others.

She took a deep breath, winced a little as her brain rocked against her skull, then got to her feet and offered them a smile. "Hello there, what's so urgent you forced me out on this brisk morning?"

Sarah gave her a quick hug, then studied her face. "You alright, mom? You look a bit peckish."

"Do I? I had trouble sleeping last night. I'm a little tired, actually." Truth enough. Evelyn saw the look exchanged between her daughters and frowned. "Really, what's going on? I have a lot to do today."

"Why don't we go get a coffee? It's cold out, isn't

it?" Alice said.

They crossed the street and walked down to their favorite locally owned coffee shop. It was a small space made homey with dark green walls and wood trim, typical coffee shop art on the walls, and a dozen tables spread around. They often would meet here for coffee and spend a couple hours chatting before walking around downtown. The warmth infused with coffee beans and baked goods hit Evelyn as they pushed open the door. The smell usually made her mouth water, but today it just made her feel slightly sick. She ordered a plain green tea and then took a seat while the lattes were made, jiggling her leg up and down and checking the news on her phone. Nothing yet…

The chairs scraped back as Alice and Sarah sat. Evelyn clicked her phone off. "So, what's this all about?"

"Right to the point, eh?" said Sarah.

"I told you that I have a lot going on today."

"Like what?" Sarah said. "Shopping? Baking? This is a little more important than that. Or is it meddling in my marriage that's on today's agenda? Thanks for those emails about the marriage retreats, by the way." She added with unmistakable sarcasm.

"Just because I don't have a job, doesn't mean I don't have things to do," Evelyn said, choosing to ignore the marriage jib.

"Sarah, stop." Alice fiddled with her lid of her latte. "Mom…we're worried about you. You've been out of sorts since you got back from England."

"And last night," Sarah interjected. "Going off the grid like that—you never do that. We think you might be avoiding us. I mean, I know I was avoiding *you*, but it's not like you to be the one avoiding *us*."

Evelyn frowned. "Don't be ridiculous, I'm not avoiding you. Just because I don't answer the phone for one night doesn't mean anything."

Alice leaned forward. "You've been reclusive since the trip mom, don't deny it. We initially thought something happened with Lena—"

"Which, we think it was beyond weird that you brought her with you," said Sarah.

"What? How did you know Lena came with me?"

"I mean, one of us could have gone, or one of the kids if you wanted company," Sarah continued.

"It wasn't about needing company. Lena and I are friends," Evelyn said. "You two need to get over that. How did you know she came?"

"Okay, but still, you have been odd since the trip, mom. It's not been like you." Alice glanced at Sarah, then continued. "We were worried, so we...did some digging."

"What are you talking about?"

"It's obvious you are keeping something from us," Sarah said. "At first we were worried maybe it was a health thing that you were trying to protect us from knowing about."

"Of course you did," Evelyn said. "It's always a health thing with us old folks, isn't it? Girls, I really must be going." She made to stand.

"We know about Edwin, mom!" Alice blurted.

Evelyn blinked. "What?" After all that had happened between last night and telling Lena about Doug, Edwin was the furthest thing from her mind and the last thing she expected to come out of her daughter's mouth.

"We were worried, so we called Mavis to ask if she has seen you and why you might be acting so weird."

"You talked to Mavis? When?" Mavis texted her this morning saying to call. Evelyn completely forgot about that…what did Mavis say to them?

"This morning. You were being so strange last night…anyway she told us all about it," said Sarah.

"About what?"

"Edwin!"

"That's it? Just Edwin?"

Alice nodded. "Well, about him, and that Lena went on the trip with you—"

"What do you mean 'just Edwin'?" Sarah said. "Is there some other major life thing going on that you aren't telling us?"

If only they knew.

"No, no. I'm just surprised is all." Mavis told them about Edwin, not about telling Lena about Doug…not that it mattered anymore. Maybe Mavis thought it was the lesser of the two to divulge. Though she could have just said nothing, but even Evelyn knew that wasn't much of a possibility. Mavis could never resist the opportunity to gossip, which was why the girls called her to start with. Well, at least Mavis tried to warn Evelyn, she supposed.

"You saw him, didn't you? In England," said Alice.

"It's okay, mom. You don't have to hide that you are…dating? Are you dating?" Sarah said.

"We just want you to be happy," Alice said. "You don't have to hide it from us."

"I…" Evelyn's mind whirled, trying to keep up. "Right, yes. I did see him. We aren't dating, we are just friends but—I don't know if we are even that to be honest. I just—"

"But would you move to England?" Sarah asked. "Because I am not sure about that, leaving all your family—"

"Sarah!" Alice said. "We weren't going to bring that up today. We are just here to let mom know, that no matter what we support her."

"I…" A lumped formed in Evelyn's throat. Would they say the same if they knew what she'd done last night? Would they support her then? For a moment she imagined telling them, *I killed someone last night. He was attacking Lena. We had no choice. But I did it, I killed him.* She imagined their faces turning pale, their encouraging smiles slipping off to be replaced by fear and confusion.

The contradictory truth hit her hard—she could never tell them and also, she could not sit across from them and act normal the rest of her life. She couldn't live this lie.

"Oh, girls."

"Mom…are you crying? Are you okay?" Sarah stared, alarmed.

"I'm fine…just a long night last night." Evelyn sniffled. "Goodness. Sorry."

"It's okay, mom." Alice reached across and grabbed her hand. "We just wanted you to know you don't have to hide anything from us. We are happy for you. And if Edwin doesn't work out, we think it's great you're even thinking about dating. You don't need to be alone."

Evelyn nodded and cleared her throat. "Right…thanks, girls. I appreciate that. I—you don't have to worry about Edwin though, it's not—it's not a thing to worry about." She needed to get out of here before she fully cracked up. She sniffed and feigned checking the time on her phone. "I'm sorry, I do have to go. Thanks for this, though. I appreciate it."

She stood and gave them both a hug before forgetting her untouched tea and hurrying out the door. She walked in the direction her car was parked, arms wrapped tight around herself, a mix of emotions raging war inside. Edwin, Doug, her family, Lena, Sean, jail…Sadness mixed with fear, warm love colliding with consuming guilt. She paused and leaned against the side of a brick building, breathing hard.

"Come on, Evelyn. Get it together," she muttered.

Right. She could do this. She was English for god sakes—more than that—she was Cornish! She didn't *do* public breakdowns. It was against her DNA. A few more steadying breaths, then Evelyn straightened her back. She continued on but stopped again when she realized what building she was standing outside of. The Public Library. Perfect! There's got to be something helpful in there. Maybe she could use one of the computers at the very least…

Evelyn pushed open the glass door and entered. The welcoming smell of books and paper comforted her. Here was knowledge, here was finally something that would help. She made a split-second decision and headed into the row of books. If she couldn't find anything here, she would try the internet, but this felt like the safer option.

As nonchalantly as possible, Evelyn made her way over to the true crime section. There was a great deal of biographies on serial killers which didn't seem helpful. A couple about school shootings, predators, kidnapping tales…gosh, this was grim.

She grabbed a couple that had self-defense in the title and flipped through them, losing hope with each book. Snapping the last shut, she shoved it back on the shelf and marched over to the computers.

She glanced around. Only a few people were in the library today, a couple of college students sitting at a table studying and a mom with her toddlers over in the kid section. She opened up a web page and typed: *if you don't claim self-defense right away, can you go to jail?*

Immediately an article popped up about Canadian Self-Defense laws. She clicked on it and scanned the article. There were various types of examples of self-defense cases: from bar fights, to robberies, to assaults. The consensus seemed to be it was up to the judge to decide if it was a case of self-defense, which it was if the person had reasonable grounds to believe they or someone else was going to be harmed, the act was made to protect themselves or someone else, or the act committed was reasonable for the circumstances.

Evelyn blew a breath out between her lips. She was sure they would meet that criteria...though it seemed to be up to the Judge to decide. What she was concerned about was that they didn't have a third-party witness...And they left without saying anything and got rid of the murder weapons...In hindsight that might not have been the best call—but the Judge would understand the panic they'd been under, right? They were in shock! No one could think straight after being a part of something like that...

Yes, the best thing to do would be to go to the police and lead them to the body. They still had time. That would show they were innocent of any wrongdoing...right? Evelyn leaned back.

She had no idea. What she needed was to talk to a police officer, who would not arrest her, and have them tell her what to do.

Something was nagging at the back of her mind. What was it? Why couldn't she think of it—

Edwin. That's what it was. Edwin had a brother who was a policeman in London.

Evelyn grabbed her phone and opened their messages. He had responded a few times to the goodbye one she had sent yesterday (was it really just yesterday? It felt like a million years ago). She ignored them and typed as quick as she could, saying she had an emergency and asked if he could take a phone call in half an hour.

Then she stuffed the phone back in her purse, exited out of the web page and hurried to the door.

CHAPTER TWENTY-NINE

The door to the condo banged open as Lena yanked her keys out of the lock and kicked off her shoes at the bottom of the steps. She took the steps two at a time then went to her bedroom, unraveled Evelyn's scarf, pulled the sweater and jeans off, and replaced them with her own clothes before dashing to the bathroom. There she leaned close to the mirror, examining the bruise on her cheekbone. It was darker than last night, a greeny-yellow tinge taking over the edges and spreading up to her eye. She touched it softly and winced. It looked a bit swollen. More make-up would not be an answer for this. She was going to have to stick to her lame story and hope her mom wouldn't interrogate her for once.

Unless she just told her everything.

The possibility of confessing to her mom dangled temptingly in her mind. She felt for a split second, the sheer relief of telling someone what happened, of spreading the burden so it didn't feel so heavy on her.

But she couldn't—not yet. She'd promised Evelyn she would give her one day. Then Lena would tell, she would have to. This was too big of a secret to keep.

One day, she told herself firmly.

She could get through one day.

Lena pulled her hair up into a messy bun, and just finished adjusting the scarf around her neck when her doorbell rang. She went to the living room just as her mom was opening the door.

"Hello? Selena? The door was unlocked."

"Come up!" Lena called.

Her mom was out of breath by the time she reached the top. Lena hurried to help with the take-out bags and set them on the counter. The smell of Chinese food filled the little condo and probably her downstairs neighbor's as well.

"Goodness, I hope your next house has less stairs. I don't know how you manage bringing in your groceries all the time." Her mom brushed her hair behind her ear and shrugged off her jacket. "I just came from Roy and Carrie's. They want to have you over for dinner to hear about your trip."

"Sure they do," Lena said, taking the containers out.

"They do. You know, you should make more of an effort to go see them." Her mom came around to the island. "They say they've barely seen you since— Selena! What happened to your face?"

Lena carefully avoided eye contact. "I fell off my bike."

"And hit your face?"

"I landed funny."

"It looks horrible."

"It's not that bad, mom." She could feel her mom studying her and tried again, "It's not a big deal. Thanks for getting all this food."

She went to grab some plates, but her mom stopped her with a gentle hand on her arm. "Selena, honey, are you sure you're alright? You sounded so strange on the phone."

"I'm just stressed. From quitting my job and everything." Lena could hear the lie in her own voice.

"Right…can we sit for a minute? I'm not hungry for lunch yet." Her mom went to the couch and sat down expectantly.

Lena followed slowly behind. The same dreaded feeling crept into her stomach that she used to get as a teenager when she knew her mom was going to try to pry information out of her. She was never very good at hiding things.

"So, why'd you quit?"

Lena's heart slammed into her ribcage at the echo of the question Sean had asked her last night as he poured her first drink. For a moment she was back there, seeing his hands offering the drink, his knowing stare, the pot floating from his lips…

"Selena?"

"Oh, sorry." Lena blinked. "I'm a bit tired. Um. I just—well—my boss is a jerk. He just pushed me too far, I guess." She felt impatient having to go over all this. It felt so trivial now, so inconsequential in the grand scheme of things. She'd gotten mad at a comment made by her boss and quit a job she didn't enjoy anyways. Who cared. What Lena really wanted was for her mom to leave so she could go find Evelyn and figure out what they were going to do.

Her mom settled into the couch. Lena suppressed a sigh. "He's always been a jerk," her mom said, ready to analyze everything. "That's not changed. What made you quit?"

"I guess I'm just ready for a change."

"What will you do now?"

"I don't know yet. I don't have a plan." Lena shifted on the couch. "I'll figure it out, mom. You don't have to worry about me. Do you want some lunch?"

"Not yet." Her mom's eyes narrowed. "There must have been something that boosted you in that direction. I've been trying to get you to quit since you started. You've never enjoyed it there."

"Mom, please. There's nothing to read into here. I just wanted to quit."

"Fine. How was your trip? You've barely told me anything about it."

Lena sighed. "It was good, mom."

"Don't sound so irritated. I just want to know how it went."

"Sorry. It was…great." Lena thought for a moment. "Actually, I loved it. There's so much history over there and…it's so different. I really loved it." A longing swept through her. She wished she was there now. Was it really just last week that they were touring around England and the biggest issue in Lena's life was the past and her lack-luster future? Now they were getting rid of murder weapons and debating how much jail time they could get. She wished she could step back in time—back to when life was mostly boring.

She missed boring.

Lena tried to suppress those thoughts and continued on, "London was amazing. We could have easily spent the whole time there. St. Ives was beautiful, though. It felt like a place that I didn't know I always needed to visit. I met this Scottish girl on the docks who let me use her paints. It was the first time I picked up a brush in—I don't know, since college."

"You painted?"

"A little. Actually, it made me really miss it. I have been planning on picking up some new art supplies and—what?"

"Oh, honey." Her mom brushed a tear aside that suddenly filled her eyes. "I'm so thrilled to hear that."

"Why?"

"It's just…you haven't been you, in so long. You know?"

Lena sat quiet.

"I don't mean to offend." Her mom rushed to say. "It's just, I feel like you have been coasting along and not…passionate like you used to be. I'm sorry, I know you have been through a lot."

"No, it's okay." Lena stared at her hands. "I actually have been thinking lately, maybe James wasn't exactly…encouraging with—"

"Anything."

"Mom."

"Well…"

"The point is…I know I haven't really been myself in a while. I'm actually not sure if I ever figured out what—who that is. Even with Cheryl I—" Lena stopped. She couldn't talk about Cheryl now. Not with everything that had just happened. Lena would break down for sure.

Her mom took her hand. "You're a gentle soul, Lena, you've always been that way. You've always gravitated towards strong-willed people. But that doesn't mean you're not strong. You'll find your way—I know you will. You need to be careful who you surround yourself with though."

Lena swallowed. "Thanks, mom."

"What about this Evelyn? She seems to be a good influence on you, getting you to go all the way to England and everything. You haven't told me much about her."

"She's…"

A seventy-year-old baker.

The widow to the man who killed James.

My accomplice.

None of those seemed to be a great first impression to give. "Very spunky," Lena said finally.

"Spunk is good. I'd like to meet her. Let's all have dinner soon."

"Right...I'll see."

"Well!" Her mom stood up. "This is an exciting time for you. You have the world at your feet now. No attachments, no job. Who knows what you will do next?"

"Yeah." Who knew indeed...The respite from reality ended and the rush of stress filled her up again. She clasped her hands to keep them from trembling.

Her mom moved towards the island. "Let's eat. Maybe after lunch you can tell me what actually happened to your face."

"Mom."

"I'm not an idiot, Lena," she said as she grabbed the plates.

Lena sat at the island. "I'm not ready to talk about it yet, okay?"

Her mom paused, "If someone is hurting you..."

"I'm okay, mom. Please. If I was in trouble, I'd tell you." Lena tried to look innocent under her mom's gaze. She felt like the worst daughter in the world.

"Okay," her mom said. "Dish up then. I have a nail appointment in half an hour I can't be late for. Do you want to come?"

"No, thanks. I think I'll just stay home and contemplate my life choices."

"Don't contemplate too much. That's a recipe for depression." Her mom sat down and scooped noodles and beef onto her plate.

"Yeah, I know." Lena filled her own plate and sat beside her.

Her mom took her phone out of her pocket and started scanning through some texts. She gasped suddenly. "No!"

"What?" Lena chewed on a piece of ginger beef. "Carrie needs you to babysit again? You're over there every day, mom. Maybe you should tell her—"

"They found a body by the river in Redwood!"

Lena froze. "What did you say?"

"A body! I've got a dozen texts from people. Oh, my word. How horrible."

No.

No, no, no.

It was happening. Lena had known it would, but it still felt like someone upturned a bucket of ice water over her.

"Do they…know who it is?"

"Not yet. Someone found it while jogging, I guess. The police haven't released any information yet—but Mrs. Henderson talked to that girl. Oh, what's her name? The one who works at the gas station?"

"Haley." Lena said, numbness spreading.

"Right, Haley, who heard from someone who talked to the person who found the body that it definitely wasn't natural causes. Can you believe it? In Redwood!" Her mom shook her head. "What is the world coming to? Oh god, I wonder who it is." She began texting furiously.

Lena watched her, feeling as if she was floating outside her own body. A weird buzzing filled her ears, dimming the continuous commentary from her mother.

Very slowly, she took out her own phone and texted Evelyn.

—*They found him.*—

CHAPTER THIRTY

Evelyn stared at the mess in her kitchen.

Bowls with dried batter were stacked in the sink, empty egg cartons with shells littered about. Flour dusted the counters with used whisks, spilled sugar, and an empty milk jug. Not to mention all the finished baking that was haphazardly covered. Muffins and loafs…the cinnamon bun dough still rising in the bowl.

It looked like a mad baker had been put into overdrive. Which she supposed is exactly what had happened. It disturbed her to see it like this, so out of order and chaotic. It wasn't like her to have chaos in her life. It went against everything she'd trained herself to be over the years. She stared for a minute longer at what was usually her safe-haven then went to the cupboard and grabbed some acetaminophen. She threw two back, swallowed without water, then set about making a cup of coffee.

She was just pouring the hot water over the grinds in her French press when her phone rang. She looked at the caller I.D. and answered, "Hello, traitor."

"Oh, no. They talked to you already? I told you to call me this morning." Mavis sounded frantic. "I've been waiting for you to call, but then I thought you probably weren't calling because you are just so mad! Are you mad?"

"I'm not mad. It's alright."

"It is not! They accosted me, I'll have you know. They would not leave me be until I gave them something. I am so sorry."

"It's fine, Mavis."

"Are you sure? I feel just awful for telling them about Edwin. I didn't say much, by the way. Just that you were talking."

Evelyn's stomach rolled at his name. She checked the time quick. She was supposed to call him in two minutes. "Don't worry about a thing, darling. We had a good chat. Do you mind if I call you later? I'm just in the middle of something."

"Okay, good. I'm so relieved. Yes, call me later."

Evelyn hung up and stared at the darkening brew. Unable to wait any longer, she pressed down the handle, smashing the grinds to the bottom, then poured herself a cup. She brought it with her to the living room, setting it on a coaster on the side table. She scrolled through her contacts to his name, then breathed in deep through her nose and let it whistle out her clenched teeth.

Just do it. Call him.

Tell him.

Once she did, there was no going back. Someone else would know.

She felt awful. How she was using him now after just ending things. It felt terribly manipulative, but it was what it was. She needed help and had nowhere else to turn. Maybe this was why they were brought into each other's lives in the first place—not for companionship to battle the feelings of loneliness in their last years on this earth, but to be a resource to help Evelyn get out of this pickle. It felt a little better to think this was what fate had intended. She was less of an awful human that way.

One more breath and Evelyn hit the dial button. She only waited two rings before he picked up.

"Hello."

His deep rumbling voice trembled through her. She always loved men's voices, their baritones so manly and sure. She clutched the phone to her ear. "Edwin. Hi."

There was a pause. "I must admit, I'm surprised you're calling, after I read your last message."

"I know—I'm sorry. I wouldn't be, except, I'm in a bit of trouble."

"What sort of trouble?"

She swallowed hard. "I have some questions I was wondering if you could pass along to your brother."

"My brother?"

"The one who works as a police officer? I'm afraid I am in need of some advice."

He paused again before he answered. "Right. Okay. Let's hear it then."

"Maybe, we will say it's about a hypothetical situation." Evelyn got up and paced around the room.

"Evie, what's going on?"

"We may have got into some trouble, Lena and I."

"What kind of trouble?"

"Maybe, bad trouble?"

"What happened?"

Deep breath. "Well, let's say—hypothetically—a woman saw a young man attacking another woman. So, she—um—she takes a rock and hits him with it. Then let's say the woman who was being attacked, also hits him with a—bottle."

Silence. Then, "Did the young man die? Hypothetically."

"Yes, I'm afraid so."

"Sounds like self-defense."

"Right, yes. But say, the women might have panicked and threw away the weapons and left the body—well moved the body a little—and now it's the next day and they are wondering what to do."

"Bleddy."

"Right." Evelyn waited. "Um…you still there?"

"Aye."

"Could you maybe call your brother? Now? Maybe just ask what would happen if they go to the police now."

"Right. Okay. I'll give you a shout back."

The phone went dead.

Evelyn stood still for a minute, her heart pounding.

Right. That wasn't so bad. Now all she had to do was wait and—

A text on her phone stopped her thoughts. Stopped everything.

—*They found him.*—

They found the body. Time was closing in on them. It wouldn't be long before they identified him as Sean, then started asking around. Before they found out about Lena being there that night…

Evelyn sat heavily on the couch. One would think at her age, she would have seen it all, dealt with it all, but this was a whole ball of wax she was not prepared to handle.

She typed back and sent:

—*It will be okay*—

She felt very much like a hypocrite.

Minutes ticked by as Evelyn sat there, cradling the phone in her hands. When it finally rang, she nearly fell off the couch. She scrambled to press the answer button. "Hello? How did it go?"

"It's a bit of a predicament."

Her heart sank

"It's obviously self-defense, but you will need to prove it. There was no witness, right? Besides the two of you."

"Right," Evelyn whispered.

"Do you know if he had priors? Any history of abuse?"

"I have no idea."

"That would help...are there markings on Lena? I mean the 'hypothetical' woman who was attacked?"

"There's bruising."

"That's good...I'm sure it will be okay, Evie." He sounded hesitant.

"But you don't know for sure? That it will be okay?"

"It should be..."

"As long as they believe us." Evelyn felt sick. They should believe them. They had no reason not too...besides the fact they tried to cover their tracks and didn't tell the police immediately what had happened...God, what had she been thinking.

"Maybe...maybe just hold off?" Edwin spoke in a low voice. "Maybe just hold off for a while and see...I don't want you to get in trouble, Evie. I'll talk to my brother some more..."

Evelyn's eyes blurred. She blinked hard, clearing her vision. This was getting more and more tangled. The longer they waited...

They couldn't wait.

It was going to get worse and worse. That was very clear now.

She didn't know what was going to happen, but she knew one thing for certain.

"I need to protect her, Edwin," Evelyn said. "She's been through so much."

Edwin was quiet.

Evelyn lifted her head. "I will protect her. I know what to do. Thank you for your help. And for—well, being a friend."

"What are you—"

She hung up.

Well, she had her plan now.

First things first, though.

Evelyn downed her lukewarm coffee, then got up and went to the kitchen. She twisted the tap, squeezed a dollop of soap into the sink, and watched as bubbles filled around the dirty dishes. The sweet smell of lemons and cleanliness rose up. She set to work—methodically working through the piles, scrubbing and rinsing away the markings of her baking. She took her time drying the dishes and putting away everything. Clearing the counter, storing the baked goods properly in containers, wiping away the flour, and sweeping the floor.

She stood back when she was done, her hands tingling from the dish soap. A bit of weight lifted off her chest.

Clean.

Orderly.

The way things should be.

Now to clean up the bigger mess.

But before she did, she needed to prepare. She wasn't exactly sure what was going to happen next, but she wanted a plan for every possible outcome, or at least, as much of a plan as she could.

She went and grabbed her laptop and opened a new email. She typed Alice and Sarah's emails at the top, then began carefully typing out what happened, start to finish. When it was done she sat back, shaking a little, then saved the email in her draft file. When it was time, she would send it. They should hear it from her.

She imagined how they would react when they read it. Sarah would initially dismiss it as a weird joke—she never took her seriously. Alice would call and call, leaving voicemails and texts, and then she would call Sarah and freak them both out. Evelyn's main worry was Sarah. She had a tough outer shell but was so incredibly fragile on the inside…She was already going through so much with her marriage and mental health and her last kid graduating this year…Evelyn wavered in her conviction for a second, then straightened her back. Alice would take care of Sarah. Alice was more than capable. Right now Evelyn had to focus on the bigger problem, keeping Lena safe.

Another thought struck her—how would her daughters tell their kids? O*h, by the way, Grandma offed someone and turned herself in to the police*. Not exactly a phone call one would expect to get.

She couldn't think about that now. If she thought about her grandkids, she might not get off the couch at all.

Evelyn sent a quick text to Lena, then checked the time. Nearly noon. Perhaps she would wait a little till after lunch. Yes, one last lunch before she set a bomb off in all her loved one's lives. Then whatever would be, would be.

She hated that saying.

CHAPTER THIRTY-ONE

Lena threw out her untouched portion of Chinese food as soon as her mom left. She checked her phone for the dozenth time.

No word from Evelyn since her last text.

She was just about to call her when a text came in.

—Got a plan, will call soon—

She tapped the phone in her hand as she paced. How long ago did they find him? How quick would they identify the body? No one would report him missing—unless maybe his work if he was supposed to be there today? He was only part-time so there was a chance they wouldn't miss him yet, and it's not like there was family who would raise the alarm. There was nothing on him that would help identify him. Sean didn't have his wallet on him when they went for their walk…she was pretty sure. Why would he have brought it? He had even left his phone behind.

His phone.

Which was currently in her purse.

She should do something with that, right? Get rid of it? Delete things on it? At least check and see if someone was trying to get a hold of him…Yes, that was a good plan.

Lena lunged across the room, slamming into her coffee table in the process. "Motherfuc—" Clenching her throbbing shin, she limped in an awkward hunch the rest of the way to where her purse was hanging on the coat rack. She located his phone and clicked it on as she moved back to the living room. There was a missed phone call from an unknown number and three texts, also from the unknown number. She could only see the beginnings of them on the locked screen.

—I know you did it—
—Answer the pho…—
—Coward. You won't…—

Her stomach dropped at the sight of the first one. For a second she thought it was directed at her until she remembered it couldn't be. What the hell was this about? Someone was angry with Sean over something. Lena tried to unlock the home screen, but it was passcode protected. She cursed under her breath. So much for going in and deleting things. She stared at the messages from the unknown number. Were they wondering why Sean hadn't answered? Would they raise the alarm soon? The area code was unfamiliar. It was likely they weren't a local person—unless they moved here and kept their number the same, which she supposed most people did…

Lena took out her own phone and googled the number. No name popped up, but it said the number was from B.C. Someone from Vancouver Island, probably? A drug dealer or something. Or didn't he say his disgruntled landlord from B.C. was harassing him last night? It had felt like he was lying, though, when he'd said that. Maybe it was his ex. Sean had said he moved away because of a bad breakup…

I know you did it…what could she mean by that if it was his ex? Lena's mind whirled. What if the breakup happened because Sean got aggressive with her—what if this woman could prove that Sean had violent tendencies? She could testify for Lena and Evelyn that he was dangerous, the ex could back them up that what happened last night had been their only option. It was highly probable that she could help them out...If things started with Sean hurting Cheryl, who knew how many women he'd traumatized over the years? Lena had seen it herself, not just last night but on their date how angry he could get...

Lena pressed the phone app and dialed the number. She took a deep breath as it rang. It occurred to her a second before someone answered that she should have rehearsed what she was going to say.

"Hello?" A female voice said.

"Hello! Hi! This is—um—my name is Lena Martin. I—this might sound strange, but I was wondering—are you Sean Whitmore's ex?"

There was a pause.

Lena hurried on. "Or...you aren't his old landlord, are you? It's just—I was just wondering if maybe you knew him? He—I—we've been hanging out a bit and—um—I was just wondering if maybe you..."

"Lena, you said?"

"Yes?"

"You need to stay the hell away from that man."

Lena sucked in a breath. "You—you are his ex, then? Has he ever done something that—"

"I'm not his ex. My daughter is. Was. He—"

She could hear the woman taking deep breaths. Lena pressed the phone hard against her ear. "Please," she said. "I'm in trouble. If there's something you could tell me—anything—about him it might help."

"How did you get this number?"

"I—I took it from his phone. I saw you texted him a

few times."

The woman was quiet. Lena waited.

"Sean Whitmore," the woman said finally, her voice hard. "Murdered my little girl."

"What? He—what?"

"He murdered her. I know he did, the bastard. The police say there isn't any proof because they can't find her—her body. I know he did it though."

"H-how?"

"I knew something was off. I could see it whenever they were together. About a year after she moved in with him, Becky started pulling away from us. She was less and less herself every time I saw her. I asked her over and over to tell me what was going on. She never would say. There were bruises though, I saw bruises on her arms. I told her she needed to leave him. She wouldn't listen." Her voice got higher and higher as she talked. "Then, five months ago, he reported her as missing."

"*He* reported her missing?"

"He said she went for a walk one night and didn't come home. The police looked into it—looked into him—but they couldn't find anything. They couldn't find her. They say the investigation is still open, but there's still nothing. I know he did it though. I know he did!" At this, she began to cry.

"I'm so sorry." Lena said, horrified.

"S-so you stay away from him! Do you understand? Stay away from that psycho."

"I—I think you are right, Mrs…"

"Nelson."

"Mrs. Nelson. I've seen Sean get…violent. He's—he's tried to hurt me too." Lena said this in a whisper.

She heard Mrs. Nelson take a long, shuddering

breath. "Will you tell them that? Will you tell that to the police here? It might help…"

"I—yes, I can, but—Sean…" She wanted to tell the woman. It was on the tip of Lena's tongue. She wanted to say Sean wouldn't be hurting any more women. That Becky wasn't the first, but she *would* be the last. There was no doubt in Lena's mind that Sean had done exactly what Mrs. Nelson said he did. It made Lena's stomach twist. "Mrs. Nelson…I am so sorry for what Sean did. There are some things…happening here. With him. I can't tell you everything right now, but I will soon. If— I might need your help, too. If you are willing."

"Yes, of course. I'll do anything."

The desperation in her voice made Lena want to weep. She thanked her and ended the call. Lena's hands trembled. That could have been her. So easily. If Evelyn wasn't crazy and followed them out there, Lena would have been just another Becky Nelson. Just another Cheryl. Another woman Sean hurt. Not hurt, *murdered.*

Sean's last words echoed again, *you bitches all die the same.*

God. How many were there? Had Sean left a trail of bodies since he disappeared all those years ago? There was clearly some sort of pattern going on…It was horrifying to think of.

Becky Nelson…the name felt familiar. Like she should recognize it. Lena opened her phone again and searched her name. The results came in immediately. News articles of a missing twenty-eight-year-old woman, Becky Nelson from Victoria, B.C. The picture made Lena's heart stop. Blonde hair, blue eyes—her look so similar to Cheryl it was nauseating.

Sean clearly had a type.

Lena scanned a few of the articles. Most of them were several months old. The story had been resurrected last month when the Nelson family made a plea to the police to do more, but other than that there was nothing.

What did Sean do with the body? Was Becky somewhere at the bottom of the Pacific Ocean? Buried in the forest? The image of Sean dragging a Cheryl looking girl across the ground made Lena want to vomit.

She needed to tell Evelyn about this. This could only help them if—when—they talked to the police.

Lena was just about to call when her phone rang. A long, unknown number calling. She picked up. "Hello?"

"Lena?"

"Edwin?" Lena said, confused. "Hi. What's—how did you get my number?"

"I remembered you worked at the paper, and I called there, they gave me your cell." He sounded out of breath. "Listen, Evelyn called me, she told me what happened."

"She did?" Lena clenched the phone.

"Yes, she did. She's not answering my calls now, is she with you?"

"No. I was just about to call—"

"Bollocks. Lena, I think Evelyn is going to the police."

"What? Did she tell you that?"

"She was going on about protecting you. I think she is going there now and is going to take the fall for it. For everything."

Lena started. "No—no, she said she has a plan and is going to call me. She—you think she is going there now?"

"I'm positive. Lena, can you stop her? She's really worried about you getting in trouble. I think she will confess to just about anything to make sure you're okay…"

"Right. Okay. Yes, I'll find her. Thanks Edwin." Lena hung up. She grabbed her purse and pounded down the steps, quickly jamming her feet in her boots and launching out the door.

Her neighbor was sitting on his porch step having a smoke. "How's it—"

"Not now!" Lena snapped, running to her car and yanking it open. She tried calling Evelyn as she drove, but it went to voicemail.

"What the hell are you doing, Evelyn." Lena muttered, tapping impatiently on the wheel at a red light. What did Edwin mean, Evelyn would say anything to protect her? Was Evelyn going to flat out lie, pretend Lena wasn't even there? What was she thinking? This was so like Evelyn to just take charge and leave everyone else to play catch-up. Lena imagined Evelyn sitting at a stainless-steel table in a dark room with one of those one-way windows, a police officer across from her, her elegantly gloved hands in handcuffs before her…The image made Lena hit her gas pedal hard and lurch forward as soon as the light turned.

She pulled into the police station parking lot. Someone was standing in front of the building. Was it? Yes! There was no mistaking that long silver braid.

Lena parked right in front, not bothering to turn the engine off, and launched out of the car. "Evelyn! Evelyn, what do you think you're doing?"

Evelyn turned, startled. "Lena? What are you doing here?"

"What am I doing? What are *you* doing? Were you really going to go in without me?"

"I—yes. I am." She drew herself up. "I was just taking a minute to collect myself, then I am going in."

"Not without me." Lena stood, breathless beside her.

Evelyn frowned. "Where is your coat? It's far too cold to go running around without a jacket."

"What were you thinking, Evelyn?" Lena said. "Why didn't you tell me you were coming here?"

"Because there's no need for you to come. I've got this handled."

"You aren't going in there without me."

"Yes. I am. I'm going to make a deal with them. I am going to tell them I have information about the body found in Redwood. I'll say that I will tell them everything if they promise you won't get in any sort of trouble."

"Evelyn—"

"I think it will be okay." Evelyn kept on. "It *was* self-defense—but just in case—you need to stay out of it until it's for certain."

"Evelyn, I'm not going to let you—"

"Yes, you are." Evelyn snapped. "You are, Lena. I won't have it any other way. Understand? It was my fault this whole thing got dragged out. I was the one who hit him—"

"You saved me." Lena was crying now. She wiped her tears away impatiently. "I would be dead if it wasn't for you."

"Then you owe me, and I'm calling it in. You will remain outside this police station until you hear from me. Understand?" Evelyn took a deep breath, then said a little more gently, "It's going to be alright. Okay? I promise. Now, you know I am far more stubborn than you, let's

335

not keep going in circles."

Lena wiped her nose on her sleeve and laughed a little with a sniff. "True."

"Good. So. I'm just going too—" Evelyn took out her phone. She seemed to hesitate a second, then tapped the screen and turned her phone off. "There. Just needed to send an email. Okay, well. I'll just—"

"Tell them about Becky Nelson," Lena said. "She was his girlfriend from Vancouver Island. She went missing and her mom is certain Sean was involved. She said she is sure he abused her. Tell them to check into that, okay? It might—help."

Evelyn nodded. "That's good. That will help back us up."

They stared at each other.

"This is…"

"I know." Evelyn moved and wrapped her arms around her. She smelled like cinnamon. "I know it is."

"Can I help you?"

They jumped a part. A police officer had walked up behind them, a coffee in his hand. He looked between them quizzically.

"Yes." Evelyn tilted her chin up. "Indeed, you can. I must speak with someone about—well—a body."

The police officer's eyebrows rose, clearly taken back. "Oh. Right, okay. You can just—follow me."

"Excellent."

Lena stood with her hands dangling uselessly at her side as Evelyn disappeared into the building. A cold gust pressed against her back, blowing her hair across her face. She shivered, wrapping her arms around herself, but she couldn't move. She stood in front of the building, her car idling behind her as she waited.

CHAPTER THIRTY-TWO

One month later

"It is *so* good to be free."

Lena snorted, popping a few pieces of popcorn from the bottom of the bag in her mouth. "You were never in jail, Evelyn."

"I know, but it does weigh a person down, the thought that one *could* go to jail."

"I'm not convinced that was ever a real danger." They followed the small crowd of people exiting the theater out into the dark, snowy parking lot.

"Well, that's easy to say now, on the other side of things," Evelyn said. She winced as they left the warmth behind for the cool, icy blast of winter. They fast walked across the parking lot to Evelyn's car, which thankfully started when she'd pressed the button from the theater. She slid in and jabbed on the heated seat. Lena buckled in beside her.

"Where to now? Drop me off at home?" Lena asked.

"This is my first night of freedom, we are *not* going home at nine o'clock," Evelyn said. "To the pub! Sarah is going to meet us there."

Lena chuckled. "Aren't you normally asleep by nine?"

"Recently yes, because I had nowhere else I could go." That was a bit of a lie, Evelyn usually tried to be in

337

bed by nine, regardless of having to abide by an eight o'clock curfew or not. She'd hated the indignity of it though, being told she had to be in her own house at a certain time. Especially because she felt the ridiculous stipulation had come from that bullfrog looking, eager beaver detective. It probably wasn't directly because of him, but it had felt like something that vindictive little man would do.

She'd been quite dismayed to see the detective she'd had to work with when she gave her confession. He was a rather short, young man with thinning brown hair and overly big eyes emphasized by glasses perched on a comically small nose. A man who had not much going for him looks-wise in a position of authority was never a good combination.

True enough, he seemed suspicious of everything she said and eager to lay some sort of charge. It wasn't until a nice, older detective with a sensibly portioned face came in that things started to look more positive. He'd been far more sympathetic and willing to listen to the whole story, not to mention they bonded wordlessly over their disdain for the bullfrog man.

As it was, the case had to go before a judge and Evelyn had to abide by a curfew until it did. Finally, just yesterday the judge decided Evelyn would pay a fine for Obstruction of Justice for moving the body and for trying to cover up the crime, which—she was told—was better than being charged with Indignity to a Dead Body (but really, she'd only moved it a couple feet into a little bit of water—it wasn't like she chopped it up or something. She said this to the young detective when he started throwing that charge around—he'd seemed less than impressed). All other charges had been dismissed on grounds of self-defense, which was solidly backed by Lena's testimony, the pictures from that night, Mrs. Nelson's testimony, and the testimony of a girl her lawyer tracked down whom Sean used to date and had also abused.

It was as good an outcome as they could have hoped for.

Sarah was already at the pub when they arrived. She waved them over to a booth by a window.

"Hello, love." Evelyn slid into the booth and helped herself to some of her nachos.

"Hi, Sarah. How are you?" Lena said, politely.

"Fine, thanks. You?" Sarah returned.

"Good."

Evelyn chewed on her nacho, watching the exchange. Her girls still didn't know how to act around Lena. Evelyn had gotten them all together a few times in the last month. They were a bit stiff in their exchanges with her—not sure how to deal with the sadness and guilt Lena's presence brought. They would warm up soon enough though, Evelyn thought, as Lena was basically family now.

"How was the movie?" Sarah asked.

"Wonderful!" Evelyn said. "A cheery romance. Quite funny, wasn't it, Lena? We stayed away from anything too, you know, *murderery*. I'm sure you can imagine why."

"*Mom*."

"What?"

"Don't joke about—that."

"I'm not!" The movie, in fact, had been Lena's pick.

If it had been up to Evelyn, she would've preferred something murderey, or at least, not romantic. Because thinking of romance lately inevitably led her to think about her empty condo and how it could be not so empty if she would just call Edwin. He'd reached out a few times, but Evelyn was stubborn and hadn't answered. She felt bad that she'd used him in her hour of need and then stopped talking to him again. But it was better for both of them to let whatever they had started go. If they both wanted companionship, then fine, they could find that in their own parts of the world. The long-distance thing was just silly. She kept reminding herself of that whenever she caught herself thinking of him.

Which was a lot. Lately she seemed to always be thinking of him, and of St. Ives. She imagined him sitting in his pub, looking out the window at the sea. She wanted to go there, to sit with him and talk about life and death by a crackling fire with a pint in hand. She wanted to listen to his warm lilting voice laughing at her stories and eat Cornish pasties with him for lunch. Then later, she wanted him to hold her hand and lay beside her, keeping her warm—keeping her company against the loneliness of an empty bed. It was too impossible, though. Their worlds too far away. There were too many factors to solve that particular problem. She pushed those thoughts away, again.

Sarah fiddled with the edge of her plate. "Well, it's my first night of freedom too, actually."

"Oh?"

"Cam's moved out, officially."

Evelyn stiffened. Lena gently pressed her foot against her under the table. "That's…a transition," she said, as neutrally as possible. Lena had been encouraging Evelyn to be more *accepting* of things, more *supportive*, particularly of other's decisions. Lena actually was a bit of a nag about it, telling Evelyn not to comment on her daughter's impending disastrous life decision and to just *go* with it.

It was incredibly annoying.

"It is," Sarah said. "It's a big transition, but it feels right, you know?"

"Uh huh." Evelyn flagged down the server, relieved to have an excuse to change the subject. Evelyn and Lena split a pot of tea and another plate of nachos. They visited some more about light things—carefree, every day, run-of-the-mill things. It felt incredibly good, because—jokes aside—Evelyn hadn't truly been able to think of anything else until tonight, when she finally knew what the outcome was, when things felt back under her control again.

After saying goodbye to Sarah, Evelyn drove Lena back to her condo complex. They arrived just as the clock flicked to ten-thirty. Evelyn stretched and yawned. "It feels like midnight."

"Thanks for picking me up. You didn't have to do that."

Evelyn waved her hand. "Oh, it's no problem. I was actually hoping you were going to invite me in when I came to get you. I'm very curious how you live."

Lena laughed. "Do you want to come in now? I have something to give you, actually. A surprise. I was saving it for later but I can give it to you now."

"Oh, I love surprises." Evelyn got out and followed Lena. "You know, you can tell a lot about a person by the state of their house."

"Uh-huh."

Evelyn bounced on the balls of her feet and rubbed her hands together while Lena unlocked her door, their breaths puffing out white clouds around their faces. They squeezed into the little landing. Lena kicked her shoes off in a haphazard way that made Evelyn cringe. She straightened them along with her own, then followed Lena up the stairs. "My goodness, that's quite a climb," she said, a little out of breath.

"So, what do you think?" Lena spread her arms and turned around the condo.

"It's…" Evelyn peered at their surroundings.

"Boring? Plain? Small?"

"Charming. It could use a paint job, though."

"I know. What's it say about me, you think?"

Evelyn looked at Lena, standing in the middle of her tiny condo, hoody bunched around the waist of her dark jeans, her hair long and tangled from the wind. Evelyn's heart squeezed. Lena looked so young and had gone through so much. "It says you are finding yourself still," Evelyn said.

Lena laughed a quiet little laugh. "Ain't that the truth. One sec, I'll get you your surprise." She disappeared around the corner and came back out carrying a canvas, the back outward facing. "I wanted to wait until, *you know*."

"Things were settled?"

"Yes. I wanted to give you something to say thank you for—well—lots of things." Lena tucked her hair behind her ear. "You know I've been taking some lessons. I'm still quite rusty. But I wanted to give you—"

"For Pete's sake, let me see it!"

Lena laughed nervously and flipped the canvas around.

Evelyn inhaled. "Oh Lena, it's—it's just beautiful."

It was a painting of a golden wheat field, the sun slowly rising, casting colors all across the sky. A flock of birds were flying in a great clump in the distance—Evelyn could almost see their swirling pattern, how they would move in and out, dancing around each other in perfectly synchronized chaos.

She moved and gently took it from Lena to study. "A new day," Evelyn said, her voice thick. "I love it. Thank you, Lena."

"It—I tried to think of something that reminded me of you. How you live each day like its brand new..."

Evelyn gently touched the birds. "I like these, they are so free."

"To remind you it's okay to not be in control all the time," Lena said, with a little laugh.

Evelyn chuckled. "I'm not that bad."

"There's one other surprise." Lena took a breath. "I've been talking to Edwin."

"Edwin?" Evelyn blinked, completely not expecting that.

"Because—we decided he is going to come here."

"What? Here? He is coming here?"

"Yes, he gets on a flight tomorrow, actually."

"But...we agreed—there isn't much sense getting so emotionally involved..."

"*You* agreed to that. He happens to disagree. For the record, so do I. You guys obviously have something between you."

"I'm seventy, Lena. I live in Canada, and he lives in England. It doesn't make sense."

"That's okay though," Lena said. "You are always going on about seizing the day and making the most out of things."

"But—how would it work? We both have families and commitments and—"

"You two will figure it out."

"You make it sound so simple."

"It is, for the most part. If you can take the emotions out of it."

Evelyn laughed, hearing her own words thrown back at her. "You've come a long way, my young apprentice." She considered it. "Okay. He will come here and…we will just…see, I guess. What happens."

Lena smiled. "Exactly."

Despite herself, Evelyn felt a thrill race through her. Edwin was coming *here*—he wanted to see her, to make something work. It was embarrassing how happy that made her. Maybe it was possible…maybe they could live part-time here and part-time there? She wouldn't mind spending more time in St. Ives…It was absurd though wasn't it? They couldn't possibly go back and forth for long. What if one of them started declining health wise?

When she tried to picture how it all looked in the future, all she saw was a great crowd of unknown factors. Maybe that was okay though…maybe Lena was right, and Evelyn needed to relax on the reigns and just see what happened…It felt very daring thinking that way. Kind of exciting.

"Right," Evelyn said. "Well, if I am going to be all free-spirited with this, then you have to do something for me."

"What's that?"

"You need to take charge of your life. Let the wind blow you less and make things happen. Get out of this depressing little condo, for starters."

"You said it's charming."

"I lied. Look, Lena, you have been through a lot. Lord knows you have—if anyone deserves to mope around and curl up in a ball, it's you—but do you really want that for your life?"

Lena looked around her condo, her arms folded across her chest. She swallowed hard and answered quietly, "No, I don't. I'm tired of living like that. I'm tired of—of being sad."

"Good. Then it's settled. I'll loosen up and let life happen a bit more, and you will tighten up and seize the day."

Lena grinned. "Shall we make a pact then? Shake on it?"

"Yes. That sounds like a good idea." Evelyn extended her hand.

"Should we—like—spit in our palms or something?"

"Don't be ridiculous. We aren't animals."

They shook hands.

Evelyn let go, feeling solemn—like something important had just happened. Her eyes felt heavy. "Good, well. I must get going. Thanks for this." She gestured to the painting, then turned quickly so Lena couldn't see her embarrassing display of emotion.

When she got home after leaving Lena's, she put her shoes on her shoe rack, hung up her jacket and crossed the room to carefully remove the picture of the lilies. She then hung Lena's painting in its place and stood back with her hands on her hips, considering it.

It could be moved up a tad, maybe tilted a little more to the left? She squinted at it, then let her hands fall to her sides. No, she would leave it as is. It was fine.

More than fine, it was absolutely perfect.

CHAPTER THIRTY-THREE

Lena looked around her condo for the last time. It looked deceitfully bigger without her and James' things taking up precious space. Nicer, maybe. The cleaners had just left; she'd come back to make sure everything was in good condition for when the realtor came to take pictures for the listing. It had taken a short amount of time to sort through and pack up everything.

Some things she packed away in boxes to go into storage at her parents' place, but most things she found she didn't want to hang on to. The wedding dishes she and James had picked out, work clothes she hated wearing, the impersonal decor...all those things went into a donation pile. A few things went into the trash— any lingering pictures of Sean, the outfit she wore the night they went clubbing, the dress she wore when they first went for supper. Anything that brought Sean to mind, she firmly discarded. It was odd when she stared at the three piles she'd made—her whole life so far, boiled down to a pile of cardboard boxes, ready and waiting for her to restart her life. Whenever that may be.

Her ring she decided to keep, but no longer was it weighing her finger down. She put it securely in her jewelry box and added it to the boxes going to her parents' place. It felt right to keep it, a memento of her past life.

Outside, a horn honked, and an engine roared in

response. Sounds that used to annoy her now felt nostalgic. It was a comfort she would miss and look back fondly on—*remember how the sounds of traffic were nonstop all the time? How hot the condo got in the summer? Remember how the smell of the neighbors' supper would linger for days, how there were so many chips in the paint it looked like someone took a knife to the walls?*

Of course, she didn't have a person to commiserate with who would understand. Whoever lived here next would get it—they would move in, hear the traffic, and immediately wonder if they'd just made a big mistake. They would come to love and hate these walls, they would stand at the window staring at the cars going by and long for the next house, the next step up the success ladder, only to look back and miss the simpleness of this time. Though some people didn't move up from the starter house—some people spent their lives in places like this, not advancing, just living. That was fine too, she supposed. She just hoped whoever bought the condo would be happy here. Happier than she'd been at least.

Lena wasn't sure how she would feel looking back. Her time here wasn't the typical bliss of a newlywed. Her memories were confusing, sad, terrifying, as well as happy—that was important to remember—throughout everything there *were* threads of happiness mixed in. It was easy to flit one way or the other, either everything was always wonderful, or everything was terrible, but the truth was it was both—terrible and wonderful, happy and sad. She would equally miss James, and as she realized now, not miss him. It was a strange paradox, but that's the way it was. For most things in life, probably.

She looked around one last time, then descended the

stairs and firmly shut the door with a satisfying click. She turned to go to her car but stopped at the sight of her neighbor, wearing a t-shirt despite the winter chill, leaning casually against the side of his condo, exhaling streams of smoke.

"Hi," Lena said to him.

"Hey," he answered, tossing his hair out of his eyes. "Saw you loading boxes the other day. You moving?"

"Yup."

"Nice. Where to?"

"Not sure yet. I'm going travelling first." Lena felt a tad prideful saying that. She was going *travelling*. She was one of those adventurous, hippy people going on a journey to *find* herself. Maybe she would write a book about it, and it would get turned into a movie. Anything was possible. Except the writing the book thing, that would not be happening on account of she would never ever get around to it. She would paint though, throughout her trip she would paint, that would be how she recorded her journey.

"Good for you," he said, taking another puff.

"Thanks." Lena took another step forward, then paused. "Hey, what's your name?"

The guy laughed. "Elliot."

"Really?" Lena said. "Huh."

"I don't look like an Elliot?"

"Not really. I thought maybe Kyle or Dan or something."

"Sorry to disappoint." He grinned and cocked his head. "You wanna come in for a beer?"

"Oh, I—" Lena stopped, considering. As part of her promise to Evelyn, Lena had made a couple of resolutions. One, to sell her condo. Two, to say yes to things instead of always no. This felt like a test, her first chance at change. She could go for a beer with her pothead neighbor Elliot, something she never ever would have done a few months ago. A few days ago, even. They would talk, maybe flirt, then she would leave. No harm, no foul.

Was that the best start to her new resolution, though? Going alone into a guy's condo she barely knew? Surely some discretion was allowed with the whole seizing the day thing. "I actually should get going," Lena said, feeling a bit guilty. "Thanks, though."

Elliot shrugged. "No problem. Hope you enjoy your trip."

"Thanks, I will. Good luck with the next neighbor." Lena gave him a little wave and continued to her car. She was *friendly* towards him at least. That was a good start, wasn't it? Besides, she already was taking a pretty massive leap towards seizing the day with her plan for an extended trip to Europe.

Her first stop was going to be St. Ives. She was going to hang out there till the New Year, working in Edwin's pub. After that, her Scottish friend Maisie was going to join her for a few weeks of touring around France, Italy, and Germany. After that, who knew? She would probably meet up with Evelyn and Edwin at some point. Maybe she would go to Scotland for a while, maybe Ireland. She had no plans other than she was giving herself six months away from reality and after that, she would see who she was at that point and go from there.

It was nerve-wracking, thinking of going, but it also felt like it was the right decision. She wanted to continue what the first trip had started in her, encourage the stirring it had created that life could be different. That it should be different.

She needed some time away from all the terrible things that had happened, some room to breathe and think about things other than her losses. Some space from the people and ghosts who had shaped her so far, so she could start shaping herself.

The idea came to her shortly after the pact she'd made with Evelyn. She had gone back to Redwood, not to the river—she vowed never to go there again—but to Cheryl's grave. Lena had stood staring at Cheryl's gravestone, at the numbers marking the short eighteen years she had on this earth, unable to speak. Lena had just wanted to apologize for not knowing, for letting Sean get away with what he'd done for so long. There was no way to prove anything, same with Becky's case, but it was enough that she knew the truth. She went from there to the city cemetery where James was buried. Lena had knelt on the frozen ground, her legs quickly turning numb and damp, and gently laid some flowers at the base of his grave.

James had been a good man sometimes, he'd also been a flawed man who had hurt her, dampened her. But, he also loved her, he would have laid down his life for her. Could that be another paradox? Maybe he hadn't fit perfectly into a good guy or bad guy role. Maybe she couldn't blame the way she was, on him, or Cheryl, or even Sean for that matter. Maybe Lena had gotten what she had tolerated. Maybe she didn't know herself well enough to know what she wanted, to be strong enough to stick up for herself. That was on her, not them. At some point Lena needed to own up to her side of things, to not blame everyone else for how things turned out.

This led to the idea to go back to Europe—to the place she liked who she was, and where she thought about things other than herself.

Her enthusiasm wavered slightly on the plane ride over. For the whole nine hours she had equal feelings of excitement mixed with fearful regret. It was by far the scariest thing she'd done yet in her life—besides, well, the whole clubbing a man to death and running away thing.

As the plane began its descent, Lena stared out the tiny window, watching the lights of London glow brighter and brighter against the surrounding blackness. Too late to go back now. For better or worse, her adventure was beginning. When she finally was allowed to stand up, she stretched and rolled her shoulders, feeling cramped and kinked together after being squashed in the little seat the whole way across an ocean. As she reached to get her bag down from the overhead compartment, she noticed a tall, blonde guy just a little way up the plane. He caught her eye and grinned; she felt her stomach flutter in response. From the look of his travel backpack, he was another person about to head out on a European adventure.

For a moment she imagined going over to him, introducing herself, letting him buy her a drink and strike up a conversation. She considered it for a moment, then broke her gaze away, slinging her pack over her shoulder.

No, this wasn't going to be that kind of trip—at least not right now. Right now, she had everything she needed, which—save for her backpack—was exactly nothing and no one. It was a different kind of alone than what she'd endured this past year, right up to the moment

Evelyn approached her in the theater. Not an abandoned by everyone and everything alone, but a choice—an intentional aloneness that strangely, didn't make her feel alone at all.

EPILOGUE

Doug saw them everywhere, it seemed.

In the mall once, at the movie theater, the restaurant now and then, a few times getting groceries on the west end of town. He noticed them at first because of the girl—she looked like a young Alice.

Then he started noticing them because of him. His name was James. Doug knew this because there was a bench near the restaurant that had his face on it, James Martin—Real Estate Agent.

It started at the grocery store. The girl dropped their eggs when she was moving the groceries from the cart to their car. The way James had snapped at her, swearing and yanking her by the arm over to the passenger side, made Doug stiffen. He almost said something then, but it wasn't his place. Evelyn was always telling him he needed to mind his own business.

Then he saw them again, at the restaurant. He was stopping by as he did sometimes, just to see how things were going. They were sitting in a booth, arguing in low tones over something. He couldn't make out what. Suddenly, James had slammed his drink down and left, brushing past Doug on the way out without acknowledging him. He watched as the poor girl sat there, red-faced, trying not to cry. Eventually she left, in an Uber Doug assumed.

What kind of man did that? Abandon his wife at a

restaurant? Talked to her so disrespectfully in public? Doug could only imagine what that man did in the safety of his own home.

Every time he saw them he was tempted to march over there and teach the young chap a lesson in common decency. Not that he saw an incident like that every time he saw them—maybe a handful of times he noticed something uncomfortable over the span of six months. It was enough for him to know there was a pattern going on.

Then, one night when he was working as a ride-share driver, he pulled up to this strip club downtown, and who should come stumbling out, but the realtor himself. It didn't surprise Doug that this was where James spent his Friday nights. Doug wondered if the girl knew. He assumed not.

James got in the back of Doug's car, reeking of booze and cigarettes.

"Alright there?" Doug asked.

"Fine, man," he responded.

"Seat belt done up?"

James glared at him. "Just drive."

Doug put the vehicle into drive, glancing back now and then at the man slumped against the window. "Rough night?"

"Nope."

Doug followed the GPS, weaving through the streets, easing out onto the highway to loop around the city, the fastest way to the address. He glanced again at the realtor. What were the chances of him ending up in Doug's car, of all cars? Or that he'd run into them so many times? It had to be a sign—Doug was a firm believer in signs. It's what led him to his wife all those years ago at a college party he hated, and later to this country so far from their home. This was fate—this couple needed some help, and Doug was the man to deliver it.

"You know, I've seen you around," he said.

"What?"

"I've seen you around."

"Oh. Yeah. I'm a realtor, you've probably seen some of my ads."

"I've actually seen you with your wife."

"What?"

Doug made eye contact with James through the mirror. "I've seen you with your wife, a few times. You don't treat her very well."

"What the fuck are you talking about."

"I'm talking about you, how you talk to her. It's not right, you should—"

"Look man, I don't know what your deal is, but you need to shut the fuck up."

Doug twisted in his seat. "Listen here, there's no—"

That's all it took. A second of distraction, of looking over his shoulder in an attempt to do a decent thing.

Doug never finished his sentence. Fate, it seemed, had different plans.

A word about the author...

Jenna Hanger, writing under the pen name J.L.Cole, lives in Alberta with her husband and two young daughters. When she isn't busy chasing her children, she can be found helping on the family ranch or writing at her desk. The Widows' Pact is her second novel, and definitely not her last. To keep up-to-date with the latest news check out her website: www.jl-cole.com or follow her on social media @jlcolebooks @jlcole1331.

Thank you for purchasing
this publication of The Wild Rose Press, Inc.

For questions or more information
contact us at
info@thewildrosepress.com.

The Wild Rose Press, Inc.
www.thewildrosepress.com

Lightning Source UK Ltd.
Milton Keynes UK
UKHW021324270123
416064UK00014B/1030